On the Way to Istanbul…

by

Kayla Danoli

COPYRIGHT

First published in 2017
Copyright © Kayla Danoli 2017

Cataloguing-in-publication data
Creator: Danoli, Kayla, author

Cataloguing-in-Publication details are available from the National Library of Australia
www.trove.nla.gov.au

ISBN: 978-0-9750287-8-0 (paperback)
ISBN: 978-0-9750287-9-7 (eBook)

Cover design: T A Marshall, Mackay, Queensland.

CONTENTS

ALSO BY THE AUTHOR

Revenge is not Enough
Harbour Plaza: built on dreams

CHAPTER 1

"What have I done? What… have… I… done? It's all Connie's fault. I shouldn't have listened to her. She won't talk me into anything again. Connie's had far too much of a hand in this whole exercise." I gazed at the mirror on the wall above the hall table and shook my head as I heaved a sigh of resignation. "I suppose, if the truth be told, it's my fault. I let her talk me into it, just as she talked me into so many things over the last few weeks. Well, there's nothing to do about it now. I just have to live with it….. at least for as long as it takes until I can do something about it."

I ran a tentative hand down the back of my neck. It wasn't as short as I thought, and not nearly as short as it looks, but how long will it take it to return to normal? And that fringe… Will I ever be able to get rid of that?

Who would have thought a haircut could be so traumatic. Connie's words echoed in my mind as I stood gazing at my reflection in the mirror. "You don't want to be messing about with hair like that when you're on holidays. It's too much trouble and it will be too hot. You need something that is easy to look after. Besides, it ages you. Go get one of those new shorter hairdos that take no looking after," Connie had said with no shortage of conviction.

…And the young dolly bird hairdresser's words came rushing back to haunt me. "This is the 60s. You don't need to be pfaffing about with all this palaver. Everything is easy care now, short and simple."

She didn't put too much effort into stifling the smile that tugged the corners of her mouth when I responded, "I'm not exactly a teenager anymore. I don't want to look like I'm trying to regain my lost youth." It all happened in a blur. Before I had finished speaking, it was gone. I had short hair. What I thought was going to be a quick haircut turned into an endurance test. Despite my strenuous protest, the young hairdresser added highlights to my hair, assuring me they would give me a 'real lift'.

As I sat there wondering how long highlighting took, another young lass emerged through the beaded curtain that sectioned off the other half of the salon. That area is a beauty parlour. Summoned by some unseen gesture by my hairdresser, the newcomer began fussing about my face. Eyebrows were tidied, eyes made up, and new make-up applied. She demanded to see my lipstick and promptly dismissed it as having gone out of fashion years ago. There followed a brief educational interlude wherein she acquainted me with new lipstick colours and the wonders of various bits of eye make-up. Then, with the morning disappeared in a flurry of beautification, I left the salon with a bag of product for my hair, various new make-up, and my purse considerably lighter.

This was supposed to be the last stage of what Connie insisted on referring to as my 'makeover'. My wardrobe already contained various pieces of clothing and shoes which, in saner moments, I would never consider purchasing. There was even a new suitcase, and within the next few days, that new apparel – and maybe even some of that new make-up – would go into that suitcase. However, in the meantime, I had to make the best of this new Marjorie Leggett who stared back at me from the hall mirror … and tomorrow would be a real test of this new-look. Tomorrow, Connie and I were rostered to work at the local library. It would be the first public outing of the new me.

My arrival at the library was greeted with much oohing and aahing, and a plethora of comments about how much younger it made me look. I managed to survive the episode. Connie was still smiling broadly at the success of her efforts when we went for ham sandwiches and a pot of tea at a local café after finishing duty at the library.

The next day was for packing and generally making the cottage okay to be unattended when I swanned off. There wasn't much to do, but I felt my stomach tightening, and I wondered yet again how I managed to get myself into this situation. Connie dropped in twice during the day, once on her way back from the shop with the paper, and then again later for a cup of tea. Her excitement at my impending departure did nothing to ease my trepidation.

As expected, although I fussed about filling in time until quite late before going to bed, I didn't sleep well. Did I sleep at all? I crawled out of bed early this morning with a thick head and a great weight in the pit of my stomach. As I stumbled through my daily routine – which was anything but routine today – I felt my stomach becoming increasingly tighter by the moment.

Oh hell, this is it. There is no turning back now. Whatever happens from here on is in the lap of the gods. I do hope I haven't offended any of them recently! "There's my taxi. It's only about 10 minutes late, which is not too bad I suppose for this hour of the day. I knew it would be late and there would be nothing but confusion at every turn. That's why I arranged everything to get me there well ahead of time." Goodness me, I'm talking to an empty cottage I chided myself. I haven't even left home and I'm talking to myself. Is this a sign of things to come?

Connie planned to come across to say goodbye. I knew I wouldn't be up to handling farewells and therefore, didn't share my planned early departure with her. As the taxi drew up out front of the cottage, I pulled the front door closed behind me and rushed down the path to the gate. The driver took my suitcase from me. I dropped the spare key in the letterbox for Connie to collect later, and dived into the taxi as the driver climbed back aboard. Connie rushed out of her front door as we moved off. I waved to her from my perch in the rear of the cab, and smiled at the thought that I would have to deal with the fallout from such a departure when I returned home.

…And then we were at Victoria Station. Suitcase in hand, I rushed inside. Feelings of panic were starting to take hold. Where did I need to go? What did I need to do? Yet again, I checked the contents of my oversized handbag; documents, foreign currency, travel sickness pills still all there. Why wouldn't they be? This was the third time I'd checked them since awaiting the arrival of the taxi, and nothing had occurred to change the situation.

I was surprised. Everything went smoothly. The only odd moment was when the young man checking my documentation commented, "You are a wee bit early – well actually, quite a bit early. Your train doesn't depart for another couple of hours." That was my plan, so he received a polite smile in response. Then, with my suitcase safely checked in, I went in search of a tearoom. I don't think I want or need tea, but a tearoom seems like an ideal place to kill time until I can board my train.

It's a wonder I didn't wear out my watch. I checked it so often while I waited. As it approached 6.00p.m., I could contain myself no longer. Armed with a chocolate bar and a pack of sandwiches, I went in search of my platform. The guard, or whatever he was, on duty there raised his eyebrows in surprise and checked his watch as I approached. I then spent the next 20 minutes or so standing around waiting with a few others until we were allowed on board the train. A few more arrived as the departure time drew nearer, but our number remained small. More or less on time at 6.50p.m., the *Golden Arrow* pulled out of Victoria Station headed for the port.

The trip was by train to Dover, then ferry to Calais, and then by train once more to the *Gare du Nord* at Paris, where some passengers disembarked, before the rest of us continued around Paris to the *Gare de Lyon*. It was from there the real part of our adventure would begin. The trip to Paris allowed plenty of time for reflection on how I came to be in this situation.

I, Marjorie Leggett, a 40-something year old (almost 50 year old in truth) emotionally damaged spinster suffered something of a midlife crisis prior to my unplanned retirement. With my whole adult life devoted to my job, the devastating breakup of an extended relationship made encountering my former long-term lover in the workplace unbearable. A fortuitous bequest from an elderly aunt came at just the right time to allow for an immediate and early retirement. The bequest, a cottage in the suburbs and a small annuity, made my retirement possible.

At first, after moving to the cottage, I sat around not knowing what to do with myself. There appeared to be no direction in my life or purpose for each day. A chance encounter at the corner shop with Connie Benson, the woman living across the road from me, led to my joining Connie as a volunteer at the local library, and began a strong friendship with the woman. The library volunteers were a close-knit group and further new friendships developed.

My wake-up call came by way of a couple of tragedies that happened to other volunteers. The first was Jean who died after a short battle with a brain tumour. She was only a handful of years older than me. Then, a couple of months ago, a second volunteer suffered a fatal heart attack. These events alerted me to not only my own mortality, but also to the hand life sometimes deals when it's least expected. Those volunteers had unfulfilled hopes and dreams. Jean's husband was much older than she was and, as he approached retirement, the couple planned to spend their life travelling. Jean would never see those places they intended to visit together.

Connie, who popped in regularly for a cup of tea or a chat, realising something was amiss, pursued the matter on several occasions until I caved in and opened up. "Oh, it's nothing really. I'm just being a silly old woman. I probably need to get away for a few days; just take a bit of a holiday."

"You are depressed. You don't need a few days away. You need a proper holiday. You need to do something more with your life, something exciting… and I don't think going to Brighton for a weekend will do it. Go somewhere exotic."

While that suggestion went nowhere for a day or two, it didn't go away. It continued to gnaw away in the back of my mind. When we next had a cuppa a few days later, I tentatively reintroduced the subject. "Where would you consider 'somewhere exotic'? Would it be somewhere like the Orkneys?"

"The Orkneys…? No, definitely not; get out of the country; go somewhere exciting."

"Where is exciting? I'm not sure I know what you mean – or where you mean."

"Well, this is 1965, and the world is loaded with interesting places to see. You could go somewhere that is exciting in a modern sense, somewhere like New York or Paris." Connie noticed my slight shake of the head in response to her suggestion and realised that 'modern' wasn't the answer. "…Or you could think about places considered exotic in previous decades. Think about places like Cairo and sailing down the Nile, Constantinople – sorry, Istanbul now. Those sorts of places were where people went in the past in search of exciting holidays. Maybe you should think about places like those."

"I don't know much about any of those places, and I wouldn't know how to begin planning a holiday there."

"Get some books out of the library. Read about those places. Work out where you want to go, and then book a tour. These days, you don't have to do everything yourself. You go on a package tour. Now, come on, what place appeals to you?"

This conversation had become uncomfortable. I was determined to end it. "Well I don't know do I… and I won't know until I take your advice and read about some places. I'll have a look at what's in the library." However, this approach only served to maintain the quandary. Although I read books about various places, going down the Nile or dashing across Europe to Istanbul remained the favoured options. Nevertheless, my interest in a trip to some 'exotic' destination was growing daily. If I could just decide on one of those destinations…!

Over the ensuing weeks, Istanbul seemed to gain favour over a jaunt down the Nile, but I remained undecided. It wasn't until the subject came up again over coffee with Connie that a winner emerged. Connie listened intently as I listed all the points for and against each place. She sat silently until my review ended before offering her observation. "I see you've done your homework and you've narrowed down the field of likely places, but I don't see what your problem is. From listening to you, it's obvious that for you, Istanbul has the most appeal." Discussion on the topic concluded at that point but, by the time Connie left, I knew I would be investigating the possibility of visiting Turkey.

It took no more than a visit to a travel agent to acquire all the information I could possibly want – and more – about visiting Istanbul, including package deals and their various costs. As with everything else in life, there were options, and too many options make decisions difficult. Then Connie's words about how people in the 1920s and 30s travelled came back to me. Back then, anyone going to Istanbul – and wanting to do it in comfort and style – would take the *Orient Express*. More research at the library had me daydreaming about such a train trip to Istanbul.

I could do it. Always frugal with my income, and with no life to speak of to spend anything on, I am reasonably comfortably off, and now with my annuity, I could afford to treat myself. Of course, the original Orient Express was no more, but its replacement, the Simplon Direct Orient Express, appeared to follow much the same route as the original and offered passengers much the same experience.

"If you leave London on Thursday, you will have quite a stopover in Paris if you want to have a sleeper cabin from Paris to Istanbul," the young woman in the travel agency advised me, her eyes gleaming at the prospect of making more bookings for me in Paris. I intended to book to leave London in time to join the last train to Istanbul in the low fare season ending on 31st May. The plan did not include a stay in Paris. I resigned myself to a June departure date. What difference did a couple of days make, I asked myself as I reaffirmed in my own mind that I did not want to spend time in Paris. Then she told me of some special deal on offer. During the first week of June, the first five people to book a sleeper from Paris to Istanbul would be eligible for the low season fare. What was she waiting for? Make my booking!

In something of a rash move, I shared my thinking with Connie after our stint at the library the following week. That's all it took. Connie was away and running with the idea of getting me off to Istanbul. "Of course, you'll need to get some more suitable clothes for the trip. Twin sets and pleated skirts won't do at all. You will need simple cool, loose clothing."

That was the start of it: my personal makeover by Connie. I was towed along to the shopping centre to choose new outfits. Then there had to be a new suitcase. That was because I didn't even own a decent sized suitcase, never before having been on a holiday of any substance. There was a bit of a battle about shoes. Despite my strenuous insistence that my sensible shoes were best for walking, and that I anticipated there would be quite a bit of walking at the various places where the train stopped, Connie, on the other hand, insisted sensible brogues didn't go with the new clothes. The outcome of that battle was a couple of new brightly coloured pairs of sling backs with low skinny heels. I couldn't see myself doing too much walking in those heels, and was a bit apprehensive about what sort of injury I might sustain if I fell off them.

How involved could this makeover become? With my travel wardrobe more or less sorted out, Connie focused her attention on me, the woman. "You'll have to do something about that hair. You need a hairdo that is much simpler to look after – something a bit more wash and wear.

"What's wrong with my hair? I've worn it this way all my adult life. Why would I want to change it now, and what exactly did you have in mind to do with it?" I absent-mindedly slid a hand up and patted my dark locks now sporting a good deal more 'pepper and salt' than I cared to admit to. Since I was about 20, I had maintained shoulder length hair and worn it up.

It took some doing, but Connie managed to talk me … me, strong-minded independent Marjorie Leggett … into visiting Connie's regular hairdresser for a 'bit of a trim and style'. Connie even made the appointment for me… and it seems she had a quiet word to the hairdresser about what the outcome of my visit should be. So, it was with a good deal of nervousness I kept the appointment, only to emerge afterwards looking a different person. Although I was still short in stature, and my once reed thin figure still sported the extra padding that had me verging on cuddly these days, apart from that, I have to admit the dowdy woman who entered the salon exited the place looking a whole lot more 1965-ish.

Although that ended Connie's makeover exercise, there were still plenty of last-minute things to do. There was the requisite documentation to collect, foreign currency to acquire, and decisions to make about what things to take with me to cope with every possible contingency. Not having travelled to any extent before, packing for the trip looked like degenerating into a nightmare until Connie came to the rescue. "Come on; on the spare bed, lay out everything you think you need to take with you." I made a token effort to comply. "No, everything; we need it laid out to see how much you have to pack and how much we can cull. Oh, and fetch your tour itinerary. We need to match outfits with places and the things you are going to be doing at those places."

While my initial reaction was to resist being organised by Connie, the results proved worthwhile. "Thank you Connie, now that we have gone through that exercise, I don't think there's half as much left on the bed to pack, and I feel a lot more confident about fitting it into the suitcase."

There wasn't much left to do: packing, cleaning out the fridge, and stopping the paper and mail deliveries. Connie agreed to keep an eye on the cottage while I'm away and deal with any emergencies in the garden. Somehow, in spite of the strong friendship that existed between us, I had never given Connie a spare key to the cottage. It was an oversight, not intentional. It made sense that someone should have a spare key in case of emergency.

CHAPTER 2

'Sunday 03 June: the adventure begins' was all I had written before a knock on the cabin door ended the update of my trip journal.

"Breakfast and morning tea will be served in your cabin. Lunch will be in the dining car," the steward informed me. "If you have a moment to come with me now, I will show you the facilities and the dining car." I joined the young steward in the corridor and he pointed off to his left towards the front end of the carriage. "The steward's station is down there if you should need me for anything." Then we set off on a quick familiarisation tour that ended back at my cabin. After announcing he would be along shortly with breakfast, he left me to my own devices again. Personable enough young man, I thought as I sat peering out the window while I waited for breakfast to appear.

Due to depart the *Gare de Lyon* at 6.55a.m., the Orient Express moved off five minutes late at seven o'clock. I felt the train chug into motion and breathed a sigh of relief. I murmured to the empty cabin, "Istanbul here I come. I do hope this isn't a mistake. I'm still not sure what a frump like me thinks she is doing on this train." The arrival of breakfast interrupted any further thoughts on the matter. With breakfast spread out on the small table in the cabin, I asked the universe in general, "How leisurely is this? Next stop Munich; how shall I spend the morning?"

Morning tea arrived, and shortly after we passed through Strasbourg. Sometime between breakfast and morning tea, I felt the onset of 'scenery overload' and I remembered the book purchased to fill in the hours on the trip. A quick rifle through my copious handbag unearthed *Ship of Fools* by Katherine Anne Porter. Although released only a couple of months previously, the book had captured my imagination. The local library had yet to obtain a copy, so I purchased my own from a major bookstore in the city.

After morning tea and another quick check on the scenery flying past, I made myself comfortable and started reading my book. The list of characters at the start of the book took some understanding, but I persisted with it, thinking it might be prudent to know who was who on the ship before moving on to the rest of the story. I found it a little slow to get going. Perhaps it was because only half my attention focused on the book, while the other half and my peripheral vision closely monitored everything sliding past my window. The story seemed so slow, I found myself stifling a yawn. That was when the view of an interesting valley caught my attention. With the book abandoned I returned to watching the scenery, and that's what I was doing when the steward came to announce lunch was served.

As I made my way to the dining car, there were a few people ahead of me, but none followed me. I concluded I must be the last to arrive for lunch. The packed dining car confirmed this deduction. Every seat appeared occupied. It wasn't until I reached the far end of the carriage that I found an empty place. I cleared my throat and spoke to the male diner already seated at the table. "Ahem, excuse me, may I join you?"

Ralph Carter looked up from the book he was reading. "Yes of course, please take a seat." I made a hasty assessment of the man now blinking up at me. Late 50s I guessed; weary eyes and mouth turned down slightly at the corners. Although quite grey at the temples, there was a thick thatch of brown hair with no evidence of thinning, while the luxuriant moustache adorning his top lip was lighter and more ginger than its lofty counterpart.

"I apologise for intruding like this, but the carriage is packed. I am surprised at how many people are on board. This appears to be the only seat available. Please don't let me interrupt you, feel free to continue reading your book."

"I assure you, your joining me is not an intrusion. I believe the train is fully booked, so I imagine every mealtime will see the dining car packed with our fellow passengers."

"I saw so few people board the train at Victoria Station. I remember seeing you and a couple of the others that I noticed at tables as I walked through the here, but I haven't seen the majority of the people in here before now."

"No, there were not many from London. Most of the passengers joined the train at Paris, after having spent some time in that city. If you have the time and you're interested in Paris, I suppose it's the way to go, the way to make the most of your trip overseas. Of course, they're not all English. There is a good smattering from all over Europe included on the passenger list, so they would need to make their way to Paris to join the train."

"Oh, there's another latecomer. Would you mind if I shuffled up so she can share our table as well?"

"No of course not; wave her over."

Sofia Elmas gave a relieved smile and hurried to the table. "I didn't realise I was so late. Is it all right if I join you?" After assurances that she was most welcome, Sofia sat down as I moved my place settings further along the table to make room for her. The steward arrived immediately to set another place at the table, halting any further conversation for a few moments. However, the young woman only picked at her food, finished eating quickly and left the table.

"She seemed very tense, nervous even. I wonder what's going on in her life. Whatever it is I don't think she is on this trip for a relaxing holiday," I suggested.

"There seemed to be something bothering her, but it is probably something we will never know about, particularly as she doesn't seem keen to indulge in conversation."

"Are you sure you wouldn't prefer to be reading your book? What's the name of it anyway?" A glimpse of part of the cover of the novel had caught my attention.

"It's a new one out... *Ship of Fools*. It's by some female American academic I think."

"It's the same novel I bought for the trip. It was getting some very good reviews and it was tipped to be a bestseller."

"How are you finding it?"

"Uhmm... Oh, I haven't really gotten into it. I've only read a few pages."

"I haven't read much more. It takes a bit of getting into... a bit slow, if you know what I mean."

Conversation seemed to flow easily between us and we stretched our mealtime until we became aware of rather pointed looks from the staff. "I think the staff would like us to go so they can get on with their work," I whispered across the table to Ralph.

"Right; have you got everything? Let's go. I'll walk you back to your cabin," Ralph replied as he gathered up his book and led me out of the dining car.

"This is mine," I said as we arrived at my cabin. "Thank you for your company. Do you have far to go for your cabin?"

"No, mine is two doors further along. I'll be able to stop and collect you in future whenever we are off to the dining car."

After a nod and smile in reply, I whispered, "Who is in the cabin in between ours." Ralph shrugged in response and I continued, "We will have plenty of time to find out. Next stop, Munich – and soon I think."

"Yes, we will be late arriving. After being a few minutes late leaving Paris, that section of the line where we had to go slowly because of all the debris the storm brought down from the hillside put us even further behind. The steward said they would make it up at Munich. We were supposed to have about two hours there to stretch our legs and look around the place, but they will shorten our stay by however many minutes we are running behind time."

Although I intended reading more of my book, my heart wasn't in it. I abandoned it in favour of staring at the passing scenery. However, my mind wasn't on that either. It kept drifting back to Ralph Carter. When I saw him at Victoria Station waiting to board the train, I remember thinking he must be a businessman. He looked so stylish in his pale grey suit with charcoal waistcoat and maroon tie. Very different from the way he looked at lunch. "I think I like the lunchtime version better," I shared aloud with my cabin, and then chuckled. I'm talking to myself again, I thought. But I have to admit, it was quite an enjoyable lunch.

He was pleasant company and we shared intelligent conversation about common interests. Above all else, he seemed a gentleman. A sobering thought occurred to me. Someone like that probably is married… although, there was no wedding ring. But, wedding rings for men are a modern fashion and neither he nor I is young enough for 'modern fashion'. This is nonsense, I admonished myself. What have I become? I didn't come on this trip to be like some teenager chasing a holiday romance. Still, the man I lunched with did seem to tick all the boxes.

The itinerary had us at Munich at 1.55p.m. We arrived 35 minutes late, but were advised the train would leave on time at 3.58p.m. That still gives me more than enough time to stretch my legs and have a bit of a look around, I thought as I negotiated the steps to the platform. However, having arrived on the platform, the question was what to do next. Which way to go? The thought of moving too far away from the train worried me. What if I became lost wandering around this place and didn't make it back to the train in time? Then, as I stood, a picture of indecision rooted to the spot, a familiar voice eased my nerves.

"…Any ideas on where to go or what to see?" Ralph Carter asked. I shook my head; no point in telling him the truth. "Well, perhaps we should wander out front to at least see what the place looks like from here."

Once we were outside the station, Ralph took charge again. "Oh good, that looks like a tearoom or café over there across the street. I don't know about you, but I could go a cup of tea about now." Ralph's assessment was correct. It was a tearoom and the woman who served us had 'a little of the English'. It proved enough to get us a passable pot of tea and a couple of pastries. Afterwards, we wandered along the street, passing an ancient looking church and a few Bavarian-looking buildings containing shops selling tourist-type trinkets. The whole while, we both kept close watch on the time, and hurried back to the train a good 15 minutes before we were due to board again.

As we waited to board, I said quietly, "I didn't see Sofia leave the train. We could have asked her to join us for a cup of tea if we had seen her."

"I have a feeling she didn't leave the train. I'm not sure why I think that but, if that is the case, she probably had a good reason to stay on board. Anyway, she most likely will join us for dinner this evening. Okay, here we go. Next stop Salzburg. I think it's only a couple of hours along the track and the stopover is only about 20 minutes or so."

Ralph was right. We arrived at Salzburg just before six o'clock. It was a brief stop. Two young men carrying what looked like guitar cases left the train, and we moved off again after the scheduled time at the station. Once the train settled down to its usual rhythm, I took another look at the itinerary. It appeared there would be a brief stop at Jesenice before continuing through the night to arrive at Ljubljana shortly after midnight. The stopover at Ljubljana again about 20 minutes before the train headed off to Zagreb. After a brief period of watching the storybook-like scenery sliding past, it was time to freshen up before dinner.

As I dressed for dinner, I giggled and shared a thought with the uninterested cabin, "If only Connie could see me now, she would be mortified." I was still in this jaunty mood when I answered Ralph's knock and joined him in the corridor to make our way to the dining car. "Wait up, Ralph. Sofia has just stepped out into the corridor. Let's wait for her to catch up so we can all go in together."

"Thank you for waiting for me. I didn't want to be the last one and make another grand entrance to the dining car," Sofia said and grimaced at the memory of all the attention she attracted when she arrived so late for lunch. There wasn't opportunity for conversation as we made our way in single file along the carriage corridors to the dining car. Although there were plenty of seats available, we again chose a table at the far end of the carriage.

While we fussed about getting settled at the table, Sofia, still standing beside her chair, gasped audibly and her hand flew to grasp the pendant hanging from her neck. It caught me off guard and my eyes began wildly searching the carriage for any sign of impending danger as I asked, "What is it? What happened?"

Sofia shook her head. "It's nothing. I… uhmm… I just remembered something, but it is okay."

"Are you sure you're okay, my dear? For a moment there you looked terrified," Ralph said.

"He's right," I added. "You look like you've seen a ghost. You're still very pale. Are you sure you're all right? Would you rather go back to your carriage to lie down for a while?"

"No, no please, there is no need to fuss. I am fine. It was just a moment, and now it has passed. Let us enjoy dinner together, no?"

That didn't have the ring of truth to it. I raised an eyebrow across the table at Ralph whose face remained unchanged, but I thought I saw something akin to concern in his eyes and in the set of his jaw. At first, conversation was stilted with everyone still a bit rattled by what had happened, but it became easier. Ralph and I prattled on about Munich and the exorbitant prices for tourist trinkets. To keep conversation on the subject flowing, I shared my experience with the others. "I had thought to buy one of those beers stein things for Connie's husband, Harry, but I couldn't believe the price on it. Anyway, if I bought it then, I would have to cart it around with me – without damaging it – until I got back to London. Needless to say, I didn't buy the stein."

"I think you will find such prices very high in many of the places the train stops at, particularly those places close to the railway stations that sell things for the tourists. There are places in Istanbul where you will find interesting things at much better prices," Sofia advised us.

"Do you know Istanbul well? I am a bit nervous about finding my way around the place..." Then I remembered my nervousness from the outset and added with a giggle, "But then I was nervous about this whole trip and anything and everything that is new seems to terrify me these days." Although my companions laughed at my comment, I thought Sofia's laughter seemed strained somehow.

"I know Istanbul quite well. I am Turkish and my family live in one of the suburbs of Istanbul. It's where I grew up." I noted that Sofia, in spite of claiming to know Istanbul well, didn't offer to show us around or point out places to go.

"So, you live in Paris now?" Ralph asked.

"No... why do you think that?"

"Oh, I'm sorry. I thought you joined the train in Paris, and I assumed you might be living there now. Mind you, quite a few from England joined the train at Paris after having spent a few days exploring that city."

"This is so for me also. I came from London a couple of days early. This is why I get the train at Paris."

An exciting new thought occurred to me. "Oh good; Ralph you live in London too don't you?" Ralph gave a half-hearted nod. "If Sofia also lives in London, all three of us will be able to get together after this trip. We'll be able to maintain contact." I could see Ralph wasn't sure where I was going with all this and had an uncomfortable feeling about it, but he nodded and was about to comment on the suggestion when Sofia cut him off.

"No, this is not so. I do not live in London. I live in Istanbul and my work is at the Istanbul Archaeology Museums. My museum sent many priceless artefacts on loan to the British Museum for a very big exhibition. Security for such material is very strong. I must travel with the artefacts to London and check when they are unpacked that everything is okay, and then supervise the installation of the exhibition. That is why I was in London."

"Oh yes, I know about that exhibition. It opened the week before I left to come on this trip. My friend Connie and I wanted to see it before I left, but the week was too busy for me and I couldn't fit it in. We wanted to have plenty of time so that we could understand it properly. It doesn't matter though as it runs for quite a long time. When I couldn't fit it in, we agreed to wait until I get back from this trip before going to see it. Your job with the exhibition seems like a heavy workload – and a very big responsibility – for just one person. Don't they need you to keep an eye on things now that the exhibition is open?"

"No, I was not the only one. At first, yes, then another … what is the word? Ah, yes, colleague …another colleague came to help install the exhibition. One more colleague came just before the opening. He was to help me give the talks – there is a word for this – to the visitors to the exhibition."

"I believe they are called 'floor talks'. That is exciting news. Connie and I wanted to go at a time when we could take in one of those. We must be sure to go when you are delivering one. Oh, but now you are returning to Istanbul. Does that mean you won't be giving the talks after all?"

"Maybe no … perhaps … I don't know about the future."

There was something in her tone – in the way that she answered – that suggested there was a lot more to that reply than we were given. "That is disappointing. I hope it's your work bringing you back home and it's not any sort of trouble waiting for you there." I twitched an eyebrow at Ralph as I finished speaking. If Sofia noticed, she didn't react. I doubt she did see, or even hear what I said for that matter. She was preoccupied and was running her eyes over everyone else in the dining car.

Although Ralph had contributed nothing to that part of the conversation about the museum and the exhibition, I thought I detected an increased interest in the discussion, an excitement even. What might have interested Ralph pricked my curiosity, but there was no opportunity then to pursue it. Sofia folded her napkin neatly, placed it on the table and pushed her chair back. "I think it is time for me to leave. If you would excuse me, I will return to my cabin."

Ralph shot me a meaningful look as he said, "Wait up; we will come with you. Most of the diners have left and I think the staff would like to see us gone too." We scrambled from our chairs to join Sofia in the walkway through the carriage. "If you will allow me, I'll walk you two ladies to your cabins." He spread his arms out to shepherd Sofia and I along. Was that a look of relief that flitted across Sofia's face, I wondered as we made our way out of the dining carriage.

At my door, the others said goodnight and saw me safely inside before continuing along the corridor. I waited a few heartbeats before quietly opening the door a fraction again, just enough to allow me to peer along the corridor. Ralph saw Sofia safely into her cabin, which was a couple of doors along from his own, then came back to his own cabin. I ducked my head back inside and eased the door closed as I saw Ralph start to turn around. I wasn't sure why I did that, but I was aware of a certain feeling of unease building within me. Was it unease, or something else… and about what? I had no idea, but there was something about tonight – tonight's conversation perhaps – that bothered me.

I wandered aimlessly through my cabin to the window and

took vague note of the darkening landscape beyond. Then, with my forehead pressed against the cold glass of my window, I tried to recall every detail of our time in the dining car this evening. I had spent many years taking the minutes of various meetings. Those minutes were not verbatim recordings, but rather where a record of the gist of the proceedings. I had learnt to read the nuances, and to incorporate those in the way I recorded the discussions. Now, in retrospect, I tried applying those same skills to analysing our time together at dinner.

This process was interrupted by a gentle tap on my cabin door. Ralph stood outside glancing nervously along the corridor towards Sofia's cabin. "May I come in for a moment please?" His demeanour suggested something was afoot, and I was keen to know what it was. I stepped aside without hesitation and gestured for Ralph to take a seat.

"I apologise for this intrusion, but I wanted to talk to you about tonight. I noticed something strange and I think you did as well. I wondered if we might discuss it," Ralph said as he stood, with his hands in his cardigan's pockets, before taking the seat I indicated.

"I was thinking about this evening when you knocked. There was something about this evening. I have no idea what it was or why I even think that. Should I ask the steward if we might have a pot of tea or something to sustain us through our discussion?"

"Make it coffee; we need something to liven up our little grey cells, Miss Marple." We enjoyed a chuckle over his reference to Agatha Christie's heroine and it helped lighten the mood by the time the coffee arrived. "Now, tell me what you made of Sofia tonight," Ralph asked.

"I'm not sure I know what you mean. I find her pleasant company, although I think she was a bit distracted in some way tonight. I hope the reason she is going home is not because she did something wrong and has been recalled. However, I have the distinct feeling there is nothing routine or ordinary about her trip back to Istanbul."

"Distracted; yes, that's one way of describing it. I think she was nervous about something, perhaps even frightened."

"I didn't buy her excuse for why she gasped like that. However, she did seem happy enough to talk about the exhibition and how she came to be in London."

"Yes, the museum stuff was interesting. I think we should pursue that a bit more. Maybe ask her to give us directions to where she works. Make like tourists." Ralph's words were somehow unsettling, and I felt my stomach tightening as our dissection of Sofia's behaviour this evening continued.

Discussions continued without any sound conclusions drawn until the train stopped at Jesenice at eleven o'clock. By the time the train moved off again, we had said our goodnights, Ralph had gone back to his cabin and I was tucked up in my bed.

CHAPTER 3

Although tired by the time I climbed into bed, sleep did not come easily. Unsettled by my earlier discussions with Ralph, I continued tossing and turning as the train pulled into Ljubljana. It was another brief stop of 20 minutes at this station. The train pulled out and we were on our way again at 1.00a.m. I hope I'm not still awake when we hit Zagreb, I thought as the train slowly picked up speed.

My last thought as I drifted off to sleep was of the strange noise I heard outside the carriage, possibly on the tracks rather than the platform, during our stop at Ljubljana. Why does it bother me? I let my mind drift back to when we were pulling into the station. We had barely stopped when I heard the thump, not close, but possibly from further along the train somewhere. Then another detail came back: the crunch of the gravel. It sounded like someone running on the gravel beside the rail line. "I must remember to mention it to Ralph tomorrow when we are alone," I murmured aloud drowsily.

I dozed off, but was not sound asleep when the sound of someone running along the corridor woke me again. I lay still, taking short shallow breaths and straining to catch any further sounds. All was quiet for a few moments then I heard it. It sounded like someone talking – yelling – somewhere in the carriage, but not too close to my cabin. It was hard to judge the direction as I lay there, so I sat up, swung my legs over the side of the bunk and swivelled my head until I worked out from which direction the sound came.

The voice I heard came from the front end of the carriage, somewhere near the steward's station I guessed. By the time I worked out where the racket came from, it had stopped. After only a few moments, I heard footsteps come past my door. They weren't running, but they were in a hurry. As they faded into the distance, I cracked open my cabin door far enough to be able to see along the length of the corridor. Two men in train staff uniforms, one of whom I recognised as the steward from this carriage, reached the door at the far end of the carriage and quickly disappeared through it.

All manner of thoughts ran through my mind. Has there been an accident? …Someone taken ill? I sat back on my bunk, a myriad of questions still fluttering through my mind. After a few minutes, I heard people coming along the corridor once more. Again, it sounded like two people. They were not running, but they too were hurrying and one of them appeared to be shouting. I couldn't make out what he was saying. It sounded like some foreign language. Another sound accompanied the shouting and, as it passed my door, I recognised the crackle of the two-way radio that the man was yelling into.

Then nothing, just silence and the usual rattle and moan of the train. However, I thought it seemed to be slowing. Wracked by mounting curiosity and hampered by indecision, I remained sitting on my bunk waiting for the next instalment of what I decided must be a significant drama playing out somewhere on the train. Nothing much happened for about 10 minutes. Then the footsteps returned. This time they made their way along the corridor at a more sedate pace. I'm not sure why, but I threw on my robe.

As I reached to open my cabin door, I thought I heard knocking on a door somewhere further along the carriage. After giving into indecision for a few more heartbeats, I eased my door open a fraction and peered down towards the far end of the carriage. Our steward was standing in the corridor speaking to a passenger through an open door. It was Ralph's cabin. Has something happened to Ralph? Should I go to see if he is okay? It is probably none of my business. But we had developed a connection – a friendship of sorts – and I am concerned for him. Still confused, I closed my door and stood there wondering what I should do.

"I must go to see what has happened. What will he think if I don't do anything?" I murmured aloud in the darkness. Footsteps retreated along the corridor again. All thought of caution abandoned, I pushed the door open and stepped out into the corridor… in time to see the steward and Ralph in a robe disappearing through the carriage's end door. Well, Ralph seems okay, but what is going on? Is Ralph a doctor? How remiss of me. I never even asked him what he did for a living. I ran through possible scenarios in my mind before coming back to what I thought was the most likely. Perhaps Ralph is a doctor... Someone is ill, and they've summoned him to deal with the situation. However, he didn't have a doctor's bag with him. Maybe that's not what's going on.

Alone in my darkened cabin, nothing was making any sense. However, I was aware of a growing uneasiness, and somehow I felt vulnerable sitting there in my night attire. Discretion seemed to suggest I should dress, so I complied – at least partially. After climbing into all my undergarments, I threw a robe over the top and sat down again to think about what I should do next. There appeared little I could do. Whatever was happening, was happening somewhere in another carriage. I could hardly go traipsing through the train looking for wherever the action might be taking place.

It was while I sat there weighing up the limited options available to me that I heard footsteps in the corridor again. I guessed there were two sets. They paused briefly before they reached my cabin. Then I heard only one set of the footsteps continue towards the steward's station. I stood waiting behind the closed door to see what might happen next. Maybe the drama was over and nothing more would happen. It must have been for two or three minutes that I stood there shallow breathing and straining to catch any slight sound that suggested the situation was ongoing.

There appeared to be nothing else happening, and going back to bed seemed like the most logical move. It was as I was climbing into bed that I heard the faint sound of a door opening and closing. Out of bed again, I rested my hand on my cabin door handle and hesitated for a moment before cracking the door open a little. It could be any of the passengers just going to use the facilities. More than likely, it had nothing to do with whatever happened previously, or so I told myself. But the rear view of Ralph, now fully dressed, retreating along the corridor told me the drama – whatever it was – remained ongoing.

I wanted to know what was happening. Not knowing was

making me feel uneasy. I finish dressing before opening the door once more and stepping out into the corridor. As I did so, I saw Ralph enter through the carriage's end door and make his way along the corridor towards me. He stopped outside his cabin but, by the time he got there, I was already standing there waiting for him. "What's happened, Ralph? What's going on? And why is the train stopping?"

Ralph appeared to consider his response for a heartbeat before choosing his words. "There's been an incident; nothing for you to worry about. You probably should go back to bed. Oh, while I have you, I wonder, do you have a camera?"

"I brought two cameras with me. One is a standard 127mm film camera, and the other is a Polaroid. Why…" Before I could finish the question, Ralph cut me off.

"Could I borrow the Polaroid – actually, could I borrow both of them? I need to take some photos right now. I would take good care of the cameras, and replace the film of course at the next opportunity."

"Uhmm   no, I don't think so. I'll come and take the photos for you. It will only take me a moment to get them."

"No… I don't think that's a good idea. I don't think you ought to do that. It's not…"

"If I can't come with you to take the photos for you, you won't be using my cameras. So, why don't we stop messing about, and I'll get my bag."

"Look, I'm not being difficult, not really. It's just that what I need to photograph isn't particularly nice to look at, and I don't think you need to see it."

I already had turned on my heel and started back towards my cabin "I'll make decisions about what I will or won't see, thank you Mr Carter. Wait here. I'll be back with you in a moment."

Ralph shook his head and threw his hands up in resignation. He knew he was beaten, but neither of us knew how things would pan out when we got to where we were going. As I said, it only took me a few moments to collect the large bag containing my two cameras and their associated bits and pieces. I followed Ralph along the corridor, past the facilities to the end door and into the next carriage, which turned out to be the baggage car. At first glance, it looked as though a whirlwind had been through that carriage.

Bags pulled out from the racks where they had been stowed, lay strewn about on the floor. Some were open and appeared to have been searched. I saw three or four with their contents spilling out onto the floor. Ralph didn't allow me to stand around too long taking in the scene before putting me to work. "Right, Polaroids I think first up. Start by photographing what you can see from the door. Get as much of the carriage in as you can. Then, follow me around and I'll indicate what I want you to photograph."

It was a slow process that took quite some time as we needed to pause between each shot to allow the print to develop properly and to be sure it was okay before moving on to the next target. I took a quick look in my camera bag between shots. It was a relief to see that I had the foresight to pack quite a bit of film for both cameras. Although, at the rate we were going, there wouldn't be much of the Polaroid stock left. Almost without warning, Ralph indicated we had finished photographing the luggage.

"There is something else we need to photograph, and I think we might need to use both cameras for that. It's a fairly grisly sight, and I'm not sure it's one I would want a woman to see. Perhaps it would be best if I took the rest of the photos." Although Ralph ended on a hopeful note, I'm sure he suspected it would be to no avail. If he did, he was right.

"I am not some giggle-headed teenager. If you can manage whatever this 'grisly sight' is, I feel confident I will be able to deal with it as well. Shall we get on with it then?"

Time was slipping away. Full marks to Ralph; it seems he knows when he is beaten. He led the way around the end of one of the luggage racks and stopped. With his hand held up to hold my progress, he asked, "Are you sure about this?"

I'm no fool. I already had worked out that the 'grisly sight' might well be a body. In a brave show of defiance, I swallowed hard and lifted my chin. "Definitely; and, if I'm not okay, I will let you know."

Ralph shrugged and heaved a somewhat theatrical sigh of resignation. He motioned me to come forward and stand beside him. Then, pointing at what lay before us on the carriage floor, he said without any particular emphasis, "That's what we need to photograph next and in some detail."

The body lay in a pool of drying blood on the floor between two luggage racks. It was obvious the young man had sustained considerable damage to his head. As he was lying face down, it was difficult to see if there were other injuries, or what he looked like. I felt the bile burn the back of my throat. After swallowing hard a couple of times, I took a couple of deep breaths, all the while being careful that Ralph should not notice my discomfort. A strange metallic smell had greeted us as we rounded the end of the luggage rack and, as I stood looking at the darkening pool of blood surrounding the body, the smell seemed to be intensifying. There was no time to stop and ponder the scene. Ralph brought me back to the reality of the task in hand.

"It's going to be tricky to get good shots because of the location, but we have to do the best we can. We need shots of the area with the body in situ. After that, we will have to go in and photograph the immediate scene and the body in close detail," Ralph explained as he waved his arm about like some tour guide describing an example of fine architecture.

Another hard swallow and a deep breath before I replied. "Right then; where do you want me to begin?" I hoped I sounded more convincing than I felt.

"I think, if you stand about here for a shot taking in the body and this part of the carriage, and then maybe try for another from over there." They were both tricky angles and, after taking my time framing them, I was happy with the results. I was still admiring my work when Ralph came and stood beside me. "These are good. Now, we really need one from the other end." I made a move to walk around the body, but Ralph grabbed my arm and held me back. "No, we can't go walking in there and damaging the crime scene yet."

"Yes, I see. The problem is, the other end of this luggage rack is affixed to the wall. I can't go around that end of the rack to photograph the scene from over there."

"Yeah, just give me a moment to think about it," Ralph said as he stood with his hands on his hips intently studying the area in question.

I left him to get on with it and walked back around to the other side of the luggage rack. Yes, I was right. I thought I had seen a large wooden crate on the floor around here. And I think it might be in just the right place, I thought as I stepped around the strewn luggage to get to the crate. The suitcases now decorating the floor had occupied the shelves on the rack above the crate. The rack itself comprised four shelves but, with the wooden crate too large to fit into the rack, it had been left on the floor and against the bottom shelf. Above the crate, the next two shelves were partially emptied when the suitcases stored there were removed. The whole length of the top shelf was empty. I guess that was because staff filled the easier lower shelves first before struggling to lift any luggage onto the top shelf.

After assessing the situation for a few moments, I had a plan. I stepped out of my shoes, placed the camera bag onto the second top shelf which I could just reach, and climbed up onto the crate. Next, I moved my camera bag up to the top shelf, and followed up behind it by using the empty spaces on the two shelves above the crate as a ladder to reach the top of the rack. When I looked down on the scene on the other side, Ralph remained hands on hips where I had left him. He started swivelling from the waist, presumably looking for me, at the same time as the flash on my camera discharged and I shot his crime scene from my lofty perch.

Aware of where I was, I inched along the top of the rack to the end where it attached to the wall. There was no crate on the other side of the rack to help me climb down. I had to climb all the way using the shelves as a ladder. Ralph seemed to have a bit to say about the foolhardiness and risk involved, and something about safety, but I was too busy concentrating on moving my camera bag down with me as I descended the rack to be too interested in what he was saying.

Another three photographs of the scene from the other end were required. After that, I was again faced with the mountaineering effort of scaling the rack and then descending to arrive back on the wooden crate on the other side. I was helped off the crate by a stern faced Ralph who still seemed to have plenty to say about my exploits. However, he did shut up after he looked at my photographs.

"Yes well, quite good," he commented gruffly. "Now we need to concentrate on the body and its immediate surrounding area. Are you right to do that?"

Somehow, although I wasn't sure how, he had managed to ruffle my feathers so my reply was a touch tart. "We have already wasted enough time listening to you carry on. Can we get on instead of standing here? What do you want me to shoot first?"

Ralph managed to suppress the throaty chuckle I heard developing by turning it into poor attempt at a cough. He strode in close to the body and indicated what he wanted in the first photos. After a few shots of the area surrounding the body, and a few of the rear of the body and specific parts of it, I was loading the last of my Polaroid film into the camera when Ralph rolled the body over onto its back.

There was that bile rising in my throat again. I swallowed hard. Although I thought I had become accustomed to the smell, it seemed to intensify when he moved the body. In an effort to maintain my show of bravado and retain my dignity, I resorted to short, shallow breaths. I hoped it would be like other bad smells and that I wouldn't notice it after a while, or that we would not be at such close quarters with it for too long. However, it seemed like the latter was unlikely. Ralph appeared completely unmoved by the tableau before him. As he scampered around examining the body, he mumbled to himself and scribbled in his notebook. The longer I watched, the less Ralph was looking like a doctor and more like something else entirely.

The young man – I guessed he was young, although it was hard to tell – had jet black hair, his one undamaged eyebrow was thick and black as were his long curling lashes. I thought he had been a good-looking lad. But the attack has been frenzied and brutal. That was obvious even to my untrained eye. His face sustained more damage than the back of his head, although I had already thought that was considerable. However, in my unspoken opinion, the most likely cause of death was a stab wound to the man's chest. The short handled knife still protruding from the wound didn't leave much to the imagination in terms of the weapon used.

More photos before Ralph started going through the man's

pockets. This produced nothing useful as far as I could tell, but I photographed every item as Ralph found it. What he didn't find, as he confided later, was any clue to the man's identity. He explained that the first line of thinking would be that the man was a fellow passenger. In the absence of any identification, Ralph would have to resort to asking staff if they recognised him. My horrified reaction to suggestion of that approach didn't go unnoticed. "It will be all right. I won't make them look at the body itself. I'll use your photos, so can you see if you can get one more clear shot of his face, please."

"… Or what's left of it," was all I could reply. Then added, "I doubt anyone will recognise him with the state his face is in now."

With the preliminary investigation completed, Ralph was keen to move on with the identification of the body. "Let's leave it for now. I need to find our steward and his supervisor to see if any of the staff recognise this man. I'll walk you back to your cabin and then make a start on the identification process."

As he locked the luggage van door behind us, I asked, "Why has this train stopped here in the middle of nowhere? Are we safe out here so far from anywhere?"

"We are about halfway to Zagreb. It is better to keep the train away from any town, particularly from the Zagreb station, for the crime scene to remain isolated and to avoid people getting on and off the train and disappearing into the town. It would be a security nightmare if it pulled into Zagreb or any other station."

"That means we are stranded out here with no protection and with the killer probably still on board. How is that supposed to keep us safe?" I demanded. "…And where are the Police? Surely they should be here dealing with the situation and protecting passengers from the likelihood of any further incidents."

"There was a slip came down off a hillside sometime during the night, depositing rocks and trees across the road. It also brought down some of the last of the snow, and has effectively blocked the road to all vehicles. The police have to drive as far as they can before making their way for the last of the distance to the train cross-country on foot."

"Humph, that hardly seems a satisfactory situation. I would have thought the Police would use one of those pumper things to travel along the rail tracks to the train. Forget about investigating the crime, the rest of us need police here to ensure our safety."

We reached my cabin as I finished venting my dissatisfaction. I unlocked my door and flung it open. As he held it open for me to enter, Ralph said, "The Police are here – me – and they are about to check out your cabin to ensure there is no one lurking in there before they head off to deal with other matters." With that, Ralph marched into my cabin before I could stop him and went through the motions of checking out every possible hiding place, even the overhead luggage rack. Only then, did he motion for me to enter.

"There you are; nobody hiding anywhere. You will be perfectly safe in here if you keep your door locked and only open it to me." I spun around ready to argue, but he was already pulling the door closed behind him prior to setting off along the corridor in quest of identification of our body in the luggage van.

CHAPTER 4

"Sir, Sir; Miss Leggett and Miss Elmas are missing," I heard the steward say as he rushed to meet Ralph who was on his way to the steward's station. As Ralph observed, and I could tell even at my distance, our steward was on the verge of hyperventilating.

"Calm down. Now, why do you think these two women are missing?"

"They do not answer their doors. Our supervisor tells us to speak to every passenger in our carriage to tell them why the train is stopping and reassure them everything is okay."

"Good God, what reason did you give them for why we were stopping?"

"Oh… I see your concern. Not to worry, Sir. We are telling them there is a problem on the line in front of us and we will be on our way as soon as it is fixed. We do not mention the …er… the problem down there," the steward said, as he jerked his head in the direction of the luggage carriage.

"Good, good; now about those missing women … Miss Leggett was with me in the luggage carriage. Miss Elmas might be a heavy sleeper, so I will go shortly to try again to wake her." Ralph might not believe his own words but they sounded plausible. The steward looked skeptical, but Ralph continued. "However, before I do that, I need to ask you if you recognised the man in the luggage carriage."

"No, Sir, but I only saw his back. I do not recognise him from that view, but I know he is not one of my passengers. It is easy to be sure, as I know there are no young single men in my carriage on this trip."

"Okay, that sounds like a good reason to know he is not from this carriage, but I'm going to ask you to have a look at a couple of photographs to see if maybe you remember seeing the man somewhere on the train. I must tell you that they are not pleasant to look at."

The steward's sharp intake of breath was fair comment on the content of photographs, but he simply shook his head and said, "No, I have not seen him."

"Thank you. Now, I need to speak to your supervisor. I need his permission to show these photographs to the rest of the staff and to ask them the same question; all of the staff not just the stewards."

"Our supervisor is supervisor for all staff on the train. He has told everyone they must give you every help and answer any questions you ask. I can call the supervisor to come here to talk with you if you wish."

Ralph said he wanted to talk to the supervisor about the body anyway, and that he thought it would be useful if the supervisor tagged along when he spoke to the other staff. The steward called his supervisor on the two-way radio and, within about a minute, the gentleman in question appeared. As with our carriage's steward, the supervisor did not recognise the dead man and had no recollection of having seen him on the train. Then Ralph, accompanied by his grisly photographs and the supervisor, set off to speak to the other staff.

It was then that I decided there was no point in hiding in the little alcove close to the steward's station any longer. I had snuck along the corridor and ducked into the space while Ralph and the steward examined the photographs. Since nothing more was going to happen here, there wouldn't be any more for me to overhear. However, I did hear later that questioning the staff netted a negative response all round, and that the supervisor assured Ralph that all his staff were present and accounted for, and that none had left the train at any of the previous stops.

With nothing more to be achieved at this time by talking to the supervisor or his staff, Ralph came back to our carriage to address the worrying news that Miss Elmas might be missing. I had to admire his restraint. It must've been a hard decision to take to interview the staff before checking on Sofia. I'm sure that, as Ralph rushed back through the carriages, he hoped he'd made the right decision.

I came out into the corridor after I heard him run past my door. He banged heavily on Sofia's door several times with no result, before he noticed what he later claimed was a strange coldness starting to envelop him. "Sofia, Sofia, it's me, Ralph. Please open the door. I need to talk to you urgently." Nothing but silence greeted him. After we stood listening to the silence for the length of a few heartbeats, he began again, but louder this time. "Sofia, Sofia, open up. I…" A faint sound we both heard from within the cabin made him stop midsentence. After what seemed like an eternity, Sofia opened her door fraction.

"What is it? What is so urgent for you to call on me at this hour of the night?" None too happy to be disturbed we noted.

Ralph ploughed on regardless. "May I come in please? I need to talk to you… and yes it is urgent." The tone of his voice left no room to manoeuvre, and Sofia knew she had no reason to fear Ralph. With an obvious lack of enthusiasm, she opened the door and stood back to let him enter. She motioned me to follow him in. I didn't need a second invitation and I didn't bother to check whether that was okay with Ralph.

Not wasting time on niceties, Ralph got straight down to business. It was true that Sofia looked as though she been in bed all night. The dishevelled bunk, her untidy hair, and the fact that she had thrown a robe over her sleepwear all suggested she had been asleep in her cabin. However, Ralph's experience told him that a criminal, including a murderer, would do their utmost to ensure they distanced themselves from the crime. He later confided that the scene in Sofia's cabin might have been nothing more than stage setting.

If something wasn't right about all this, Ralph seemed to decide maybe a shock tactic would shake something loose. He withdrew the grisly photographs of the body from his pocket, flashed them in front of Sofia, and demanded, "Do you recognise this man? Have you seen him before?"

Sofia's hand flew to her mouth. She recoiled from Ralph and sat down heavily on the bed. As she cowered away from him, she asked in a voice little above a whisper, "What is this about? Why are you showing me these photographs – these horrible images?"

"Do you recognise this man? Have you seen him on the train, or seen him around anywhere at all?"

"No, I don't think so. Why are you asking me this?" Then, apparently sensing Ralph's growing impatience, she added, "It is very hard to see what he looked like, but I don't think I know him."

"Are you sure? Please take another look. Maybe there is something about him you might recognise." Sofia shook her head violently and looked genuinely frightened by Ralph's questioning. He softened his approach and tried to smooth things over. "I'm sorry I was so brutal, but the steward thought you were missing earlier. He had to wake all the passengers to tell them why the train was stopping and got no response when he tried to wake you. We were concerned something might have happened to you as well. Did you hear the steward when he came through the carriage earlier?"

She nodded and replied without lifting her eyes from her hands in her lap, "Someone did bang on my door and call out my name. I didn't recognise the voice, so I thought it safest to do nothing in the hope they would go away…. and they did. No one came to my cabin after that until you came." That seemed like a plausible explanation and Ralph appeared to accept it. Sofia continued, "Who is this man, do you know? It looks like this terrible thing has happened on this train, but it doesn't look like he had an accident. Why have we stopped here where there is nothing? Are we safe here? Are we safe on this train?"

They are not unreasonable questions, and Ralph appeared to agree. We both noticed how nervous Sofia appeared in spite of all the assurances Ralph gave her. I couldn't help thinking that there was more to this woman than met the eye. I wanted to know more about Sofia and, as it turns out, Ralph needed to know more about her as well, including why she was so nervous and unsettled at dinner the previous evening. He chose his next words with care to avoid having her clam up and refuse to speak to him.

"I am sorry, Sofia, but I think I need to ask you some other questions. I need to know what is going on with you. I'm not saying I think it is that you are involved with the murder that happened on this train, but I think you are frightened about something; very frightened, I would say."

"Why are you asking me all these questions? You have no right. What have I, or anything about my life to do with you? Who do you think you are; the police or something?"

"I am the Police. I am a detective with the London Metropolitan Police Department, and I have been asked to handle the preliminary investigation into the murder that occurred on this train tonight. I didn't ask to do this, and I didn't expect to have to do anything like this while I was travelling. I just happen to be a policeman who was asked to take care of things until the local coppers arrive. Now, maybe your situation has nothing to do with what occurred here tonight, but I need to be convinced of that. You see, I think there is a connection – maybe a tenuous one – but some connection nevertheless, between this terrible thing tonight and whatever it was that frightened you earlier this evening."

A gentle tap on Sofia's door prevented any further discussion. "Who is it?" Ralph demanded, the anger in his voice startling both Sofia and me.

"It is your carriage steward, Sir. Is everything all right? Is Miss Elmas there, and is everything all right with her?"

"Yes, Miss Elmas is here. There is no cause for concern. I will talk to you again later."

As he finished speaking, Ralph looked down at Sofia. She seemed unable to meet his eyes but found her voice. "I think I need to talk to both of you. You have been so kind to me, and I need to talk to someone I can trust."

We all settled as best we could in the close confines of Sofia's cabin. Even Ralph chose to sit now. The cabin seemed almost claustrophobic. "Maybe I should see if we can use a dining carriage. It might make everyone feel a bit more comfortable and would give us a bit more room," Ralph suggested. "There should be no one in the dining carriage at this hour, so it would be okay for us to talk privately."

"No. Please, I would prefer to stay here if you both are okay with squashing in like this. I feel safer here at the moment." Ralph's suggestion of relocating seemed to have agitated her. We both rushed to assure her we were fine with the current arrangement and Ralph, keen to hear whatever she was going to tell us, encouraged her to begin.

"I know, Marjorie, you were disappointed to learn I was going back to Istanbul and would not be giving the floor talks at the exhibition in London. I think you thought something had gone wrong with me at my work." I started to protest. "It is okay, but thank you for your concern. However, it is nothing like that. Something has happened to my family, and I was put in a … a difficult position. So, I ran away from London."

"Did this have something to do with the exhibition – with the artefacts, I mean?" Ralph asked quietly.

"You know! How do you…."

"How do I know what Sofia? What is there to know about what happened at the British Museum?" I'm sure my mouth gaped as I looked at him incredulously. What was he doing? This was not at all like the Ralph I thought I knew.

"What happened….? Nothing happened. That is why I ran away, so it couldn't happen. I couldn't do what they wanted if I wasn't there. But I think I have put my family in serious danger."

"Perhaps you should tell me about it. Please start at the beginning so I can understand exactly what it's all about." Ralph studied his boots as he spoke, but I could see the deep furrows in his brow as he weighed up Sofia's first bit of information.

"They wanted me to steal artefacts. It didn't matter whose artefacts they were, whether they belong to the Istanbul or the British Museum, so long as they related to the early Ottoman Empire. This meant they wanted things that were to go in the exhibition, or things that we decided not to include. Of course, I refused to be involved. I knew such things would make big money on the black market but they would be lost forever. There were threats. I tried to ignore them."

"What sort of threats, Sofia…. and who is 'they', do you know?" Ralph asked, but now he studied Sofia's face intently as he asked his questions.

"At first, the threats were quite vague. They didn't say what would happen, just suggested it would be better for me if I did what they asked. Then they became more specific. There was suggestion someone would get hurt. I thought they meant me, that I would get hurt if I didn't do as they asked. As to your second question, I don't know who 'they' are. I have some ideas, but they are so… so… so impossible to be correct."

"Yet these threats were still enough to make you run away.

There must've been something more specific to frighten you so much that you had to escape." Ralph was now leaning forward as he spoke. Resting his forearms on his knees, he leaned in quite close to Sofia, his voice quiet and gentle. I felt that tightening of my stomach that I was becoming so familiar with on this trip. I looked from Sofia to Ralph and back again. The atmosphere in the cabin was electric. I realised Ralph was trying to connect with Sofia in a special careful way. He was trying to gain her trust, to get her to open up. I sat motionless and said nothing lest I break the bond developing between them.

"No, that's not exactly how it happened. A friend works in … in the diplomatic service I think you call it. His family and mine have been close friends forever and I have known him all my life, since we were children together. At one time, he wanted to marry my sister, but this couldn't happen at that time. There were all sorts of reasons why not. However, they remained close friends. I know he didn't approve of, or like, the man she married. None of us did, except maybe my father who believed he was a good catch."

"Was this man one of those who threatened you?"

"No. No, I'm sorry. I forgot what I was to tell you. This young man, this friend, accompanied some politicians – some dignitaries – to London for the opening of the *Treasures of the Ottoman Empire* exhibition. As soon as he arrived in London, he came to find me to tell me he was very worried about my sister and my family. He tried to visit twice before he left Istanbul. He thought they might have something for him to bring to me in London. Although he rang the bell many times on both occasions, no one answered the door, yet all the lights were on and he thought he saw shadows of people moving about inside. Then, the day before he was to leave for London, he visited the market. He saw one of the staff from my family's home there and asked her why she was not at work. All the staff members were forced to take leave. They were not told how long they would be on leave, but that they would be contacted later and told when to return."

"Has this happened before – all the staff being sent on leave? Maybe your family were going away for a few days or something and didn't need the staff."

"That is not so. There were no plans for them to go away and, if they did, they would want the staff to stay at the house to watch over everything and keep it safe. I tried to ring my mother and my sister several times, but they do not answer and they do not reply to the messages I leave."

"This is all you have to suggest something is wrong? If you were worried, couldn't you ask the local Police to check on the house to make sure they were all right?"

"I think that is not a good idea. Things in Istanbul are different from the way they are in London – in England. Also, I am worried that, if the Police call, everyone will say they are okay and then terrible things might happen after the Police leave."

"Okay, I can accept that things are different in your country. But is that all there is causing you so much concern?"

"No. My friend came to see me on the day of the exhibition opening. He had to make arrangements, check on security and everything for attendance of his dignitaries at the opening. He told me two men from Istanbul had slipped unofficially into London the night before."

"Unofficially….? What does that mean? Are they illegal immigrants and, if they are, how did they manage it? Are you sure they weren't just interested citizen coming to look at the exhibition?"

"Yes, I think 'illegal' is correct but I do not how they do it. The reason my friend knows about their arrival is because the government – the Turkish Government – watches one of those men closely all the time."

"Are you telling me one of those men is under constant surveillance?"

"I suppose that is what you call it. He is the brother of the man who married my sister. The two brothers, my sister's husband and his younger brother, are not … I don't know how to say it. They are not honourable men. They are involved in all sorts of things the Police believe – serious crime sometimes – but the Police always are unable to prove it. If they were not watching this man, the embassy would not know two men arrived illegally in London."

"You think their arrival had something to do with what they asked you to do?"

"At first, I think they come to do rough stuff to me because I say I will not do what they want. I get frightened and with my friend's help, I run away from London as soon as the exhibition opening is over. Then, when I am in Paris, it starts to make more sense. Maybe it is not me they want to hurt. Maybe it is my family. Perhaps this explains the situation with the staff, and why nobody answers the phone or the door."

"Are you suggesting you think your family is being held hostage? That they are in danger if you do not do what these people want?"

"This seems the most likely explanation. I believe my sister's husband is behind all of this. He is a very bad man. None of us wanted her to marry him, but he is very smooth and turned her head. At first, my father thought he was a very good catch. He is the second son of a rich and influential Syrian family that my father had done business with for many years. The head of that family is very honest – a good man – but his eldest son, who will take over from him eventually, maybe is not so good. And the second and third sons are total rubbish; criminals. I don't think my sister and my father know how bad they are, or maybe they don't want to know or to believe."

"How bad are we talking about here? Are they just petty criminals … just theft, breaking and entering, that sort of thing?"

"No. They are bad, seriously bad. There are suspicions that they have abducted people and been responsible for some murders – responsible, but not doing the actual murders, you understand? They are rich, but they extort more money wherever they can from local businessmen or other people who have money. They threaten to damage the business or put the owners out of business in some way. Or they find something embarrassing in someone's past and threaten to make it public if the person does not pay up."

"You know this how? If so, surely the police must know and must be able to do something about this. How do these two brothers continue like this without getting caught and brought to trial?"

"I know because I have friends in the diplomatic service and in the… I think you call it the Secret Service… who tell me these things. The authorities can do nothing because none of the victims will talk to them in case something bad happens to them or their families."

"You say you think your family is being held hostage, but what do you plan to do when you get to Istanbul? What can you do? Your sister's husband will not be happy to see you. He expects you to be in London doing what he wants, stealing artefacts for him to sell on the black market. How long were you in Paris? They might have tracked you there, and might know you are on this train."

"I don't think so. I didn't go straight to Paris. First, I went to Amsterdam, before making a long trip through a few countries to come to Paris. I only arrived there late the day before I caught this train for Istanbul. When I was in Paris, I had a quick meeting with my friend who was taking his dignitaries back to Istanbul. He told me the two men, the illegal immigrants, are still in London."

"Do you believe that? Something frightened you at dinner in the dining car last night. I think you saw someone, and that person frightened you. Am I right?"

Sofia shook her head and, to me, it appeared that she was either going to deny it, or refuse to answer. The young woman became agitated, but eventually, with a sigh of resignation, nodded at Ralph. "Yes, I thought I saw someone I knew, but I think I imagined it. It was only a glimpse of a man. Then he was gone and I never saw him again. After a while, I decided I must be wrong. I told myself it was one of the other passengers that I saw, and not the person I thought it was. Although I tried, I couldn't convince myself and I became frightened and thought it best to be careful. If it was the man I thought it was, I could be in danger."

"Okay, I think I understand why you would be cautious, but who is the man you thought you saw? Whose presence on this train would frighten you so much?"

"Oh, I think I am being silly. You will think me a fool. My friend tells me this man is still in London, but I think I see him on the train. The man I thought I saw is the brother of my sister's husband. Then you show me a photo of a... a ... a body. I do not think I know that man, but his face is such a mess, I am not sure. Now I'm not sure about anything anymore. Maybe I did see the brother of my sister's husband in the dining car. Maybe that body is something he has done. I do not feel safe out here in the middle of nowhere, with nothing around, and no one to help. What if that man is still on the train, are any of us safe?"

This reminded me of that sound I heard earlier in the night, before they found the body. Although I was aware I might interrupt Ralph's questioning, I chose at that point to mention the sound I heard rather than wait till later to mention it. "Sometime after we left Ljubljana, I heard something that might be relevant. I was dozing off again when I heard the noise, so I can't be sure about what I heard. However, there was a thump, followed by a brief strange noise. I can't be sure about that either in the light of all that has happened and been said since, but the sounds I heard could have been somebody jumping off the train running on the gravel beside the railway line."

"That is interesting. I need to talk to the train's staff again to see if the man Sofia thinks she saw was on the train at some point, and whether they have discovered anyone who wasn't where they should be. I'm hoping the Zagreb police will arrive shortly and I can hand the whole thing over to them."

"Do you have to go...? Oh, I'm sorry... of course, you must do what is necessary. It's just that I feel safer with you here." The pleading in Sofia's voice wrenched at both Ralph and me.

I felt I had to do something. "I'll stay with you, Sofia. I'm not sure how much use I would be, but I am sure that together we would be more than a match for anything unwanted that came through that door." I have to admit my words did not reflect the lack of bravery I felt. "Ralph, I wonder if we should try moving Sofia to another cabin, just in case someone has already worked out where she is. Our cabins are too small to take her in with one of us, and I don't know if there are any spare cabins."

"That gives me an idea. I'm going to slip out now, but I will be back in a moment. In the meantime, keep the door locked and open it only to me." Ralph opened the door slightly, looked both ways along the carriage and was gone, pulling the door closed behind him without a sound.

I tried a weak smile at Sofia. "As if he needed to tell us to keep the door locked...," I commented as I checked no intruder could get in through door or window.

Ralph was gone for a couple of minutes. He beamed triumphantly as I let him back into Sofia's cabin. "There is a spare cabin. It's a family sized one, and it is ideally located. So, if you could pack your things, Sofia, we will have you somewhere else in a jiffy."

Sofia stood unmoving for the few heartbeats it took for Ralph's words to sink in before she sprang into action. "I have not unpacked. It will take only a moment to throw these couple of things into my bag," she said as she gathered up a few items of clothing.

Then, after another check to make sure the corridor was empty, our furtive convoy departed Sofia's cabin.

CHAPTER 5

"Well, will you look at that … who would have thought this was here?" I exclaimed as I followed the other two into what was to be Sofia's new cabin. "I suppose I never thought about it before, but when you look at it, there is quite a long distance between my cabin door and Ralph's. I didn't know they had such large cabins on this train."

"They gave me a master key so I could come and go from the baggage car whenever I needed to, so I've used that to get us in here. The fact that it is such a big cabin is a good thing. Nobody is likely to think of looking for Sofia in a family compartment, but it also gives us a chance to all be in here together a little more comfortably than in any of our individual cabins. Now, I will leave you two to get settled as I must go to talk to the staff."

There wasn't much 'getting settled' to do. Sofia preferred to keep her bag packed in case she needed to escape quickly. We two women settled awkwardly opposite each other. Conversation was scarce. That night's events seemed to overshadow all other thoughts, and we really didn't know each other well enough to be making small talk about common interests. In the way of small talk, I made the comment that I was a little surprised that the nights remained so cool although it was the start of summer.

"We are still quite high up in this part of the country, so even the days still will be cool. However, even in Istanbul, at this time of the year the nights can be quite cool, while the days become warmer as we move through summer. Your outfit is very practical for this time of the year and for the temperature we are experiencing tonight."

I glanced down at my pale blue twinset and grey checked skirt and giggled. "My friend Connie would be horrified if she could see me now. I wear this sort of outfit most of the time. Not when I was working, of course. Then, I wore suits or two-piece outfits. When I decided to come on this trip, she had me buy some new clothes and shoes. I'm not really into this 'mod' fashion, but I managed to find some things that I didn't mind and felt I would wear without feeling too self-conscious."

"But your hairstyle is quite modern and it suits you perfectly. Why would your friend be horrified to see you now?"

"She supervised my packing for this trip to make sure I didn't add any of my 'old stuff' into the case. I wasn't quite happy about it so, after she left, I added a couple of my favourite outfits without her knowing about it. This is one of them. I should have a photo taken in it so I can surprise when I get back."

"Yes, it is very different from the clothes you wore earlier, but I think it suits you and is very practical."

"At first, I thought Connie might be right. Not wanting to appear old and dowdy, I wore my new clothes. When Ralph boarded the train in London, he wore a three-piece suit. Then later, I saw him in the dining room, he was wearing what I think must be his favourite sort of outfit: casual slacks and a cardigan over a soft shirt. He seemed perfectly comfortable and at home dressed like that, so I thought, that's good enough for me too." We both had a chuckle over the prospect of what Connie might make of the whole thing, before I continued with the story of my makeover. "The hairdo is all Connie's idea as well. She conned me into going to the hairdresser that she uses after arranging for everything beforehand. It didn't matter what I said, it all happened and I found myself leaving the salon with the new hairdo, my face made up, and with a bag full of new cosmetics – which I'm sure I won't remember how to use."

"I'm sure it will come to you. With your beautiful fine skin, I don't think it matters if you don't know how to use it. Just leave it in the bag."

Conversation came to a halt at the sound of someone at the door. We both relaxed as Ralph announced, "It's only me."

Once we all arranged ourselves comfortably once more, Sofia and I focused on Ralph, who seemed blissfully unaware that the atmosphere in the cabin was heavy with expectation. I decided it was time the waiting ended. "Well…?" I asked as I extended my hands, palms up, at Ralph.

"Well what?"

"Are you deliberately messing about, or do you have something to share with us?" I'm sure my exasperation was clear in my tone of voice.

Sofia rushed in to prevent the situation becoming difficult. "Please Ralph, did you find out anything while you're away? We are anxious to know what you found out about any missing passengers, or the man I thought I saw."

"Oh, I see. Sorry, I was a bit preoccupied with trying to sort out something in my mind. Not a lot to report, I'm sorry. No male, or any other passenger is missing, and none of the stewards remembers seeing anyone fitting your description of him. However, a couple of the staff remembers seeing someone who might fit the description in the dining car last evening. They seem to remember he came in for dinner but left again when there were no seats available. There wasn't anything unusual about that. It's common when the train is full. The latecomers go away to wait for a while until some of the diners leave before coming back to try again for a seat in the dining car. No one remembers seeing the man come back later."

"So, it might have been him leaving the train that I heard." Ralph nodded in agreement with my comment. "But he wasn't a passenger. Does that suggest he boarded the train covertly somewhere with the clear intent to commit some sort of mischief?"

"Mischief…! If that photo Ralph showed me is of mischief, I do not want to see something that is horrible," Sofia said. There were a few moments of silence after Sofia's outburst. Everyone shuffled and fidgeted as they wondered what to say next to ease the tension.

It fell to Ralph to ease the situation. "There was some good news. The Zagreb Police should arrive shortly. They radioed through while I was speaking to the staff. It seems the rough country they are crossing on foot is slowing them down. Someone will come for me when they arrive and I probably will be gone for a bit afterwards while I bring them up to speed and do a handover with them." Because the steward, along with everyone else apart from we three, was unaware of the changed cabin arrangements, Ralph slipped back into his own cabin to await the arrival of the Police.

Some 15 minutes elapsed before the steward came to announce the arrival of the police and to ask Ralph to accompany him to the dining car where they were to meet. Ralph reported four officers sat sipping steaming coffee when he walked in. To get it over and done with an out of the way, introductions were immediate and perfunctory. While the others rearranged themselves to make room for him to sit down, Ralph assessed the new arrivals: one officer in charge (ex-military he guessed), one female officer, and two others he categorised as 'foot soldiers'. The introductions did not include mention of rank. This left Ralph to work out the pecking order for himself. He said inclusion of rank would have been a waste of time anyway, as it wouldn't mean anything to him. In his own case, Ralph stated that he was a detective, without qualifying it further.

The brief meeting, apparently consisted of Ralph's delivering a succinct report on his involvement. While he spoke, he tabled one set of all my Polaroid photos to be pass around. The set of Polaroids, having completed their passage around the table, returned to the officer in charge and disappeared into his briefcase. From the outset, something told Ralph he should retain a copy of everything. It was to this end that he had me take two photographs of everything. "I congratulated myself on my foresight. Although I have no idea what I will do with the extra copy, somehow it was comforting to know I still have it," Ralph admitted.

With the preliminaries out of the way, Ralph led the group in single file to the baggage carriage. He unlocked the door and stood aside for the others to peer in, but extended his arm across the doorway to prevent entry. "It might be worthwhile for you to have a good look at things from where you are now to acquaint yourself with the overall situation before going any further." There were nods all round. The officers murmured comments amongst themselves in a language Ralph didn't understand.

"Right then, are we ready to go in?" More nods, and the officer in charge gestured for Ralph to lead on. "The body is around here behind this rack. I have left everything in situ including replacing everything in pockets where it was found. No identification was possible from the material found on the body. As it seems no one can identify him, it might come down to relying on clothing labels for clues. There is not much of that to go on either, but what there is might mean more to you than it does to me."

After the officer in charge expressed his thanks in one brief starchy sentence, Ralph was in no doubt he was being dismissed. He wished them well and made his way back to the carriage door, followed by the two foot soldiers, one of whom carried a heavy-looking backpack. Once outside the door, the officers ignored Ralph, produced a role of crime scene tape from their backpack and began stretching it across the entrance to the carriage. Ralph received the message loud and clear: his involvement was at an end. A bit miffed by his treatment, he turned on his heel and started down the corridor. He slipped the master key he held in his hand into his pocket. His intention was to hand it over but that changed. Ralph finished his report with his comment about the master key. He chuckled, "Sod 'em, I thought as I strode along the corridor. Until and unless someone asks me for it, the key stays with me... And, we can continue to access this compartment with ease."

As the officers were still engaged in roping off access to the baggage car, Ralph went to his own cabin to avoid drawing attention to our appropriation of the larger cabin. He tried reading his book until he thought it safe to venture out into the corridor without being seen. After about 15 minutes, he gave up on the book and checked the corridor. No one about, so he went along and let himself into Sofia's new cabin. We had the blinds down to prevent anyone outside seeing in, and Ralph found Sofia and me sitting opposite each other chatting about nothing in particular.

"I am no longer involved in the murder investigation," he announced as he sat down on a bunk. "I won't be allowed back in to the baggage carriage, so I won't know what happens after this."

"Do they know about me and the man I think I saw in the dining car?" Sofia asked quietly.

Before Ralph could answer, I added my question to Sofia's. "Did you tell them about what I thought I heard after we left Ljubljana?"

"The answer to both your questions is 'no'. I did not mention either matter. Don't ask me why, because I don't know why I didn't. I know I should have, but something – some instinct perhaps – told me not to. If any of it turns out to be relevant later, I can mention it then and say I have only just learned of it." He gave an exaggerated wink and tapped the side of his nose as he finished speaking.

"What do we do now?" Sofia asked. "Do we just sit here waiting for something to happen, waiting for someone to come after me?"

"Hmm, good questions, and I have been giving that some thought. I think we should carry on as normal, except you should continue to use this cabin and not your own. I will give you the master key I still have."

None of this was particularly comforting, and something else occurred to me. "It will be breakfast time shortly. What happens when they go to deliver breakfast to Sofia's cabin and she is not there – and neither is her luggage?"

"I need to leave some clothing lying about in there; some clothes hanging up, something thrown on the bed, even my hat in the luggage rack. That way the steward will think I have gone to the facilities, but I am still using the cabin."

Unaware, I had pursed my lips as I studied the opposite wall while I weighed up Sofia's suggestion. "Then what happens? Do we try to smuggle your breakfast tray back here without being seen?"

"No. It would be better if I return to my cabin to eat breakfast and leave the tray outside afterwards as normal. That way, we would not arouse suspicions." Ralph gave a slight shake of his head in response to her suggestion. "You do not think that is wise? I think it is a practical way to do it," Sofia challenged him.

"No. It is a good idea; very practical," Ralph conceded. "I'm amazed by how quickly you two women can come up with creative solutions to problems." We 'two women' exchanged a look, but chose to let his comment go by.

There was no one in sight when Ralph checked the corridor, so Sofia and I, armed with items of Sofia's clothing, followed him to her cabin. It took us longer than expected to arrange the clothing to look haphazardly strewn about to our satisfaction.

After some encouragement from Ralph, we completed the task and returned to the larger cabin. "Right, now that you're settled in safely again, Sofia, Marjorie and I will return to our cabins to wait for breakfast and maintain the façade that all is normal with us," Ralph said and added a meaningful look at me to be sure I understood.

Breakfast came and went. "There remains some delay with the track," the steward advised when he delivered breakfast. "However, they think that maybe soon we will be able to progress again." The three of us discussed the steward's comments later when we returned to the big cabin.

"Does that mean the police are letting the train go on to Zagreb now, or were the steward's comments just a ploy to keep passengers settled for a bit longer?" I asked.

Ralph studied some indeterminate point in the distance before answering. "Hard to say, but I think they are either going to have to get the train moving again soon, or come up with a new excuse for the delay. They might get away with a lengthy delay due to a supposed blockage of the track in winter but not at this time of year, and passengers will start to question this delay if it stretches on much longer." Ralph peered out the window and scanned the countryside as he spoke. "It is getting light outside. If they haven't already removed the body, they will need to do it soon if they want to spirit it away under cover of darkness so passengers remain unaware."

"What was that sound? Did that sound like the train getting ready to start?" Sofia asked. There was no need for an answer. A few moments later, we felt the shudders as the train began to move again.

"Next stop Zagreb, in a bit over an hour I estimate," Ralph announced. "We probably should take some time to work out how we should proceed from here, although I think the threat to Sofia has passed."

"You are right, we need to talk about what to do, but why do you think I am now safe?" Sofia asked.

"If what Marjorie heard was the murderer running from the train, you should be safe as there is little likelihood he would have tried to get back on the train."

My head suddenly felt empty. I felt as I couldn't remember anything from the itinerary. "Before we do any serious planning about how we go on from here, I'll duck back to my cabin to fetch my itinerary. It will tell us all the places the train is supposed to stop at between here and Istanbul. All the times will be wrong after tonight's delay, and I doubt they will be able to make up as much time as we've lost. We will have to recalculate all of the times." It took me only a few moments to go to my own cabin, grab the documentation that I'd left lying on my bunk and be back in the corridor again.

My timing was fortuitous. I paused in the corridor to watch the steward. He knocked on each of the cabin doors and spoke briefly to the occupants. I took a few swift paces to stand in front of the door of Sofia's new cabin. Then, in a voice that I hoped Ralph and Sofia would hear, I commented aloud, "Good heavens, here comes that steward again. I do hope he is not bringing more bad news."

Sofia half opened her door and stepped out to stand beside me in the corridor. Ralph followed her, but moved quickly to stand in front of his own door. By the time the steward reached my cabin, he gained the impression he was interrupting a conversation being held in the corridor between myself and Sofia. Before the steward could deliver his message, Ralph, now standing in his cabin doorway, demanded, "What's going on now? What's all the fuss out here about this time?" As he spoke, Ralph bustled along the corridor to join Sofia and me.

"Ah, thank you for joining us, Mr Carter. Now I only have to deliver the message once instead of three times," the steward said.

"That does save you a bit... Philippe," I said as I peered at his name badge, "But what information have you brought us this time? I hope it's not more bad news."

"I'm sorry, but yes... well no, not very bad news." His audience giggled as Philippe tried desperately to sort out what he had to say. "We will soon arrive at Zagreb. The stop there is normally only 35-40 minutes. Today the train must do some shunting operations. Our stop will be a bit longer. Everybody must leave the train at Zagreb while we are stopped and the shunting occurs. We apologise if it is an inconvenience, but it must be that way. However, it is an opportunity to walk around and stretch your legs, and maybe look at a bit of the place or have a coffee."

Along with my best Oscar-winning portrayal of frustration, I muttered, "I suppose if it has to be, then we will have to get off. I must say, this trip is not going as I expected. No, don't go apologising. It's not your fault, Philippe. I know that. We will get off with everyone else, won't we?" My two companions nodded their agreement. It was a beaming steward who continued on his mission, believing he had somehow managed to avert a potentially sticky situation.

"I do not want to get off the train," Sofia whispered when she gauged the steward was out of earshot. "I will not be safe out in the open like that. It is better if I managed to hide in my new cabin."

"No, I don't think that's the case. If you stay on the train, there will be no one around you. You will be alone and it will be an ideal opportunity if someone wants to make an attempt on your life. It is much better for you to come with us, and for we three to stick together the whole time," Ralph said.

"I'm sorry, Sofia, but I think Ralph is right. You must come with us. We should stay together. I don't think anyone will try something when there are people around and when we are with you," I said.

It was gone 9.00a.m. when the train pulled into Zagreb... only about six hours behind schedule. As the three of us stood looking out from Galvi Kolodvor, Zagreb's main station, we were greeted by the sight of the regal-looking Hotel Esplanade. "It doesn't seem too far away. Why don't we go for a walk for a better look at the place?" I suggested.

"This is ridiculous," Sofia complained, "All of us walking as though we are joined together."

Sofia had a point. I understood what she was saying. "Ralph, I must admit it does feel a little odd huddled like this, and I suspect it must look a bit strange to anyone observing us. Are you sure we need to carry on walking so closely together, especially when there are so many people around us? Surely no one would try anything in this sort of situation."

"Perhaps I was being a touch overcautious. In fact, we might be drawing unnecessary attention to ourselves by being like this. Okay then, let's relax a little and behave more naturally," Ralph suggested. He heard both of his companions heave a sigh of relief as we added a little space between us.

"What a lovely area this is," I commented as I strode along taking in the sights.

"It is King Tomislav Square. I agree it is a lovely place to walk, not crowded and a nice way to get to the Hotel Esplanade," Sofia said.

"This place is magnificent. I might have been tempted to overnight here if I'd known about this hotel. I believe the war took its toll on the place," I murmured as we wandered around the hotel.

"They certainly did a good job on restoring the place. There is no sign now of what it became during the war," Ralph said.

While I was enjoying strolling around, there were other necessities in life besides architecture, and I made noises accordingly. "The information we were given as we left the train was that we had at least an hour and half to take in the sights before the train might be ready to leave Zagreb. That gives us reasonable time for a cup of coffee I think."

No need for any further discussion; there was no argument. We wandered into the coffee shop and Sofia and I instantly went into raptures at the sight of the array of pastries and other sweet treats. "You would feel like royalty even if you only have a glass of water in here," I said. "It's so elegant, even down to the starched white tablecloths. You're almost terrified you might spill something on them."

Ralph soon put an end to our brief thoughts of grandeur. After checking his watch, he announced, "We should get back to the station. If we leave now we won't have to hurry to get back within the hour and half they suggested we might be spending here."

As it turned out, we had plenty of time. When we arrived back at the station, the train was not yet waiting there. With nothing else to do, and reluctant to leave the station again, we sat on one of the benches on the platform to await its return. After about 15 minutes, the familiar rattle accompanied by the squeal of brakes announced the arrival of our train. It was another few minutes before we were allowed to board.

We stood at once, hoping to be able to board straight away. We were wrong, and spent the subsequent waiting time standing on the platform idly observing everything around us. Ralph leaned in closer to me and murmured, "That's a different baggage car that's on there now." I blinked in surprise and followed his gaze to the carriage in question. "I noticed when we left the train that the one we had then was dark green in colour, not the dark grey one that's attached now."

"So that's what the 'shunting operations' were about."

Ralph ran his hand across the stubble now apparent on his jawline as he gave the matter some thought. "I suspect the Police have isolated the carriage as a crime scene. They probably had to take the train somewhere to drop off our carriage and connect the new one. If they want to continue to keep the whole incident hush-hush, I suppose someone then had to transfer all the baggage from one carriage to the other. I'm not sure how they would have dealt with those cases that were opened. Interesting to think about, but I'm not sure we will ever know what they did."

Then, the carriage doors opened and everyone's focus was on returning to their cabins. I later admitted that I had inspected my cabin closely after I came back, but didn't detect any sign of anything having been disturbed or anyone having been in there. Sofia giggled and admitted she had done the same, even checking under the mattress on the bunk she had been sleeping in.

And then came the now familiar shuddering, slow laborious movement as the train eased away from the platform. We were on our way to Belgrade.

CHAPTER 6

After inspecting our cabins and stowing anything we had been carrying, as if summoned by some unseen trumpet, the three of us congregated in the corridor. "It's about five hours to Belgrade I think. That should give us plenty of time to talk through a few things, and to work out what's going on and how to proceed," Ralph said with a view to taking charge of the situation. However, the sight of the steward coming towards us again put our planning on hold.

"Good afternoon… oh sorry, it is still morning for a bit longer. In case you're wondering, I wanted to let you know that lunch will be served in the dining car from 12.30p.m.," Philippe advised us.

As the steward walked away, I raised my eyebrows in question at Ralph and asked, "Is it worthwhile getting started on our planning? There is only about another half hour before lunch. Why don't we agree to leave it until afterwards? We could meet in Sofia's compartment then without having to watch the time or worry about the steward coming to interrupt us until afternoon teatime."

Lunch happened. No time wasted over it, and no one took much notice of what was served. Soon after, we reconvened in Sofia's compartment. Not sure how to begin, a few moments of shuffling and uncertainty occurred before Ralph took charge.

"Unless I am mistaken, I don't believe either of you has asked why I am on this train. I thought that I should…"

I interrupted before Ralph could say any more. "Why would we ask? What is so special about you, or about your being on this train? Sofia has explained why she is on board. She is going home. I simply assumed you were on the train because you were on holidays, taking a trip the same as I am. Is there something more sinister about your presence here?"

In the few moments it took Ralph to consider his reply, Sofia cut in. "Given everything that has happened, and that you were conveniently on hand to deal with the murder, there were moments when I wondered if you were here for a reason. Now that you bring the matter up, I think it is something other than a holiday that has you on this train."

"You are right, Sofia. There is a reason I'm here. I don't know that I would call it sinister, Marjorie, but I am here because of my work. The main reason I wanted to have this discussion was to inform Sofia about an incident that occurred back in London after she 'ran away'. How that incident led to my being on the Direct Orient Express is a long story, but I think it's one that perhaps you both should know."

Sofia and I exchanged a look before I answered. "I'm not sure... is this something... damn... what I'm trying to say is, this all sounds like something pretty iffy to do with some crime, and I'm wondering whether you should be telling me about it. I suspect it involves Sofia either directly or indirectly, and that she needs to know. But are you sure you want me to stay to hear it too?"

"I asked myself that question," Ralph admitted. "I decided it was best if we all knew the story and understood its implications so, unless you have some objection, I think you too should hear what I have to say."

I didn't have any objections. Besides, I was curious as all hell now that he had said that much. Ralph cleared his throat and hummed and hawed for a few moments while he gathered his thoughts before launching into his spiel in a way that took both of us women by surprise. "Sofia, have you heard from anyone associated with the exhibition since you left London? Any of your work colleagues perhaps, or maybe one of the organisers tried to contact you?"

"No. There has been no contact by anybody, but I expected that. Nobody knew where I was or what I was doing, and that's the way I needed it to remain. I certainly didn't try to contact anyone and I am unaware of anyone trying to contact me. Why is this important?"

"I'll get to that. Now, as I understand it, you left London immediately after the night of the exhibition opening. Is that correct?"

"Not exactly; I was at the Museum for most of the next day, went home a bit early in the afternoon and left London soon after. I spent the night in a hotel before catching the ferry to Flushing and then went on to Amsterdam. This feels much like an interrogation. Am I under suspicion of having done something, having committed some crime?"

"Surely not, Ralph. What is it you're getting at with all these questions? I'm finding it all a bit unsettling. It must be worse for Sofia. Perhaps you should get on with the story, and get to the point." I could feel the heat of the red smudges developing in my cheeks resulting from my rising indignation at the way in which this supposed 'discussion' was progressing.

"I do not mean to upset anyone. I am simply trying to find out how much Sofia knows about what happened in London after the opening of the exhibition. That way, I will know how to explain things so that it makes sense and no one is confused. After all, I am a policeman and I have spent many years asking questions in a certain way. I don't mean to sound like I'm interrogating anyone. It just comes naturally after all these years I suppose."

Ruffled feathers somewhat smoothed, apologies flowed from all those assembled. Once a neutral environment was established once more, Ralph got on with his story.

"Let's see now, it would have happened on the night you left London. That is, the night you spent at a hotel before catching the ferry across the channel. An incident occurred at the British Museum, in the space where your Ottoman Empire exhibition was set up."

There was a sharp intake of breath from Sofia and her hand flew to her face. "No, oh no, please don't tell me something terrible has happened to the artefacts."

"Maybe if I just continue the story, your questions might be answered as I go along. So, where was I? Oh yes, an incident on the night you left London; well actually, it was early the next morning. There was some sort of dinner or function on that evening after the museum closed. It went quite late, but one of the workers had arranged to come in afterwards to do something with the artefacts in the exhibition. Straight after the function, he firstly went to an off-site storage facility to collect a piece of material. There was no problem with that, as security knew he was coming. He collected whatever it was and left."

"Hmm, I think I know what that might be about. Sorry, my apologies for interrupting; please continue." Sofia motioned Ralph to go on with his account of what happened.

Ralph continued his story, including every pedantic detail as only a police officer delivering his findings could do. "Once this person had whatever he went to the storage facility for, the man returned to the British Museum. By the time he arrived there, it was around midnight. The place was deserted except for the cleaners. On his arrival, he went to the storage area. The cleaners reported seeing him enter the building and rush through in that direction. Soon after, they saw him go into the area of the Ottoman Empire exhibition."

"Yes, it is as I thought," Sofia murmured. Ralph shot her an irritated look but continued without hesitation.

"Sometime later, they don't know how long but think it was only a few minutes, the cleaners heard worrying noises coming from the exhibition area. They went to investigate and found the man they saw earlier lying unconscious on the floor. He had a nasty gash to the head and had been stabbed in the chest area, but he was still alive. The cleaners called police and ambulance and whoever else. The injured man was carted off to hospital. However, in their subsequent search of the premises, the police found the body of a security guard at the bottom of the rear stairwell."

Sofia shaking her head in disbelief, made a kind of quiet keening sound. When Ralph stopped to draw breath, she exclaimed, "This is terrible. There is so much more to all of this than what happened to those men. There are political implications. It is my fault. I should have stayed to do my job as I was supposed to."

"Then it might have been you lying on the floor… and maybe in an even worse condition than the current victim," Ralph pointed out before attempting to take up his story again.

"What about the exhibition?" I asked. "Was anything stolen or damaged?" While waiting for an answer, I moved closer to Sofia and put an arm around the young woman's shoulders.

"Ralph, Sofia is very distressed by all this. Should we maybe leave the rest of the story until later?"

"No, no. I need to know what happened. I am concerned for those men of course, but I must know about the exhibition, about the artefacts. Please continue the story."

"Well, if you're sure…" Ralph hesitated but continued. "It is believed the man opened one of the display cases, probably to add whatever it was he collected from the off-site facility. He was found on the floor in front of that case, which had its lid open. The man had chocked up the false floor of the case to enable him use an antique looking hand drill to make two small holes in the board."

"The Cyrus cylinder…! It would be the case that held the Cyrus cylinder. Was it taken?" It seemed to me that Sofia was hyperventilating. I began rubbing her back, and quietly urged her to calm down and let Ralph share the rest of the story.

"If you're okay…" Ralph began. Sofia nodded, and I indicated to Ralph that he should carry on. "I don't know what this Cyrus cylinder is, but one large object remained in the case. There was no sign of the object that the man retrieved from off-site storage, but it is believed he was in the process of installing it in the case when he was attacked. There had been an attempt to take the other object as well – that is, the large object that was already included in the exhibition – but something seems to have prevented that. It took the police a couple of days with the help of the museum people to work out what they think happened. In the end, they determined some small seal – I think that's what it was called – was missing. Nothing else appears to have been taken. Sofia, I know this is terribly upsetting for you, but does this make any sense to you? Can you suggest any explanation for what happened that night?"

"O-o-oh yes, I'm sure I know exactly what happened. The public, including you, might not know about all the politics and protocols involved in mounting this exhibition. The loan of so many absolutely priceless artefacts to the British Museum was a big deal. When this sort of situation happens there is a lot of red tape – bureaucracy – involved. I'm not saying there shouldn't be, but it gets in the way and slows the work down. This was a huge exhibition and all this other stuff meant that we were working like crazy right up to the last minute before the opening. There were so many other behind-the-scenes things taking up time: meetings, discussions with dignitaries, inspection tours for dignitaries, and so many more things that take time."

I was aware of the deep furrows creasing my brow as I wrestled with all the information being provided by Ralph and Sofia. I must have missed some important point along the way. All I had gotten out of it so far was confusion. "So how does all that contribute to the situation that night of the attack?"

"That's a good question, Marjorie. What's the relevance of all that, Sofia?" Ralph also looked a bit perplexed by Sofia's comments.

"As I said, we were busy right up until the official opening. Just before they opened the doors for the visitors to enter, a colleague and I had a quick walk around the exhibition to make sure everything was as it should be. We identified several little things, very minor things – cosmetic effects really – that we would fix once the opening was over: move something slightly, turn something around a little bit more, reposition a text panel so it's easier to read... nothing major. These things were not obvious before setting up the whole of the exhibition was finished. There was no time to take care of these things during the day of the opening, so my colleague and I planned to do these changes before we opened the next day."

"But, as it happened, you weren't there that next day, so you don't know whether those things were done or not," Ralph commented. "I still don't see how this relates to the incident I told you about."

"One of the things we planned to do something about was the case holding the Cyrus cylinder. The case looked a little too empty and our attention was drawn to it by visitors' comments. It seems quite a few visitors who know a bit about antiquities thought the Cyrus cylinder was a seal. Although the text panel in the case beside the object explained its history, it seems people still thought it was something other than what it was. I suppose, if you don't know too much and you see something that is cylindrical with a hole through the middle and carved on the outside, it's not unreasonable to think it might be used as a seal. However, the Cyrus cylinder was never intended for that use, and is far too big to have been used in that way."

"I read something about that object in the pamphlet advertising the exhibition. Its history was fascinating and I was looking forward to seeing it when we visited the exhibition," I told her.

"To help people better understand, we decided to change the display in that case – just a bit. Our thinking was to select an appropriate seal from the British Museum's collection and place it in the opposite corner of the case to the Cyrus cylinder. We chose a seal from photographs of the collection and my colleague arranged for the production of an appropriate text panel that told a bit about the seal, but also drew viewers' attention to the difference between the two artefacts in the case, and their different purposes. What you have described as occurring that night is consistent with what we planned to do. My colleague retrieved the seal from the off-site storage, and was in the process of installing it in the display case when he was attacked. You said something was stolen, but not the Cyrus cylinder. It probably was that seal he was about to install in the case that was stolen."

"Yes, I think that probably is correct. What I don't understand, is why he was drilling holes in the false floor of the case," Ralph said.

"I think you said it appeared that the attacker tried unsuccessfully to remove the Cyrus cylinder. That might be because the cylinder is tied to the false base. It would still be possible to steal it but it would take a bit longer as he would need to free it before he could take it away. We use nylon cord that is clear and looks like fishing line to tie the artefacts in place. The cylinder has several strands passing through the hole in its centre. They are secured beneath the false floor. The holes that were drilled in that board were to take the cords that would have secured the additional seal in place on the board. It is likely my colleague had not yet secured the seal in place when he was attacked. Therefore, when the attacker couldn't easily free the cylinder, he chose to grab the seal and go."

"That makes sense. The cleaners were working just outside the exhibition area and, when they heard the noise coming from inside, they dropped everything and ran into see what was happening. It is likely that the sound of the cleaners approaching frightened off the attacker before he had a chance to free the cylinder from its tethers. I think we both agree that the most likely scenario is that the attacker's intent was to steal the Cyrus cylinder. How significant is the theft of the seal?" Ralph asked.

"The theft of any artefact is significant. It undoubtedly will find its way onto the black market and disappear forever. However, it is fortunate that, while the seal we intended to use is ancient and significant in itself, it is not significant in the overall terms of either of our collections or the exhibition. I don't believe someone would kill a man and almost kill another just to steal a relatively unimportant seal."

"I agree with your assessment of the situation, and of the seal as being relatively unimportant. In the case of the latter, the British Museum seems to share your opinion and does not wish to pursue the matter of the stolen object. Of course, that doesn't mean that the incident itself is over and done with. There is a murder and an attempted murder to investigate."

Further discussion on the subject was halted by the sound of a trolley loaded with afternoon tea trays being rattled into the carriage. Ralph cautiously peered out into the corridor. With a frantic motion to me, he stepped out into the corridor and I followed him. We made a show of strolling up to my cabin door as the steward wheeled his trolley towards us. "Your timing is excellent," Ralph told the steward. We were just heading for Miss Leggett's cabin to take afternoon tea together. Miss Elmas will be joining us directly she returns from the other end of the carriage."

The steward gave a knowing nod in response to the last comment to indicate he understood that Miss Elmas had gone to use the facilities. "In that case, I will leave three trays with you," he said, smiling at me, and proceeded to unload the trays, leaving very little room in my cabin for the people who were to partake of the afternoon tea they held.

When we heard the steward and his trolley rattle past on his return from delivering afternoon tea to the other passengers, we waited a couple of minutes before venturing back to Sofia's compartment. Sofia opened the door, and Ralph strode in carrying one tray out in front of him. I followed him struggling somehow to balance one tray on each hand. I stepped sideways through the doorway so as not to bump the trays, and heard Sofia giggle. "What's so funny?" I demanded. But it was good to hear her giggle.

"I was not laughing at you Marjorie. The way Ralph was carrying that tray reminded me of someone who was carrying a bomb that was about to explode. He looked almost terrified."

"…And I was. I was quite terrified I would slosh the tea out of the pot and all over that pristine white cloth in the bottom of the tray," Ralph said with a mock shudder, which generated peals of laughter and helped lighten the atmosphere a bit. Conversation took on a lighter note while we disposed of afternoon tea. Then, with the trays placed outside my door to maintain the charade, we returned to the compartment and prepared to pick up from where we left off before the steward's interruption.

As Ralph closed the door behind us, and before we had time to sit down, Sofia asked the question that troubled her all through afternoon tea. "Ralph, you have not mentioned the injured man's name. Do the Police know his identity?"

"Ah, yes, I believe they do. I hadn't mentioned it because I can't remember it."

"If I told you a name, would it help you to remember?"

Ralph shrugged and then nodded. "Give it a shot. It might help."

"The man I think it would be is the one who was to work on rearranging the display case. He is the colleague who also was to deliver some of the floor talks. His name is Altan Sadiq. Is this the man who was taken to hospital?"

"Sadiq… Altan Sadiq…. Yes, that sounds about right. I can't be sure you understand, but I think that sounds like the name. They say he will be okay, if that helps you feel better," Ralph added when he saw Sofia's reaction to his confirmation of the man's name.

"Thank you. Yes, it helps a bit. The whole thing is shocking, but somehow it is worse when it is someone you know and like." Ralph, at a loss as to what to say, found himself shuffling from one foot to the other as he tried to work out what to do next.

In an effort to rescue the situation, I asked, "Are we going to stand around for the rest of the ride to Belgrade, or shall we get comfortable?" With that, I moved a couple of paces away, smoothed the covers and sat down on one of the bunks. "I have to admit that it's been an intriguing story, but I think it all started when you sounded a bit miffed that we hadn't asked why you were on the train. I must confess that, after so much time and conversation expended on the matter, I still don't think I know why you, Ralph Carter, are on this train." I felt the other two looking at me as I made myself comfortable. "It seems to me that you wanted us to ask, probably because there is another story you are dying to tell us."

"Oh, did I not say?" Ralph said in mock surprise. After a resounding chorus of 'no' from us, Ralph allowed himself a chuckle as he began to explain. "Another young chap was also seen in the museum on the night of the incident, that is, another besides the cleaners, the attacker and his victims. This is where the story gets a bit tricky. That other young chap is the nephew of the Minister for Culture, the Honourable Geoffrey Durnsford, who just happens to be some distant in-law of our Police Commissioner. Young Durnsford is suspected of being involved in the crime in some way and that has rattled the corridors of power a bit. In addition, the Turkish government is making all sorts of noise about the incident."

"I imagine my government might have plenty to say about the incident, although the only thing that should really concern them is the attack on the Turkish national, Altan Sadiq. Even so, I can understand how an attempt to steal the Cyrus cylinder would make them very nervous. I am sure there are many within their ranks who are calling for our artefacts to be returned to Turkey before some other incident occurs."

Ralph heaved a sigh of resignation. "Yes, I believe that is the case. That is what has been happening. Those investigating the incident say there are indications that there was insider involvement. Because of this..."

"What does 'insider involvement' mean? Are they suggesting that someone from the museum was involved?" Sofia asked before

Ralph finished speaking.

"No, not exactly; my colleagues investigating the case are playing it a bit cagey and not saying what they have, but they are suggesting the 'insider' is at the Turkish end of things. The Turkish Embassy officials in London took great umbrage at this and wasted no time in relaying the information back to Turkey. That stirred up a whole lot of trouble which nobody wanted and, as I understand it, precipitated a major investigation by Turkish authorities of everyone involved with the Istanbul Archaeology Museums. The Turks also insisted that the Met send an officer to assist with the investigation."

Ralph stopped to draw breath and it was obvious he was trying to collect his thoughts about how to tell the next part of the story, but before he could manage that, I interrupted his thinking. "Are you the representative they are sending to help with the investigation? That must demonstrate much confidence in your ability."

"If only…," Ralph said and added yet another sigh. "The truth is, at home, nobody is particularly interested in what the Turks are going on about. We are interested in capturing the attacker who killed and injured people that night. If we happen to uncover any others who might have been associated with the attempted robbery that would be a bonus… but it is not the main focus of the Met's investigation. If I was honest, I'd say their main focus at the moment is proving young Durnsford had nothing to do with it and clearing his name, but that might be uncharitable of me. However, they find themselves in a situation where they have to at least appear to be interested in the Turkish point of view. None of the detectives wanted to go, and we already have a heavy caseload to deal with. I believe the powers-that-be looked around to someone who wouldn't be missed if they went to Turkey. I suspect that 'let's send Carter' was an easy solution to the problem. So, here I am on my way to Istanbul."

"I… don't… understand," Sofia said. Her confusion at what she heard was clear. "I'm sorry, Ralph, but I don't understand. Are you saying that there was some evidence suggesting someone from our archaeology museums was involved, or was that something they told the Turkish authorities to make them go away?"

"Surely, they wouldn't say that if there wasn't some evidence to suggest it." I was quite shocked – almost put out – by the suggestion that it might be otherwise. "…I mean, if there wasn't some evidence to incriminate someone from the Turkish side of things."

"I cannot say. No… I am not holding anything back. I have not seen any evidence. I have not seen any case files. The truth is, I haven't had any involvement. However, if you're asking for my opinion on the matter, I would say that it might be possible that they found some evidence to suggest it was an insider job. But, if I were a betting man, I think my money might be on a disinformation exercise."

While everyone else was mulling over Ralph's comments, I stole a glance at my watch. "Look at the time." It caused a flurry of time-checking as the others also checked their watches and agreed it would soon be four o'clock. "I did a quick calculation when we got back on the train after Zagreb and worked out that we should be in Belgrade around four o'clock. Has anyone heard what time they expect us to arrive?" After receiving a negative response from the other two, I continued. "If we are going to be there by four o'clock, we must be pretty close by now. It's hard to know where we are with the blind down like that all the time." I raised the blind about halfway up and peered at the countryside flashing by. "Well, that wasn't particularly helpful. I have no idea where we are, but somehow it's not what I expected to see if we were close to Belgrade."

"No, that does not look like close to the city. I think we have a way to go yet," Sofia said.

"By the way, is it just me, or does this train seemed to be going slow this afternoon?" I asked.

"I had the same thought myself when we were having afternoon tea. It might have something to do with the countryside we're going through, or the state of the track. It would be nice though to know what time we might arrive at Belgrade. I think I might go in search of our trusty steward to see if he can shed light on anything," Ralph said.

"I'm sorry, I don't wish to appear rude, but this afternoon has brought so much to think about. Would you both mind if I had some time to myself? I think I would like some time alone to think through everything Ralph has said and to get my head around what it all means." Sofia looked from one to the other of us and was relieved to see us both nodding.

"Of course, my dear, it has been a lot to take in. And I know that I for one could do with a little lie down before we get to Belgrade," I confessed as I followed Ralph out the door.

CHAPTER 7

"Ah good, there you both are," Ralph said as I let him into my cabin.

"Yes, Sofia just came to see if I knew anything more about our likely arrival time in Belgrade and what our options are for while we are there. The program suggests we have an hour or so to stretch our legs and look around, but all timings seem to have gone out the window after that long stop this morning. We were thinking they might see Belgrade as an opportunity to make up some lost time."

"Our ever helpful steward suggested we should arrive at Belgrade somewhere between 4:30 and five o'clock. He has received no definite information yet about our time of arrival but expected to hear something soon to pass on to passengers, and that would include details of any changes to the stopover time. And in case you are going to ask, I queried why the train appeared to be going slower than normal. He assured me it was something technical, nothing serious, and not to worry about it."

I gave an audible sniff of scepticism. "Great; telling us not to worry is the best way of ensuring that we do worry."

"I'm wondering if it had something to do with that replacement baggage carriage they added it Zagreb. It looks an older model than the one we started out with," Ralph suggested. "I must say, Sofia, you do look a little brighter than you did earlier. Is there anything from earlier this afternoon that we need to discuss further?"

"That is possible, but I think I still need more time to think about everything. Other things that we did not discuss are bothering me now that I know as much as you told us."

It seemed we had little time to indulge in further conversation on the topic anyway. "Whatever our arrival time, it won't be too much longer before we arrive at Belgrade. Maybe it is best to leave the topic alone until later this evening, after dinner perhaps. We should spend the next little while preparing for whatever our stop at Belgrade involves," I suggested.

It was only about five minutes later, while we were discussing what we might do in that city that the steward arrived with news. "Our arrival time at Belgrade is 4.50p.m. Our stop will be for about an hour, and the train will depart again at about 5:55p.m. All passengers are encouraged to take advantage of the stop to stretch their legs and maybe take in the sites around the station area. Dinner will be served at about seven o'clock, but this will be confirmed when we get underway again."

"Well now we know," Ralph said, "So, what shall we do while we are there?"

No one else spoke up, so I put forward my suggestion. "I think I would like to have a bit of a walk about. I have nothing special in mind, except maybe just having a bit of a look at the place. It will be good to get the legs working again after being cooped up on the train all day."

"I too would like to walk. Our walk around Zagreb felt good, and I think walking around Belgrade might help to clear the head." Sofia looked at Ralph as she finished speaking, hoping for support for the idea of going for a walk. He rose to the occasion.

"Okay, in the interests of us remaining together and because I too fancy a walk, there is consensus that we will spend the stop at Belgrade taking in the sights on foot."

Almost right on the dot of the advised time, the train screeched to a halt beside the platform at Belgrade's main station, pronouncing the name of which was beyond most English speakers. It appeared that most passengers shared the need to exercise their legs. As soon as the train was stationary, passengers rushed for the doors and streamed out onto the platform. Hesitant once on the platform, some stood around in small groups apparently unsure what to do next. Others boldly strode off in all directions to begin their exploration of the immediate environs. We were amongst the latter.

With no particular plan in mind, we strode through the station and out to the street beyond. "Oh, look at that building over there," I exclaimed. "It looks like it belongs in a storybook. Can we go over for a closer look?"

"You don't see something like that every day," Ralph

commented. "Let's head across the square to see it."

"It is a hotel," Sofia informed us. "The building I think you are talking about is the Hotel Moskva. It is something of a landmark here in Belgrade and, although it looks and is an old building, its modernisation includes a spa centre and a gym."

"It's amazing. I must have photos of it. Come on you two, stand in front of it so I can get you in too." After a series of shots from various angles I spotted something else that impressed me. "What's that building over there? It looks old as well, but not as artistic as the Hotel Moskva."

"The building across the street from the Moskva is the Balkan Hotel. It also is a very old hotel but, now refurbished inside, it is quite modern. Come, I will show you something at the Balkan," Sofia said as she started off across the street. Ralph and I obediently followed her across to the Balkan where she led us into the hotel's 'Orient Express' restaurant. It comprised a restaurant, lounge and shisha bar.

"It's just beautiful in here," I sighed as I let my eyes roam over every corner of the restaurant. "The interior is quite distinctive and so refined. If you wanted to treat yourself, you would arrange to spend an overnight stopover here."

"We still have quite a bit of time to fill in. What else should we see while we are here, Sofia?" Ralph asked.

"Uhmm, I think Knez Mihailova Street. It is not too far and is quite beautiful."

After all our sightseeing, we found ourselves hurrying to get back to the station on time. Breathless after our brisk walk, we arrived on the platform as they opened the carriage doors for passengers to reboard the train. There were three other passengers from our carriage queued up ahead of us. "What is it, Sofia? What's the matter... what did you see?" I swivelled my head all round to see if I could see what the problem was as I asked the question.

"No, nothing; it is okay."

"Then why are you so nervous? Something has put you on edge. What is it?" I persisted, as it was obvious something was amiss.

"It's nothing. It's just being out here in the open makes me feel very vulnerable. I think I would be an easy target like this, no?"

The elderly couple at the head of the queue to enter our carriage seemed to have all sorts of trouble getting themselves and their various bags of shopping on board. No one had boarded our carriage since we tagged onto the end of the queue. All five others waiting for the elderly couple to get out of the way became fidgety and impatient. Ralph, idly listening to Sofia's and my exchanges, realised as I did the truth in what Sofia said. She was a sitting duck out here in the comparative open.

Without warning, Sofia found herself pushed forward into the back of the person in front of her. At the same time, Ralph grabbed my arm and pulled me up to stand beside him. "What… What has happened?" Sofia asked as she looked around wildly.

"Nothing has happened," Ralph reassured her. "You were right about being exposed out here in the queue, so I took steps to correct that situation. With Marjorie and me standing up close behind you like this, you are covered from all angles. I don't think there is any likelihood of an attempt on you at this time, but we need to be careful."

"At last…!" I said in a stage whisper as the elderly couple, laden with their shopping, disappeared into the carriage. "I was beginning to think we might be better off going to the next carriage to board and then making our way back along the train to our own cabins." Just about to board the carriage, the woman ahead of Sofia shot me a filthy look and hissed, "We will all be old one day… even you." Mortified by my own insensitivity, I felt the colour burn its way up into my cheeks.

The steward, exasperated by the tardiness of his passengers in boarding the train, had come to the rescue. He took the shopping bags from the elderly couple before hauling them aboard. Then, he remained at the door to deliver his latest message to each of the passengers as we boarded. "It is now confirmed that dinner will be available in the dining car from seven o'clock. Our scheduled time to leave Belgrade is six o'clock."

When we arrived at my cabin, Ralph asked, "Well ladies, what is our schedule for this evening? Do we want to continue our discussions between now and dinner?"

"N-o-o … No, I don't think so. There isn't much time before

dinner. Why don't we leave it for now and discuss at dinner what we might like to do for the rest of the evening?" I suggested and was relieved to see Sofia nodding.

"Yes, I think that is the right way," Sofia agreed. "I think I might like to have a lie down for a few minutes before dinner. Perhaps we should leave it and see how we all feel after we've eaten."

"That suits me," Ralph said. "I think I'll try reading a bit more of that book. Marjorie, I take it you haven't had an opportunity to read much more than I have. I'm beginning to think I'll have a lot of book to read when I finally get home after this trip."

We saw Sofia safely to her compartment before we went to our cabins. Ralph was still trying to get comfortable with his book when I tapped softly on his door interrupting things. "Marjorie, is everything alright?" He checked the corridor for any impending disaster about to descend on us. "Nothing has happened has it?"

"No, everything is fine. I just wanted a quiet word if I may. I noticed that even when we were walking about the streets, Sofia was on edge and I wondered what you think her situation is likely to be from now until we get to Istanbul. Do you think someone is trying to harm her, and are they likely to try something while we're on the train?"

"It's difficult to say. I'm not sure we've heard the whole story from Sofia's point of view, so I don't know how to assess her situation properly. My concern is that, whoever murdered two people and severely injured a third would stop at nothing if they intended to harm Sofia. I am beating myself up about being so lax about everything while we roamed the streets of Belgrade. My thinking is that we should not become complacent and should proceed as though an attempt on her life could be imminent at any time."

Not exactly the comforting words I wanted to hear. "That's a scary thought, but it is in line with my own thinking. I guess the other question I have is, do we share our thoughts on the matter with Sofia?"

"I don't think there is any need to. Sofia's nervousness is evidence enough for me that she is fully aware of the gravity of the situation she finds herself in – we all find ourselves in."

We passed a brief time until dinner in our respective cabins before being amongst the first passengers to make their way to the dining car. As soon as we all settled at what has become our customary table, Ralph surprised us. "I don't know about the rest of you, but after the long day I've had, I could really go a glass of something to relax me. What about you two, could I interest you in a drink of some sort? Perhaps a sherry, or maybe I could get us a bottle of white wine. What do you think?"

A drink of some sort sounded good. "I don't think I feel like a sherry, but a glass of white wine would be very nice. What about you Sofia, would you like a glass of wine?" Sofia nodded enthusiastic support of the idea.

As a few other tables were occupied when we arrived soon after seven o'clock, there was a bit of a wait for our food to start arriving. This gave us time to enjoy the wine. By the time our entrées arrived, we were feeling considerably more relaxed.

Conversation over dinner was light and of no consequence, focusing mainly on what we had seen in that small corner of Belgrade. We lingered after finishing our meal to drain the last of the wine before returning to our cabins. There was agreement we would reconvene in Sofia's compartment after taking about a half-hour to attend to personal matters and freshen up.

Later, I stepped out of my cabin and saw Ralph unlocking his cabin door. "Ah Ralph, are we getting ready to meet again? I'll just be a few minutes if you want to do that."

"Take your time, Marjorie. I'll be a little while yet, but you go ahead and join Sofia when you're ready." Ralph flopped down on his bunk and threw his notebook onto what passed for a table in his tiny cabin. I'll probably have to apologise to Marjorie later, he told himself. I brushed her off rudely and almost slammed the door in her face. "What do I do now?" He asked the universe. "This is a pile of shite. What the hell is that all about?" His empty cabin didn't respond, certainly didn't miraculously produce any answers, so he opened his notebook. After a couple of deep breaths in an attempt to lower his anger a few notches, he began reading slowly and carefully.

It was useless. His mind wasn't on his notebook. It wandered back to that time earlier in the evening when they returned to their cabins after dinner. Every moment came back with such clarity.

Still trying to get comfortable with his book, Ralph's planned reading time went the way of so many well laid plans when a knock at his door interrupted everything. "Excuse me Sir, I apologise for interrupting you, but there is a radio message coming through for you in a few minutes. Please come with me now to take the call."

As Ralph told it, when he opened the door, the train's staff supervisor standing there came as something of a shock. He expected either me or Sofia to be there. The supervisor's presence was a surprise, but his message further compounded that situation. "I'm not sure I follow you. What's this all about? Who is supposed to be calling me?"

"Sir, I cannot answer those questions as you would wish. All I know is that it will be a confidential call, for your ears only I believe. I'm not sure about the identity of the caller, but I think it might be the Police. We don't have much time. Please, we must go now, Sir."

As they started along the corridor, a worrying thought occurred to Ralph. "Has something happened – on board this train, I mean? Has there been another incident that warrants police involvement?"

"I'm sorry, Sir, I do not have this kind of information. My instructions are only to take you to my work area so that you may take the call in private. We must hurry. The call is due in a couple of minutes."

I thought we were hurrying, Ralph thought. If he goes any faster, I'm going to have to trot to keep up. Then they entered the first carriage behind the engine. The supervisor stood aside and held open the door for Ralph to enter. "So, this is your office," Ralph said as he surveyed the space.

"Not exactly an office I think, but it is my workplace. You will take the call on that radio there. I will stay to make sure the call starts okay, and then I will leave so you will have privacy." Ralph, ex-Airforce – but a long time ago – didn't think he would need help, but wasn't sure what sort of modern foreign-made equipment might be in use.

Ralph looked at the radio and shrugged as the supervisor pointed to it. It didn't look any more complicated than others he had used in the past, and it confirmed his initial thought that he could manage on his own. However, something suggested that the supervisor had instructions on the procedures to follow for this call, so Ralph chose not to interfere. After the supervisor finished speaking, there was barely enough time for Ralph to settle comfortably at the desk before the call came through.

As previously outlined, the supervisor took the call, confirmed Ralph's presence and handed over to Ralph before quietly disappearing out the door and closing it behind him. Ralph felt decidedly wrong-footed. He had no idea to whom he would be speaking, wasn't sure what it was all about and, whether it really was the police (which police?) that were calling him.

No point sitting here wondering, he told himself, and pressed the button on the microphone. "This is Ralph Carter. Please identify yourself and the reason for this call."

After a moment of hiss and crackle, an accented voice cut through the ether to provide a name and rank, neither of which Ralph understood. There was a slight pause. Ralph thought he heard the shuffling of paper. Then the voice was back. "It is fortunate for us you are on board that train at this time. We had a call from the London Metropolitan Police for some assistance in a matter with which I believe you are familiar."

Ralph cut in, "Excuse me. Who is 'we'? And what particular matter are we talking about?" The disembodied voice, not bothering to mask its frustration at the interruption, said Ralph's supervisor contacted them and that it was in relation to the same matter that had him on the train to Istanbul. Ralph stifled a groan at the sound of his supervisor's name. Bob Brent never had much time for him, Ralph thought, and the immediate thought that followed was that whatever this call was about, it was something no one else would take on, and was unlikely to enhance his career prospects in any way. "Huh, career prospects… What career…? That stalled years ago." Ralph was startled when his caller asked him to repeat what he had said.

"Christ, I must have been thinking aloud," Ralph murmured as he tried to regain some lost ground. "Sorry, I asked for confirmation this call is in relation to the incident at the British Museum. Can you confirm that, please?"

"Yes, that is so. We believe Miss Sofia Elmas, who recently worked on a major exhibition at the British Museum, is a passenger on your train. The Metropolitan Police believe she is involved in the recent crime at that museum. They asked us to observe what she does when she first arrives at Istanbul, to note where she goes, who she meets, and subsequently to apprehend her and arrange for her extradition to London. You are on that train because of your secondment to us to assist with another related investigation. As such, you have the same authority as our officers."

Ralph gripped the microphone so firmly, his knuckles turned white. He sat staring at it, unable to believe what he had heard. As though through a fog, he heard his name called repeatedly. It penetrated the numbness that enveloped him, snapping him back to reality. Again, another white lie: "I'm sorry. A moment please while I complete the notes I'm making." As he tried to unscramble his confused thoughts, Ralph whispered to himself, "It is well there are no visuals associated with this call." Then, with his brain and mouth fully in sync, he delved what the call was about. "Okay, I'm with you now. What is it you expect me to do? So far, that remains a mystery to me. Oh, and you had better tell me what this Miss Sofia Elmas is supposed to have done, or what her involvement in the London crime is supposed to be."

"Evidence suggests Miss Elmas is guilty of committing the crimes both at the museum and on your train."

"I don't… That's not…," Ralph spluttered into the microphone as he tried to find the right words, but the deafening clanging of warning bells in his mind made him stop to rethink the situation.

The disembodied voice was becoming impatient. "What are you trying to say? Do you know something about this?"

More clanging… and becoming louder. "Er, no, I don't know anything that helps. I was going to say that I find it hard to believe a woman could commit those crimes. The murder here on the train was brutal, a frenzied attack. I wasn't directly involved in the London investigation, but I understand it was similar."

"Maybe, but that is not my concern. My only concern is to observe Miss Elmas when she arrives home, and then to arrange her extradition. Your job while you are on the train is to stay close to the woman. Do you know who she is?"

"Yes, I know Miss Elmas."

"Good. You must stay close to her; befriend her. Watch everything she does. If she leaves the train for any reason, you must go with her. Follow her or join her, whatever, but do not lose her. We will take over tailing her when she gets off the train in Istanbul. Is there anything you need clarified, or anything else you need to ask?"

Once Ralph assured him that he had all he needed, the call ended. Stunned by all that happened, Ralph stared blankly at his notebook open on the bench in front of him. Unable to move, he remained glued to his seat. A gentle knock on the door broke into the whirlpool of thoughts he tried to translate into something that made sense. "Yes?" He rasped in response to the knock. It was all he could manage. Even his vocal cords had gone into shock.

The door opened a fraction. The supervisor thrust his head into the narrow gap. "Is it all right for me to enter? I think your call has finished, no?"

"Yes, please come in. The call is finished. I was finishing my notes. I'll be on my way now. Thank you for allowing me to use your area." He didn't know how many carriages he walked through, or how long it took him to return to his own cabin. Ralph was too stunned to think, and found his way back to his cabin purely on autopilot, or instinct, or something similar.

As he revisited his call and the new instructions he received, he walked up and down his small cabin in an attempt to realign himself with the here and now. "Follow procedures," he counselled himself aloud, and headed for his bag parked in the corner of the cabin.

About half an hour later, a notepad sported several pages of his scribbled thoughts. "It doesn't make any sense," he murmured to himself. Again, he addressed the universe in general. "How can they think she did it? What have they found? What evidence have they got to make them think that?" Just as well he wasn't expecting a response. He didn't get one. Accompanied by a sigh of resignation, he threw down his pen and checked his watch. After hurriedly stowing his notes in his bag, he rushed to pound on Sofia's door.

She looked a little put out when she opened the door, and stood in the doorway blocking his entry. "It's getting late. We thought you might have decided to give our meeting a miss. We were just talking about calling it a night ourselves. Is it worthwhile getting together now, or should we leave it until tomorrow?"

Oh dear, she is definitely not a happy traveller, Ralph told himself as he went into placating mode. "Apologies, I lost track of the time. I understand if you two ladies would prefer to call it a night. I'm not sure how much more we have to discuss anyway, but I'm sure there is nothing urgent."

Something was not right here. "Perhaps we should leave it overnight," I suggested. "I think we must be just about at our next stopping place. I can't remember what the place is called. I remember its name is all consonants and no vowels. I've no idea how you would pronounce it. I checked the schedule earlier and adjusted the times once more. I think we should be there at a bit after nine o'clock and, if my calculations are correct, that will be in about 10 minutes. We will be there only about 20 minutes. I think I'd like to be in bed by the time we stop so that I'll be ready and able to sleep for a few hours after we get going again."

"That sounds like a good idea, Sofia agreed.

"Okay, I'll go along with that. I'll see you in the morning." With that, Ralph spun on his heel and marched back to his own cabin. He noticed a certain weariness had crept up on him, and he welcomed the opportunity firstly to be alone and then to have an early night. The train made its scheduled stop and then moved off again on its way to the city of Sofia. As Ralph later reported, the way things were shaping up for him, he thought he still might be awake when we got to the next town, as sleep showed no signs of visiting him.

Sleep was elusive for me as well and, after tossing and turning for about an hour, I decided to sit up and read for a while. On my way to retrieve the book from across the cabin, my trip documentation caught my eye. Without too much thought, I picked up the trip itinerary, added it to my book and took them both to the small table. My intention being to read my book, I went to place the itinerary to one side – and stopped. "Well, we've had the stop at the place with the unpronounceable name. Let's see what comes next and what we will be missing out on," I murmured as I unfolded the itinerary.

My conversation with myself continued as I scanned down the page. "Ah, that's right, next stop Sofia." I calculated the revised time for our arrival. "Well, if my calculations are correct, that's another place we're not going to see. We are supposed to have almost an hour in Sofia but, if we don't arrive there until nearly 4.00a.m., I don't think passengers are going to want to get off to stretch their legs for an hour at that time of the morning. What had I planned to see during our stopover in Sofia?"

I searched through my notes attached to the itinerary and found a very brief entry for Sofia. "It doesn't look like I'll be missing out on much. All I noted was the Communist Party headquarters building, and maybe the new film production studio that they're establishing, that is if it's operating yet." I folded up the documentation and pushed it to the other side of the table. I couldn't help but giggle as I'd drew my book over to me. "Good God, I really must be going senile. I've begun having conversations with myself… And I'm having another one now." I grabbed my book and slammed it opened at the marked page and wondered yet again whether a book about a 'ship of fools' was an appropriate choice for this journey.

As is so often the case, although wide awake when I started reading my book, after about half an hour I realised I was struggling to keep my eyes open and I really didn't have a clue what the last couple of pages were about. I closed the book, left it lying on the table, and slid into bed. Although somewhat revived by that spurt of activity, within a few moments, I was sound sleep.

CHAPTER 8

I awoke to a cool morning, and with a thick head. I had not slept well and the stop at Sofia disturbed what little sleep I had. I drifted off while we were stopped at Sofia, but the shudder and rumble of the train as it pulled away from the platform woke me again. I seem to have fallen asleep almost immediately once we were underway, but the rest of the night was restless and plagued by dreams that, although not quite nightmares, where frightening. Instead of scrambling out of bed as soon as I awoke this morning as is my usual practice, I opted to stay snuggled up with the bed-clothes pulled up to my chin.

After dozing on and off for the best part of half an hour, I shook myself free of whatever had engulfed me and sprang out of bed. Disoriented by the upheaval of my normal routine, I splashed cold water on my face and dressed as I tried to wake up properly. An early riser from habit, I was amazed to find there were only a few minutes before breakfast would arrive. I spent that time rushing about tidying my cabin before the steward arrived with my tray, and all the while hoping the activity might rev up my system enough for me to be functioning normally by the time that happened.

Ralph had not spent a good night either. He claimed he climbed out of bed this morning feeling decidedly below par. He had slept – he knew he slept – but didn't feel as though he had. He had hoped to be bright and fresh this morning to be able to make sense of the previous evening's radio conversation. Breakfast arrived and he greeted it unenthusiastically. With no interest in food, or anything else much that morning, he toyed with his breakfast for over half an hour without eating much. With a final nibble at a piece of bacon, he gave up, placed his tray outside the door and dressed to face the day.

Washed and dressed and feeling a little more human, he said he wondered what to do next. Should he see if the women were awake, or should he wait until we made some move towards him? He said later that it was clear to him that last night ended with him being well and truly out of favour. He suspected that, as a result, we might choose to do our own thing from now on and cut him out. It wasn't until much later that he admitted that, given the strong message he received in the previous night's radio call, such an outcome, while probably justified, would not be an ideal situation for him. As he recounted it, he told himself as he hauled himself upright and marched to the cabin door, "No, it's up to me to make the first move." Before leaving, he paused to check his appearance, pulled his cardigan down snugly and smoothed the front of his slacks before stepping out into the corridor.

His timing was perfect. Ralph summoned up his most affable demeanour as he saw me coming towards him from the facilities at the far end of the carriage. I smiled and tried for a cheery 'good morning'. He smiled back, and bravely asked how I had slept.

"Terribly," I grumbled. "I don't know what was wrong with me. It wasn't only the train's stopping and starting that disturbed me. I just didn't seem capable of deep sleep at all and woke with a woolly head this morning."

Ralph chuckled. "Well that only makes two of us so far this morning. Have you seen anything of Sofia yet today?"

"No-o-o, and I'm a little concerned. I heard the steward bring her breakfast tray at the same time as he delivered ours. A bit later I heard him come back and knock on her door again. She mustn't have answered it because, when I came out later, her untouched breakfast tray remained outside her door. On my way back just now, I was going to see if you were awake to ask if you had any thoughts on what we might do."

"I don't have any ideas, but I am developing an uneasy feeling. Let's try knocking on doors, starting with her cabin door. I don't think she will be in her cabin, but it's worth checking that one first. If – or when – we don't get any response, we'll try pounding on the compartment door."

"And if we don't get any response there…? I do hope she is all right. Like you, I have a very uneasy feeling about this."

With my questions still unanswered, we stood outside Sofia's cabin while Ralph pounded on the door and called Sofia's name. As expected, there was no response. We exchanged worried looks before moving along the corridor to stand outside the compartment we had moved Sofia into. I confessed to Ralph, "I don't know why I felt so worried when we got no response from her cabin. We didn't expect her to be in there anyway."

While I stood helplessly looking on, Ralph began his repeat performance. He pounded heavily on the compartment door and shouted, "Sofia. Sofia, it's Ralph. Are you all right?" Not a sound was heard from inside.

Futile though it seemed, I tried my luck. I knocked gently and called softly, "Sofia, I'm worried about you. Please open the door. Is something wrong? Please let me know you are okay." I was no more successful than Ralph was. Ralph saw the worry etched across my face as I turned to look at him. He put a hand on my arm in a bid to comfort me, but I got nothing from it. "Now I really am worried, Ralph. She couldn't sleep through the racket we made. What do we do now? What else can we do is the question, I suppose."

Ralph shook his head gently as he studied the toes of his shoes. "I feel something is definitely amiss. I gave Sofia the master key I had, so we can't go in to see if she is okay. I know it might bring her wrath down on me for invading her privacy, but I have an idea, and I think it might be the only thing we can do. Wait here, I'll be back in a moment."

Perplexed, I watched Ralph stride off along the corridor only to return a few moments later with the steward. Philippe, the steward, appeared uneasy about something, but I noted Ralph's set jaw and guessed there had been an exchange of words. As we gathered outside Sofia's compartment, Philippe almost wailed at Ralph, "As I have told you, there should be nobody in this compartment. There is no passenger booked to use this compartment."

Ralph, appearing unmoved by the steward's performance, pointed to the door and demanded, "Open the door!" After shooting Ralph a none too pleasant look and shrugging, the steward threw open the door and stood off to one side without as much as a quick glance inside the compartment.

The compartment was empty. None of Sofia's belongings remained in it, but the bunk was rumpled. It had not been slept in, but looked as though it had been sat on. "Are there any other empty cabins or compartments in this carriage?" Ralph asked the steward, who nodded a silent response. "Which ones…? Come on man, we could have a serious situation here. Let's get those other cabins checked out."

As Ralph gestured to the steward to move along the corridor to the next unoccupied cabin, an elderly woman from a cabin close to the steward's station rushed out into the corridor shouting, "Philippe, Philippe, come quickly please." The steward hesitated, unsure which passenger to deal with first. Ralph helped him with his dilemma.

"Give me your keys and tell me which cabin numbers are empty, then go and sort out the woman's problem. Come on, move yourself. It might be serious." The steward thrust his keys into Ralph's outstretched hand and rattled off some numbers before bolting back along the corridor to the woman now standing in the middle of the corridor frantically waving her arms in the air.

With me close on his heels, Ralph rushed in the opposite direction along the corridor until he came to the first supposedly unoccupied cabin. He knocked rapidly and called out, "Hello. Is anyone in there?" When there was no response, he quickly unlocked the door and peered inside. It was empty, and there was nothing to indicate anyone had been there. We moved systematically along the corridor checking all the cabins the steward identified as unoccupied. We found nothing until we came to the last cabin at the end of the carriage. "Unless they were booked out, I doubt they would put anyone in this cabin. It's not a great location being opposite the facilities as it is," I suggested as Ralph fumbled with the keys.

"The steward gave us this number so, in the interest of being thorough, we will have a quick look in this one as well. I have to admit that, so far it's not looking good," Ralph said.

"You don't think she might have slipped off the train at either of those stops we made during the night? Surely she wouldn't have been tempted to do something like that," I asked.

As he pushed open the door to the last cabin, Ralph spoke over his shoulder to me. "I sincerely hope not, but we are running out of options. There are not too many other places she could be unless she managed to find somewhere in another carriage."

"I thought this was supposed to be empty," I said. "It's obvious someone is using the cabin. This must be where Sofia moved to. I don't understand why she would do that."

Ralph had the cabin door open for only a couple of seconds before I spoke, but that was long enough for me to see the personal belongings strewn throughout the cabin. He pushed the door open wider and took a quick look inside before responding. "It's not Sofia who is using this cabin. All the kit strewn about in here belongs to a male. I don't know who might be using it, but it's supposed to be empty."

"What's the steward up to, making out the cabin is empty when he's got someone stashed away in it?" I realise my voice was creeping higher in accord with my level of alarm.

Intuition kicked in. Ralph caught me by the shoulder and spun me around. "Quickly, come back to Sofia's cabin with me. I don't think we should be seen standing around outside this cabin for too long." A few seconds later Ralph unlocked Sofia's cabin door and we quickly slipped inside.

"Why have we come back here?" I didn't have a clue what was going on. All I felt was confusion as I looked around the cabin. "We know Sofia is not here, or in the other compartment, so how does coming back here help find her?"

"For goodness sake, woman, just give me a moment to think. I know she's not here, or anywhere else in this carriage. Just give me a few minutes to think the situation through." His rebuke brought the colour to my cheeks, but I bit my tongue and sat down heavily on the bunk without comment. However, it didn't take long for the situation to get the better of me and I started to fidget. I raised the blind and peered out of the scenery flying past without really seeing anything. Ralph hadn't said anymore since his rebuke, and in my mind, finding Sofia was going nowhere.

I stood up with the intention of telling Ralph I was going back to my own cabin but he startled me with an unexpected comment. "Might be worth a try…," He murmured more to himself than to me. Then, he spun around to face me, "There is one place where we haven't looked that she might consider a safe place to hide.

Come on; let's see if we can find the right key to get in."

We stood rocking and swaying in the cramped space between the two carriages as Ralph tried the various keys on the steward's keyring. "Please hurry, Ralph. I don't feel altogether safe out here, especially as I don't think anyone would be too happy about finding us breaking into the baggage carriage."

"We are not 'breaking in'. We have a key. Yes, and before you argue, I know we are not supposed to be down here. Aha, jackpot! Come on, quickly, and close the door behind you."

Apart from the fact that it looked a bit older and the racks looked a bit more knocked about, this carriage didn't differ much from the one we had started out with. The one major difference was, the last time I was in the baggage carriage, luggage and other stuff was tossed about everywhere and the contents of some cases spilled out onto the floor. Without thinking, I gingerly picked my way to the far end of the carriage and peered around the end of the rack. I felt more than a bit sheepish when I looked over my shoulder and found Ralph standing with his hands on his hips watching me. A rising red tide of embarrassment crawled up my cheeks again.

"If you don't feel comfortable, you can go back to your cabin," Ralph said quietly, "But this is not the same carriage remember. There is no body in this carriage, no blood on the floor, and nothing else to suggest a crime has been committed." As he finished speaking I thought I heard something. I stiffened and turned my head sharply to the right. With my chin elevated and my mouth slightly open, I strained to hear if the noise I thought I'd heard would come again

Ralph stood still and followed my lead. He hadn't heard anything, but then he had been speaking. He still couldn't hear anything… nor could I. Not wanting to speak, he waved his hand at me to get my attention. When I was facing him, he whispered so quietly he wasn't much more than just mouthing the words. "What…? Did you hear something?"

I too wasn't going to speak, so my reply was an almost imperceptible nod. Although I hadn't heard the sound again, I had worked out where it came from. With my hand still down by my side, I swivelled my right wrist to point to an area behind the luggage rack to my right. Ralph leaned in close and whispered in my ear, "Ignore what I said and walk to the door. Make as much noise as you like while you're about it."

My first instinct was to ask what he was up to, but I had second thoughts and simply raised my eyebrows at him in question. His response was to motion me to move towards the door. Okay, I'll play along. I shrugged, turned and slowly took the first couple of steps. As I did so, Ralph announced loudly, "No, nothing here, just another waste of time. Let's go."

When I reach the cabin door, I wasn't sure what I was supposed to do next. I put my hand on the handle to open it and then glanced around for Ralph in the hope of getting further instructions about what to do next. I was in time to see him step around the end of the luggage rack, the opposite rack to the one I had peered around to check for bodies. A commotion broke out but through it, I heard Ralph's voice clearly. "It's okay. It's okay, Sofia, please listen to me. It's okay, we mean you no harm. Why are you down here? Did something happen last night?" Was I imagining things? Above the noise of the train I thought I heard something.

I rushed around the end of the luggage rack to join Ralph and a distraught Sofia. I threw my arms around Sofia and held her tight. "What has happened to frighten you so badly? We are here now. Come back to the compartment with us and tell us what has happened." Sofia shook her head frantically and freed herself from my grip.

"I can't. It is not safe for me. ... And I think if you are seen with me too much, it might not be safe for you either. It is best I stay here on my own. I need to think about whether to try to leave the train somewhere or to stay on board until we get to Istanbul."

After taking a moment or two to think about what Sofia had said, Ralph moved in closer and, keeping his voice low, asked the question that that had come to him. "Did you see someone on board who frightened you again?" Sofia shrugged and gave a half-hearted nod. "I see. There is someone in the end cabin of our carriage, someone in a cabin that is supposed to be unoccupied. I do not think the occupant is a paying passenger, nor do I think he is supposed to be on board. Did you see who the occupant of the cabin was?"

"No, I didn't know anyone was in that cabin. I was going to the facilities and had my door open a little when I realised I didn't have my toothbrush. I went back to get it and, as I approached my door again, I saw, reflected on the window on the other side of the corridor, a man coming my way along the corridor. My cabin was in darkness, so I eased the door closed until it was open just a crack, and I waited for the man to pass. He wore a big hat – strange in the middle of the night, no? It was difficult to see his face clearly, but I think it was the same man I saw on the train before. He went past without stopping; didn't even look at my door. I waited for quite a while before risking a quick look up and down the corridor. There was no one about."

"You didn't see where the man went?" Ralph asked although he already knew the answer.

"No. He had disappeared when I checked the corridor. I guessed he must have one of the cabins further along the carriage from ours."

"What happened after that? How did you come to be hiding down here?"

"I remembered you said the key you gave me was a master key. I had noticed that a few cabins were unoccupied, so I decided to try to find one to hide in. It wasn't until I was out in the corridor and about to start trying doors that I realised I didn't know which cabin belonged to the man I was trying to hide from. As none of the staff seemed to be able to identify him when you asked earlier, I assumed he was not supposed to be on the train or in any of the cabins. The risk of coming face-to-face with him when I opened a cabin door to see if it was unoccupied was too high."

"That was good thinking. I'm pleased it occurred to you before the whole thing went pear-shaped. So, when you tried to find a different cabin, what made you come to the luggage carriage?" Ralph was becoming officious. As I listened to him dragging the details out of Sofia, I couldn't help but think it was becoming an endurance test for all involved. I kept my thoughts to myself – for the moment anyway.

"I was out in the corridor. I didn't know what to do, to go back to the compartment or to look for somewhere else, but I knew I couldn't hang around out there in the corridor. Then I thought of the baggage carriage. When I got to the door, I remembered it was a different carriage from the one we started with. I almost went into a panic when I realized that, because I thought the key might not fit this new carriage. I was desperate; I had to try. It worked. I went back to the compartment, collected my belongings, and snuck back here."

"I still think that steward has a lot to answer for. I'm sure he is up to no good. I can't believe he didn't know someone was in that cabin." There had been nothing to convince me that wasn't the case.

Sofia looked confused. Ralph stepped in to help her. "The steward was going to check on the empty cabins with us but something else came up. He gave me his keys and told me which ones were unoccupied. We tried all the cabins he mentioned, and of course found there was somebody in the last one. Marjorie is firmly of the opinion that the steward knew someone was in that cabin, probably illegally, and that the steward had a hand in the man's being there."

"Well, explain how else anyone could sneak on board and occupy a cabin if the steward wasn't aware and wasn't helping him? Where would he get a key for the cabin? From the steward, that's where."

"Marjorie dear, please think about it for a minute. Do you really think the steward would give me his keys and tell us the cabin was empty if he knew someone was using that cabin? Do you think he would risk us uncovering everything?" Ralph did have a point.

"I'm sorry, you are right. I'm just being a silly old woman. However, it does occur to me that it is a while since the steward gave you his keys. Unless it was some major calamity he had to deal with, by now, he should be wondering where we are in what we are up to. So, with that in mind, what do we do now?"

Ralph stood with his hands in his pocket and studied the toes of his loafers as he tried to come up with the answer to that question. After a few moments he looked from Sofia to me and back again. He began speaking hesitantly as if still sorting out some of the details. "I think... Maybe we should... Yes, that's what we need to do. Right ladies, here is how we proceed. You two will remain here while I go in search of the steward. I will acquaint him with the fact that the end cabin is occupied, and then I think I'll try to set up something that looks like he's bringing me to the baggage carriage to collect something from my luggage."

The proposal didn't sound too solid to me. I turned to Sofia in the hope that I would see something in the other woman's demeanour that would allay my own developing concern. Ralph noticed my action and the fact that I was wringing my hands. He said, "You will be safe here. No one is likely to come look-ing for you down here. Sofia has hidden safely in here for a few hours now and, if we hadn't come looking for her, probably would remain undiscovered until we reached Istanbul – if she was discovered at all. I don't know how long I will be gone but it shouldn't be too long. Just make sure the door is locked after I leave."

As Ralph opened the door to the carriage, he froze. Although he had opened the door not more than a crack, he sensed move-ment in the corridor ahead of him. He angled around to enable him to see a reflection of the corridor in the carriage windows. He exhaled in relief and tried to get his heart rate under control again. Reflected in the carriage windows was someone in a train staff uniform. It was the steward searching for them. Ralph opened the door a bit wider and gestured frantically to the steward to join him, and then immediately put his finger to his lips as a warning to the steward not to say anything. Ralph's antics appear to have spooked the steward. It seemed to take him forever to join Ralph as he cautiously made his way down the corridor, swivelling his head left and right and interspersing it with the occasional glance over his shoulder.

"Come on," Ralph hissed in the steward's ear as he opened the door wide enough for the steward to pass through. "We'll go into the baggage carriage. We can talk in there." The steward took a cautious half step backwards, his face displaying his doubt about complying with Ralph's request. "For goodness sake man, you're safe. I'll explain everything. We can talk properly – in the baggage carriage."

Ralph let himself back into the baggage carriage. The steward followed close on his heels. As soon as he opened the door, Ralph announced in something akin to a stage whisper, "It's all right, it's only me and the steward." Sofia and I materialized from behind the luggage rack and then, perched on whatever was convenient, we all helped bring the steward up to date on everything we had discovered.

"I cannot believe this, a stowaway on this train… in my carriage and I was not aware," Phillipe said. He shook his head in disbelief. "I will never be able to live this down." In spite of the gravity of the situation, we giggled at his discomfort. "I must find this man and arrange to throw him off when we arrive at Svilengrad… which will be soon," he added after checking his watch.

"No, you don't want to go doing that. If this is the man we think he is, he is dangerous," Ralph warned. "You must let the Police take care of things. Perhaps you should tell your supervisor everything and have him radio for the Police to meet the train at Svilengrad. If you prefer, bring your supervisor here to us and we will explain the situation to him."

"Of course, you are right. I will go now to talk to the supervisor. Will you wait here or go back to your cabins?"

"Here…!" Sofia said. Ralph and I nodded in agreement. After casting a worried look over the three of us, the steward hurried out of the carriage.

This whole business of someone stowing away on the train was beyond my comprehension. "Do you think the man is still on the train? I mean, I know his belongings are still in that cabin, but where else could he be if he is not hiding in the cabin with his stuff? Surely he wouldn't be brazen enough to wander through the train at will and expect not to be discovered."

"I think he is still on the train. He has no fear of being 'discovered' as you put it because, as far as the staff members are concerned, he's just another passenger. His only real worry is our steward, Philippe, working out that there is someone in this carriage who shouldn't be here. Sofia, when did you see the man, was it soon after we went to our cabins, or after our stop at that place with the unpronounceable name? If I know when you saw him, I'll be able to work out whether he had an opportunity to leave the train when it stopped after that."

"After we went to our cabins, there was one stop. It was not long after that I saw him, maybe half an hour or an hour after we were on our way to Sofia. Yes, I think it was nearly eleven o'clock."

Ralph began thinking aloud. "So, his only chance to leave the train after that was at Sofia, and I can't think of any reason that would make him get off the train there. If that assessment is correct, I think it's fairly safe to assume he is still on the train somewhere. The next question then is how he accessed that cabin. The empty cabins are not left unlocked, so where and how did he get a key to that last cabin?"

"And how did he know that one would be empty," I added as Ralph finished speaking. "Does all that mean he's had help from someone… from an insider? Someone with knowledge of this carriage gave him a key?" I asked. "That brings us back to the steward again, doesn't it? How else would he get a key and be able to roam around without anyone taking any notice?"

Sofia giggled. "I think Marjorie does not like our steward. I wonder what he has done to make her distrust him." Although she directed her comments to Ralph, she looked at me from under a raised eyebrow. Sofia's comments did the trick.

They served as a wake-up call for me. I realised how unfounded my comments had been. "I will make him several mental apologies for my comments against him." Everyone grinned and somehow it seemed to lighten the atmosphere.

It was nearly half an hour later when the steward tapped gently on the baggage carriage door, opened it cautiously and came in, followed closely by his supervisor. Once again, the whole story of the 'non-passenger' in the supposedly empty cabin was retold, and the fears for Sofia's safety explained at great length. Ralph took pains to make sure that both the supervisor and the steward understood the type of man they were dealing with in regard to the stowaway in the end cabin. Again, Ralph stressed that they should not approach the man directly, but should alert the police at Svilengrad and ask for their assistance.

"It is less than half an hour until we arrive at Svilengrad. I must hurry to radio ahead," the supervisor said before rushing out of the carriage.

The steward watched him go and then turned to speak to Ralph. "Our stop at Svilengrad is about 40 minutes. If the police are waiting when we arrive, removal of the man should not delay us."

"Y-e-s, that's true, but the first thing they have to do is to find the man. They might be lucky and he will be hiding quietly in the cabin when we stop. However, he could be wandering about the train somewhere, in the facilities, or having a drink in the lounge car. It will be difficult for the police if he is not in his cabin, since they don't know what he looks like."

"Only Sofia knows what he looks like. We don't know, so we wouldn't be able to help the police. What if the police coming on board gets him stirred up? What is he likely to do… how will he react?" This last question I directed to Sofia.

"I cannot say. I only know that the man is dangerous, and I believe he would stop at nothing to save himself."

Ralph realised he needed to save the situation that he assessed as building towards panic. The last thing needed right now was panic amongst passengers, especially his two female companions. A quick look at the steward suggested he too was sliding in that same direction. "Right, we need to pull ourselves together. It's imperative that we all act normally. You, Philippe, need to get back to your station to do whatever it is you do at this time of the day. Then, looking at Sofia and me, he continued. "Our priority is to get Sofia safely back into that compartment."

"No, no. I am safer here."

"No, that is not the case. You are not safe alone anywhere on this train while there is a risk this man is still roaming around. We cannot stay with you. The risk is that we would be missed, and that could alert the man that something is going on."

That news had both of us feeling nervous and more than a bit despondent. We disappeared back behind the luggage rack to allow Ralph time and space to think. Ralph spent the next few minutes alone wandering up and down the centre aisle of the baggage carriage as he tried putting together a plan to spirit Sofia back to her compartment unseen. According to his calculations, we should be arriving at Svilengrad station in about ten minutes and he had an uneasy feeling about how things might play out over the next hour or so.

CHAPTER 9

The previous night's radio call weighed heavily on Ralph's mind. There were two issues at stake now. The first and obvious priority was keeping Sofia safe from the man she feared intended to do her harm. However, Ralph found the second issue more troubling. He could not support the police's theory that Sofia was responsible for the two serious crimes that occurred in the last few days. Time spent with her, gave him to believe she was incapable of such atrocities. He struggled with his instruction to stick with her and to ensure she was available to be arrested on her arrival in Istanbul. Torn between duty and his belief in the woman, he decided he needed more time – and more evidence – before making his own assessment of her guilt or otherwise.

From the whirlpool of conflict and confusion dominating Ralph's mind, one compelling thought emerged. One way or another, it was clear Sofia was in danger. The message that emerged from his deep thinking was that he had to keep her safe, not only from the man, but also from the police, until he could be sure of what was happening. And time was running out.

Soon they would be pulling into Svilengrad station. If the supervisor had followed his instructions, police would board the train there. It was likely their instructions could include taking Sofia into custody. It became clear that remaining in the baggage carriage was not in her best interest. Any alternative he came up with didn't have much to recommend it, but getting Sofia safely back into the compartment still seemed the best option.

If he was going to do this, it needed to happen now, before they reached the station. Ralph caught his breath. Was the train beginning to slow? He hurried to the carriage door and quickly slipped into the intersecting space between the baggage carriage and their sleeper carriage. "A glass panel in this door would be nice," he muttered to himself as he wiped a sweaty hand down the seam of his trousers. With his hand resting on the door handle, he took a deep breath, held it and exhaled slowly before cracking the door open a fraction.

He couldn't see down the corridor, so focused his attention on the windows opposite the cabin doors. No reflections, no sign of movement. Ralph eased the door about a quarter of the way open and cautiously peered around it. The corridor was empty. No time to lose, he rushed back into the baggage carriage and rounded us up. "Hurry; grab what Sofia has here with her and follow me. Sofia, give me the key to the compartment." They were already on their way to the door as he completed delivering his instructions. "We must be quick and silent. Stay a couple of paces behind me. That way, I will reach the compartment door first and have it open so you can continue straight in."

It was decidedly claustrophobic with three bodies and Sofia's bags crammed into the space between the two carriages. The way we randomly lined up had Sofia sandwiched between Ralph and me. "Marjorie, you will be tail-end-Charlie, so please make sure the door is closed behind you". With one last look over his shoulder to make sure everyone was ready to go, Ralph cracked open the door. After again checking the windows and finding no sign of anyone, he opened the door further to inspect the corridor. "All clear; here goes nothing," Ralph murmured as he pushed the door wide open and hurried off along the corridor.

"I don't believe this," I heard Ralph murmur as he closed the compartment door behind me. "It was too easy, but there is still more to do. Right, that's stage one of the plan completed. Sofia, grab everything that is yours and bring it with you. There must be nothing left in here to suggest someone has been using the compartment."

I was confused and concerned. "We just got here, Ralph. Are you saying we have to move again?" I demanded. "If we keep doing this, we are going to get caught."

"Marjorie, please, just do as I say. We can discuss your misgivings later. Come on, look lively everyone. No, Marjorie, you take that small bag. I'll take this big one. Now, here's what's going to happen. If the corridor is clear, Sofia and I will go back to my cabin with these bags. Marjorie, you dart along to your cabin. Everyone stays put after that until at least 15 minutes after the train leaves the Svilengrad station. Everyone right to go...?" We both nodded.

Ralph went through his checking-the-corridor routine, and a scrambled exodus from the compartment followed, with me as the last one out responsible for ensuring the door was closed properly. As I unlocked my door, I stole a quick glance towards Ralph's cabin. I saw him disappear inside and close the door behind him.

I sat down heavily on the bunk and dropped Sofia's small bag onto the floor. "I don't consider myself old, just middle-aged," I told the cabin, "But I'm sure all the rushing about involved in this cloak and dagger stuff is playing havoc with my blood pressure." I took a few deep breaths and sat very still in a bid to slow my heart now thumping wildly in my chest.

The train was drawing up to the platform. I raised the blind and peered out as the station sign and baggage trolleys parked at the end of the platform flashed past my window. And then, with screeching and shuddering, we had stopped. Not many people waited. I cast an anxious eye over everyone on the platform. None of them looked like police officers, but then, what do police officers look like? How would you tell them from ordinary citizens if they weren't in uniform?

There was a feeling of relaxation seeping over me. "Why am I starting to relax?" I whispered to myself. What does the fact that I didn't see any police mean? If the police are not here, it means no one is going to try to take that bloke off the train. Sofia will still be in danger... And we'll all be nervous wrecks worrying about her safety by the time we get to Istanbul." Then another stray thought came to me with such force it made me catch my breath.

"It's not only Sofia who is in danger," I gasped as that thought crystallised. "We all could be in danger by association." I sat bolt upright as the reality of our situation sank in. "Good God," I exclaimed. Ralph always took the lead I realised. Whenever we had to move as a group, or a situation looked a bit tricky, Ralph always led the way. If something were to happen, Ralph would be first in the firing line, metaphorically and literally. A cold numbness invaded my body and I suddenly felt very afraid.

Not afraid so much for myself I realised, but for Ralph. At that moment, I knew beyond all else, I did not want anything to happen to Ralph.

Footsteps in the corridor drew me back to the here and now. More than one pair of feet I thought; maybe three or four people by the sound of it. I held my breath. The muffled thump of boots on the carpeted corridor continued past my cabin. I strained to follow their rhythmic but hurried progress. Good, I thought. It sounds like they have passed Ralph's cabin. It must be the Police. I hope they manage to nab that bloke and remove him from the train so we can breathe easy again.

If they did manage to get him, how would they get the bloke off? Would they bring him back down the corridor and out onto the platform through the main carriage door, or would they try to spirit him off without the public seeing? Whatever was happening, it seemed to be taking a while. I checked my watch. That didn't tell me anything. I hadn't noted the time we arrived at the station or when I heard the footsteps in the corridor.

Time does seem to progress much slower when you are waiting for something, I told myself. We are supposed to have a 40 minute stop at Svilengrad. There were few people getting on or off the train. Would they shorten our stopover to help makeup some of the earlier lost time? "At this rate, I'm going to be sitting here wondering until the train moves off again," I told the empty cabin. However, I kept a close eye on the comings and goings on the platform… just in case something interesting happened out there.

The train shuddered and groaned as it began moving again. I checked my watch once more. I suspected the stop was less than 40 minutes, possibly more like half an hour. With Ralph's instruction in mind about waiting 15 minutes after leaving the station before leaving our cabins, I began calculating what time that would be. I realised I didn't have enough information. When I looked out the window again, we were still passing various bits of the station's infrastructure. Some sort of freight depot slid past followed by what looked like a small room set atop high steel supports, and then a set of signals were left trailing in our wake.

When I craned my neck to one side, up ahead I could see a

white fence running across to the track. I assumed the fence prevented access to the station complex from beyond that point, and it marked the end of anything to do with the station. Is this from where I should start timing my 15 minutes, I wondered, and not from when the train first started moving again? After pondering the question for a couple of minutes, I checked my watch yet again. The train had been underway for about the required time. How much longer should I wait before going to join the others?

I was still pondering that question when a knock on my door made me jump. I threw open the door to be greeted by a smiling Ralph and Sofia. "May we come in?" Ralph asked. Beneath Sofia's smile, for the first time, I noticed something else. Had it been there all along and I simply hadn't noticed it before, or was it a recent arrival? Sofia looked weary, haggard even. Not surprising given her situation, I told myself, but I wondered if there wasn't more to it than that.

We didn't stay in my cabin, but adjourned to Sofia's compartment. As soon as everyone was comfortable, I had to ask the question. "Did the police come on board? I didn't see anyone who looked like them boarding the train, but I did hear some suspicious footsteps in the corridor."

"I think somebody – several bodies to be correct – came past heading for the facilities end of the carriage. I assume the point of interest was that last cabin. There was nothing that I heard beyond that to indicate what happened there. I didn't hear those feet come back along the corridor, so I assume they left the train from that far end of the carriage," Ralph said.

"I do not think they found the man there. He would not go quietly and I think we would have heard some noise to indicate what was happening. I don't know what to think now." Sofia gave a gentle shake of her head as she finished speaking. Both Ralph and I were watching her viciously wringing her hands.

It must be a 'woman thing', but I am surprised at how often Sofia's ideas so directly align with mine. I voiced that opinion. "Although I don't know anything about the man in question, that was my thinking as well, Sofia. Ralph, what are your thoughts on what happened?"

"I don't know what happened, but I don't think they apprehended anyone unless he was comatose at the time. However, the fact that we didn't hear them come back through the carriage is curious. Perhaps we should try to catch up with our ever helpful steward as soon as possible to see if he can shed some light on what happened – that is, if anything did happen."

That's all very well, I thought, but it's no comfort at all to me and I doubt to Sofia either. "If they didn't catch him and remove him from the train, what does that mean? Did he manage to elude them and, therefore, he is still on the train, or did he leave the train earlier but left his belongings behind?"

Ralph seemed to consider my question for a moment before answering. "There is another aspect of this that we haven't considered. Right from when we checked the supposedly empty cabins, we assumed that stuff belonged to the man Sofia has seen on board, the man she thinks is her brother-in-law's brother. What if that's not the case? What if we were wrong and all the kit in that cabin belongs to some other chap?"

Silence reigned as Sofia and I considered his remarks. Our silence didn't bother Ralph. Although he had posed a couple of questions, he wasn't looking for a response. He had been merely thinking aloud, and found that having verbalised those thoughts, his belief that we might have been wrong strengthened. In the end, it was me who broke the silence. "Do you really think we might have made a mistake, or is that just a ploy to make us feel safe?

"Are you saying that the man I saw might still be on the train? I am not safe yet?" Sofia asked.

"Possibly," Ralph answered economically, "But there is something else I need to talk to you about, and I think we need to do that about now. Before we begin that though, has anyone worked out our new time of arrival in Istanbul?" Both Sofia and I shook our heads. We hadn't looked that far ahead, having been too focused on the here and now and staying safe.

"I know it will be late," I began after some thought. "After the last long stop, I calculated we wouldn't arrive until sometime in the evening instead of around lunchtime. But, I think they have been catching up little bits of time wherever they could, so I don't know how late we will be now."

"Okay, if you ladies will wait here, I will go and have a chat with our steward about a couple of things. It shouldn't take more than a few minutes if he is at his station."

"You'll be pleased to get home," I said to Sofia.

"I am not sure. No, of course you are right. I have to admit I will be much happier to be off this train. What concerns me now is what I might find at home. I do not think I will find everything all right, but I don't know what to expect, or how bad things might be."

That was intriguing. Sofia had indicated previously she thought things might not be as they should be at home, but this sounded as though she had some idea of what the situation could be. I was about to press her for details of what she thought she would find at home when Ralph reappeared. "See, that didn't take long at all," he announced.

"True, but did you learn anything useful?" I asked.

"I did indeed. Phillipe expects we should arrive at Istanbul sometime between eight o'clock and 830p.m. tonight. I hope…"

"So late…!" Sofia exclaimed.

"Is that a problem for you? I was about to say that I hoped our arrival wouldn't be a problem for us booking into our hotel. I hadn't thought a late arrival might be a problem for you."

"Oh, I don't know… They don't know I'm coming you see. It would have been better – more convenient – for me to arrive during the day." I felt myself frowning at her comment. I couldn't see how arriving at her parents' house at any time of the day could be a problem, unless it was in the middle of the night and she had to wake up people. But, Ralph is asking the questions at the moment and, not wanting to interrupt, I didn't voice my surprise at Sofia's comment. To that end, I waited for Ralph to continue, but he seemed to have disappeared into his own mind and nothing was forthcoming.

"Ralph, do you think we might have a problem checking into our hotels? I was hoping to ask a taxi to take me to the one I am booked into as I have no idea where to find it, even in daylight hours."

"The hotels are used to tourists arriving late," Sofia assured me. "Some of the big ones man their reception desks all night, while others continue to have theirs manned until very late. I don't think you will have problems unless you have booked into one of the smaller places." It was at that point that Ralph and I discovered we were booked into the same hotel.

I was relieved. "You can't believe how glad I am to hear we are staying at the same hotel. When I left London, I was so nervous because I had never done anything like this before. Now that I know the train, I am quite relaxed about being here." It wasn't quite true I admitted to myself, but they didn't need to know that. "However, now that we are about to arrive in Istanbul, I am beginning to feel terrified again of the unknown."

Sofia leaned over and patted my arm. "You'll be fine… And it appears you will have Ralph to look after you."

Her comment made the heat rise in my cheeks again and I quickly turned my head away to look out of the window now that it's blind was only half down. What on earth am I blushing about? Blushing for no reason, talking to myself, I must be starting to lose my marbles. It's all Connie's fault. I should never have let her talk me into this. Through the turmoil of my thoughts, I heard my name being called.

"Marjorie, Marjorie, are you alright?" Ralph asked. "Something seems to have upset you. Was it something we said?"

"No, nothing like that; I was just feeling a bit nervous about finding myself alone in a strange place." The lie came so easily I surprise myself, but then it wasn't a complete lie. In an effort to divert attention away from me, I asked, "Did the steward volunteer any information on what happened at Svilengrad – or if anything did happen there?"

"Well, he was enlightening," Ralph replied. "Three plain clothes police officers came on board and the supervisor took them to the end cabin of this carriage, hence the foot traffic we heard in the corridor. Nobody was in the cabin, but they bundled up everything that was there and took it with them. They questioned the staff, but that went nowhere. They were going to leave an officer on board in that cabin. However, in the end Phillipe thinks they decided the man wasn't still on board, and leaving an officer here would be a waste of a resource. As a last resort, they checked out the baggage carriage in case someone was lurking in there. When they found nothing, they left from the off side at the rear of the train so as not to draw attention to themselves."

Lunch was just about over when the staff supervisor approached our table. We had lingered over our lunch today much longer than anyone else in the dining car. I don't know whether it was because we felt safe there, or because we are a bit low on energy and adrenaline after all the excitement earlier today. A few minutes before the supervisor arrived at our table, I commented about the staff giving us very pointed looks, and I half expected them to come and ask us to leave if we lingered much longer. The supervisor was most apologetic for interrupting our lunch, but insisted Ralph go with him then to take an urgent call. As they walked away from the table, I thought I heard Ralph say, "What, another one?"

Unsure whether we should remain in the dining car until Ralph returned, or if he would expect us to return to our cabins, I sought Sofia's thoughts on the matter. "I am not sure what he would want us to do, but I think I feel safer here although all the diners have gone. I don't know how safe the two of us would be making our way back through the train alone. Many of the passengers disappear into their cabins for a snooze after lunch, so the corridors usually are empty. I prefer to have some people around I think."

"Okay, that decides it. We will wait here until either the staff throws us out, or Ralph comes looking for us here when he can't find us in our cabins." Now that we've decided to remain in the dining car, what were we going to talk about? It wouldn't be possible to discuss our usual topic of conversation – murder on the train and Sofia's safety – because of the close proximity of the dining car staff. I don't think either of us is an exponent of the art of small talk, so hanging around in here waiting for Ralph could become something of an ordeal.

"Do you know what is going on with Ralph?" I was a bit surprised by the question and wasn't sure what she meant, so I shook my head. "What is this call he must take? The staff supervisor appeared to act a bit strange when he came for Ralph. I am wondering if there is more to know about all the things that have happened on this train. Would Ralph keep information from us, do you think?"

It was a very good question, and one that occurred to me as well. I didn't think Ralph would hold anything back if it was crucial to our well-being… At least, I hoped he wouldn't. This call he had to take was a bit worrying though, and I don't think he was too happy about it either. It's probably not a good idea to share those thoughts with Sofia at this stage. She seems concerned enough as it is about her safety and that of her family. Still, I couldn't let her question go unanswered or she would begin to wonder if she deliberately was being kept in the dark. "No, I don't know what's going on with Ralph. I'm hoping he'll tell us what this was about when he gets back. But, in answer to your last question, I don't think Ralph would withhold anything from us. I feel sure he has shared everything he knows up until now, and I think he is probably as much in the dark about this whole business as we are."

Ralph looked grim when he returned to the dining car about half an hour after he had left us. He had checked our cabins first to see if we had gone back there after he went to take his call before realising – or hoping perhaps – we were still in the dining car. I saw Sofia stiffen as Ralph approached our table. She too noticed how grim he looked, and the frantic wringing of her hands began again. There is too much tension all round. I felt the need to do something, to say something that might ease the atmosphere.

"Oh good, you're back. Perhaps we should head back to our cabins. I'm sure the dining car staff is on the verge of chucking us out." Ralph's training kicked in and he rose to the occasion to play his role.

"I do apologise for abandoning you like that, sometimes you just have to do what you have to do. I think retreating to our cabins for a post-prandial nap might be in order. I might even have another go at attacking that book that I'm struggling with."

Eager anticipation seemed to govern the speed at which we made our way back to Sofia's compartment. I barely waited until everyone was settled before putting Ralph on the spot. "What was that all about, Ralph? I've no doubt it does involve all of us, or at least some of us, and we believe we need to know. If it is something to do with your work in London that is confidential and has nothing to do with us, we would not expect you to share it with us. However, if it does impact on us and relates to what's been happening on this train in any way, I think you owe it to us to share whatever information you have."

"Thank you for that, Marjorie, but let me say that I had no intention of keeping anyone in the dark. I am still trying to sort out a few things in my mind. I had thought I would wait that until I'd made sense of it all before sharing it with you. However, as it may take some time for me to make sense of it, if I ever do, I had all but decided to share what little I know with you before you made your demands."

There, it was happening again. I felt the burning in my cheeks as they reddened in response to Ralph's thinly veiled rebuke. How is it that this man can do this to me all the time? I doubt I have blushed as much in my whole life as I have while I've been on this train. I let his comment go by as I sat demurely with my eyes lowered and my hands in my lap. The hope was that Ralph would see this as some sort of act of contrition and get on with whatever he was going to tell us.

Sofia wasn't about to take any chances that he might change his mind. "Yes, that's well and good, Ralph. We understand that we are rushing you and that perhaps you haven't managed to grasp all of the details yet. We might be able to help you with that, if you share what you know. Can we get on with it, please?"

I held my breath, half expecting Ralph to explode. Instead, there is a deep rumbling chuckle that broke into a full-bodied laugh. "Okay ladies, I get the message. If everyone is comfortable, I will tell you about my radio call. In fact, there are things I want to share with you about both my calls, but I have to say at the outset, some of the information I need to share will be upsetting for some, if not all of us."

"After that, I almost feel sorry I started all this. However, I am a firm believer that it is easier to cope with something if you know what it is. I don't doubt that you are right and that some of what you need to tell us will be disturbing, but I think we are all made of fairly stern stuff and each of us will cope with it in our own way." I looked to both Sofia and Ralph as I finished speaking for any sign of dissension. There was none. Ralph took out his notebook, laid it on the table, and cleared his throat in readiness for the news he was about to deliver.

"There is good news, and there is not so good news." Ralph began. "The good news is that the killer, as we have been calling him, from the end cabin is no longer on the train. The fingerprints taken from that cabin match the prints from a body found beside the line a short distance prior to Svilengrad." Ralph paused.

"I don't know that I consider that good news," I interjected. "The question now is: who killed the killer? I assume he was killed and didn't just happen to fall from the train. ...And is whoever killed him still on the train?"

"That's two questions, Marjorie, and you are stealing my thunder."

When will I ever learn to bite my tongue? I didn't want to interrupt Ralph. I wanted to hear his information and, more importantly, I did not want another rebuke. I apologised and encouraged him to go on, which he did. "As I was saying, there is good news and not so good news. The fingerprints confirm the man found dead beside the railway line was the one from the end cabin. The not so good news is that it appears he met with foul play as you assumed, Marjorie... And yes, whoever killed the killer might still be on this train. It appears the police did not give the staff the whole story but it was, in the main, the truth. The police did not find the man they were seeking on board the train. It wasn't until sometime later that his body was found by a member of the public who notified the police. However, what the police chose not to tell the staff was that a blood stain was found on the top step at the off-side door to the baggage carriage."

"That was the door the police left the train by after their search wasn't it?" I risked the question in the interest of clarification.

"Yes, that is correct. It was when they were leaving that they found the blood. They can't be sure it belonged to the man in question until DNA results come back, but they are confident there will be a match."

We had forgotten about Sofia and her connection, although somewhat distant, to the man we believed occupied that end cabin. If our assumption about his identity was correct, news of his demise might come as something other than a good news story for Sofia. Ralph and I must have remembered the connection at about the same time. We both spun around to look at Sofia. She had her elbows planted on the table and her face buried in her hands. Her head seemed to be shaking ever so slightly from side to side, and I thought I heard soft keening sound coming from her.

"Oh Sofia, that was insensitive of me. I apologise for breaking the news in that way. I forgot you knew the man, if our assumption about who he was is correct." Ralph looked genuinely distressed by what he saw as a callous act on his part, but I was just as guilty, prattling on asking questions without as much as a thought for Sofia.

She had been weeping. Sofia's cheeks were streaked with tears when she looked up in response to Ralph's apology. "No, no; do not apologise. There is nothing to apologise for. If the man is my brother-in-law's younger brother, I feel no grief for his death. I was so sure he was at the bottom of everything that has happened that it is now distressing to find that maybe he was only a small part of it, and that we are not safe yet."

After allowing a moment for us to regroup and recover our equilibrium, I made a move to get the flow of information restarted. "Ralph, do we know how he was killed? I mean, are we sure that he wasn't killed accidentally while trying to leave the train before it reached Svilengrad?"

"The police say his injuries confirm it was murder. He had been hit on the side of the head. The blow wouldn't have killed him. It probably stunned him or, at least, made him groggy and disorientated. They believe some sort of struggle ensued but the killer managed to overpower the man and get him to the carriage door before stabbing him and bundling him off the train. It was the stabbing that killed him, not the fall from the train."

Sofia seemed to have regained her composure. She sat nodding at Ralph's information relating to the man's death. Both Ralph and I took a moment to make sure she was okay. We need not have worried. Sofia had taken it all in and now had a question to ask, the same question as likely was on all our minds. "Are you saying the killer – this second killer – is still on this train? Is that the opinion of the police?"

"They are unsure about whether that person is still of the train or not, but their suspicion is that he left the train at Svilengrad. They believe the sequence of events suggests the killer needed to commit the crime and dump the body before the train reached Svilengrad where he disembarked. They also are of the opinion that the killer might have joined the train at Sofia, and was only on board for that one leg of the journey."

"…But they have nothing to substantiate any of those hypotheses?" I asked.

"No, it appears not. It is all speculation. Regardless, I think it in our best interest to assume danger still exists on this train and that we should act accordingly."

There was no argument from Sofia or me. Ralph seemed pleased about that, but went on to alert us to the fact that afternoon tea would be served soon. "I think it would be wise for all of us to be in one of our cabins when the trays are delivered. I have a pack of cards in my bag. Perhaps we could be sitting at a table supposedly enjoying a game."

"My cabin is the first one Phillippe delivers to. It would simplify matters if we were all in my cabin when he arrives and he will know in an instant where we all are," I suggested. The other two agreed and, after Ralph had retrieved his pack of cards, we relocated to my cabin and made ourselves as comfortable as possible around my small table and in such a confined space. Ralph dealt out cards to each of us in some random fashion that I am sure has nothing to do with the rules of any game. Each of us picked up our hand of cards and tried to look as though we knew what we were about. I for one didn't have a clue. I can't remember ever having played cards in my life.

The rattle of the trolley laden with tea trays along the corridor put an end to the dress rehearsal. Ralph threw a few cards onto the centre of the table and said, "For credibility; there is more we need to discuss, but it can wait until after we have tea and when there is no likelihood of our trusty steward coming to interrupt. We all picked up our cards and were quite intent on our game when three trays were delivered to my cabin.

CHAPTER 10

The tea tray trolley and Phillippe, our steward, rattled off along the corridor and disappeared from the carriage. Ralph sprung up and shut the door. As he walked back to the table, he looked grim and said in a fairly gruff voice, "Right, now we come to that first radio call I had. I'm sorry, but it's all bad news." Across the table from me, I saw Sofia stiffen as she braced herself for whatever was to come next.

"Not more bodies…?" Sofia asked in a strangled little voice.

"Er… No, not more bodies… Well, none that we don't already know about anyway." Then Ralph began a fairly detailed account of that first radio call that reminded him he had been seconded to the local police to assist in the investigation of the incident at the British Museum. "The call came through soon after we found that body in the baggage carriage. I'm not sure how to word this next bit, so I'm just going to dive straight in. I'm sorry, Sofia, it will upset you I'm afraid. The reason they called me was that they suspect your involvement in the British Museum incident and in the death of the unknown man in the baggage carriage."

Sofia gasped and her hand shot to her mouth. "How can this be? How can they believe I was involved in such terrible things?"

"I have to say, I don't know. I don't know if they have any sort of evidence that they think links you to either of the incidents other than the fact that you supposedly were in the right place at the right time to have been involved."

"No, no! I have not done these terrible things. I did not know about them until you told me. So, they think it was me. What do they want you to do about it, now that you have all the powers of a local police officer?"

"My instructions were to stay close to you, to make sure nothing happened to you, and not to lose you. They seem concerned that you might slip away and disappear somehow. I'm afraid, their intention once you arrive at Istanbul, is to arrest you and arrange

107

your extradition back to London. I am supposed to make sure you are available so that can happen."

She looked aghast she stared towards the end of the table at Ralph. Then her anger kicked in. "So, all your looking after me, and taking care of me to make sure nothing happens to me is because of your orders, and so you can fulfil your duty and hand me over to the police when we arrive in Istanbul."

"Oh, Sofia, no that's not what we were about. That's not why…," I stammered as I searched for words to explain that our motivation in trying to keep her safe is based on friendship and nothing else, but Ralph cut me off.

"No, Sofia, I promise you that's not the truth. We were already concerned about you before that radio call and I think, even you might agree if you think about it, that we had already established something of a friendship before that call. I did not tell the police that I knew you or that Marjorie and I were associating with you. I do not believe you were involved in either of those incidents. However, I can't help feel there is more that you haven't told me. I don't know what that might be, but perhaps it's about what you think is happening in Istanbul rather than anything to do with those two incidents."

I was horrified. How could Ralph be prepared to hand Sofia over to the police when we got to Istanbul? I don't know too much about the police over here, but I don't have a lot of confidence about the way she might be treated. I started to protest. I knew my cheeks were bright red, but this time it was from anger not embarrassment. Before he said anything more, Ralph was about to find out how angry I was. But I didn't get the chance to say anything.

"I will tell you both now that I have no intention of handing Sofia over to the police, and that has been the case since I took that call. However, that brings us to the next part of this conversation: how to spirit Sofia off this train and away from the police once we arrive in Istanbul. I did tell them that the train was running late and I didn't think we would arrive at Istanbul until maybe around ten o'clock. I know that's not right, but I thought it might delay them and give us a bit of time to get away. The comment in response was that they would be at the station a little earlier in case the train made up some time."

"I do not see how this can happen. If the police are determined to arrest me, then I will be arrested," Sofia said in a quiet voice.

"It is true that they are quite determined, and that is why whatever plan we come up with needs to be foolproof. I think we need to pool our creative talents in order to come up the best possible option for getting Sofia off this train, and away unseen and free."

Although the conversation was on a serious note, I laughed. The other two looked at me almost in disgust. I felt obliged to explain. "I'm sorry, I know the situation isn't funny but let me tell you about something that is. Ralph, since you mentioned the police would be at the station to arrest Sofia, my mind has been working overtime. I'll admit I've only been half listening to everything you've said since then, because I was trying to work out how I might be able to sneak Sofia away from the train, the police, and you."

"Please tell me you've come up with some wonderful plan that can't possibly fail," Ralph said as he ran a hand over his face.

"Not exactly... but, between us, I think we can work up a vague idea I have into something that will achieve what we want."

"Oh Marjorie, it is so good of you to try, but I do not want you getting into trouble with the police."

"That's all very well, Sofia, but let's hear what Marjorie has to tell us about this idea of hers."

Since my plan wasn't all that well-developed at this stage, it didn't take me long to outline my thinking. As I explained the concept, some of the details began to clarify in my mind. I was aware that time was running out. The steward had indicated eight o'clock or a bit later as our anticipated arrival time at Istanbul. Our original itinerary had us arriving at lunchtime but, due to all the lost time along the way, we now would be some eight hours late. When he delivered the afternoon tea trays, Philippe had indicated that, due to our late arrival at Istanbul, dinner would be available in the dining car from six o'clock.

Those timings meant that, whatever plan we came up with,

we had to be able to implement it in the short period between finishing dinner and arriving at Istanbul. We could not afford to forgo dinner as such a move might draw attention to us. We would need to be amongst the first diners to arrive for our meal, eat fast, and leave the dining car as soon as possible. Another issue I saw as an impediment to our fast get away from the train was the waiting around for our luggage to be unloaded.

My mind was so focused on the logistics of our operations, I had forgotten about the others in the cabin with me. I stared at my hands flipping over the cards on the table in front of me until the silence in the cabin intruded on my thinking. I looked up to see the other two watching me. "Oh, I'm sorry. I was thinking through some of the logistics associated with tonight's escapade. Apart from anything else that could go wrong, another thing that occurred to me was the danger involved in hanging around on the platform while we wait for our luggage to be unloaded."

"Ah yes, I see what your concern is. However, we won't have to wait for our luggage." Ralph looked smug as he made his statement.

"Eh…? I don't think I fancy abandoning my suitcase and being stranded in Istanbul without a change of clothes," I said.

"We don't have to abandon our luggage. How many bags and bits and pieces have each of you? I guess what I'm really asking is, can each of you manage your own luggage by yourself as we make a dash for a taxi?"

It seems we each had a medium sized suitcase in the baggage carriage as well as an overnight-type bag in our cabins. In addition, Sofia had her handbag, and I had my camera bag and an oversized handbag. With a bit of careful repacking, I was confident my camera bag would fit in the top of my overnight bag. In the mad dash to the taxi, I would have my handbag over my shoulder and one bag in each hand. I knew they weren't heavy as I'd carried them out to the taxi when I left home. Sofia also was confident she could pack her handbag into her overnight bag, leaving her with just two bags to carry. Ralph's cabin bag was a bit larger than an overnight bag. He needed the extra room for the papers and files relating to the British Museum case that he brought with him.

At the close of our deliberations, the conclusion was that each of us could manage our own luggage from train to taxi when the time came. "We won't want to try running with our luggage," Ralph advised. "If we run, we will draw attention to ourselves. A brisk walk would be safer."

"That doesn't eliminate the problem of hanging around on the platform waiting for our suitcases to arrive," I reminded him.

"But we won't be waiting on the platform for our luggage. We have a key, remember. Soon, the carriage will become very quiet as people retire to their cabins to get ready for dinner and to pack whatever is in their cabins in readiness for our arrival at Istanbul. That's when the corridor should become deserted, and it will be an ideal time for us to steal our bags out of the baggage carriage."

"Oh, of course, I had forgotten we have that key," Sofia said. "I'll give it to you now, Ralph, so you can open the door when we go for our suitcases."

"Okay, that's part of the plan sorted out," Ralph said as he glanced from Sofia to me. "That only leaves the small matter of how we smuggle Sofia off the train without anyone realising who she is."

"Ah well, that's where my initial plan comes in. It'll just take me a moment to explain exactly what I have in mind." Both my companions leaned forward in a show of eager anticipation, and I ran through my plan in a quite detailed way. When I finished, I looked from one to the other and found them both wearing wide smiles and nodding enthusiastically. "If you think that idea will work, there is only one other thing that concerns me about this whole operation." Sofia and Ralph exchanged a look and I noted the confusion on both faces. I took a moment to organise my thoughts more fully before explaining what that concern was.

"Ralph, you and I are booked into the same hotel. Under other circumstances, Sofia would go to her home. I think our current situation requires a change of plan for all of us. It is obvious that Sofia can't go home, not tonight anyway. And, if the police fail to find us at the railway station, it won't take them long to find us at our hotel. I imagine we want to delay any future encounters with the police for as long as possible."

"That's good thinking, Marjorie. As you indicate, it would be unwise for us, along with Sofia, to check into our hotel tonight – or for a few days perhaps."

Sofia spoke slowly as she gathered her thoughts. "I … think … it is true that the police would find you – find us – very quickly if we went to your hotel. It might be safer if we went to one of the smaller more out of the way hotels. Although they are small, there are a few that are quite good. I think one of those would be better."

"I think that's a good suggestion, Sofia. We are in your hands on this one. Neither Marjorie nor I have the knowledge of Istanbul to select alternate accommodation." As Ralph finished speaking, Sofia mentioned the name of the hotel, and explained why she thought it was a sound option for us.

"There are a few three-star hotels that I think would not offend anyone too much. They are reasonably priced, but don't have the extra bits like mini bars and refrigerators in every room. I'm thinking of places like the Sultan's Inn, Deniz Houses, and even the Naz Wooden House. Maybe not this last one as it is very small – only about seven rooms, I think. They might not have anything available for all three of us, and we don't want to be running around all night looking for somewhere to stay. All those I mentioned are tucked away from the main areas but are close enough to restaurants and the main sights to be able to walk to most places."

We agreed with her suggestion and, as she would be directing the taxi driver to take us to wherever, it was up to her where we spent the night. While we sat there feeling pleased with our planning, Ralph left the table and checked the corridor. "Not a soul in sight; come on ladies, look lively. We are about to raid the baggage carriage."

My heart was thumping in my chest as Sofia and I ran after Ralph to the end of the carriage and waited in the space between the two carriages for him to unlock the baggage carriage door. It took longer than I anticipated to locate our suitcases. I felt the tension in my stomach tightening with every passing moment but, finally the three of us were lined up at the door waiting to return to our own cabins. Ralph went first, and checked the corridor.

He held up his hand to stop us moving forward. "We need to wait a moment. There is someone on their way back to their cabin from the facilities. I'll check the corridor again shortly to see if it's clear."

I put my suitcase down and wiped my sweaty palm on my skirt. Then, there was no time to think. Ralph was waving us through to follow him. Sofia and I raced out of the baggage carriage, Sofia slamming the door behind her, and then all three of us were galloping awkwardly along the corridor with our suitcases thumping against our legs as we ran. In my haste to open the cabin door I fumbled with the key. "Come on, come on! Get it open," I urged myself quietly.

At last, I had it open. I raced in, threw the suitcase on the floor and slammed the cabin door closed behind me… And then I stood there in the middle of my cabin, giggling as the tension associated with carrying out our 'robbery' dissipated. I would never make a real thief – or any other sort of criminal. I would probably die of a heart attack or something similar from all the nervous tension involved.

After sitting on my bunk for a couple of minutes to settle my pulse back into something resembling normal rhythm, I checked my watch. There wasn't much time before the dining car would open and I had a bit to do. My first priority was to change. We agreed that we would 'dress for dinner' tonight. For me, this meant wearing the same outfit as I had on when I boarded the train. This was one of my new straight through, easy-fit frocks – shift dresses, I think they are called – and a pair of those shoes with little heels that I still wasn't too sure about. Ralph said he would follow my lead, and wear the suit and tie he had on when he left London. Sofia said she would follow our example. The whole idea of dressing for dinner was that, should the police ask questions later, passengers and staff would remember seeing us as we were dressed for dinner – and not as we intended to be dressed when we left the train.

The clothes I would wear later, I laid out on my bunk in readiness, and placed my sturdy walking brogues on the floor beside the bunk. That left repacking my overnight case to take care of. A part of that process was digging out a couple of scarves that I had stashed in the bag somewhere. It was easiest to repack the bag by tipping everything out and starting from scratch. I put the two scarves on the bunk with my outfit for later, repacked the rest of the contents as best I could to ensure there was enough room left for the outfit I will be wearing to dinner and my camera bag to go in on top later.

At a couple of minutes to six o'clock Ralph tapped on my door. I grabbed one of the scarves and draped it around my neck before opening the door to find Ralph and Sofia waiting in the corridor. We were the first diners to arrive and went straight to our customary table. As the caterers hadn't planned on having to serve dinner this evening, many items were off the menu. Nevertheless, there was still plenty to choose from, and I don't think we three were too interested in food anyway. We ordered and ate quickly. Quite a few diners were seated as we left, and we made a show of making inane comments such as 'good night', 'the trip's nearly over' and 'Istanbul here we come'. All of this nonsense just so people would notice us and remember what we looked like this evening should others begin asking about us in the near future.

As we walked back to our carriage, I took the scarf from around my neck and handed it to Sofia. She understood and just nodded her thanks. Then, it was into our cabins for final preparation for whatever lay ahead in Istanbul. I changed quickly into my 'get away' outfit, and packed the last few items into my overnight bag before closing it. There was one last thing I needed to do: taking the scarf I had kept, I folded it into a triangle, brushed all my hair back out of sight, placed the scarf over my hair and tied the corners under my chin. "….As I would for a walk in the English countryside," I told the mirror as I admired my handiwork.

The information we received during dinner was that we were now expected to arrive at Istanbul at about nine o'clock. I was now ready to go, but it seemed like I was in for a long hour and a half wait before the next phase began. For want of anything else to do, I sat and stared out the window into the black night as what little I could make out of the scenery flashed past. My mind roamed off of its own accord to places I had no intention of revisiting, not at this time anyway. It took itself back to the end of 1964 and that traumatic time when a small annuity and an equally small cottage inherited from my aunt made it possible for me to resign from full-time employment.

It's funny the hand life deals you. I had not known about Aunt Edith until a couple of years before she died. Aunt Edith was my mother's sister who had fallen out with the family after some wild escapade in her youth. Ostracised, disowned; she was never spoken of by any of the family after that. When my mother died about three years ago, Aunt Edith saw the funeral notice in the paper and plucked up courage to track down her only niece, me. While not exactly close, Edith and I developed a sound friendship in the brief period before she died. She had no one else to leave anything to, so I got the lot. Although inheriting the cottage meant giving up my small flat in the city and moving to a quiet residential suburb, it all came at exactly the right time. My unplanned retirement, facilitated by the inheritance, came on the heels the breakup of a long-term relationship with my employer.

Why was my mind dredging up this stuff now? Perhaps it had something to do with family relationships and the decisions we make. Sofia is obviously concerned for the welfare of her family at the moment, but I can't help wonder what sort of mess she might find if, and when, she is able to go home and sort things out. Yes, perhaps it's thinking about Sofia's situation that brought back those painful memories from a while back. I told myself that's what it was, and there was nothing more to it than that. Still, the memories were disturbing, and I did not need to be disturbed tonight. I had a feeling clear thinking would be called for.

The train was slowing, and up ahead I could see the station and its well-lit platform. I mentally shook myself, and forced my mind to run through everything we were supposed to do as soon as the train stopped and the doors opened. There it was, the familiar sound of the train coming to a halt beside the platform. The screeching and shuddering died away and was replaced by the clunk of the carriage doors being thrown open and the sounds from the platform drifting in.

With my handbag over my shoulder and bag on either side of me, I stood just inside my cabin door waiting for the knock from

Ralph to tell me we were on our way. It seemed I waited a long time, but in reality it was no more than a few moments. There was the knock on my door and, in a couple of quick movements I was out in the corridor and at the tail end of our trio as we headed for the carriage door. We didn't run along the corridor, but our pace was brisk. The platform was a little lower than the carriage doorway, necessitating a climb down one step to reach it.

Ralph, as a leader, went down first. He left his main suitcase on the top step, carried his overnight bag down with him, and then when he was on the platform reached up to get his suitcase. With his bags placed off to one side, he took Sofia's bags from her, allowing her to climb down unhindered. Then he repeated the performance with me. And there we were. The three of us on the platform with our luggage, and before any of the other passengers had disembarked. Although we walked off together, Sofia was actually directing our passage from the platform, through the station and out to the taxi rank.

What a different group we were from the one that dined together such a short time earlier in the dining car. I wore my pleated skirt and a twinset with my heavy jacket unbuttoned over the lot, a scarf tied over my hair, and was comfortable in my sturdy walking shoes. Ralph had abandoned his suit in favour of casual slacks, a soft unbuttoned polo shirt, loafers and a plaid flat cap pulled down firmly on his head. I did a double take when I opened my door to him earlier. The luxurious moustache was gone. What a pity, I thought. It suited him. Sofia had more trouble sorting out a suitable wardrobe for the occasion, but eventually managed to find enough casual items to be in keeping with the rest of us. She had my second scarf tied over her hair in the same manner as mine, and both she and Ralph wore their casual jackets jauntily unfastened.

As the rush had not yet begun, we went straight to the first cab on the rank. The driver helped Ralph load our luggage while Sofia and I slid into the back of the vehicle and scrunched up to leave enough room for Ralph. Then it was time for Sofia to star. The image of a very English family on holidays left little doubt that we would have none of the language. So, it was up to Sofia to give the driver directions, but without any indication that she was a local.

She was brilliant. As she leaned forward to speak to the driver, she tripped over and stammered through a phrase in Turkish that ended with the name of the hotel. To me, it was a credible rendition of someone who couldn't speak the language but had learnt the odd phrase to use on the trip. Then I felt it was my turn to add a bit more realism to our charade. "Oh, aren't you the clever one, Lass, learning a bit of the language like that and all. Harry, isn't our Lorraine ever so clever. You an' me, we would no' be able to learn that." We had agreed our adopted names beforehand and somehow managed to remember them.

"Aye, you done good, Luv, learnin' a bit of the lingo like that. Like as not, it will come in very 'andy while we're 'ere in Istanbul."

The taxi pulled up in front of a nice enough looking hotel, and the next act of our charade began. "Beryl, you got your 'andbag 'andy, you pay the man while I get our bags," Ralph – sorry, 'Harry' said as he opened the door. I went through a rigmarole that I hoped the driver understood to mean I didn't know how much to pay.

"Lorraine luv, ask the man 'ow much for the fare." Sofia stumbled over a few words and the driver said the amount. 'Lorraine' repeated it for me, and I fished my purse out of my oversized handbag. With a selection of notes splayed out in my hand like a hand of cards, I asked 'Lorraine', "What did he say?" She repeated the amount. "Oh goodness, 'ow much is that? I don't understand this funny money. Will one of these notes be enough?"

At that point, 'Harry', who had finished unloading our luggage, stuck his head in the window. "Don't forget he'll be expecting a tip, Beryl."

"God, how much is a tip supposed to be?" I flapped the handful of notes about for a moment to highlight my confusion – which was only partly staged. The reality was that I did find this foreign currency confusing, and having to do the mental arithmetic to convert it to values I understood in good old English money was exhausting.

Lorraine leaned over and pointed to one of the notes. "Mam, give him that one. I think that will cover it." She must have been right, and it must have included a considerable tip. The driver smiled widely and bobbed his head in thanks a few times as we scrambled out of the vehicle. Sofia later confided that the extravagant tip would buy the driver's silence. It was a sort of loyalty thing. He would be sure he had no helpful information to give about his big tippers if the police came asking questions.

"Right," Ralph said, "We can't stand out here all night. Best we go in and see if we can organise somewhere to sleep for the rest of the night." I dived into my cavernous handbag and brought out a phrase book.

I handed the book to Sofia. "A prop… it will help give our lack of the language more credibility." She laughed as she took it from me. Then we picked up our bags and, with Sofia sandwiched between Ralph and I, we followed Ralph to the reception desk. It was time for 'Lorraine' to star again. She stumbled over a phrase to ask for a room. The young man on duty at the desk gave her an indulgent smile and replied with a couple of words. The inflection used I took to mean he had asked a question.

Sofia flapped about through the phrase book as she leaned towards me seeking assistance. Of course, to be able to 'help' her, I needed my glasses. More ferreting about in that huge handbag… and more time-wasting for a few moments. "Ah, 'family'… he's asking if we want a family room," Sofia said.

"Oh aye, Luv, tell him yes we want a family room," I said accompanied by much enthusiastic head nodding. That bit was done, but it had taken so long, another five people were queued up waiting for attention. But the drama wasn't over yet. The receptionist rattled off a few more words. Sofia looked confused and indicated she didn't understand. He grabbed the guests' register and spun it around on the desk to face us. After stabbing at the next blank line with a well-manicured forefinger, he pointed to all three of us and mimed writing. "Oh 'Arry, I think he wants us to register. You make a start."

After filling in his details, Ralph slid the register along the desk to me. I struggled not to laugh at what he entered. Nevertheless, I had to follow suit. Ralph's entry read 'Harry Buxton, double glazing salesman, 43 Waterloo Bridge Road, London'. So, I became Beryl Buxton with a ditto to indicate of the same address. As I finished writing and was about to give the register to Sofia to fill in, the receptionist said something else.

"Uhmm… I think he is asking for some sort of ID, Dad. What do we do about that?"

Another three people joined the ever-increasing queue waiting for service. "No problem, Lorraine luv, I'll give him one of my business cards. That should do it." As Sofia wrote her entry in the register, Ralph fished out his wallet and extracted a business card. I got a quick glimpse of what was on it as he slapped it into the receptionist's outstretched hand. I didn't get a chance to read everything on it but I did see the name: Harry Buxton.

Somehow, I didn't think a business card was going to suffice as an ID, but the crowd waiting behind us was becoming rowdy and impatient. I saw the receptionist glanced at them a few times and on one occasion gave them a 'calm down' sign with his hand. They were not about to calm down. If anything, they were becoming abusive. The receptionist was beginning to look flustered as the waiting crowd stepped up their harassment. In desperation, he held up both hands in resignation, one still holding Harry's business card. Then, nodding his acceptance of the situation, the receptionist reclaimed the register and produced a key from somewhere below the desk. He held the key's tag out to Ralph and pointed to the large numerals on it. It seems we are to be in room 21.

Ralph took the key from him and nodded knowingly. The receptionist then pointed towards the far end of the back wall and held up two fingers. "Oh dear, I do hope he is not being rude because we've been holding 'im up," I said to Ralph. Quick to understand that we didn't know what he was trying to tell us, the receptionist changed his sign language. This time, he pointed straight up in the air with his index finger and raised and lowered his arm couple of times before giving us the two finger message again. This he followed by pointing to the far corner of the back wall again.

"Ooh look, that's where the lifts are," Sofia said and gave the receptionist a smile and a nod. He smiled back and gave the one and two finger signals again. Sofia beamed at him and thanked him. "Okay, come on let's head for the lifts," Sofia said as she picked up her bags. Once we were in the lift, I asked, "Okay, now we are here, where are we going?"

Sofia leaned over and pressed the button with a '2' illuminated on it. "I think his sign language indicated that our room is up on level 2. I guess we'll find out whether I'm right or not when we get there," she said with a smile.

Once were on that floor, it only took us a moment to find our room, which was almost directly across from the lift. I was unsure about what to expect, but was pleasantly surprised. As we entered the room, directly in front of us was a small sitting area. It contained a round dining table and chairs and, further across towards the outside wall, were a couple of lounge chairs and a TV. To our left, the rest of the room contained built-in wardrobes, a double and a single bed and their associated bedside tables. Three doors led off from that main room, one opened into another small room containing a single bed, and the second door opened into the bathroom. The final door led out onto a small balcony. Our accommodation was clean and proved quite comfortable.

We agreed it was too late for any planning to occur. After settling in and freshening up, we fell into bed. I was allocated the double bed and Sofia had the single bed in the main room. Ralph took the single bed in the other room. At the outset, I was hesitant about us all being in the one room but, as it turned out, that hadn't happened. However, we had agreed that, for safety, we should stay together and not be separated.

By the time we turned in, I think we were all so tired and exhausted from the night's tension and excitement, we would have slept anywhere as long as the police couldn't find us.

CHAPTER 11

We all slept late, not surfacing until our requested late breakfast arrived. The pot of tea was terrible and I was a bit strenuous in my disapproval of it. Sofia giggled. "You are in Turkey now. Maybe it would be safer to drink coffee." Ralph and I exchanged a look at her comment but said nothing. There were no plans in place for the day, so breakfast dragged on longer than expected. If it wasn't for the arrival of staff to collect our breakfast things, who knows how long it might have stretched on. No one seemed in any hurry to bring it to an end.

Once the breakfast clutter disappeared, Ralph called us all to order and reminded us we were in desperate need of a plan to take us forward until we sorted out the mess involving Sofia. I was concerned for him and said when we were out of Sofia's earshot, "Ralph, while I know we are driven by nothing but the best intentions, I'm concerned that what we've already done, apart from whatever we might plan to do from here on in, will impact on your career. Not only could you end up in serious trouble here, but your superiors may take a dim view of your involvement with the local police on the museum incident enquiry not going smoothly or according to plan. It could end your career."

He grunted in response and shook his head slightly. "What career...? My career stalled years ago. I don't lick boots or tug the forelock as people might like. I can live with myself because of it, but it has closed off any further progression up the rankings ladder. Don't get me wrong, I love what I do and I believe in its ideals. Investigating crime has been a big part of my life and I feel as though it's in my blood. But the rest of the nonsense that goes on does not appeal to me. I realise the consequences that might accrue as far as my so-called career is concerned, but my sense of what's right and where my duty lies is more important to me that any so-called career." There was no response to that other than a shrug. I was presumptuous in bringing the matter up in the first place.

As soon as we were all together again, Ralph kicked off what turned out to be a heavy planning session. "There's a lot to think about," he began. "We have a number of separate issues to deal with that are all part of one major situation. I think our approach in the first instance should be to come up with a broad plan that identifies what we want to achieve. From that, we can work out each of the steps involved, including timings and who does what. Are there any different thoughts on that?"

Of course there was no argument or 'different thoughts'. Well, not from me anyway, as I had been turning over in my mind how we were going to tackle the problem. It was all a bit too overwhelming for my tiny mind to cope with, so I welcomed Ralph's taking the lead as we settled down to hard work.

"Right, before we can really start to think about a plan, Sofia, I think we need more information from you." Sofia looked startled. "No, don't get concerned about it. I believe we need your input on such things as what you think might be happening at your home, any thoughts you have on who might be involved and why, and I guess the other big thing is how difficult you think the next phase of this operation is going to be."

Silence reigned for what seemed like a long time, but it was probably no more than a minute, before Sofia began to speak. "I find it difficult to provide worthwhile information. From the beginning, I thought my brother-in-law and his younger brother were behind it all. My assessment of the situation was that they engineered a plan to steal artefacts and sell them on the black market. As I said before, they are from a very wealthy family. My brother-in-law works in his family's business. He is their representative here in Istanbul. But he is not the heir to their empire. There is an older brother." Ralph and I nodded to signify we remembered her earlier comments.

"The younger brother of my brother-in-law, who is the third son of the family, does not work at all. All his life, he has been an embarrassment to his father. After he was in trouble a few times, his father threw him out, but continues to pay him a huge allowance. This provides him with plenty of money but also allows him plenty of time to make more trouble. Both brothers are greedy. They always want more money, and I think they resent the eldest brother's position and his being treated differently – better – than they are."

"Do you think this is this another example of that age old situation where money becomes the root of all evil?" Ralph asked.

"No, not really, but please let me finish. The story is complicated and I need to think on it as I go along." Ralph apologised and Sofia continued.

"My father continues to pay my sister an allowance but, once she married, he set it up so that her husband could not get his hands on her money. It caused some friction in the marriage in the early days but, although I think my brother-in-law still resents that situation, he appears to accept it. As I think I said before, in the beginning my father and sister could not see what the brothers were like, or maybe they didn't want to see. My father saw the second son of his wealthy Syrian friend as a good match for my sister. My sister is what you English might call 'flighty'. She did not complete University – was too busy with her social life – and has never worked. Marriage to someone who could maintain her position in society and keep her as she was accustomed was probably the best future my father saw for his daughter."

"You said there was some friction between the two men early in the marriage. Did that make your father change his mind about the man he chose to marry his daughter?" I asked quietly. I wasn't sure whether this was 'off limits' territory.

"How could my father and my sister not see what her husband was like as time went by? I am sure they both came to realise what sort of men he and his brother are, but they do not say anything. Maybe it's about saving face and not wanting to admit a mistake was made."

"You said your initial thought was that these two brothers were behind what happened at the museum. However, now I detect a little uncertainty in what you said. Is your belief still the same?" Ralph asked.

"I don't know what I think now. So much has happened, so many murders. Perhaps I don't want to believe these people who are associated with my family are capable of such things. I do not like my brother-in-law. I have made no secret of that, and he has made no secret of the fact that he does not like me either. However, that someone would try to involve me in all this as they have, is beyond what I think those two brothers would do."

"S-o-o, does that mean you have changed your opinion, or do you still think they are involved?" Ralph persisted.

"About my brother-in-law, I do not know. I am not sure whether he might be involved or not. But, his brother I still think has involvement, although I do know how much or what that is."

"Oh, gracious me, I forgot something. Excuse me for a moment please, ladies, while I fetch something from my bag." Ralph disappeared into his room and returned a few moments later carrying a folder. He placed it on the table without opening it, clasped his hands on top of it and appeared to retreat into deep and troubling thought. At last he looked up but hesitated a bit longer. It seemed to me that he was trying to decide whether to share something with us or not. This was going nowhere and it was obvious that whatever it was troubled Ralph, so I took the initiative.

"Ralph, you seem as though you have something serious to tell us or show us. After all we have been through in these last few days, whatever it is I'm sure Sofia and I will cope with it."

"That's just the problem. I'm not sure what it is I have to show you. But, I think you are right. I need to show you, and then we will see where this goes." He was being so mysterious, I didn't know whether to fear the worst or get excited as I watched him lift the cover of his folder about half an inch and slide something out.

"After dinner on the train last evening, as I went past the staff supervisor's work area, I decided to use the master key I still had to enter and have a quick look around. I knew the supervisor was still in the dining car and probably would be there saying his farewells to the diners for a while. I don't know why I did it or what I expected to find, but I think it paid off. On what passes for his desk, I found a few pieces of paper lying on top of an envelope. A quick scan of the paper proved it was of no interest; staff rosters and the like. Then I took a peek in the envelope. It contained only one item. I slid it out about half its length before I turned the envelope over and I realised it contained a photograph. On a mad impulse without a thought behind it, I pocketed the contents of the envelope before arranging everything as I had found it."

"That was frightfully dangerous, even rash. Why was the photograph worth the risk?" I asked as I felt my stomach tightening. I doubted it was a photograph of the supervisor with his wife and children. And, given the way Ralph was behaving about showing it to us, I had no doubt it would be unpleasant in some way.

"In a moment, I will turn it over so you can see for yourselves. But first… Sofia, at some stage, you thought the man you saw on the train was your brother-in-law's younger brother but later, you seemed unsure. That uncertainty was compounded later when we discovered that it was likely the man you saw probably was the same man as was occupying that end cabin. Is that an accurate assessment of the situation?"

"Y-e-s, that is correct. I am quite confused about all of it now."

"Okay, in a moment I will turn this photo over for you to look at. I must warn you both that it is unpleasant but not too gruesome. Please look carefully at the photo to see if you recognise the person in the photo as the man on the train, or anyone else that you might know." Before turning it over, he slid off a paperclip that held something to the front of the photograph. Both Sofia and I were leaning forward over the table, eager for the big moment to arrive. After taking a deep breath, he slowly flipped over the photo.

We both sat back at the sight of the photo. Sofia gasped and her hand flew to a medallion she wore around her neck. I reached across, grabbed her other hand and held it tight. Ralph was right. The photo was unpleasant. When would a photo of a dead body not be unpleasant? But it was nothing nearly as horrible as that first body I had photographed in the baggage carriage, or as shocking as the photos of it that Sofia was shown. All colour drained from Sofia's face and she seemed unable to speak. I rushed across and put an arm around her shoulders and held her for a moment. As I stood beside and slightly behind her, I raised my eyebrows in question at Ralph. What was so upsetting about this photo to make her react this way?

A carafe of water and glasses were on the bench behind me. I let go of Sofia and poured a glass for her. Her hand shook as she took the glass from me. The first couple of gulps she took made her cough and splutter. "Just sip it; little sips are best," I counselled her. After a few sips, she put the glass to one side, thanked me, and then picked up the photograph. I watched her force herself to take a long, close look at it. She sat studying it for a few moments before putting it back on the table and pushing it across to the centre. After a long time spent staring at some unknown spot on the table top, she slowly raised her eyes and spoke to Ralph.

"Tell me about this photo please. What do you know about it, other than you stole it from the supervisor's area?

"Hmmm… are you sure?" Sofia nodded impatiently. "Okay, the photo was upside down in the envelope. I recognised the police insignia on the front of the envelope. So, I turned it over to open the back of it and slid out the photo, exposing about half of the back of the photograph. When I turned the whole thing over, I realised the photo had gone into the envelope 'head first', so to speak, and the part I had exposed was the lower half of it. I realised straight away that it might be of interest and, not wanting to hang about in there any longer than necessary, I turned the envelope over again, ripped out the photo and shoved it in my pocket, before closing the envelope and putting it back on the desk as before. There was no time to hang about looking at the photo but, the bit I had seen – the lower half of it – showed a body lying on what looked like gravel."

"Then what happened," I asked.

"Well, nothing really; I got out of the supervisor's area in a hurry, went back to my cabin and spent the rest of the time on the train getting ready to leave it and disappear into the night. I only remembered the photo when we were talking a few minutes ago. My first decent look at the thing was when I went to get it from my bag." He focused on Sofia as he continued. "There was a brief note attached to the photo by a paperclip, which I removed before I showed the photo to you. I believe it is a photo of the body of the man that was found beside the line by a member of the public. It is probable the police asked the supervisor to show that photo to his staff and maybe the passengers to see if anyone recognised him. The photo shocked you. What can you tell me about it?"

Ralph pushed the note that had been attached to the photo across the table to her. "This is what was attached to it. I can't read it because I don't understand the language. Are you able to tell me what it says?"

Sofia slowly extended her hand and took the note, which appeared to be handwritten on a piece torn from the bottom of a larger sheet. "It is addressed to 'The Supervisor', and it says the attached is a photo of a body found beside the railway line about 15 kilometres before Svilengrad. The writer says it is believed to be the man they looked for on the train when it arrived at Svilengrad. It asks the supervisor to show it to his staff and others to see if anyone recognises the man or remembers seeing him on the train. There is a signature that I can't read, but that is all."

"Thank you. We already know that the fingerprints of the body match those found in the end cabin of our carriage. So, I think it is safe to assume the note is correct and the body found beside the line is indeed the body of the man occupying that end cabin. My question now is do either of you recognise him or remember seeing him on or around the train?"

"Yes. Yes, I know this man. It is the younger brother of my brother-in-law. It is the man I thought I saw in the dining car that first time we ate together there. I can't believe this. I always thought his lifestyle would eventually bring him an unpleasant end, but I did not expect this, or that I somehow would be involved."

"You are not involved. None of us is, unless there is something else you need to tell me," Ralph said as he looked hard across the table at Sofia.

"No, I have told you all I know. I do not know anything about this," her angry outburst caught both Ralph and I by surprise. Ralph spoke quietly to her to settle her down again before asking if she had any ideas about what might be happening.

"I am confused. I thought those two brothers were behind whatever has happened to my family and the attempt to get me to steal artefacts. But, now this brother is dead. I don't think my brother-in-law would do that… not to this brother who he was fond of. Does this mean someone else is in charge of whatever is going on, and this brother was only a small part of it… a 'foot soldier' as I think I have heard you call them?"

"That might be the case, or it could be someone else altogether – a competitor – with exactly the same goal in mind, and who saw fit to remove the competition." When Ralph finished speaking, he let the silence drag on while we digested what he suggested.

If Sofia thought she was confused, I promise she is nowhere nearly as confused as I am. "Ralph, let me check that I have all this right. The brother appears to have been involved in something dodgy, whatever it was. There could be someone else who is running the show, or who was in competition with the brother for the same prize, whatever that might be. And the BIG question for me remains: what is it they were all involved in?"

Sofia went to say something, but changed her mind and chose to study her tightly clasped hands on the table instead. The look of concern on her face made me wish she had gone on with saying whatever it was that occurred to her. My instinct told me it probably was important and it might not be good news. Ralph watched Sofia for a few moments. When she didn't speak, he did so instead. "Your assessment of the situation is correct. And, I don't think your big question is any great mystery. We saw that on the occasion of each of the murders, suitcases in the baggage carriage were searched. It is obvious I think that the persons involved – probably those who were murdered – were looking for something they believed someone on board this train had secreted in their luggage."

When Ralph finished speaking, we both turned to Sofia expecting her to comment. She said nothing but, when she looked up from the table, she found us both looking at her. "What…? I have nothing hidden in my luggage! Search my bags if you want. You will find nothing that is not mine, and should not be there."

"Don't be silly, Sofia. Nobody is suggesting there is anything you shouldn't have in your luggage. We were wondering what your thoughts were on Ralph's idea of what this whole thing is about." She took a moment to digest my attempt at placating her.

I seemed to have some success. She apologised before making a couple of false starts on sharing her thoughts with us.

"Why would they search the cases if they were not looking for something? I think that 'something' might be an artefact. Perhaps it is the seal taken form the British Museum that they look for, but I don't think so. The seal is valuable, but not so valuable it is worth killing two people for. Oh, I cannot stand this! Every time we look at what happened, we find new questions. We never find answers."

"Maybe we don't get answers, but we have uncovered a few facts, which should help direct us towards those answers," Ralph said.

Sofia tilted her chin up defiantly. "Well, here are more questions that we don't have any facts for. What was the object they searched for, and who stole it... oh, and who brought it onto the train? We have possible suspects and ideas about a possible object, but no facts to help us work it all out so we know how to go on from here."

I found myself nodding in agreement with her statement. "I agree with all of that, Sofia, but because we don't have anything we could call clues, we have to work out how to get more information. At least, I think that's how I see it. Perhaps Ralph has better ideas on what we should do next."

For the next few minutes we debated a few possible scenarios that Ralph came up with regarding what the object might be and how it got onto the train. We agreed the most likely object was an artefact, but left it at that as we had no idea what or how many might be involved. How it came to be on the train was more problematic... and we weren't sure that it – whatever 'it' was – ever was on board the train. If it was on board the train, where was it now?

I was beginning to develop a headache, and we still were no further advanced with planning what to do today. Things needed moving along. "All this speculation is fine but we are wasting precious time debating all the real or imagined possibilities. Time is of the essence I believe. How long do we have before the police track us down and we all end up behind bars? We have to act; to make the most of what little time we might have. To my mind, finding out what the situation is with Sofia's family might be somewhere to start."

"With any investigation," Ralph began, "The first thing that happens is all the facts and the possibilities are identified to inform any planning that occurs. We need…"

I am over all this police procedural stuff. My response was a tad sharper than perhaps needs be. "We don't have all the facts and we are unlikely to be able to gather them. We are not, in this instance, 'the police' conducting an investigation. Right now, we are on the other side of the equation, and I for one would prefer not to end up behind bars. So, can we get on with planning what we might do for the rest of the day – and even tomorrow perhaps – starting with what we might do about some lunch?" I looked up as I finished speaking to find both Ralph and Sofia, mouths slightly agape, staring at me. "Well okay, let's start with something easy. Come on, what are we going to do about lunch?"

Ralph burst out laughing and Sofia joined in. "As you say, let's start with the easy one: what are our options for lunch?"

"It is not too far to walk to find places where we could eat, or we could remain here in our room and order room service, Sofia suggested. "Will we be safe if we go out?"

"I am not sure what will keep us safe," Ralph admitted. "However, if they are looking for us, and the three of us are seen out and about together, we might draw attention to ourselves by wandering around as a threesome. I would be happy to risk going out for lunch if we don't go to the main areas of the town, but find some little out of the way place close to here. But, I would also be happy to stay in and order room service."

"There are a few places close to here that cater for people from the suburb. One of those would be the best. If the three of us together might draw attention, you two could go for lunch together while I go on my own to check out where my family lives."

"Let's do both of those things," Ralph said. "The three of us will find somewhere 'suburban' to eat. Afterwards, we will walk Marjorie back here to the hotel before Sofia and I check out her home." I started to protest. I didn't particularly want to be left alone at the hotel, but I also didn't want to miss out on what might happen later. My attempt at a protest fell on deaf ears. Both of the others assured me I would not be going with them to check out the house.

We agreed it was still a little too early for lunch and that we should wait another half hour before leaving the hotel. That gave me a chance to ask a question that had been gnawing at me since we registered last night. "Ralph, what's with the business card you gave the receptionist last night? That was all a bit convenient wasn't it?"

"Convenient... Yeah, I suppose it was." He pulled his wallet out of his back pocket and extracted another of the business cards, which he held up by the corner so I could read it. It looked the same as the one I'd had a brief glimpse of last night. The headshot of a smiling Ralph with a trilby perched jauntily on his head occupied one corner of the card. It stated that Harry Buxton was a painter and decorator, and a double glazing specialist, and provided a phone number for contact. It provided no physical address for the business.

"A man of many talents…," I said as Ralph returned the card to his wallet. "But how come you had that card?"

"Just recently, I did a bit of undercover work for one of our investigations. We were trying to find a particular house, so I posed as a double glazing salesman and knocked on doors along a particular street, ostensibly looking for potential customers. The business cards were part of the act, and the phone number belonged to someone at the Met who would deal with calls in the unlikely event anyone rang the number. When we were thinking of names to give ourselves, I remembered Harry Buxton and later, on the way to the hotel, I remembered I still had a few of his business cards in my wallet." We all enjoyed a giggle about it and it lightened the atmosphere between us before we prepared to leave the hotel in search of food.

As we stepped out the hotel door, Sofia pointed off to her right. "That way goes to many of the sights that attract tourists and leads to the main square. We will go this way," she said pointing off to her left. "There is a little shopping mall a few minutes from here. I remember there were – what do you call them? – cafeterias, I think you call them, where we can pick what we want to eat without having to ask for something from a menu."

It took almost ten minutes for us to reach the mall. We settled for the first cafeteria we came to, and I had my first introduction to the local food. "Oh dear, I don't recognise any of these dishes I don't think. What are they, Sofia? I don't usually like anything too hot or too spicy." Ralph echoed my preference for plain food, and Sofia proceeded to point out the dishes she thought would suit. Her advice was excellent, and the food was good. We idled away quite a bit of time after we finished eating just watching the local population drifting past on the street. Then it was time to head back to the hotel. I did so with a heavy heart.

Although I understood the logic in not having the three of us tramping around in Sofia's neighbourhood, I wasn't happy about being left behind, and somehow I felt nervous about being alone. Without knowing how long the other two would be gone, I filled in some time straightening up the room and unpacking a little more of my case before turning to my book as a last resort.

With the two lounge chairs arranged facing each other up against the wall and below the window, I slipped off my shoes, sat in one chair and put my feet up on the other. After sorting out where I was up to in my book, I settled down for what I knew could develop into a long read while I waited for the others to return. Ralph was right. The book was taking a long time to find top gear. Although I persevered, I wasn't absorbing much as my mind wanted to wander off to elsewhere. I gave up on the book in favour of inspecting the world outside the window. With my elbows planted on the windowsill and my head resting in my hands, my mind drifted off.

It skimmed over events that occurred on the train between Paris and Istanbul. Then it spent a few brief seconds thinking about my companions before, unbidden, my mind chose to wander further back into what these days I considered to be forbidden territory. It revisited the events that had me on this trip, before venturing further back to the situation that precipitated my move to the suburbs and the establishment of my friendship with Connie. Perverse as it is, my mind insisted on performing its own comparison of Ralph with my former long-time lover. I tried to stop it, but it persisted. From there, it floated on to examine that long-term relationship that now seems so long ago. And which had remained forbidden territory for all its duration.

Was I kidding myself in thinking of that man as a 'lover', and was what we had really a 'relationship'? At the time of my resignation and immediately after, I couldn't convince myself about either of these descriptions. Perhaps what we had was nothing more than a convenience… something that filled the gap in each of our lives. We never went anywhere together. He came to my flat on a regular basis for all those years. There was the occasional touch, a stolen kiss or cuddle at work. After all, he outranked me and such behaviour, should it be discovered, would not have gone down well with the firm. Still, I was naïve enough to believe that the day would come when he would do 'the right thing', and I allowed myself the occasional thought of a happily ever after scenario.

It didn't happen like that. I still felt the shock and pain of his last visit to my flat. That night I discovered what an utter fool I had been. He arrived unexpectedly at around nine o'clock that evening and, without any preamble, announced he would be getting married on Saturday. He was marrying the woman who had been his live-in 'housekeeper' for about 25 years and his fiancée for the past five years. "So, this will be the last time I come around. How about we have a drink to mark the occasion?" he said, and produced a bottle of wine from a carrier bag. We did not have a drink or open the wine. In fact, I don't know what happened between when he made his big announcement and when I slammed the door on him after pushing him out onto the doorstep. No, there was no comparison between that man and Ralph Carter. I vaguely remember wondering where that last thought had come from.

There were voices. They whispered close to me. Through half opened lids, I saw shadows moving about. It was dark. …Why was it dark? I was wide awake now and sprang up out of the chair. "Relax Marjorie; take it easy. It is only Sofia and I returned from our tour of the suburbs." I glanced out the window. Twilight, installed for some time now, was sliding into night.

How long had I been asleep? It must be at least two hours I reckoned. Sofia turned on the lights. I stood there blinking to adjust to the real world and rubbing my neck, stiff from being at a strange angle in the chair for too long. The fact that I had fallen asleep after revisiting those memories of that painful upheaval in my life must mean that I have moved on.... and that, after all this time, those memories have lost their sting.

"We have ordered room service for dinner. I hope you are happy with what we are getting." I finally found my voice and reassured her that whatever she had ordered would be fine. Now sufficiently awake, I was curious about how their afternoon's sortie into Sofia's home territory went.

"No dramas," Ralph said, "But nothing much to show for it either. We are none the wiser for our afternoon's outing. However, dinner will not be a protracted affair tonight. We are going out again."

"Will I be going with you this time?"

"Eh…? Yes, of course; we are all going. It will be cool out tonight, so we will need to rug up. Wear dark clothing if possible and, as we will be on foot for some of it, walking shoes please."

There was no time for further discussion as room service arrived with dinner at that point, and I was left with my curiosity chewing at me for a bit longer. Dinner was excellent and I discovered I was hungry in spite of having eaten well at lunchtime. As soon as we had finished, Ralph went over tonight's operation with us. They had detected no sign of life at the house this afternoon. Sofia had tried calling the house from a public phone but the call went unanswered. The purpose of tonight's exercise is to check for any lights in the house, or anything else that might indicate people are inside.

And then it was time to go. Bundled up in our heavy jackets, and Sofia and I with our heads covered by scarves, we exited the hotel and scrambled into a waiting taxi. Neither Sofia nor I carried handbags. I had slipped what I considered 'essential items' into the huge pockets of my jacket, adding to its weight and making it even more cumbersome. Although not wanting to be left behind again, I had some misgivings about this expedition we were undertaking. My stomach began churning as soon as the taxi pulled away from the hotel.

CHAPTER 12

Sofia's tutoring beforehand allowed Ralph to give the driver our destination address. I had no idea where we were going but, after a few minutes of dashing along unfamiliar streets, the taxi slowed to a standstill outside a bar on a corner. There was the usual delay as we sorted out money to pay the fare, before the taxi sped off and we were left standing on the pavement. Although the bar behind us appeared a popular place with the locals, I doubted it had anything to do with our endgame. "Come, Marjorie, we walk from here. It is not far, but we should stay close together," Sofia whispered to me. Mystery solved; we were not going into that establishment. I don't think I would feel any easier about going into that bar than I do about what we are about embark on.

'Not far' turned out to be a bit more than three blocks – long blocks. It wasn't difficult walking but, after the first short distance, there was a pronounced shortage of street lighting. Although our path had quite a smooth surface, it is unnerving not being able to see what you are walking on, or if you are about to bump into or trip over something. In the short time since we left the hotel, the weather seemed to have taken a turn for the worse. The wind had gotten up, and to my mind we were in for a squall or something similar. I found myself wondering whether squalls and the like are a part of normal weather conditions in this part of the world. The folding umbrella in my pocket received a reassuring pat. It had been added to my pocket more out of habit than anything else. At home, you wouldn't dream of going out without an umbrella… 'just in case it rains', which it always does, particularly if you didn't bring an umbrella.

A take-away food carton whipped along by the wind blew across the path in front of us. Sofia, leading our procession, picked it up and opened it out. Strange thing to do; I raised my eyebrows in question at Ralph. Because it was so dark, he had no idea I had done so, and I was left to wonder about it alone. My curiosity was compounded a while later when Sofia picked up a stick, part of a dead branch brought down by the wind.

Soon, a considerable fence blocked our progress. It didn't cause any undue interest from my two companions, but they had been here – or somewhere near here – earlier today. Comprised of substantial brick columns interspersed by panels of metal palings topped with sinister looking spikes, I judged the fence to be nearly nine feet high. Once I got over the sight of such a huge barricade, I noticed what lay beyond it.

The enormous house loomed out of the dark night as an even darker shape. I blinked a few times to be sure my eyes were working okay. They were, and the more I looked at it, the more details of the house became clearer. "What is this place?" I asked in not much more than a whisper. There was no reply. I turned to look at my companions. They both looked at me, and even in the darkness, I could make out the confused looks on their faces. Then the truth dawned on me. "Sofia, is this your home? Is this where you live?"

"Yes… well no. It is my family's home. I haven't lived here for about three years. I have a small unit close to where I work. They do still keep my apartment here for me. If I'm here for a special occasion, a function of some sort, and it is best to stay overnight, I stay here in it. My sister and her husband have their own apartment in that part of the house." Sofia pointed to indicate where her sister's apartment was located, and explained that the servants' quarters were on the ground floor at the rear of the building.

"It looks like a medieval manor house, only a bit more decorative with all those fancy additions. It must be very old."

"It is very old. Nothing much has changed on the outside, but inside has undergone a lot of modernisation over the years. It has belonged to my family for generations."

Ralph halted any further discussion about the house. "I think we should get on with what we came to do. Are you right to proceed, Sofia?"

"Yes of course, I am sorry, I have been wasting time." With that, Sofia picked up a stone and placed it in the cardboard takeaway food box, which she had managed to reform into a box shape. However, the box was now inside out. This meant that the coloured outside surface was now inside, while the exterior of the box stood out stark white in the darkness. Without any warning, Sofia hurled the box over the fence. It landed with a loud thump some distance inside the fence. She and Ralph stood tensed for a short period of time. I wasn't sure what I should do or what was supposed to happen in response to the box's landing on the other side. As I was about to ask what the box thing was all about, Sofia brought her arm back and, with a grunt, hurled the stick she carried over the fence and well into the front yard of the house. Then, everyone waited again. Once more, nothing happened.

"Good...," Sofia said. I thought I detected a note of relief in her voice.

"Good what...?" I asked. "I'm confused. What did chucking those things over the fence prove that was so good?"

"No security guards are on duty. If there were, someone would come out to investigate what happened. No one did, so I think it is safe to assume they were told to take leave along with all the servants. This is strange. It is not normal. There is all the more reason for the security guards to be on duty if nobody is in the house. But it is good for us tonight. Come; let's see what we can see. This way..."

For a brief moment, I wondered where we were going to go. The path we were on ended at the fence. There was no way in except through the big gates I could see further along from where we stood. Ralph and Sofia already had moved off. It took me a few quick steps to catch up to them as we headed off to our right along the fence and away from the gates. About four metres past the path, we reached a corner and turned it to make our way along the side of the property. The same wrought iron and brick construction continued along this side until we had passed the rear of the house. Our conga line stopped suddenly and I crashed into the rear of Ralph. "What...?" I demanded as I ran a hand down to straighten my clothes.

"Shhh...," Sofia hissed. "Look there is a little spot of light coming from that window. It looks like the curtain is caught up somehow and is letting a little light escape from the bottom corner."

"Do you think we can't see any other lights in the house because all the other drapes are closed properly?" Ralph asked.

"No, I don't think so. That area of the house is the kitchen and servants' quarters. It has heavy drapes. The rest of the house does not have such heavy curtaining. If other lights were on, we would not see light, only a soft glow coming from the windows. But, we would know there were lights on in there."

"We need to move on to check out the rest of the place as quickly as possible." At Ralph's suggestion, we set off again along the side fence. After the palings panel we had looked through, the next long section of fence was all brickwork with two heavy wooden gates set in the middle of it. Ralph doubled back to the last palings section and peered to his right through the fence before returning to join us. "What's the long building in there that runs end on to this section of the fence? Is there a reason this part is all brick?"

"Uhmm… I think it was because they needed a big gate here, but it did not need to be a fancy one. A long time ago, that building was the stables. The horses, carriages and all the harness was kept there, and the drivers – coachmen I think they are called – had rooms on the upper floor. It has changed a bit over the years. Now, the family's vehicles are kept in there."

"So, it's what we might call 'the mews'," I suggested.

"I do not know this word," Sofia said.

"I think we can agree it was the mews," Ralph said. "They needed the double gates to get the carriages in and out… and now the vehicles use it."

"In the early days, yes, I think the horses and carriages used these gates, but they are not used much now. If any of the family needs a vehicle, a driver brings it around to the front door to collect them. That building's doors are at the back. The vehicles reverse out of the building, drive around the back past the tennis court and the pool, and along the other side of the house to the front door. The servants have a van to collect supplies from town. The van doesn't go around to the front of the house. It uses this gate, and any deliveries that come to the house come in through here. So, this entrance doesn't get much use anymore."

"You mentioned a tennis court and a pool. Where are they

located?" I asked. This place was one amazing revelation after another.

"They are on the other side – past the garage building. They stretch back that way." Sofia waved her arm towards an area somewhere ahead of us. When they take vehicles out of the garage, they drive between the end of tennis court and the pool and the stables."

"There are stables as well…? I thought you turned the stables into a garage." I was beginning to wish I could see this place in daylight, if only to understand the layout of the property.

"Yes, the old stables were renovated to become the garage. A new stables built along modern lines were constructed further back on the property. That area comprises the stables building, a feed store and an exercise yard. My father has a few racehorses – three or four, I think. My sister and her husband have horses as well, not for racing but for pleasure. We should keep moving. I want to see if anything is happening anywhere else on the rest of the property."

We began moving along the fence again. The solid brick section gave way to the earlier arrangement of panels of metal palings between brick columns. Although I could make out the distant stables building in the dark, the white painted fence around the exercise yard stood out sharply some distance up ahead of us. However, in the area between the garage and where Sofia indicated the new stables were, another building stood out in the darkness.

Sofia gasped and stopped suddenly, causing a concertina effect on our procession. Ralph and I slammed up against Sofia. "What…?" I whispered as I untangled myself from Ralph. Then I noticed where the other two were looking. I followed their lead and looked through the fence towards the other side of the property. Oh yes, I see what all the excitement might be about, I thought to myself.

Near the far side fence and presumably behind the pool and the tennis court was a small cottage. The fact that there was a cottage there wasn't what caused the excitement. It was light streaming out from every window that caught our attention. Although I realised that anyone, even one of the servants, might live in the cottage,

Sofia's reaction suggested this was not what she expected to see. I leaned in as close as I could and whispered, "Who lives there… or maybe I should be asking does anyone live there?"

"No, no one lives there now," Sofia murmured. The man who looked after the horses used to, but there has been nobody there for a few years now."

"Is it possible your parents put somebody into the cottage in recent times without you knowing about it? You did say you haven't lived here for a few years," Ralph asked without taking his eyes off the cottage.

"That is not possible. I was here about a week before I went to London to look at a new racehorse my father bought. There was no one in the house then and my father was talking about having it removed to make room for some special swimming pool for the racehorses. I think it is unlikely for things to have changed so quickly. We should continue down to the back fence to see if anything else has changed."

With exaggerated care to avoid making any sound, we began moving along the fence again. We moved past what I assumed was the stables and the exercise yard with the white painted fence. There wasn't as much as a pause to look at the stables complex. With Sofia in the lead, we kept moving past the exercise yard to be confronted at the next palings panel by what she called 'the orchard'. "That was our orchard, and this next area is our vegetable garden. It supplies most of the fresh vegetables for the house all year round. I saw a dense patch of trees but we didn't stop to look at them. A perfume I was unfamiliar with saturated the heavy night air. I assumed it came from some of the trees in the orchard that were in flower, but it didn't seem important enough to ask about it. Sofia was in 'tourist guide' mode as we continued along the fence.

After the densely planted orchard with all its trees, we passed another neatly laid out area. This was the vegetable garden that kept the house supplied with produce for most of the year. That it managed to do so wasn't surprising. It seemed to cover a huge area. A low shrubby hedge marked the boundary between the vegetable garden and whatever came next, and we hurried on behind Sofia to see what that might be.

What we came to was another cottage set about midway across the property. I thought I could make out shrubs and the remnants of well laid out garden beds at the front of the cottage. There was only a short distance between the rear of the cottage and the back fence of the property. Another all brick section confronted us as we reached that part of the side fence running past the cottage. A fancy double wrought iron gate was set in the middle of the brickwork. I waited for our tour guide to explain but, when nothing eventuated, I felt obliged to ask about the cottage.

"It has always been the gardener's cottage. Maybe 'gardener' is the wrong word. The person who lived here was more like a groundsman, someone who looked after all of the grounds and supervised the gardeners. The wife of the last one who lived here was the family's cook. I think she was here for ever. She was quite old when they left. I think she only left because her husband was old and not well and wanted to retire. The woman who was the wife's assistant took over as the cook, although she was already an old lady. The man who took over looking after the grounds did not move into the cottage. He lives in town in his own home with his family and comes here to work every day."

The cottage appeared in complete darkness. It wasn't hard to accept that the place remained unoccupied. As we stood looking through the palings before the long section of solid brick wall, I became aware of a distinct change in the weather. The wind, now colder and with a discernible dampness to it, came in strong gusts. "It feels like it's going to rain at any minute," I said, stating the obvious.

"As I haven't observed anywhere along the way that might provide cover, I suspect we are all in for a hosing if it does rain." Ralph had barely finished speaking when a streak of lightning followed immediately by a tremendous clap of thunder prevented any further conversation. I thrust my hand into my pocket and grabbed hold of my folding umbrella. It wouldn't cover all three of us, but it might keep one or two of us relatively dry – if the wind didn't blow it inside out. Lightning and thunder now put on a continuous display and I thought I felt the first warning drops of rain.

"Wait here," Sofia said as she moved further along the fence.

"What's she doing?" I whispered to Ralph. He shrugged and we both continued to watch in silence, and in the hope that it will make sense before we got thoroughly drenched.

Sofia rushed to the fancy wrought iron gates. Then, standing slightly towards us, she stretched her hand out and placed it on the centre hinge of the gate nearest to us. She took a couple of carefully measured sidesteps back towards us while running her hand along the brickwork. We both craned our necks for a glimpse of whatever had halted Sofia's sideway passage along the fence. A bolt of lightning provided a split-second glimpse of her doing something to the wall. We heard a soft grunt, followed a few moments later by a soft 'aha', which we interpreted to mean there had been some sort of Eureka moment.

Between the claps of thunder, we heard her call, "Come here. Come to the gate with me." Those odd drops of rain were becoming more plentiful. There was no doubt the heavens were about to open and the deluge would begin. Nevertheless, we hurried forward to where Sofia appeared to be fiddling with the gates. It wasn't until we reached her that we realised she was unlocking the gates.

In spite of perhaps not being used for some time, the gate swung open with barely a sound that was lost amid the thunder. Sofia went through and held the gate open just wide enough for us to follow her. After gently pushing the gates together, she slipped a key into her pocket and rushed forward. "Come. Follow me before we get wet. There is a small area at the back of the cottage where we can take cover until the storm passes." No argument required. Ralph and I wasted no time in following her around to the back of the house where a small awning stretched across a concreted area.

With the wind blowing the way it was, during heavy gusts, the rain seemed to be coming parallel to the ground. To stay dry required us to plaster ourselves against the rear wall of the house. The only place to sit was on the two concrete steps leading to the back door. At very close quarters, we made ourselves as comfortable as possible on those steps. Unlike anything I was used to, it seemed a fierce storm. Sofia assured me they weren't uncommon but didn't happen too often. After sitting huddled together for about 20 minutes, we noticed the wind had dropped and the downpour eased to a drizzle.

All of us were becoming restless. It wasn't comfortable perched in such close proximity on those steps. It was cold and, no matter how hard we tried to avoid it, we were damp. After about another ten minutes, the rain appeared to stop altogether. However, when we ventured out from under cover, a light mist still lingered on the night air. We moved back under cover but Sofia wanted to press on. "You two stay here where it's a bit drier. I want to see if I can get a look at what's going on in that other cottage and who is in there."

Ralph was quick to respond. "I don't think that's a good idea. I've had more experience at this sort of thing. I'll go. You stay here with Marjorie." I suppose it was predictable that Sofia was not about to entertain that idea.

"You don't know what you are looking for. You don't know what is normal and what is not. If you see anyone in the house, you will not know who they are and whether they should be there or not. I have to be the one to look."

"Anything I see in there, according to what you said earlier, is not normal. The place is supposed to be empty. You might not know anybody you see in the cottage either. So, why don't I go and then describe to you anyone I see inside?"

"If you insist on going to have a closer look at the cottage, it is up to you, but… I… will… be… going. Now, are you coming with me, or are you going to stay here?" Sofia made it clear there was no room to negotiate, so Ralph said he was going with her. Sofia then turned to me. "Right, we should not be too long, Marjorie. You will be all right here until we get back. If anything worries you, the gate is unlocked. Let yourself out and wait outside for us."

She must be joking! Wait here alone… not likely. Sofia wasn't the only one quite adamant about how thing were going to play out. I was not being left here alone or waiting outside the gate while goodness knows what might be happening near that other cottage. There was a brief exchange of ideas, but Sofia was in a hurry to get moving, so the battle didn't last long. We set off along the inside of that same fence we so recently explored from the outside.

The grass was wet and had grown long in the absence of

gardeners over the last week or so. In places it rose as high as our ankles and clung there in wet trailing strands. I don't know whether it still misted rain or if it was just that the air remained heavy with moisture, but it was like walking through a curtain of vapour. There was a strong temptation to use my umbrella, and I giggled to myself about the reaction that attract from the other two.

It seemed to take ages to carefully pick our way back and across to a patch of shrubbery a few metres from the side of the target cottage. The three of us crouched down behind the low scraggy shrubs would have presented an intriguing sight for anyone who happened upon us there like that. Although no drapes were pulled, at first we saw no one inside. Then, after about a minute, a man wandered into view through one of the windows. He was in what I guessed to be a sitting room of some sort. His constant prowling around in that space suggested he was impatient or worried about something.

Another man joined him after a short time, and a heated exchange appeared to take place between them. It ended with the second man trying to hold back the first man who was considerably bigger than his colleague. The first man shook off the restraining hand, turned on his heel and strode from view. Sofia muttered a couple of words –I interpreted them as swearing in her native language. She raised herself up off her knees.

Doubled over in a crouch, she ran to another patch of shrubs a short distance away. From there, she could see into windows in the back part of the cottage. The second man to enter the sitting room disappeared as he followed his colleague out of the room. As soon as he was out of our sight, Ralph and I followed Sofia's example in rushing to the next lot of shrubs. Comprised of fewer and with less dense foliage, this clump of bushes didn't offer what I considered good concealment. Already wet from having nestled in close to the other shrubs, the wet leaves and cobwebs in this group simply offered more of the same. For me, all this huddling in wet bushes was fast losing its appeal.

I wasn't watching the house. I was fussing over somewhere more comfortable to place my left knee when I heard Sofia gasp. Ralph heard it too. "What… what is it Sofia? What happened?"

"Look to the far right of that bedroom. You can just see a man reflected in the mirror. That is my brother-in-law. His face looks bruised."

"Yes, I see him. You're right. He looks like he has taken a bit of a beating. If nobody is supposed to be in this cottage, why would he be here?" Ralph asked.

"I do not know … Oh God! That's my sister."

A young woman came into view and stood beside the man who was her husband. From our vantage point, and although the tableau inside was being played out as reflections in a dressing table mirror, it was clear the husband was mouthing off. He had plenty to say, and he was angry. His young wife, a slightly less stunning version of Sofia, tried to placate him… or at least get him to shut up. She didn't seem to have any success. The husband carried on his tirade. The faint sound of raised voices seeped through the brick walls of the cottage to reach our ears.

His verbal outrage came to an abrupt end when one of the men strode up and punched him in the face. The attacker was the first man we saw enter the sitting room earlier. Sofia's hand flew to her mouth. I thought I heard a soft strangled scream. Ralph spun his head around sharply to look at Sofia. He put a hand on her shoulder. She nodded a couple of times to indicate she had herself under control again.

The blow almost knocked the husband off his feet. The only thing preventing his hitting the floor was the fact that he fell back against his wife. She did her best to catch him and hold him upright. They both staggered for a brief moment before regaining their feet. Blood poured from the husband's face. From what I could see, it looked like he sustained a busted lip and some damage to his nose. Blood flowed freely from both sites.

Not a wise move, my girl, I thought as I watched the young wife launch a verbal attack of her own. No doubt she protested the attack on her husband and his injuries, whether they were deserved or not. But, the only outcome likely from her protest at her husband's treatment was a dose of the same for herself. I watched in horror as the man who struck her husband strode towards her. Sofia sprang up and was halfway to her feet before Ralph managed to yank her down again.

"What do you think you will be able to do? Going in there will not help matters. It will just give them another person to rough up. Be sensible. We need to move away from here to somewhere we can talk more freely to work out a plan." Sofia struggled against Ralph's grip but couldn't shake him off. And Ralph, realising the moment he let her go, Sofia would be out from behind the bushes and pounding on the cottage's door, maintained a firm grip. Good God, I thought, what did she think she could do to help? One thing I was certain of was that Ralph and I were of an age that precluded us from being of much help in storming the bastion.

Relief came when the other man – the second one we saw enter the sitting room – stepped between the wife and her would-be attacker. Although it appeared to take some effort, this man restrained his colleague and held him back. Something of an argument broke out between the two men. It only lasted a few moments before things settled down again, although the would-be attacker continued to look less than pleased with the situation.

Sofia visibly relaxed. Ralph risked loosening his grip on her. "Come on, Sofia, be sensible. Let's get away from here. We need to work out what to do." It only took a curt nod from Sofia and we were all on our feet and running in that uncomfortable doubled-over posture back to that first patch of shrubbery. Without stopping, we retraced our steps to the cottage where we had sheltered from the storm.

Nobody bothered to return to the steps. We stood in a tight cluster under the rear awning and spoke in not much more than whispers. Ralph took charge. "I think we can agree your sister and her husband are not in that cottage of their own accord. It looks as though they are being held hostage. It's possible it's a part of the same operation that has seen the body count rising – including the husband's younger brother – and which we think is about stealing artefacts to sell on the black market. The police need to know what's happening here, but we can't tell them without ending up behind bars ourselves. Anyone got any bright ideas?"

I shook my head. While I agreed with his assessment of the situation, I think we are caught between the proverbial rock and a hard place. Sofia hadn't responded to Ralph's comments. She appeared to be deep in thought. Ralph watched her for a moment and was about to speak to her. I laid a hand on his arm to stop him and gave him a little shake of my head. He shrugged and said nothing. The silence stretched on for what seemed like a long time before Sofia returned to us and shared her thoughts.

"My mind is so confused. I have a few thoughts about what we might do, but I don't know if any one of them is better than the others, or if any of them will work." Ralph encouraged her to stop worrying about whether they made any sense, and to just outline for us what those thoughts were. "My first thought is about whoever that person is inside the main house. Is it one of the servants kept on to cook for them, or is it one of 'their' people – one of the ones who have my sister and her husband?

"Yes," Ralph agreed, "As we can't see in through any of the windows, we have no way of knowing who is in there. What are your other thoughts?"

"There are weapons in the main house…"

"Are you suggesting those men holding your family might have taken the weapons? From the way this operation had panned out so far, I feel sure they would have come prepared with their own weapons."

"No, I wasn't thinking they had taken our weapons. They are not just lying about. You have to know where they are to be able to take them. I wondered if those weapons might be useful to us. I can shoot and I assume that you, as a police officer, know how to."

I saw Ralph give a gentle shake of his head. Before he could speak, I jumped in. "Well, that leaves me out of any planned heroics. I've never held a gun in my life and I'm fairly confident I don't want to do so now." Ralph gave me an indulgent smile, much as a parent might give a child.

"Nobody expects you to take up arms, Marjorie. In fact, none of us should be thinking of going down that track. Any other ideas you want share, Sofia?"

"I don't know that I should bother to tell you, because I am going to do it anyway… whether you approve or not." Ralph attempted to protest, but Sofia continued speaking and prevented it. "I am going into the house to see who is there. No Ralph, don't waste your breath, just listen. I am not going to enter and call out to see if anyone is home. I am not so stupid. I know the house very well. It is my home and this is about me and my family. I will be careful. I need to be so I can do whatever I can to help save them. And, Ralph, no you are not coming in with me. If something happens to me, you two must get away and do whatever is necessary for your own safety. There is no negotiation on that. That is what is going to happen. Come; instead of standing here talking, we need to make our way to the front of the main house."

Ralph held his hands up in resignation, and we both fell into line again behind Sofia to once more make our way along that side fence and around to the front of the main house.

CHAPTER 13

The last stage of our trek along the side of the house was the most nerve-wracking. Here there was nothing but manicured lawns with nothing to take cover behind. I expected that, when we were level with the front corner of the house, we would cut across to sneak along the front wall towards that huge wooden front door. Sofia had other ideas. She took us right to the corner where the side fence met the front fence. About a metre in from the front fence, a well-trimmed hedge ran all the way across to the main gates before continuing on the other side of the gates. While the hedge didn't relieve all my tension, at least behind it I didn't feel quite so exposed and vulnerable.

"We know there are no security guards on duty, but we still should be careful. I want to check the gates first," Sofia said as we walked along the front fence. We walked erect and, hidden by the tall hedge, wasted no time on taking too many precautions about being seen. Just prior to the gates, we came to a halt. Sofia took a few heartbeats to check nobody was about before making her next move. "Wait here. I want to check the gates to make sure they can be opened if necessary."

Neither Ralph nor I had time to argue before she moved out from behind the hedge and over to the huge wrought iron gates. We saw the gates move slightly apart and then close again. Sofia was back with us within moments of having gone off on her own. "It is good. There is nothing to prevent the gates being opened from inside. Come; I will show you how to do that in case there needs to be a quick getaway from here." She didn't reference her statement to specific people, but I knew she was referring to Ralph and me when she spoke of 'needing a quick getaway'.

It was a stroke of luck that the clouds chose that moment to part and let enough light through for us to see the gates' locking mechanism. By the look of them, these were quite ancient heavy gates. Access to the crude but effective locking lever from the outside was prevented by the strategic placement of a large ornately carved plate behind which the lever was located. Sofia had Ralph try operating the lever to familiarise himself with it.

Then, there appeared nothing else to wait around for. The three of us moved back behind the hedge. I knew this was the point at which Sofia would leave us to enter the house. I felt my stomach churning. "I am going inside now. Stay here behind this hedge. If anything happens, or if I don't come back in half an hour – no, make that 45 minutes – let yourselves quickly and quietly out of that gate and get away from here."

"How are you planning to get past that imposing front door? Are you planning to ring the bell or knock?" Ralph's sarcasm made it clear how he felt about this whole exercise. Sofia, rather than be offended by his comments, just giggled.

"No need for any of that," she said. "I shall use my key." She held up a bunch of keys for Ralph to see before moving off, and was still chuckling as she walked sedately to the front door.

*****

Sofia stopped before stepping up onto the raised concrete expanse that served as a doorstep and removed her shoes. She tucked them in behind one of the two large decorative urns that stood one on either side of and a short distance out from the front door. In bare feet, she padded soundlessly to the door and slipped her key into the lock. The lock released without a sound. Sofia pushed the door open a few centimetres, held her breath and waited. Nothing happened and not a sound of any concern was heard. She pushed the door open just wide enough to allow her to slip inside before gently closing it behind her.

Once inside the house, her problem was what to do next, where to look first. Still, the only light visible appeared to come from the kitchen area. It made sense to see what was happening there before doing anything else. The coloured ceramic tiles were cool beneath her bare feet as she stole silently along the corridor leading to the kitchen and the staff quarters at the rear of the house. With the house closed up the way it was, the air was redolent with the aroma of a recently cooked meal. Lamb tagine she thought, her favourite. The so-familiar perfume of cinnamon, cardamom and coriander hung in the heavy night air.

A short distance before the kitchen door, she paused and stood still for a few moments. No voices came from the kitchen. The only sounds emanating from somewhere in there were the scrape of slippers on the tiled floor, and the noise of pans being washed. Sofia edged closer and checked for voices again before risking a peep into the kitchen. At first, she saw no one. She poked her head in a little further and caught sight of the kitchen's only occupant.

The elderly woman at the sink was no stranger. She had been a part of the family of the place since she first came to work in the house as a young girl, long before Sofia was born. Now, believed to be in her mid-eighties, the woman had been a house-maid and then the cook's assistant before becoming the cook. A position she held for decades until she suffered a serious stroke some years ago. The family paid for a long period of special re-habilitation for its long serving staff member. This resulted in few outward signs of the damage the stroke caused.

There remained some slight loss of strength to her right side. However, the stroke's most notable legacy was the woman's ongo-ing speech impediment. Her speech was unclear and find-ing the right words sometimes presented a challenge. Since the stroke, speaking seemed to exhaust her. Some of the family and key staff members learned sign language to be able to communi-cate with her without causing her undue stress. She couldn't work for a long time. The then cook's assistant, a woman already in her sixties, stepped up to the position of cook and a new assistant was engaged. Once the elderly woman completed her rehabilitation, the family was not prepared to consign her to the scrap heap. She came back to help out in the kitchen, for a couple of hours a day at first, but then for as long as she liked whenever she liked.

As Sofia stood watching the woman and wondering what to do next, it occurred to her that the old cook seemed smaller tonight, shrunken somehow. She couldn't stand there watching her all night. The woman might turn around and get a fright. Sofia softly called the woman's name. "Fatima, Fatima; it is Sofia. Is it safe to talk?"

Her hearing unaffected by the stroke, the woman heard her name called and spun around to face the source of the voice. With a quick glance over her shoulder, the woman dropped the pot she held in the sink and came across to hug Sofia. Tears rolled down her face. Sofia feared her own tears would start if she didn't do something to avoid it.

"Are any of my family here in the house?" The woman shook her head. "Are there any other servants still here?" Another shake of the head. "I know my sister, Yasmin, and her husband are in the horse-trainer's cottage. Is everyone else okay?" Sofia indicated to the woman to use sign language to respond, and she promptly complied. The story unfolded quickly and in concise bites.

Her parents had gone to visit Sofia's aunt who was ill and lived up in a mountainous area of the country. About two days after they left, three men arrived and forced Yasmin and her husband into Sofia's father's office. It sounded like a terrible fight occurred in there before Yasmin, accompanied by one of the men, came out and told all the staff to go on leave… now. They were told to be gone within the hour, and would be contacted when it was time to come back. The old woman, Fatima, ignored them and pretended to be deaf and mute. With her back to the man, Fatima continued to prepare a salad for lunch while managing to sign to Yasmin to tell them that the old cook, was deaf and mute.

This seemed to please the man. He said they would need someone to prepare meals for them, so the old woman should stay. The two women kept their ability to communicate by sign language to themselves. They took over the cottage and had been there ever since. Two days ago, one of the men left. He seemed to be the one in charge. The other two men remained. The old woman's assessment of the men: they were 'bad men, very dangerous'.

After warning the old woman not to mention her visit, not even to Yasmin, Sofia said she had something to do and then she would leave to go to organise help. While talking with the old woman had confirmed Sofia's assumption about what had taken place, it was disappointing that the woman did not know why or what the men hoped to achieve. However, she did warn Sofia, that the men had mentioned her name several times and she thought they were looking for her. That eradicated any doubts Sofia had that what was happening to her family was connected to what happened at the British Museum.

One last hug and Sofia was off to complete her mission. She made her way soundlessly and unerringly through the darkened house to what was once the children's nursery. Long now used as somewhere to store unwanted pieces of furniture and ornaments, it also held a secret. Sofia made her way over to one of the brightly painted walls, quietly shifting bits and pieces out of her way as she went. Decorated long ago by a local well-known artist with images from children's fairy tales like all the other walls of the room, this wall was the same except for one small detail.

Sofia bent down and pressed the nose of an image of a playful kitten chasing a butterfly along the skirting board. A panel of the wall swung out towards her. She stepped into the long narrow space running between the decorated wall and that of the neighbouring room. This 'gallery' stretched off on both sides of the opening and ran the full length of the wall. With the panel pulled almost closed behind her, and having checked that the drapes were closed, Sofia withdrew a small torch from her pocket and began her search.

It was ages since she was last in here and it took her a while to work out where what she wanted might be stored. After searching along the wrong part of the passage, she retraced her steps and soon found what she was looking on the other side of the opening. Then it was decision time. What should she take? She wasted a few moments dithering over her choices, but soon had her roomy jacket pockets weighed down with their precious cargo.

Before stepping out through the open panel Sofia checked her watch. Her excursion had taken longer than she anticipated. Never mind, it had been worthwhile. After returning the torch to her pocket, she stepped out from the wall cavity and pushed the panel back into the wall. As she heard the mechanism lock it into place, in the darkness, she winked at her favourite image on the nursery's walls. "Keep your secret safe," she whispered to the playful kitten still chasing its butterfly.

There was no need to hurry. The others would be on their way back to the hotel by now if they followed her instructions should she be delayed. It wasn't how she planned for things to happen, but it didn't matter. In a couple of minutes, she, like the others, would be safely outside that perimeter fence. There was no light at all in the house now. Fatima had gone to bed. As she cracked open the front door, she remembered the key to that small gate near the gardener's cottage and reminded herself that she must put it back in its hiding place before she left. Then, after a moment to listen for any untoward noises outside, she was out through the front door. Grabbing her shoes as she rushed past the decorative urn, she continued toward the main gates in her bare feet. She would put her shoes on again when she was safely out through those gates.

*****

With my back to the house, and the little torch and my wrist under my jacket, I took a quick look at the time. How else were we going to know when things had reached the critical stage?

And then we waited. I turned my back to the house again and was about to check my watch once more. "Don't do that," Ralph said. "It is nowhere near a half hour since she left."

"She changed that to 45 minutes, remember?"

"Yes, I do remember, and I know we have a long while yet to wait."

Time drags so slowly when you are doing nothing more than waiting. My legs were starting to stiffen from standing in the one spot and being so cold. Ralph noticed my fidgeting. "If your legs are stiffening, try marking time. Don't lift your feet too high, just a couple of inches will do. It will get the circulation flowing again." It felt a bit strange but it did work. And time continued to drag on. If only I knew what was happening in there, I thought. It's the not knowing that's the hardest to bear. I was well into feeling sorry for myself when Ralph leaned over and whispered in my ear. "There hasn't been any ruckus come from inside, so I assume nothing untoward has happened. It might be time to check your watch again."

No, we hadn't heard anything from inside, but I wasn't sure whether that was a good thing or not. What if Sofia had been overpowered, knocked out perhaps, and was now down in that cottage with the others? I turned my back and went through the performance of covertly checking the time. I couldn't believe my eyes. After recounting and recalculating several times, I had to admit that only 35 minutes had elapsed since Sofia walked out from behind this hedge. I told Ralph the outcome of my deliberations. He smiled and nodded. It was obvious I hadn't told him anything he didn't expect to hear.

While my fingers itched to check my watch again, Ralph appeared to remain unconcerned. At last...! He suggested I check the time again. I wasted no time complying. So close; 43 minutes had elapsed since Sofia left us to enter the house. Still nothing had been heard from in there. I tried telling myself that was okay, there would have been a commotion of sorts if something had gone wrong. Sofia would try to warn us in some way if she got into trouble. What if she couldn't? What if she had been knocked unconscious… or worse? All this time to think was not doing me any good at all. At this rate I would be a nervous wreck in no time.

To hell with waiting for Ralph to tell me to check the time again, the 45 minutes will be up by now. I checked my watch: 47 minutes now gone. "Sofia said to wait for 45 minutes. Ralph, it is now 47 minutes since she left. What do we do?" I was torn. Part of me wanted to rush to those gates and flee down that path to somewhere to catch a taxi. An equal part of me wanted to find out what had happened to Sofia. How we might do that I had no idea. Would we rush into the house, ready to take on whatever we found there, or should we backtrack to that cottage to see if Sofia had been taken to join her sister and brother-in-law?

My befuddled mind registered that Ralph said something but didn't take on board what it was. "Eh…? Sorry, I wasn't listening. What did you say?"

"I said you have to add a contingency allowance. I was responding to your comment about the 47 minutes by telling you that, in such circumstances, a ten percent contingency allowance needs to be made. In which case, we would need to wait at least 50 minutes… and, if we stay that long, why not make it an hour."

"That's ridiculous. Why not make it breakfast time and be done with it?"

"Now who is being ridiculous, Marjorie? If you want to leave now, we will. I don't think it will hurt us to wait a little longer, not too much longer though."

"And then what do we do?" Although I still whispered, I realised I was beginning to sound like a fish wife. But this conversation was going nowhere I wanted it to, and I was wound up tight enough already without Ralph's unhelpful comments.

"Then we go back to the hotel as she told us to do. And, before you ask, then we wait some more until she comes back to the hotel. If she doesn't return by morning, I will go to the police and try my luck at getting to speak to the only bloke I know of who is involved in everything that has happened… and to whom I am supposed to be on secondment."

"Wait until morning…? Anything could have happened in the meantime. She could be dead by then."

"Shush! I think I saw the door move. Yes, it has opened a little way. Look out, some's coming out!" We bobbed down and pressed ourselves in tight against the bushes. I would feel safer if these shrubs were more luxuriant, I thought as I strained my ears for any approaching sounds. When I recognised the approaching 'someone' as Sofia, I moved forward.

"Who's there…? What are you still doing here?" Sofia said after first giving a yelp of surprise – or fright.

"It's only us and we didn't mean to frighten you," Ralph rushed to reply. "We were just about to leave when I saw the front door open a little way. Now we can leave together." Sofia beckoned us to follow her and, within seconds, she had opened the gates and we were on the outside watching her put her shoes on. When we reached the start of the path we had negotiated earlier, Sofia stopped.

"There is something I must do first. Go a few metres along the path and wait for me there. I will be gone only a few minutes. If anyone comes along in the meantime, continue on the path until you reach that bar on the corner." After assuring us she was not going to enter the estate again, she jogged off into the blackness of the night.

"I hope she isn't too long," Ralph murmured as he watched Sofia disappear from view. "That storm looks like it's about to return at any minute. I hope we can avoid getting drenched before getting back to the hotel." His hopes were in vain.

True to her word, Sofia returned after a few minutes. She ran up to where we waited. My heart missed a beat. Why was Sofia running? "What's happened? Why are you running?"

"Nothing has happened. I only need to be careful when I go past that cottage where they are. But we must hurry. The storm is coming again."

The earlier rain made the path slippery and hurrying was hazardous. Before we reached halfway along the path, the heavens opened and the rain bucketed down. Sofia and I, with an arm around each other's waist, huddled under my umbrella, leaving Ralph out in the open to contend with the downpour. By the time we reached the corner and went around to stand in front of the bar, all three of us were drenched. "One good thing about the rain, it washed off most of the mud gathered from kneeling behind shrubs." I thought it a relevant observation on my part. We already looked so bedraggled a taxi driver would think twice about having us in his vehicle. Had the mud remained caked to our knees, we definitely would have been left standing on the street.

At almost the same time as we arrived in front of the bar, a taxi pulled up in front of it and discharged its passengers. We scrambled in as the last passenger disembarked, giving the driver little chance to drive off without us. Although a little lighter now, the rain continued all the way back to the hotel. After the cab dropped us out front, we took a moment to assess our appearance before entering the hotel lobby.

"Now…! Come on. The coast is clear." Sofia and I took a split second to register Ralph's words before following him. The lobby seemed twice its previous size as we took long and hurried strides towards the lifts. Once we were on our way up to our room, I ventured to ask what prompted our rush through the lobby.

"I saw the receptionist leave the desk and disappear into a

back office. It was probable he wouldn't be gone long. In our present dishevelled state, I thought it wise to reach the lifts without being seen and having our appearance render us memorable." We agreed with Ralph's assessment of the situation, and I think we all heaved a sigh of relief when we were safely in our room once more.

Later, when we were clean and dry, Sofia told us what she had learned while inside the house. Intriguing as it was, in my mind it raised another big question: what do we do now? We couldn't storm the cottage to free Sofia's sister, Yasmin, and her husband. And going to the police for help could be tricky. The dread of ending up behind bars in a Turkish prison still loomed large in my mind. My hope was that Ralph had a plan. As it turned out, he didn't.

Discussions stretched for quite some time as we explored every scenario from the possibly practicable to the ridiculous and everything in between. Sofia was all for attacking the cottage and freeing the hostages. She was a little light on for details of how we might manage that. In the end, it fell to Ralph to come up with the most workable solution. "I think our only option is for me to contact Inspector Yazar." Both Sofia and I began to protest, but Ralph silenced us. "I am supposed to be seconded to work with him on the British Museum incident investigation. It will be a little unusual given the circumstances of my late appearance, but not unexpected."

"How will you explain not having contacted him until now, and not following his specific instructions?" I asked, as I could see such an approach having an unhappy ending – possibly for all of us.

"Yes, there is likely to be the odd complication. I will claim Sofia and I were separated when we arrived at Istanbul station, and I felt obliged to try to make the situation right before reporting to him. A lot of how the meeting progresses will have to be off the cuff. He already is not happy about what he sees as his investigation being lumbered with me, so he might not have too much difficulty believing a story about my bumbling ineptitude."

Regardless of Ralph's brave face, I don't believe he is any

more comfortable about the likely outcome of such a meeting than I am. Discussion of such an approach stretched on for some time without resolve. My eyes were heavy and I was trying to stifle yet another yawn when Sofia brought the evening to an end. "Marjorie is having trouble staying awake and I don't feel much better. We have said all there is to say on this matter. It is time for sleep. If any new ideas come to us in the night, we can discuss them in the morning before making any risky moves."

She was right, I was tired. But sleep was a long time coming. A feeling of foreboding lay like a lead weight in the pit of my stomach. I knew Ralph's going cap-in-hand to the police was the only real solution available to us, but it involved such risk. He might not be allowed to leave the police station once he identifies himself. That thought caused my stomach to tighten. Somehow, I didn't think Turkish jails were the greatest places in which to find oneself.

I realised my reaction to the thought of Ralph locked up behind bars wasn't the only thing causing the wave of fear that I struggled with. It also was the prospect of not seeing Ralph again for some time – if ever – again that troubled me. Silly woman, I told myself. You're carrying on like a teenager again. Ralph probably sees you as just one more thing he has been lumbered with on this trip. There we go; that's another horrible thought I've given myself to keep me awake for a bit longer.

In spite of everything, I did manage to sleep soundly and didn't wake until past my usual time. Breakfast was a desultory affair; sparse snatches of conversation about nothing of significance throughout the meal. None of us came up with any new ideas as a result of having slept on our problem. It wasn't until we sat sipping our coffees that anyone felt brave enough to broach the subject of what to do about Sofia's sister and brother-in-law.

While there was tacit agreement that the only option was for Ralph to approach the police, it took a while for anyone to voice that opinion. Once there was verbal consensus, immediate action on implementing the plan followed. Ralph made the first move. "Well, I had better get ready. It's probably best to do it early before the day becomes too busy and people become inaccessible due to other commitments." A few minutes later and wearing his suit, he came to say goodbye before heading out. We both pleaded with him to take care how he proceeded, before Sofia rushed to him and kissed him on both cheeks. She thanked him profusely for his involvement. Ralph looked a little embarrassed and brushed her comments aside.

I don't know what came over me. I rushed to him and hugged him tightly as I whispered in his ear, "Please be careful and come back safely to us." He nodded and murmured that he would do his best. But I swear that was not the only response I received. I don't think I imagined it. He returned my hug! Gently but positively, he hugged me back. What an emotional rollercoaster that created. Already sick to the pit of my stomach with fear for his safety, part of me now struggled to contain the elation that brief contact produced. I felt the tears well up as Ralph strode to the door. With one hand on the doorknob, he turned gave us a brief nod and was gone. The sound of the door closing behind him seemed like the sound of finality.

The book I'd been trying to read since starting on this trip failed to take my mind off Ralph and what might be happening with him. Sofia spent her time prowling around the room until I gave up on the book yet again and suggested we order coffee. I still preferred tea but, in the interest of simplifying life, I was adapting to drinking coffee instead. Besides, all the tea I had since leaving Paris wasn't too great. We lingered over coffee for as long as possible while becoming increasingly aware that lunchtime was fast approaching.

We tried dismissing Ralph's non-return as a good sign. Maybe he had become involved in developing some sort of plan… or, perhaps an actual rescue mission was underway. Neither of us believed a word of it, and speculation about what was happening ceased for want of credibility. Soon all conversation fizzled out. With nothing better to do, we took a couple of chairs out onto our tiny balcony. Sofia filled in a few minutes pointing out the various sights we could see from the balcony and explaining what they were all about. It was interesting – to a point. I'm sure both of us were only half engaged in the exercise as our thoughts continued to be with Ralph.

Lunchtime slipped by without much notice. It was almost

two o'clock when my rumbling stomach suggested there was no point in dying of starvation over something we couldn't do anything about. Anyway, obtaining and eating lunch would fill in a little more time. We agreed it was too risky to go out for something to eat so, unappealing as it was, we would have to remain in our room and make do with room service once more. We were in the process of deciding what to order when a sound had us both on our feet.

Someone fumbled with a key outside our room. Sofia ran on tiptoes to press herself against the wall near the door, snatching up a small bronze statuette from the bench on her way past. I felt as though I was standing in a tub of wet concrete. My feet didn't seem to want to respond to my instinct to follow Sofia's example. At last they were moving. Although the delay was no more than a split second, it felt like I was glued to the spot for several minutes.

I heard the key inserted into the lock. The door would open at any moment. No time to join Sofia on the other side of the entrance. My chair scraped back. I was moving. I needed a weapon. I can see nothing that serves the purpose. The coffee pot from earlier is still there. I grab it and head for the wall. Sofia and I look like bookends on either side of the doorway. The door swings open. The arm and shoulder of a man slide around the door. The rest of him remains outside as he struggles to remove the key from the lock on the outside of the door. Sofia hefts her statuette above her head ready to strike. I, following her lead, lift the coffee pot high above my head. The dregs of this morning's coffee rain down on me. I gasped at my sudden drenching. Thank God the coffee was cold now.

"What on earth are you doing, Marjorie?" Ralph's entrance to the room came to an abrupt halt. He looked at me in disbelief.

"Please close the door, Ralph. I feel a big enough fool without having any of the other guests witness me make a spectacle of myself." Then everyone was laughing… except me. I was on my way to the bathroom to clean myself up and to try to regain some dignity. My companions' laughter followed in my wake.

When I re-emerged to join the others, they were seated at the table. "We ordered lunch, including something for you," Sofia said and waved the room service menu at me. I sat down to join them without a word, my dignity still bruised from my earlier performance. "Thank goodness you are back. Now Ralph can tell us about his morning. I didn't want him to start until you were here to listen as well."

"Well yes, about my morning… it didn't start off too well, but I think it ended okay." On his arrival at the police station, Ralph asked to speak to Inspector Yazar, whom he was told was out of town today. After much carry on and wading through the language barrier, the officers rang another man to come and speak to Ralph. This was Inspector Yazar's second in command, Captain Volkan. Although sceptical about Ralph's story at first, Volkan was quick to assess all the information he was given. Less than half an hour after they met, Volkan and Ralph were in an unmarked vehicle and on their way to Sofia's parents' estate.

"We parked about a block before the property and walked the rest of the way. I took him over where we went last night… only on the outside of the fence. I didn't mention going onto the property as I would have had to explain how we got in. As I didn't tell him Sofia was with me, I would have been hard pressed to come up with a story he was likely to believe. But, through the fence, I pointed out the cottage and what I had witnessed there last night. I did embellish the story a bit."

"If you didn't say I was with you, who was with you?"

"Nobody… I was alone. I thought that, when you did a runner, you might have gone home – to your parents' house, that is. I did lay it on a bit thick. Although I didn't see you in the cottage, I was concerned that you too might be held hostage there."

"That is so clever, Ralph. I take it Volkan swallowed your story," I said.

"It seems so. He tried contacting Yazar after we checked out the estate but couldn't reach him. In the end, he went off to make plans and put together a small squad. It looks like there might be some action tonight. I've been told to meet them on the path just before the fence at eight o'clock tonight."

"We will have an early dinner and be there waiting for him a little before time so we will be able to have a look to see if there are lights in the cottage again this evening."

"No Sofia. You and Marjorie will not be involved tonight. I spent the better part of the morning explaining that you gave me the slip, so how the hell would you even know about tonight's operations? You can't be seen with me. I do not want Marjorie involved in anyway, and there is still a warrant out for your arrest. Best you both remain here at the hotel. This is Police business only." Sofia made to argue, but Ralph gave her a dismissive wave of his hand. She settled back in her chair, but there was no mistaking her anger. "Now, as last night was late and tonight looks like being hectic and possibly late again, after lunch I intend to take a long nap." Any further discussion was curtailed by the arrival of room service. True to his word, immediately after lunch, Ralph disappeared into his room until six o'clock.

As soon as Ralph emerged, Sofia took us to a small eatery tucked away in a back street a short distance from the hotel. It was a quick meal followed by a brisk walk back to the hotel before Ralph, outfitted for the evening, climbed into a taxi and disappeared into the night.

There was that gnawing in the pit of my stomach again. Whatever Volkan planned for this evening was sure to be dangerous for everyone involved, and that included Ralph. A heavy feeling hung over me as I rode the lift with Sofia up to our floor. Sofia was restless and paced the room continuously for a few minutes. All of a sudden, she broke the heavy silence that prevailed in our room. "Are you happy to stay here in our room tonight?" No, of course I wasn't, but what else could we do? "Well, I am not going to stay here. What I intend to do is go to my parents' house. I will not be a part of the police operation, and I will stay out of sight. But I will make sure my sister and her husband are safe and the others do not get away."

"I understand where you are coming from, but how do you plan to do any of that? We would be two females on our own. What can we achieve that the police can't? We would have no protection. Getting arrested might be the least of our problems.

We could get killed."

"Ah, but we do have protection." Sofia went to her jacket and delved into one of its huge pockets. "We have these," she said as she brandished a couple of handguns aloft.

Goodness me, what am I getting into, I asked myself as Sofia and I, rugged up against the night chill, climbed into a taxi. The clang of the handgun in Sofia's pocket hitting the door as she climbed in reminded me of the scary heavy weight hidden in my own pocket.

CHAPTER 14

Unsure of who we would find or what was happening at Sofia's parents' estate, we had the taxi drop us on the corner in front of that rowdy bar again. Although only small, this bar looks like the place to be. A continual stream of taxis dropped patrons at its door. Almost drowning out the bar's live music, the sounds of the raucous patrons flooded out onto the street along with the heady aroma of spicy Turkish food. We waited until the next couple of taxis disgorged their contingents of passengers before slipping around the corner unnoticed amid the throng of bodies exiting the cabs and entering the bar.

A short distance along the path, I again broached the subject of that heavy 'thing' in my pocket. "Sofia, I still don't think I should be carrying this." I had my hand in the pocket and pushed it out towards Sofia to confirm what I was talking about. "As I said before, I don't know the first thing about guns. I've never fired one before; never even handled one. They frighten me, and this one in my pocket terrifies me."

"Don't be silly, Marjorie. Guns don't hurt people. It's the people who use guns that hurt other people. I'm hoping we won't have to fire them. But, in any case, I'm not asking you to use yours. If the worst scenario happens, just wave it around. It doesn't even have to be loaded. That way, it can't possibly do any damage and nothing scary is likely to happen."

None of that was reassuring, and I held fast to the wish that I did not have this weight in my pocket. Nevertheless, it was there and we were now halfway along the path to the estate. Sofia, leading the way, came to an abrupt halt. I peered around her to see what was happening. A short distance ahead of us along the last block before the estate, a number of vehicles were parked beside the path we were on. One was a very ordinary looking light coloured sedan. The other vehicles were a dead giveaway for what was happening up ahead. Their blue and white livery and the word 'Polis' emblazoned on their doors and hoods left little to the imagination.

"We are just local residents out taking in the night air. Nothing funny or unusual about that, so stay relaxed as we wander up to see what is happening." I mentally thanked Sofia for that piece of advice, but I acknowledged it probably would be easier said than done. In the event, it wasn't too difficult at all. The cars were deserted. Nobody challenged us as we sauntered past. "We must go carefully now," Sofia whispered. "They might have men stationed near the front fence." I didn't need any encouragement to 'go carefully'. My nerves were so tightly wound, I would quite happily have stood right where I was and not gone any further.

As we drew closer, one police officer caught out attention. His position, a short distance along the side fence from the corner, suggested he was a sentry, the backup should anyone try to escape from the property. A line of shrubs marked the front boundary of the last property before the estate. We pressed ourselves into the shrubs and watched and waited. The sentry wasn't stationary. In a bid to keep warm and keep his circulation flowing, he wandered a few metres further along the side fence before turning to returning to the corner again.

"We must be ready," Sofia said as she gripped my arm firmly. "As soon as he starts to move further along the fence, we must run to the front gate; silently, no noise to attract his attention. And then we wait there until he goes along the fence again." She showed me the bunch of keys in her hand.

The sentry moved off again on his patrol along the fence. Everything seemed to happen automatically. Before I thought about it, we were pressed in hard behind the far pylon of those huge front gates. I watched Sofia carefully pick through her bunch of keys before selecting one that she held on to. The sentry would soon be at the corner of the fence again. Sofia, with her lips close to my ear, whispered, "When he moves off again, I will unlock the gate and open it a little way. We must be quick. Run to that hedge where I found you last night. We will have to wait there until the sentry goes again before we run to the front door."

My lungs were taking in rapid shallow breaths. Was I hyperventilating? I wasn't sure but, if I continued like this, I suspect I will soon faint. I forced myself to take a few long, deep breaths, holding each one for a second or two before exhaling. This seemed to steady my breathing pattern and I felt less light headed. There was little time to congratulate myself on gaining such control. Sofia hissed, "Get ready. He's moving again." I risked a glance around her, and confirmed the officer was a couple of paces further along the side fence. "Now...! Let's go." Sofia had inserted her key in the gate by the time what she said registered with me.

Sofia swung one gate open just wide enough for me to slip sideways through the opening. I raced to the hedge and pressed myself against it. Sofia arrived beside me a couple of heartbeats later. I went through the controlling my breathing exercise again. There is no doubt; I am not cut out for all this cloak and dagger stuff. However, I didn't have time to think about it. Sofia was whispering in my ear again and, although I didn't think it possible, I felt my stomach increase the flip-flops it was doing.

"The next part is the most dangerous for us. We will have no cover when we run from here to the front door. Once we are at the door, I will unlock it and we will slide inside, but we will be in the open until we go inside. I do not know what we will find inside. I hope it will be like last night and that only the old servant will be at the back somewhere."

Oh great; I hadn't thought it a picnic so far, and now she tells me it is going to get dangerous. I watched in stunned silence as Sofia checked her handgun and then replaced it in her pocket. Common sense told me it took the sentry a while to saunter along the fence as far as he did and back again, but it felt like it took only a few seconds. Sofia's tightening grip on my arm told me we were about to embark on the 'most dangerous' part of our journey.

Then she said that one word, "Now," and I followed her across the lawn to the front door. She reached the door with her hand outstretched. Without hesitation the key slid into the lock. I banged into her. My understanding was that, as soon as the door opened, we would charge inside. That was not what happened.

Sofia only opened the door a few centimetres, just wide enough to check for lights on inside the house and listen for sounds. Unaware of this step of the plan, as soon as I saw the door start to open, I charged forward, and banged heavily into a stationary Sofia.

After untangling ourselves, Sofia pushed the door open a little wider and, laying a warning finger to her lips, slipped into the dark and silent house. As far as I could see, no lights were on anywhere in the house. There weren't any sounds, but there was an all-pervading eerie stillness. Sofia tapped me on the shoulder to get my attention and then pointed to my feet. "Take your shoes off and carry them," she whispered. "If we do not find anyone, we can put them back on."

With that, she set about removing her own shoes. I followed her example although I thought carrying my shoes around might prove something of a hindrance if we encountered a situation that required us to take action. I might as well have been blind. With no knowledge of the interior of the house, and with it in darkness, there was nothing I could do but stick close to Sofia as she made her way confidently towards the back of the house.

She gave me the signal to stop. I watched her continue along the hallway and enter a room a short distance up ahead. A few moments later she whispered to me to join her, and I found myself in an enormous kitchen. "It seems the old lady who has been cooking for them has gone to bed. At least, I hope that's what's happened and nothing unpleasant has occurred." To help me interpret Sofia's comments, I tried scanning Sofia's face in the darkness but could only make out an even darker shape in the surrounding darkness. We were on the move again. Sofia effortlessly navigated her way through to the opposite wall, which I discovered was an external wall of the house.

At one of the windows, she bent down, carefully peeled back one corner of the drape and peered out into the night. As with the previous evening, the first cottage was well lit. I could see people moving about inside and recognised the ones I saw from the previous evening. "Can you see anyone else?" I whispered.

"Like who… Who would you expect to see and where?"

"Well, I was wondering about the police and Ralph. I assume they are around here somewhere, and I expected that from this vantage point we might be able to see them." I knew they had to be out there somewhere but, try as I might, I saw no one except those in the cottage. The absence of police made me nervous. Maybe they were still outside the fence. A fat lot of good they're going to do out there, I thought. They need to be in here, on the grounds getting ready to do something. Although, I have to admit I had no idea what that 'something' might be or how they could rescue Sofia's sister and her husband unscathed.

Sofia gave a gentle tug on my arm. "Come, we need to get closer."

"Closer to what…?"

"Closer to the cottage; we can't do much hiding in here in the kitchen."

"Are you mad? What do you think we can do? We should stay in here. If we go out there we may interfere – even ruin – whatever the police are planning. That could have serious consequences for the very people we're trying to rescue." I did not feel inclined to venture out of the kitchen. And I had even less inclination to go charging into that cottage – if that was Sofia's plan. I thought I might have upset her as it was a few moments before she responded.

"I don't know. I haven't a plan. I just want to get a little closer to see what is happening. Maybe once were out there, we will see something that we can do, something that might help the police. One thing I am certain of is that we are useless hiding in here. You may stay here if you wish, but I am going out there to try to get closer to the cottage."

It was quite clear her mind was made up. She would be going outside. My dilemma was whether to go with her – against all my better instincts – or to stay here in the kitchen, or somewhere in the house. While I dithered trying to work out what I was going to do, Sofia interpreted my silence as a negative response. "Okay, if you are going to stay here in the house, this is what you must do at some point in time. You will have to get yourself safely outside. Not just outside the house, but outside the fence." She then rattled off a whole lot of instructions about how I should proceed.

That all seemed too complicated, and perhaps a touch more risky than going outside and trying to get closer to the cottage. Faced with two unpalatable options, I saw wisdom in taking the one that put me with someone who at least knew their way around the place. "All right, let's get out there. How are we going to go about this without bringing the world down upon us?"

There was no plan. She had already told me that, and now it became obvious. I had expected her to rattle off a whole lot of instructions and, moments later, we would be out in the garden. Wrong-footed by my response, it took her a minute or so spent studying the kitchen floor tiles to formulate a plan. But, once that happened, my instructions came thick and fast. In no time, I found myself huddled amongst shrubs once more.

Storms threaten again tonight. The air felt heavy and damp. There was little breeze. I felt a few drops of moisture on my face. Was it rain or just dew shaken from the leaves of the shrubs? Please God, don't let it rain tonight until all this is over. With no idea how long we would be out in the open and exposed as we were now, I did not wish to add a drenching to the joy of it all. It probably was a waste of time my appealing to that Higher Authority. We hadn't spoken since my Sunday School days, but perhaps He is feeling accommodating today.

Soft sounds nearby brought me back to reality. I tensed to match my already tight stomach and held my breath. A touch on my arm almost made me cry out. I looked down at Sofia's hand resting gently on my arm. "This way," she whispered. "No sound; there is someone in the bushes over there." I turned to whisper that it probably was the police, but she already was inching away from me along the hedge.

Sofia's next move made me catch my breath. After a moment's hesitation at the end of the hedge, crouched over, she ran across about five metres of open ground to another hedge. This left me alone behind the long hedge running parallel with and some distance out from one side of the cottage. It seemed those other sounds I heard were coming closer. What if it wasn't police? Should I risk following Sofia, or trust to luck and stay here? Not exactly brave when it comes to things I can't see and don't know about – particularly in the dark – I shuffled sideways as quickly and quietly as possible to the end of the hedge. Then a couple of deep breaths and I was off and running bent over almost double to join Sofia.

My knees complained. I am too old for all this nonsense. At my age, I should be sitting with my feet up watching TV, not scrambling around in the dark praying it doesn't rain. That was as far as I got with feeling sorry for myself. Sofia was tugging at my arm and motioning with her head for me to follow her. Where on earth are we going? This hedge started about a metre in from the side fence of the property and ran about halfway across the front of the cottage and out from it about the same distance as the previous hedge we hid behind. There wasn't too far we could go before running out of hedge. My concerns were unfounded.

When we reached the far end of the hedge, Sofia whispered, "I think this is a good place for us. We don't want to be too close if anything starts happening." I risked a look over the top of the hedge… and instantly pulled my head down again.

"I saw figures moving over there," I whispered to Sofia, "Over where we were hiding before."

"Something is about to happen I think; stay ready."

Stay ready for what, I thought. Does she know more about what's going on out there than I do? I let that question exercise my mind briefly until all hell broke loose. Shouting, banging and crashing about somewhere close by shattered the silence of the night. I parted the foliage a little to see through to the front of the cottage. Dark-clad figures rushed about. One dealt the cottage door a final blow with a battering ram. The door flew inwards a short distance and hung at a drunken angle. It had come off its top hinge preventing it from flying open all the way. "Does the cottage have a backdoor," I asked.

"Uhmm… yes it does, on this side at the rear. Good thinking…" For a moment I wondered about my 'good thinking'. All I did was ask a question.

A woman screamed. "Yasmin…!" While she uttered only a quiet strangled little cry, it was as well Sofia's voice was lost in all the noise of the ongoing raid. And then, in a whisper, "Be ready. You must be ready with your gun."

Be ready with my gun… for what? There was no chance to ask the question. Noises came from along the side of the cottage. The shouting inside the building drowned out most of the sounds, but they were still loud enough for me to work out they were coming towards me. Desperation welled up over me. I checked the front of the cottage. All the bodies occupying that area earlier had disappeared. No doubt, everyone is now inside and party to the racket we can hear from in there.

Out of the corner of my eye, I saw Sofia move. She was now at the very end of the hedge and poised to pounce. "Please don't do anything silly," I whispered. Perhaps she didn't hear me, or maybe she chose to ignore me. There was no response. And then I saw it: a strange black shape writhing and stumbling through the darkness. The shape paused in the last of the darkness before the softly-lit area at the front of the cottage. It appeared to suffer a moment of indecision as it writhed from side to side on the spot.

Then it all happened. That dark shape found a burst of power as it sped from the darkness, past the lit up area at the front of the cottage, and came on towards our hedge. I found myself holding the handgun Sofia had given me. How did that get there? I don't remember taking it out of my pocket. And, more importantly, what did I plan to do with it? It wasn't loaded. I didn't know how, and I had no intention of shooting anyone. Perhaps I should heed Sofia's advice. If needs be, maybe I could wave it around while trying to look threatening… and somehow managing to avoid fainting from fear.

As the shape passed through the lit area, I could see it comprised two people locked together. A large man dressed all in black. With a thick trunk-like arm around his captive's throat, he propelled Yasmin along in front of him. In slow motion, my shocked mind took stock of the situation. He – one of the bad guys, whoever he was – was escaping and using Yasmin as a human shield.

Again, I found myself almost praying Sofia would stay hidden behind the hedge and wouldn't try anything stupid. There was no point in confronting the man. She couldn't shoot at him without hitting Yasmin. He might have a weapon and would shoot Sofia if she came out from behind the hedge. Was I breathing? I feel so light headed. Perhaps I have forgotten to do so. No time to worry about trivial matters such as breathing. The man and his captive had reached the hedge. I plastered myself hard against the shrubs and I definitely didn't breathe. Sofia, buried in the shrubs, stayed put as the dark shape continued on its way past us.

I gasped in horror. The dark shape had progressed no more than a metre past the hedge when Sofia made her move. She spun away from the hedge and, still crouching, took a couple of quick silent steps towards the shape. Her action had her no more than arm's-length behind the man. I could see her arm outstretched towards him, and I had no doubt her handgun was at the end of it.

Not sure what I was supposed to do, I hesitated until I saw the man trying to turn towards Sofia. Up to this time, Sofia had said nothing. Perhaps the man felt her prod him in the back with her weapon. Something had alerted him to her presence and he tried to drag Yasmin around to position her between him and Sofia. Although Yasmin only appeared a slip of a girl, her strength was obvious.

At last my feet decided to move. I had no idea what I was supposed to do – what I was going to do – but I knew I had to help Sofia with what could develop into a nasty situation. My knees complained as I stood upright and bounded out from behind the hedge towards the trio. As I went, I checked my grip on the handgun and, for a moment, wished it was loaded and I knew how to use it. However, I remembered Sofia's advice to just wave it about and look threatening. Not confident about how to look threatening, I tried to recall an old James Cagney movie and the way those actors might have behaved.

What the hell was I thinking? Forget about Sofia's advice on how to look threatening. "Stand still; do not move," I growled in English… And almost giggled when I remembered nobody probably understood me. Then, at last, common sense kicked in. My first attempt resulted in not much more than a croak, but then I found my voice.

"Help, help," I screamed as loud as I could. "Help… Someone come and help us please." For a moment I thought nobody had heard. Nobody came rushing up to help as I had hoped for. Sofia and the 'dark shape' appeared frozen in surprised for a few moments by my actions. Then I heard rustling coming through the bushes behind me. Oh God, if that's another one of them coming out to help his mate, what do I do now?

"What's going on here?" A very English voice demanded. "Identify yourselves. What's happening?" Nobody replied; nobody moved. My brain slowly regained momentum and turned up the memory. That voice was somehow familiar. And then the memory locked into place properly. It was Ralph. Who else could it be with such an authoritative English voice in the middle of suburban Istanbul?

"Ralph, over here; it's me, Marjorie. One of them was trying to get away. He is holding Yasmin captive. Sofia is here too." By the time I finished speaking, Ralph was standing by my side.

"What in God's name do you think you're doing? Give me that thing," he demanded, and held his hand out for me to give him my gun. Ah now, this could be embarrassing, I thought.

I leaned in close to him to whisper in his ear. "It's … not loaded … I'm afraid … And I haven't a clue how to use it." He froze and looked at me in disbelief. So, I leaned in close again and whispered once more. "Sofia's weapon is loaded, and I suspect she knows how to use it." Ralph gave an almost imperceptible shake of his head, but quickly regained control of the situation. He thrust his hand at me again and gave me an exaggerated 'give me' invitation. Obedient as I am, I placed the weapon in his hand. Without consulting Sofia on the matter, Ralph assumed control. Things happened in quick succession after that.

"Sofia, order him to let her go." Sofia obeyed and a string of Turkish growled through the darkness. The man appeared disinclined to comply. He stood his ground, but seemed less interested in trying to drag Yasmin around to shield him. Ralph recognised it was all a ruse. "Sofia, tell him again to let her go or I will shoot him. Explain that I will not hit Yasmin because I will take a headshot and that, if he does not comply immediately, he should spend his last few seconds preparing to meet his maker."

My heart was beating some sort of frenzied jungle rhythm. I felt sure I was going to be sick at any moment. What was Ralph playing at? He couldn't shoot anything, not with my gun anyway.

With my mind in such a whirl, some part of still managed to note Sofia growl out Ralph's instructions in a string of Turkish. These two people surprised me. They were so in control; so authoritative. Meanwhile, I was trembling heap of jelly, of no use to anyone, including myself. If things go badly all of a sudden, I don't know what to do.

Ralph followed up Sofia's instructions to the man by motioning him to get down on the ground, and he astounded me by using a Turkish phrase. It struck me as sounding a bit odd combined with Ralph's very English accent, but it was evident the man understood. Then, in quiet English, he again spoke to Sofia. "Go around the man to Yasmin. Give him a wide berth as you go. See what you two women can work out between you."

Then Ralph called my name softly and motioned me over to him. As I was only standing about a metre away from him, it didn't require much effort on my part. "Do you have ammunition for this weapon?" he whispered. I nodded and gave him to understand it was in my pocket. I felt his left hand slide into my pocket. How stupid can I be? We are all in grave danger right now and yet, his hand sliding into my pocket caused such a thrill. Get a hold of yourself, Marjorie, I told myself. It only lasted a second. He slid his hand in to the pocket, grabbed the magazine that as if by magic was loaded, and withdrew his hand again.

At the same time, Sofia began moving in accordance with Ralph's instructions. The man, momentarily distracted by Sofia's movement, turned his head slightly to follow her circuit around him. I heard a faint click come from Ralph's direction. I switch my attention back to Ralph. He was no longer holding the loaded magazine.

Now it was my turn to play a part in the drama. "Marjorie, everything is under control here. You need to run to the cottage to alert the police to the situation we have here. Some, I think, understand English, but you won't need to be an expert at charades to get them to follow you to us." Although tempted to question such a move, I bit my tongue. We had spent all our time in Istanbul avoiding the police and now he wants me to go and draw attention to myself – and Sofia.

The strip of lawn between the hedge and the cottage was not as well cared for as the rest of the yard I had encountered so far. At some point it became infested with woody weeds. They appear to have been mowed along with the rest of the grass but not eradicated. This rendered them sharp woody protrusions in the otherwise soft grass. My bare feet suffered no ill effects from wandering around outside until now. I hopped and hobbled my way across that strip of grass to the cottage, and rushed inside without daring to stop to inspect the damage to my feet.

I don't know that I had thought about what I might find inside the cottage. All I know is that the scene that greeted me was unexpected. Three burly rough looking men were hand-cuffed and lying face down on the floor in the living room. With their weapons trained on the men, two officers in navy blue police uniforms stood guard over them. Voices and the sound of cupboard doors banging came from further back in the cottage, from what I assumed were the bedrooms.

Although what was happening in the cottage shocked me, my arrival caught the police officers by surprise. A shout greeted me as I entered the building. I don't know what he said, but they weren't words of welcome. And, while one officer continued to train his weapon on the men on the floor, his companion who had shouted at me now trained his weapon on me. In response to instinct, I raised my hands. This was not going as I hoped so far. "Help," I yelled. "Help, please," and I gestured with jerks of my head to indicate 'outside'.

Whether it was the officer shouting at me or my plea for help is unclear, but it brought two more police officers from the back rooms. One, with silver stars on his shoulder, stepped forward. In quite good English, he asked who I was and what I wanted. At last, I might be getting somewhere with my important mission. It only took a split second for my mind to assure me this officer didn't need to know who I was. There were more important things he needed to know.

"One of these men tried to escape." I waved my arm in the direction of the men on the floor. "He took Yasmin with him as a hostage. Ralph Carter, the English detective seconded to you, is holding the man and Yasmin outside." Another wave of my arm to indicate where outside. "He needs your help with his prisoner." I studied the faces around me in the hope of finding some indication that my message had gotten through. Nothing obvious anywhere; and the face of the bloke with the stars on his shoulders still registered hostility.

I searched my mind for what else I might say to generate some action. I felt desperate. I was letting Ralph down. He could be in serious trouble out there. It was at that point that I lost it. "Oh, for Goodness sake, Detective Carter could be lying out there seriously injured, and the man and Yasmin could be long gone by now. Don't just stand there. Do something!"

"Please put your arms down, Madam, and show us where this is happening." I heard what the chap with the stars said. His English was clear enough. But, somehow, I wasn't quite sure about putting my hands down. Anything could happen. I didn't have much confidence in my present situation. Then he spoke again. "You look ridiculous standing there with your arms in the air. Put … your … hands … down! Come on, woman, lead us to Detective Carter."

Okay, so I'm a bit slow and not very trusting, but I finally got his message. I lowered my arms and turned towards the door… and stopped in my tracks. My arms shot up into the air again. "What are you doing, woman? Why are your arms in the air again?" He looked confused, but maybe only half as much as I felt.

"You shouted something at me when I turned to leave. I thought I did something wrong." I was rattled and I wasn't sure I was making any sense – even to myself.

"I called my men to come with me when I follow you. When you arrived, you suggested the situation was urgent. Do you think we might get on with it now?" After dropping my arms, I turned to head for the door once more, but not before I noticed the grins on a couple of the officers' faces. As Ralph had said, some of them do understand English and were enjoying my discomfort. "By the way, is this some English custom I am not aware of?" I had no idea what he was asking about.

In need of a clue to help me formulate and answer to his question, I looked over my shoulder at the officer. There was nothing there to help me, so I shook my head and shrugged as I tried to work out what he meant. "…To go about barefooted in a strange place in the middle of the night?" That's all he wants to know. That's a relief, I thought. For a moment, I had visions of all sorts of inquisition looming ahead of me. I pulled one shoe out of my jacket pocket and waved it at him.

"…Didn't want to make a noise, so I took them off earlier. …Haven't had time to put them back on." I spoke in staccato bursts as I tried to concentrate on minimising the damage to my feet as we crossed that patch of weeds to the hedge. As I reached the hedge, I called out. "Ralph, it's only me and the cavalry. May we join you?" I called out as I didn't want to startle him and maybe distract him from his task as we came crashing through the hedge. But my chirpiness surprised me. Maybe I was starting to relax. I hope there is nothing on the other side of this hedge to change that.

"Come on through," Ralph replied, but his response was all but lost in the sound of police boots trashing the hedge as they charged through the shrubbery.

Although I had achieved my mission and Ralph's prisoner was now safely in the hands of police officers, any relief of tension I felt earlier disappeared. There was no sign of Sofia. Yasmin was still there, but now sat on the ground off to one side. Instinct screamed at me that this was not all over, and that life was about to get even more complicated.

CHAPTER 15

With the man now handcuffed and somewhat subdued, the police were keen to reunite him with his colleagues. The idea seemed not to appeal to the man. It took several officers to manhandle him through the hedge and into the cottage. As that operation was under way, Ralph had a quiet word to the chap with the stars on his shoulders. "Perhaps the young lady might be more comfortable in the house and would welcome the opportunity to clean up a bit." Although a little reluctant to do so, the senior officer agreed before striding off after the struggling mass of bodies and following them into the cottage. Before he walked away, the officer asked Ralph to join them in the cottage.

Ralph helped Yasmin to her feet. I rushed over to her, concerned that being touched by another strange man after all she had already been through might upset her. Once she was on her feet, Ralph took charge again. "Take her into the house and do what you can to make her comfortable." Yasmin heard what he said and started staggering towards the main house. Ralph grabbed me by the arm as I made to follow her. "Don't hang about in there. Get her inside, make sure she is okay, and then get back to the hotel. Don't waste any time getting away from here."

Stunned by his instruction but determined to follow them, I started to walk off. Then I remembered a question that bothered me since I came back with the police. "Where is Sofia? Is she all right?"

"Back at the hotel by now I hope. If she happens to still be in the house, get her away from here. The pair of you should not waste any time hanging about here."

I might not understand it, but I received the message and felt a degree of urgency about departing the place. As Yasmin and I approached the backdoor of the house, I wondered if we would be able to get in. Yasmin wasn't likely to have her keys on her, and I doubted the door could be opened from the outside without a key. No point in keeping that concern to myself, I decided.

"Will we need a key to get in?"

"Yes. The door will be set so that it locks after anyone enters. That is how it is done at night."

"Well, I don't have a key, and I suspect you don't have one either." We had reached the concrete pad at the back door and were at the point where, under normal circumstances, someone would insert a key in the lock.

"It is not a problem." Yasmin took a couple of steps away from me and over to a strange animal sculpture positioned at the side of the concrete slab we stood on. She did something and, with a grunt, flipped its head to one side. She repositioned the animal's head and joined me at the door again. The moonlight glinted off the key Yasmin held up triumphantly before she slipped it into the lock. It took me more effort than I imagined to push open the huge wooden door. Yasmin, so weak from her ordeal, never would have managed it on her own.

We went through the house, switching on lights as we went, to a separate area that I assumed was the couple's apartment. It was on the first floor in that part of the house where Sofia indicated Yasmin and her husband had their own apartment. Yasmin was eager for a shower and change of clothes… and it became obvious my services no longer were required. Although we turned on lights, there were a few wrong turns along the way before I found myself back on the ground floor near the front door.

Sofia's shoes no longer were near the door where she left them when we first entered the house. I took that as a positive sign that Sofia had left and was on her way back to the hotel. Ralph's instructions to leave the place carried with them the tacit message that my departure should be as covert as my arrival. That brought to mind the police officer who patrolled that short distance along the side fence. Any plan to escape from the estate needed to factor in that obstacle.

I stood by the door for a few moments while I tried to formulate a plan. Once outside the front door, I wouldn't be able to get back inside the house, and I would have to cross that open expanse of lawn before reaching the safety of the hedge that bordered it. My first task was to check on that police officer stationed at the side fence. The first window on that side of the front door might provide a good observation point. First, I slipped my shoes on… and immediately almost regretted it. In the silent house, their leather soles seemed deafening on the ceramic tiles.

Heavy drapes covered the window. I eased one side a short distance away from the window frame. With the side of my face pushed hard up against the wall, I scoured the area along the part of the side fence I could see for any sign of the police officer we saw there earlier. I could detect no movement anywhere in my field of vision. Best I look for a bit longer, I told myself. Is it possible it would be so easy to let myself out of the front door, cross the yard, and be out through the gate and on the path without being challenged by anyone?

"There is no one out there." I spun around to face the speaker. Yasmin stood a little distance away from me. "I'm sorry. I did not mean to startle you. Is there something outside that worries you?"

"No, I was checking on a police officer who was out there earlier near the fence."

"As I said, there is no one out there now. They are all at the cottage. Have you seen my husband? I am worried about him."

"I haven't seen your husband, but I expect he is still at the cottage helping the police understand what has been happening here. I hate to do this, Yasmin, but I must go. I have to leave right now and I think it is important the police don't see me leave. Once I go outside that front door, I will be quite exposed. I need to be sure no one sees me until I am out of the gate and heading down that path."

"I understand. I will go outside before you and, if there are any police about, I will distract them so you may leave without being seen."

"That sounds a bit risky for you. Are you sure you are up to this, and that there are no other bad guys lurking in the bushes?"

Yasmin assured me the only 'bad guys' were the four the police had in custody in the cottage. Without a single question about my urgent need to leave unseen, she was determined to assist. I followed her to the front door. It occurred to me that once we were outside and that door closed behind us, Yasmin would not be able to get back in. I voiced my concern. Yasmin gave me a wry grin and held up a bunch of keys. "I live here, remember. I have keys. Come, we must get you away from here."

It was all so easy, it was unnerving somehow. Yasmin went out first and, leaving the door a little ajar, walked to the side fence and checked along it. Then she came back, opened the door wider and beckoned me out. "I will walk you to the gates and open them for you."

I protested, saying I knew how to open the gates and that there was no need for her to risk being outside with me. That wasn't quite true, but I had watched Sofia open them the previous night and it hadn't looked too complicated. However, my powers of persuasion proved somewhat lacking. "Come on, you are wasting time. Hurry…!" Okay, I know when I'm defeated. With Yasmin in the lead, we trotted to the gates, and moments later, I had started down the path.

The euphoria at having made safely it off the estate evaporated within the first couple of metres on the path. It probably was the sight of the police vehicles that remained parked beside the path that reminded me I still wasn't out of the woods. Common sense told me no officers would be at the vehicles. But my gut kept nagging me about what if one of them comes back to get a vehicle for some reason. Although scarcely able to breathe, and with my heart thumping loud enough for the whole neighbourhood to hear, I thrust my hands in my pockets and sauntered past like some local resident out for an evening stroll.

Once I reached the next block, I stepped up my pace to double time. I reached the corner and was disappointed at the lack of taxis. What do you do when you don't speak the language and you don't know how to call for a cab? While I wrestled with that dilemma, I stood with my back hard up against the front wall of the bar, hoping to be invisible to any police that happened to pass by. Fast approaching the realisation that I might have to go into the bar to find someone with enough English to help with my problem, I was relieved to see a taxi approaching.

By the time it had disgorged three giggling young girls and a seedy looking older chap, I had my hand firmly on the doorhandle. As soon as the last of them scrambled out, I dived in and gave the driver my best attempt at the name of our hotel. I didn't check the time, but there were still many people about. The mysteries of the nightlife of Istanbul continued to occupy my mind when I realised the taxi was pulling in to our hotel.

Through the lobby, into the lift, and at last I was standing outside our room. My breathing slowed down to almost normal, and I took a few deep breaths to help the process along before opening the door. So preoccupied with my situation, I hadn't given a thought to what I might find when I opened that door. So, it never occurred to me to knock before opening it. And, why should I? After all, this is where I am staying – this is my room.

As I closed the door behind me, I realised that Sofia should be back here by now. The sight of an empty room halted me. Some tiny part of my mind expected Sofia to be standing waiting in the middle of the room. She wasn't. Nobody was. Then something else caught my attention. Out the corner of my eye, something moved... And it moved in my direction. My instinctive scream was more like a strangled whimper as my hands shot up to defend myself.

Crisis averted and normalcy returned within moments, but the experience left me weak kneed and in need of a sit down. Unannounced as my arrival was, it put Sofia on high alert. Once more she and the bronze statuette took up the position they adopted for Ralph's return this afternoon. The thought of how close I came to being clobbered with that statuette had my heart racing again. It took a while and a couple of scotches from room service before we were able to laugh about it.

We took the last of our drinks out onto the balcony and settled down to discuss the evening's events. It didn't take long for discussions to move to Ralph and what might be happening with him. The one thing neither of us wanted to voice, but ultimately had to, was how would both Sofia's and my disappearances from the crime scene impact on Ralph. There was little doubt that officer in charge would not be impressed by our absence, and more so by the fact that Sofia had escaped being arrested yet again.

Although it was late and the events of the night were catching up with both of us, neither of us was prepared to go to bed until we knew about Ralph. By three o'clock, our eyes were heavy and our heads were beginning to droop. Nevertheless, the sound of someone opening the door had us both wide awake and on our feet in an instant. Ralph looked as bad as I felt. His face was washed out and his eyes red-rimmed as he eased himself into the nearest lounge chair.

"Why are you both still up? I would have expected you to be in bed hours ago. Good to see you both arrived back here safely though." We explained our concern about what might be happening to him and how we couldn't go to bed until we knew. "Well, I'm here now, and still in one piece. So, perhaps you should take yourselves off to bed. That's what I will do as soon as I have cleaned up."

"…But what happened? Is everything all right for you with the police, and are they still looking for Sofia?" How could I go to sleep when I didn't know what our situation was?

"There will be time enough to talk tomorrow. Now, get yourselves off to bed so I can do the same."

Sofia and I exchanged a look and a shrug. It was clear we were not going to get anymore tonight. We climbed into bed. I expected to be awake all night worrying about what Ralph might have to tell us in the morning. Instead, I think I fell asleep the moment my head hit the pillow.

*****

Sun streaming in through the open door to the balcony woke me. It was late but I had no idea of the time. Sofia slumbered on, although she too showed signs of being disturbed by so much light in the room. Ralph, looking much refreshed after a good night's sleep, wandered in from the balcony. "Apologies for waking you, but you had to wake sometime if we were ever going to have breakfast this morning. Should you nudge Sofia to see if she wakes?"

"No need to do that. I am awake. At least, I think I am."

Breakfast arrived just as we were beginning to speculate on how much longer it might take. It wasn't until we finished eating that discussion of the previous night's events began. There wasn't much for Sofia and me to contribute, so we encouraged Ralph to tell his side of the story. It was what happened after we left the estate that we wanted to know about. He began slowly and, in spite of our encouragement to hurry to the interesting part, he told the story in his own way from beginning to end. When he reached the point in the story where Yasmin and I went back into the house, both Sofia and I leaned forward on our chairs, eager to catch every word.

"They took the bloke who was trying to make a getaway with Yasmin back to the cottage and dumped him on the floor with his three colleagues. A couple of the officers were in the back room, a bedroom I think, with Yasmin's husband. He was badly knocked about and eventually was taken away in an ambulance. But, before that, he spent a fair amount of time telling the officers everything that had happened over the last couple of weeks. It all came to an end in the cottage fairly quickly. The ambulance took the husband to hospital, and a police wagon arrived to cart the others off to the cells."

"What about Yasmin? Where is she? What happened to her?" Sofia's concern for her sister was understandable and it was amazing she waited this long to ask after her sister's welfare.

Ralph smiled at me before turning to speak directly to Sofia. "After taking Yasmin back to the house, Marjorie made her way back here. Your sister showered and changed before waking the old servant to tell her about what had happened and that it was all over."

"We assumed you went back to the police station when every-one left the estate. I was worried about how your relationship with the police stood after we chose to disappear on our arrival at Istanbul." In fact, I was concerned about how the police might view all three of us. They would not be pleased that Ralph had acted outside the terms of his secondment, and they would have taken a dim view of his not handing Sofia over to them on our arrival. No doubt, I would be seen as complicit and wouldn't be viewed in any better light than the other two. The big question was: did we still have to hide from the police? I looked at Ralph and waited for him to continue his report.

"Yes, I went back to the police station with the others. The lower ranked officers looked after the arrest paperwork for the four chaps from the cottage while I spent time with Inspector Yazar. He had a fair bit to say and plenty of questions to ask and, overall wasn't terribly impressed with my behaviour. However, it appears I redeemed myself to a great degree by discovering what was happening at the estate and bringing the police in to rescue Yasmin and her husband."

"Do they still want to arrest me?" It was a simple question, but it spoke volumes about how both Sofia and I felt about her current uncertain situation.

"I was getting to that part of the story." Ralph's reply had a tart edge to it. "We will be able to leave this hotel and behave normally once Sofia signs an undertaking to be bound into my custody while we are in Istanbul and that she will return to London with me when I return."

Sofia's hands flew to her face and tears well up in her eyes. "O-o-oh, thank you, Ralph. Where do I go to sign this document, and how soon may it be done?"

"The paperwork will be ready late this afternoon. In the meantime, you can pledge to remain in my custody."

"I do … I pledge, or whatever it is that I am supposed to say, and Marjorie is my witness."

"Good; that sorts that out. Now, there is one other thing to think about." Sofia and I exchanged a look. Things did seem to be going too well up until now. "Marjorie, your trip only included four days' stay in Istanbul before you boarded the train again for the trip back home. I might have to stay on for a few more days – possibly as long as three or four – to tie up loose ends. This means Sofia also will have to stay here with me for that time. You have not done any of the things you expected to do while in Istanbul, and your time here is almost over. So, you have a decision to make: go home according to your original booking, or stay longer and return with me and Sofia."

It wasn't the most difficult decision I've ever had to make. I had no real plans for what to do with my time in Istanbul, other than whatever the usual tourist things might be. However, the thought of having to make the return trip to England alone terrified me. "I would prefer to travel back with the pair of you if possible. Perhaps, while we are here, Sofia could show us – or me if you are busy – what there is to see in Istanbul. Mind you, I'm not sure how I go about changing my booking, and staying in this hotel, instead of where I was booked into, has cost quite a bit already."

"The hotel will not be a problem. All of us can stay together in my parents' house until we are ready to leave Istanbul. We can check out of this hotel as soon as Ralph says it is okay." The thought of staying in the big house on Sofia's parents' estate had a certain appeal and, if our meals were included in the arrangement, it would be perfect. Both Sofia and I looked at Ralph in the hope of some indication of when we might check out of the hotel.

"I think we should pack and move out as soon as we are ready this morning. That would allow us to be installed and settled in the big house before Sofia and I head to the police station this afternoon to complete that important paperwork. While we are there, I will endeavour to find out how long I am likely to be needed here. Then we will be in a position to deal with our train bookings."

"Today is Monday. I am supposed to board the train tomorrow to return to London. I suppose they will need some notice of my change of plan, or they might want to make me pay again for the return trip." This holiday had the potential to become an expensive experience. I could afford it if I had to, but I watch my pennies closely to ensure they don't run out too soon.

Both Sofia and Ralph assured me we would be able to negotiate the changes to my travel and book theirs as soon as they were finished at the police station this afternoon. With our day now planned, we got busy with packing and preparing to depart the hotel. However, our actual check-out proved something of a circus.

There were two people manning the reception desk when we arrived in the lobby with our cases. The same young man who checked us in on our arrival was the one free when we approached the desk. He didn't do an eye-roll at the sight of us but came very close to it. After heaving a heavy sigh, he mimed asking if we were leaving by pointing to our cases and then sweeping his hand off towards the hotel's front door. It seems no longer needing to be in hiding put all three of us in a jovial mood. Although it was clear the young man was asking if we were checking out, the three of us exchanged looks and shook our heads and shrugged.

If at first you don't succeed... The young man tried again.

This time, after repeating his previous performance, he added a wave goodbye. It was all too much for Sofia and she began giggling. "For goodness sake, put him out of his misery, Sofia," I said as I tried to stifle my own giggles.

It doesn't take too long to tell someone you are leaving and ask for the bill. When Sofia finished saying all that to the young man, he seemed too stunned to move. He stood staring wide-eyed and with mouth slightly agape as Sofia repeated her request. To further complicate his day, Sofia asked for a three-way split of the bill in line with what we agreed was the easiest way of paying for our stay. It took a while, but finally we were out of the hotel and loading our luggage into a taxi.

A large swarthy man with an impressive black moustache met us at the front door. His welcome home to Sofia was akin to what the return of the prodigal son must have been like. "Sofia," rang out from somewhere above us. Footsteps clattered down a staircase and, moments later, Yasmin was throwing her arms around Sofia. Then it was my turn, followed by an extra-long hug for Ralph.

We were expected. Sofia phoned Yasmin from the hotel so as not to alarm anyone by our unannounced arrival. The large man who met us at the door was a member of the family's security staff. I learned later he was in charge of security. He resumed duties after Yasmin called him last night. As he drove up to the house to start work, he passed the convoy of police vehicles and ambulance leaving the estate. Inspector Yazar left one police officer to keep an eye on things at the house. For Yasmin, after what she had been through, one police officer was not enough.

By the time we arrived, there were three of the family's security people on duty and various other servants also were back at work. Our bags were taken from us and whisked upstairs to our rooms. When Yasmin's welcome came to an end, she led us to our rooms – with Sofia protesting all the way that she was capable of showing us to our rooms. My room astounded me. It was huge, dark and cool. Light flooded in once the drapes were pulled back.

The centrepiece was a huge old wooden four-poster bed with elaborate covers and fancy valence. Other furniture included two bedside cabinets, a wash stand along one wall, and a desk and chair against the other. A luxurious lounge chair and matching footstool, along with a low side table were placed near the window. Huge timber wardrobes with elaborately carved decoration on the doors occupied space along the wall on either side of the door. This was a room more luxurious than anywhere in my cottage could ever aspire to be.

Lunchtime was fast approaching by the time we had settled into our rooms. Sofia collected us and took us down to a sitting room of sorts off from the dining room. In response to Sofia's enquiry, Yasmin said she had been told she would be able to visit her husband in hospital after lunch. He had been heavily sedated since being admitted but should be awake and up to a visit by then. Although one of the family's drivers would take her to the hospital, one of the security staff and the police officer would accompany her and wait at the hospital with her. "Ah, if you take the big car, you could take me as well," Sofia suggested.

"You want to come to the hospital with me?" There was no mistaking the surprise in Yasmin's response. It seems Sofia's dislike of the husband is no secret.

"No, you can drop me at my unit on your way so I can collect my car." Then, turning to Ralph, she added, "Once I have my car, I will come back to collect you and we will go to the police station... unless you need to accompany me to my unit as part of our 'arrangement'."

"No, there is no need for me to do that, but I would like to go with you if it is possible." He was assured there was plenty of room in the vehicle and, by the time we were summoned to lunch, it was settled that I would be the only one left at the house for the afternoon. Oh well, maybe I can give that book another try.

Lunch was an enjoyable spread of cold meats and salads, and it stretched on for some time as we questioned Yasmin about the events leading up to her rescue last night. She must be remarkably resilient. I was sure that, were I in her place, I would remain a nervous wreck for days after being rescued. At last, it was time for people to depart and for me to retire to my room for a long lazy afternoon.

In response to my being gently but persistently shaken, my eyelashes struggled to untangle themselves. As my eyelids began to part, a face swam into view. "Sofia... what is it; what's happened?"

"I'm sorry, Marjorie, but I needed to wake you. Dinner will be ready in about 20 minutes, if you want to freshen up beforehand."

Asleep ... dinnertime ... What time is it? Sofia, having delivered her message about dinner, left my room. While some of me was awake, my mind seemed to slumber on. If I had been asleep – and it certainly felt like I had been – how long had I slept? With all of me finally in sync, I groggily went through the motions of getting myself ready to join the others for dinner. They all looked a lot brighter than I felt when we gathered in the sitting room to await the dinner gong. I was awake sufficiently now to want to know how things went this afternoon at the police station.

"We thought we would be too early. After we collected my car from my unit, we went to the police station. I expected to have to sit around and wait until all the paperwork was ready to sign. However, they were happy we arrived early. They had other matters for me to deal with, and it managed to take all afternoon to complete everything." I scrutinised Sofia as she spoke and listened for any inflections that might indicate her reaction to this afternoon's events, but there was nothing. Ralph helped ease my curiosity.

"The police needed to interview Sofia, take her statement and all that sort of stuff before they trotted out all the documents for her to sign. I had to do a report on everything that happened on the train, discovering Yasmin and her husband being held hostage – everything. It took all afternoon. We were only back here about ten minutes before Sofia went to your room."

"Is that everything taken care of now, or is there still more for you to do?"

"Sofia is finished – until we get back to London, that is – but I will be at the police station again for most of tomorrow. We will start to pull together everything we know about all that has happened since the incident at the museum. So, until after that at least, I will be in detective mode again, and you ladies will be free to entertain yourselves."

"What about our return to London? Am I still boarding the train for the return journey tomorrow, or are we all going back later?"

"Ah, the train; yes, I forgot to mention that. Unless something changes, we all will board the Direct Orient Express on Friday to return to London. I have vouchers for Sofia and my tickets. I also have a police directive for the change to your booking. It seems prudent to take care of the bookings first thing in the morning. Then all of us will be free to get on with the rest of our day." For a fleeting moment I wondered whether we would be able to book sleepers at such short notice, but there was no point bringing that up now. The sound of the dinner gong had us on our feet and moving towards the dining room. I paused before entering the room and caught both my companions by an arm to detain them as well.

"There is one vital question we haven't addressed, and I think it's important we do so while we are alone. How safe are we now? Is it the belief that everyone has been rounded up and that there is no likelihood of any further problems for any of us?"

"No, I wouldn't say that. It is true that the situation has changed somewhat, but the problem has not gone away. The threat still exists to some degree and in some way. We might discuss this further after dinner." As he finished speaking, Ralph spread his arms and shepherded Sofia and me into the dining room. His 'status report' – that's how I thought of it – took the edge off my appetite. How were Sofia and I supposed to 'enjoy ourselves' for the next few days if it was unsafe for us to leave the security afforded by this house?

Further discussion of our situation was not possible for some time after dinner. Yasmin joined us in the sitting room. She reported on her visit to the hospital and indicated her husband probably would remain there for a few days yet. She too would be at the police station tomorrow. Ralph explained the police needed a formal statement from her, but they also wanted to explore her memories for even the slightest clue that might lead to who was behind the whole operation.

It wasn't until Yasmin headed for bed that we were able to resume discussion of the situation regarding our ongoing safety. Apart from the next few days in Istanbul, there was that long return train trip ahead of us. Memories of all that happened on our last train journey remained fresh in my mind, and I suspect in Sofia's as well. Our discussions turned it into quite a late night. That didn't worry me. I had slept soundly this afternoon. But, the other two looked wilted as we made our way up to our rooms. My room was the first we came to, and I paused before opening the door. "Ralph, I am pleased to report that persistence pays off. I got stuck into that book we both have been struggling to read. It is quite intriguing once you get into it."

"What is the book?" Sofia asked.

"*Ship of Fools…*" Ralph and I chorused in unison.

"Ah yes. An interesting book… I enjoyed reading it." Pity we didn't know that earlier; I might have made more effort with it sooner.

In spite of my afternoon siesta, I slept soundly all night and awoke refreshed this morning. Beyond planning our days, breakfast lacked general conversation. At a 'civilized hour', a driver would deliver Yasmin to the police station and then hang about to bring her home afterwards. Sofia would drive the three of us to arrange our train bookings – and interpret for us as required – before delivering Ralph to the police station. Sofia and I loosely left our plans for the rest of the day as 'sight-seeing'.

Then the day got underway properly and Sofia was weaving her way through early morning traffic on the way to the Direct Orient Express booking office. Ralph sat up front with Sofia. I sat in the back, and spent the journey wondering what sort of target we presented as we moved through the various crowded streets. It seems no one was interested in us this morning and, to my surprise, we arrived without encountering any threat.

CHAPTER 16

Our train bookings for Friday – the first available train with a sleeper carriage – was much easier than I expected. With our Friday departure from Istanbul now in place, we dropped Ralph at the police station and went back to the house. This surprised me as I half expected we would set off around Istanbul to take in the sights. Unsure initially where we were going, I said nothing until we were on the street leading to the house.

"We could have started our sightseeing, but I thought you might want to collect your camera first. Perhaps our morning coffee might be a little earlier than usual. We could have it before we head off the see the sights." Everything Sofia said made sense, so that's what we did.

Over coffee, we mapped out where we would go and what we might do. Our plan included having lunch down by the Bosphorus at some eatery that Sofia was fond of because of its good food and spectacular views across the Straits. We agreed to leave the regular 'tourist' sights until Ralph was with us, and confine ourselves to those things which would appeal to us as women, and drive Ralph mad if he had to endure them. Our first stop was a marketplace in a large square in the centre of the city. I felt I had walked my legs off by the time Sofia suggested we go for lunch. Besides, my purchases were becoming heavier by the minute. It was a relief to get back to the car and throw my bags on the back seat. However, in spite of having to lug it around for the rest of the time, the morning's shopping had been worthwhile. I now had some little thing for everyone who mattered back home.

Lunch was wonderful, and the view over the water seemed almost entrancing for me. Nevertheless, it had to end. Sofia shattered the magic of the moment by suggesting we go back to the house. "We've had a busy morning. Perhaps we should go home and rest for the remainder of the afternoon." I felt it was me the suggestion was directed at. My temptation was to tell her I was not such an old lady yet that I needed an afternoon nap every day.

After a moment's reflection, my eventual response was something different.

"Perhaps we should go back to the house. Ralph might be finished at the police station by now. It would be rude of us to be out enjoying ourselves while he sat back there twiddling his thumbs. Besides, it would be good to know what came out of their discussions this morning."

Ralph wasn't at the house when we got there, but arrived a short time later. Yasmin, who had visited her husband in hospital before lunching with friends, came back a little while after Ralph. We chatted over a pitcher of iced tea before Yasmin announced she had letters to write and left the three of us to move on to more serious topics.

In Ralph's opinion, his time at the police station was well spent. They managed to pull together everything they knew about what happened at the museum and on the train. There seemed little room for doubt now that everything, including what happened here at the house, was all part of the same operation. No, they still did not know who the mastermind was, or even who the key players were. All those (mostly dead) ones we knew about were thought to be mere foot soldiers and not the brains – or the money – behind it all.

We still sat going over everything we knew when Sofia checked her watch. "Time has flown so quickly this afternoon. I asked the kitchen for dinner to be a little earlier tonight. I hope you don't mind, but I want to go after dinner to talk to some friends. They might know something to add to the story."

An early dinner was not a problem, but Sofia's going off alone at night did not sit well with Ralph and brought his immediate veto of the proposal. He assumed his police officer status. He ordered Sofia not to leave the house alone, and his preferred option was that she not go out at all. The eventual compromise was for one of the security staff to accompany her and stay close by the whole time… but not close enough to hear what was being discussed. They finally agreed.

With Sofia gone, Ralph and I sat talking for quite a while. It was our first real opportunity for some getting-to-know-you time. In many ways, in Ralph I had found a kindred soul. The disappointing lot life had dealt Ralph was different but similar in many ways to what life had dealt me, at least that's what I thought at the outset. At first, our discussions centred on our current lives and in Ralph's case, his career. It was a good start. I didn't think it would go anywhere too personal, but I managed to wreck that. It happened when Ralph was talking about the downside of a copper's life.

"A young copper's life is hard enough – low pay, long hours, call outs – but it gets worse when they marry. Wives become disenchanted fairly quickly. It's no better when you move up the ranks a bit, and a detective's life makes planning anything impossible. They miss kids' birthdays and other special occasions because they are working a case, and tickets purchased for a show go unused or the wife goes alone. Coppers choose a hard life for themselves. They need to be dedicated to stick with it."

"It is hard for the wives as well. I'm sure the life you describe is not what they envisaged when they married a copper. It must put an awful strain on a marriage."

"From what I know of it, they either stick around but, as the frustrations mount, the marriage breaks down, or they take off – sometimes with the kids, but sometimes they leave them behind so the wife can start a new life."

While Ralph didn't say he was married or had experienced first-hand any of the things he mentioned, his tone of voice and body language suggested that was the case. Perhaps our lives had travelled more parallel lines than I thought. It seems neither of us had fared too well in the love stakes. Our conversation became an awkward silence. I stifled an imaginary yawn and feigned struggling to keep my eyes open. It worked and I think we both were relieved by it.

Sofia still had not returned when we went up to retire for the night. Although we went through all the motions of turning in for the night, I knew neither of us would sleep until we knew Sofia had returned safely. That did not occur until nearly 1.00a.m. But that wasn't the only thing occupying my mind and preventing any hope of sleep. So Ralph was married; add another disappointment to my life story. How could I be so stupid as to think he might be available, let alone interested in me? Already it felt as though there was a wedge between us. To somehow retain my dignity, I had to maintain a 'normal' relationship with Ralph until we were back in London. After that, I would never see him again. I could go home and lick my wounds and get on with my disappointing life.

I must have been dozing, but the sound of footsteps past my door changed that and, in an instant, had me lying there rigid with fear. Apart from the soft footsteps, the house was quiet. I forced myself out of bed. With my ears straining for any unwelcome sound, I cracked my door open a fraction. Then I heard it. It wasn't so much an unwelcome sound as an angry one. "Where the hell have you been until this time of the morning?" Ralph demanded. It could be only Sofia he asked that question.

Perhaps Ralph had the right to ask but, by asking he could create an ugly situation. Sofia wasn't a child and we were her guests in her parents' home. I headed downstairs, struggling into my robe as I went. They were standing in a lobby area just inside the front door. Even at a distance, I could see the anger on Sofia's face. Time I stepped in before things became worse.

"Thank goodness, you're back okay. It was such a relief when you came in. I wasn't able to sleep a wink until I knew you were okay." My interruption seemed to work. Sofia relaxed and rushed over to wrap her arms around me, while Ralph looked embarrassed and studied his slippers. The air still needed to be cleared a little more, so I waded in. "I thought I heard raised voices as I came down. Is everything all right?"

"That was me I'm afraid. I was so relieved Sofia was home, I carried on like an outraged parent. I do apologise, Sofia, but I was concerned for what might have happened to you." Ralph continued to look sheepish as he delivered his apology.

"Well, now we are all up and about, how about we have a cup of something before we go back to bed? While we are about it, Sofia might fill us in on how her night went and whether she learnt anything useful from it." A cup of something was the last thing I needed right now, but I thought it might help restore relationships… and I did want to know what Sofia found out.

Cocoa…! The last thing I thought this kitchen might produce was just what we needed at this hour of the night. Sofia, quite at home in the cavernous kitchen, produced mugs of steaming cocoa for everyone and we took them through to a different sitting room from the one we used earlier. This one had enormous overstuffed lounge chairs, each with its own ornate side table. Quite comfortable and elegant, but I wondered how I might maintain my dignity as I climbed out of the well- upholstered chair whose cushions now enveloped me.

Sofia sat forward on the edge of her chair. "I am sorry for causing you so much concern. It was not my intention to give you cause for worry. It was just a case of the way the night progressed that made me so late. But it was worthwhile. My friends gave me some good information, although they probably didn't know how important it was when they were telling me. I have lots of notes, but I need to make sense of them before I try to explain it to you. You are curious, I know, but I think we should drink our cocoa and go to bed. After breakfast we can take over my sitting room for a … an autopsy …. No, a post-mortem … I do not know how you English call it … but we will be able to discuss tonight without being interrupted. Thank you both for worrying about me. It is a long time since anyone has cared so much." As she finished speaking, Sofia blinked hard a few times to control the tears that had welled up.

"Of course we care about you. We have come through so much together. I like to think we are now friends. But I also must remind you that you are supposed to be in my custody. I don't know if I would get out of Turkey alive if anything happened to you after I let you go off alone." Ralph said gruffly, but added a wry grin. We all giggled. The world was back on its proper axis again, but it was time to try for some sleep in what was left of the night.

*****

Compared to the rest of the house, the modernity of Sofia's sitting room came as a surprise. Furnishings were light and airy, with nothing overly feminine about the apartment. We took our places around a small circular dining table, each one of us with a notebook in front of us. This was Sofia's show. She knew it, and settled straight into her role. "Before breakfast, I tried to make sense of my notes and to arrange them in some order."

"The friend I went to see last night was the one who contacted me to tell me he thought something was wrong here at home. He took me through the sequence of events: the unanswered phone calls, the unanswered visits to the house, meeting one of the servants in the marketplace and being told that all the staff had been sent on leave. This man and I have been friends for years. Our families go back a long way together. So, he knew that, if my family were away, they would want the staff here at the house keeping an eye on things."

"That was very astute of him, but it was a guess on his part. He could have been worrying you about nothing. As it turns out, he was right. However, I think his contacting you must've been based on more than just that," Ralph said.

"Yes, you are right. He did not want to create a fuss over something that might turn out to be nothing. Before he contacted me, he spoke to two other mutual friends who agreed that this was not normal behaviour for my family. It was after that he decided to contact me. When I told him of my being put under pressure to do something illegal, it confirmed for us both that something was not right at home. Like me, he thought my brother-in-law somehow was involved. Before we made our plan for me to disappear from London, he contacted those two friends here again and asked them to check on the house and to try to speak to some of the servants."

"He must be a true friend indeed. In this case, you are lucky to have such loyal friends." My comment might have seemed a bit unnecessary, but I felt there was more to this 'friend' that we'd heard about. However, my comment seems to have hit a nerve. Sofia fidgeted and looked embarrassed.

Without lifting her eyes to meet mine, she murmured, "He would like to be more than a friend and, perhaps one day, that might be so."

Ralph cleared his throat, more to get the conversation back on track than for any other reason. "Did this friend of yours know anything about the man who was murdered at the Museum?"

"No, he did not know that man – the guard, I think you said he was – but he does know Altan Sadiq, my colleague, who also was stabbed in that incident. My friend has tried to talk to Altan but they, the authorities I suppose, are blocking all contact."

Ralph appeared to consider Sofia's comment for a while before speaking again. "That would be unusual, particularly since your friend has such an important position in a quasi-political sense. How did he hear about the attack on your colleague?"

"He wasn't told directly. It was the group of dignitaries that he was looking after who were discussing it on their way back to Turkey. The leader of that group had been told because it was a Turkish national who had been involved and was now in hospital. It seems the dignitaries were not very happy about the way things were handled. The police had Altan under guard and none of the visiting Turkish dignitaries were allowed access."

"It is likely they would have been denied access immediately after your colleague went to hospital. He had to undergo surgery and was critically ill and, as is often the way, my colleagues might have been overly cautious and denied all access by outsiders. Still, that situation should have only lasted for a day or so until the patient was deemed fit to receive visitors. I don't know for how long he was critical after his surgery, but it would be strange for such high-ranking politicians to be denied access once he was able to talk. Perhaps the police needed to interview him first while his memories of the night were still fresh or, perhaps they did interview him and something he said caused them to isolate him, possibly for his own safety."

This was all beyond my understanding. Politics and police procedures are a foreign world to me. "Has your friend been able to contact Mr Sadiq since that time?" I thought Ralph's comment relevant. In the time immediately following the incident, Mr Sadiq might not have been able to speak to anyone, but by now he should be on the mend.

"No, he says he has not been able to contact Altan. He does not know where Altan is now. The hospital says they have no patient by that name. My friend is not convinced that is true, and suspects that is what the police have instructed them to say if anyone asks about Altan."

I could see how that situation would be upsetting for Sofia and her friend. "Ralph, have you heard anything more about Sofia's colleague? Do you know if he has recovered sufficiently to be released from hospital? If his injuries were as serious as you make out, it would require a miraculous recovery for him to be released already."

"No, I don't know anything of his current situation." Ralph paused and studied his fingertips for a moment before continuing. "I did enquire about his condition and whether he had any useful information to add to the investigation. I was told he was 'coming along quite well' and that it was 'still early days in the investigation in London'. So, I think you will agree with me when I say I was fobbed off. If nothing else, this tells me I will not know anything more until I get back to London. I'm sorry, Sofia, I can't be more help than that."

After a long discussion with her friend last night, they went to see the other people who were aware of the strange situation at Sofia's parents' house. This couple had raised the alarm in the first place. This explains how the night had managed to drag on so late. Full marks to the security officer who accompanied her, he stuck with Sofia the whole time and insisted on driving her and her friend to where they wanted to go rather than let her out of his sight.

What Sofia had failed to mention earlier was that one of those other people they went to see is part of a special task force set up by the Ministry to investigate the black market trafficking in Turkish artefacts. This came out in the next part of her report on the night's meetings.

"I would like to meet him," Ralph said. "He is likely to be more useful than anyone else I've spoken to in the last couple of days. I might be on secondment to this mob, but it is obvious I am being kept out of things… being kept at arms' length from information and everything that's happening."

"I could arrange for you to meet him. Perhaps, if he is free, after work tomorrow evening."

"One thing though, does he speak English?" Sofia confirmed that her friend was fluent in English. "That makes it easier. However, if you can arrange for me to meet him, it would be best if I spoke to him alone. That way, he would not feel reluctant to speak for fear of compromising the work he is involved in."

"Perhaps I will ask him to come to dinner. Then, after dinner, Marjorie and I will go off and leave you two alone to talk freely." Ralph agreed with her suggestion and Sofia went off to call her friend. The fact that the man would be at work at this hour of the day seemed to be of no consequence. A few minutes later, Sofia was back and announced that her friend, Koray, would be joining us for dinner.

Ralph said he wanted to set aside some time during the day to think about the questions he might ask Koray tonight. With that in mind, we set about planning our day. That hit a snag almost at the outset when Ralph said he was required to attend the police station again today. A police car would arrive to collect him at two o'clock.

We spent the morning visiting the more usual tourist attractions including the Hagia Sofia, and wandered through the gardens between it and the Blue Mosque to view the tiles from which the Mosque gets its name. Then, followed visits to the Arasta Bazaar and the Topkapi Palace, before we lunched at a small place in the main shopping area. Our return to the house by one o'clock gave Ralph some time to think about his meeting tonight before going to the Police station. That left Sofia and I with a lazy afternoon to fill in. A long chat with Yasmin helped pass the time. She advised Sofia that she had called her parents. Sofia and Yasmin's aunt was much improved and their parents would be returning either late on Friday or Saturday morning.

"I will be on my way back to London by the time they arrive," Sofia said thoughtfully. "I hope you haven't told them what happened here while they were away."

"No, of course I didn't. Do you think I would want to worry them or cause them to rush home before they are ready? I will tell them when they are here and can see that everything is all right again. My husband should be out of hospital by the time they arrive home." That little outburst killed any further conversation between the sisters, and Sofia and I were left alone shortly after when Yasmin flounced off to her apartment.

It was after six o'clock when Ralph returned from the police station. His good news was that he had completed everything the police required of him – other than escorting Sofia back to London – and he would be able to spend all Thursday with Sofia and me. We left Ralph alone to plan his meeting with Koray before we reconvened in the sitting room off the dining room at 7.30p.m. Sofia's friend arrived a few minutes later and joined us in the sitting room. As soon as we finished dinner, Sofia and I excused ourselves and withdrew to Sofia's apartment.

Somehow, Sofia and I filled in a couple of hours with chat about nothing in particular. Then I asked her about her job at the museum. It sounded fascinating and that discussion filled in the best part of another hour. By then, it was late and we had exhausted our conversation. We agreed a cuppa of some sort was just the thing before bed. On our way to the kitchen, we found Ralph and Koray heading for the front door. We all walked with Koray to let him out of the gates before resuming our quest for something to drink prior to going to bed.

Ralph looked so smug and full of renewed energy as we busied ourselves in the kitchen. He refused to elaborate further than to say his meeting with Koray was interesting and informative. It was clear there was no hope of dragging anything more than that out of him, so Sofia and I gave up on the topic.

*****

Thursday was our last full day in Istanbul. Following on from our conversation last night, Sofia suggested showing Ralph and I the Archaeology Museum where she worked. At first Ralph was reluctant, citing the ongoing risk as the reason. After giving the matter some thought, he announced that he thought a visit to the museum would be safe enough given the high level of security that was in place throughout the complex.

Just a short distance from the Topkapi Palace that we visited yesterday, the museum complex is comprised of three separate sections. As a trained archaeologist, Sofia works in the Archaeology Museum which houses artefacts that tell the history of

Turkey and of Istanbul. The other two sections of the complex are the Museum of the Ancient Orient, and the Tiled Pavilion of Mehmet the Conqueror. We explored all three sections, lunching at a cafeteria along the way. I am so glad we did this. It told me so much about this place in which I had spent such little time and of which I had seen such a tiny portion.

The day was fast drawing to a close when we returned to the house. As we sat sipping iced tea, one of the security officers delivered Ralph a message. A car would collect him at eight o'clock the next morning to take him to the police station. Concerned by the message, Ralph asked to use the phone to call Inspector Yazar. We were to board the train tomorrow for our return to London, and none of us wanted any further delay.

When he returned after his phone call, Ralph informed us that tomorrow's meeting at the police station was to finalise some paperwork and shouldn't take more than about an hour. I don't think any of us had much faith in that statement. Yasmin, her ever bright and bubbly self, joined us for dinner. Her husband was being released from hospital in the morning. He had been requested to attend the police station on his release to sign statements, or something along those lines. That meant it was likely Yasmin would not be back at the house before we left for the station.

We said our goodbyes at breakfast before Yasmin and Ralph headed off on their day's missions. Back in my room, I dressed for the trip home and packed ready to leave. After that, unsure where Sofia might be, I went along to her apartment and knocked gently on her door. It was answered immediately, and I could see she had been reading a book. Sofia gave me a strange look as I walked in. "What are you wearing? What have you done with all those lovely clothes you have been wearing here in Istanbul?"

"They were outfits my friend, Connie, had me buy to 'jazz' me up a bit. The loose fitting shift dresses suited the warm days here, but I don't think they are really me. It will be cool on the train again as we travel through the mountains. This sort of outfit is more suitable for the trip, and it's what I wear at home."

"It makes you look too old. You should think about wearing those other new clothes when you are back in London." I started to protest about not feeling comfortable in things that were brightly coloured and a bit too short for someone my age." We agreed to disagree and Sofia let the topic of my clothes drop.

"Have you done everything in readiness to depart?" she asked. I confirmed I was ready to leave.

"Good. I would like to take my car back to my apartment in town. I will need a security guard to come with me and another to drive one of the vehicles from here to bring us back. I thought you might like to come along too. If nothing else, it will help fill in some time." No sooner suggested than we were on our way to Sofia's apartment near the museum where she worked. Ralph already had returned when we arrived back at the house.

Although our train was not due to depart until 2.30p.m., we needed to be at the station at least an hour beforehand to get our-selves checked in and settled on board. Sofia requested lunch a little earlier than usual, and at 12.30p.m., we were on our way to the station. Station attendants were surprised by our early arrival but checked us in and took our luggage. We were then left to our own devices until passengers were allowed to board the train at 1.30p.m. With nothing else to do, we found seats with a view of our platform and made ourselves comfortable while we waited.

Conversation was scarce during that period and amounted to no more than sporadic comments about the time, the weather, or the lack of other passengers waiting to board the same train. I sensed rather than saw Ralph tense. As I turned towards him to see what it was that had caught my attention, Ralph stood up. "If you ladies will excuse me, I'm just going to go for a bit of a look around." Why would he suddenly want to have a look around? My pulse stepped up a notch as he spoke. We weren't even on the train yet, surely no drama would happen here in the open in broad daylight.

Sofia didn't appear to notice Ralph's comment. In response, I smiled sweetly at him and said, "We'll be here when you come back." Inane I know, but I wasn't thinking too clearly. While I feigned disinterest in his departure, I watched his reflection in the various panes of glass as he made his way to a newspaper stand some distance along from us. His show of rifling through the multitude of reading matter on offer looked false, and fell in a heap when two men approached him.

Alarm bells clanged loudly and I caught my breath. Who were those men? Was Ralph in trouble and needing assistance? It took what seemed too long for me to realise that the trio near the newspaper stand were engaged in conversation that did not appear to pose any threat to Ralph or anyone else. The reflections of the two men disappeared from the glass in the door I'd been using to monitor the trio. I watched as Ralph hurriedly grabbed a newspaper and paid for it. Then, with the paper tucked under his arm, he adopted a nonchalant saunter as he made his way back to where Sofia and I sat.

As Ralph resumed his place on our seat, he flapped the newspaper about as he selected a page and folded the paper open to read it. My mind was in turmoil. Who were those two men and what did it they mean to us? Should we expect more trouble on the journey home and, if so, what level of danger might that be? Why was Ralph being secretive about his meeting with them? I feared whatever the meeting was about, it suggested bad news for us.

Okay, I told myself, sitting here wondering about it isn't going to make me feel any better. I want to know what is going on, and it seems the only way I'm going to find out is to ask. In my mind, I did a quick run-through of how I would pose the question to Ralph. There was no point in being diplomatic, I decided. Just ask the question straight out so there can be no confusion about what it is I want to know and how determined I am to find out. I took a deep breath and opened my mouth to ask the question at the same time as the public address system announced our train was ready for boarding.

The announcement came in several languages, the first of which was Turkish. This caught Sofia's attention and she started gathering up the bits and pieces she had with her. "We can board now," she said as the English version of the announcement squawked out over the station. On Sofia's comment, Ralph folded his newspaper and stood up ready to move towards the train. The moment was lost. I would have to wait until an appropriate moment later to ask my questions.

We located our cabins without too much fuss, and I was intrigued to find that Sofia again had a compartment sandwiched between mine and Ralph's cabins. There were few people entering the sleeping carriage, so we left our doors open as we settled ourselves in for the long trip. That exercise didn't take long and, by the time we were installed, there was still about a half hour to wait before the train was due to depart.

CHAPTER 17

For want of something better to do while waiting for the train to get under way, I wandered along to Sofia's compartment. The lack of activity in the carriage struck me as odd. Although there was still a bit of time before we departed, surely passengers would be keen to come on board, locate their cabin and be settled in by the time the train pulled out.

Ralph wandered along to join us a few minutes later. We were engaged in a 'nothingness' kind of conversation about the trip back to London when a knock at the door interrupted us. "Philippe…!" Sofia yelped. "You will look after us on this trip back to Paris too?"

"Welcome aboard again. Yes, Miss Elmas, I am your steward for your trip back to Paris. Let us hope we do not have the same kind of excitement as we had the last time we were all together on this train." We giggled at his delicate way of describing the dramas of the previous trip before he announced, "There are not many passengers booked for the sleeping carriage for this trip, so I will have plenty of time to look after you all very well. Now, normally we do not have afternoon tea when we leave Istanbul. However, as I have so few to look after, I thought we might make an exception this time. Would you care to take afternoon tea?" Of course we would. As soon as we said so, Philippe hurried off to organise it.

It was hospitable of Philippe, but most importantly he confirmed what I suspected: there was an unusual lack of passengers in this carriage. I don't know why that fact insisted on occupying my mind, but for some reason it intrigued me. I shared my surprise with the others. "I realise that passenger numbers can fluctuate on every trip, but I find it somewhat extraordinary that there are so few other than us in this carriage on this trip. Does anyone else agree with me, or am I finding intrigue where there is none?"

Sofia shook her head. "I too found it surprising but, as you say, the train will not always be packed. There already have been two other trains to Paris this week. Perhaps this is not the most popular day for people wanting to make the long trip, and it is more suited to those only making short trips to the places along the way."

"You might be right, Sofia," Ralph conceded. "It is the end of the week. Perhaps most of the passengers are people who come into Istanbul to work or whatever during the week and then go home for the weekend." While Ralph's comment was not short on logic, it didn't ease my anxiety about why there were so few in the sleeping carriage. However, any further discussion of the matter was curtailed when Philippe arrived with afternoon tea.

Afterwards, we retreated to our cabins, not to emerge until the agreed time to congregate again for dinner. The dining car was full, but not so full that there were no spare places anywhere. So, there were plenty of people on board, just not in our carriage. My unease is deepening by the minute and I am no closer to finding out why that should be.

At 3.30a.m., I woke when the train pulled into Svilengrad. I drifted back to sleep, only to be woken again as the train pulled away from the station. As an automatic reflex, I checked the time. "Why would the train spend an hour at Svilengrad at this hour of the night?" I whispered to the universe. I could accept a short stop of, say, 20 minutes to allow passengers on and off, but more than an hour seemed unjustified. That was sufficient to put my mind into top gear again, and all the possible scenarios it came up with made sure I had little sleep for the rest of the night.

Not enough sleep leaves me grumpy, or so I discovered as I dealt with breakfast. I felt decidedly unsociable, as Ralph discovered when he knocked on my door soon afterwards. He had his copy of *ship of Fools* tucked under his arm. "I wondered if I might have a moment to discuss this blasted book with you. I haven't had a chance to get into it properly. I know you have managed to press on with it. I'm wondering if you would recommend I stick with it or abandon it in favour of something else. Is it worth persevering with it? Does it improve as you get into it?" I hadn't invited him in, and now stood there blinking at him. Is that why he has come to talk to me, or is there some other issue he wants to discuss? Well, he can jolly well come clean and be honest about why he has come to see me.

"I really couldn't guide you on that, Ralph. I suppose it all comes down to your taste in literature. If you give it a good shot and still can't get into it, abandon it. I think it is as simple as that. Now, was there anything else?"

"No. No, I don't think so. Thanks for your advice." Guilt overwhelmed me as I watched Ralph walk back to his own cabin.

Of course he hadn't come to talk about the book we both had been trying to read. But what was my performance all about? It wasn't a lack of sleep that made me so rude. It might be because Ralph is keeping me in the dark about his meeting with those two men before we boarded the train. More likely, it was about something else altogether. And that was not Ralph's fault... well, not entirely. So, why was I taking it out on him? If he had said he was married... But why should he, and why would I expect him to? It wasn't his fault that I'd taken to fanciful notions like some vacuous headed teenager.

This, my fantasy that Ralph and I might share some 'chemistry', was just another of life's disappointments at play. "Grow up," I told myself. "You want to know about those men; go and ask him."

"Marjorie, is everything all right?" Ralph had every reason to look confused, just as I had every reason to be embarrassed about my previous performance.

"I wanted to apologise for being rude before. My mind was preoccupied with something else and I forgot my manners. May we restart that conversation?"

Ralph chuckled as he closed the door behind me. "You know darn well I didn't come to talk to you about a book. So, what's on your mind? It wasn't to discuss the book that brought you to my door."

"No, you're right. I suspected you hadn't come to discuss the book, and that's not why I'm here either. Perhaps if you tell me why you came to see me, it might also help explain why I came to see you." We danced a verbal *pas de deux* around one another a little longer before traction was achieved and we gained momentum in the right direction. But it took my asking my question to finally get Ralph down to business.

"Ah yes, those two men… They are what I wanted to talk to you about. I wasn't being secretive. I just wasn't sure how to go about it without alarming you. Both of those men are police officers who are part of a small group I worked with while we were in Istanbul. They are travelling to Calais with us on the train, and then they will cross the channel to London with us. They will be with us, but not obviously with us, if you know what I mean."

"I take it that their role is to watch over us during the trip, to step in if a situation or danger arises. I understand that, but what I don't know is what we are likely to encounter. It is apparent that some threat remains, whether to all three of us, or if to Sofia alone is unclear. It's only natural that I would prefer that all danger had disappeared and that we would be safe on the trip and after we were back in London. However, as that appears to be not the case, then I need to know the truth of our situation. I can cope with most things if I know and understand what they're all about."

It took Ralph little time to explain our situation, and it was much as I expected. Even the police were not sure if a threat still existed and, if it did, how it would manifest. However, they believed that Sofia would be their main target – whoever 'they' were – but Ralph and I would not be excluded if we were in the way.

To me, the situation seemed a bit like fighting ghosts or wrestling water. How do you triumph when you can't get hold of the enemy, let alone know who the enemy is? It was a sobering discussion with Ralph and not one that did anything to lift my spirits. The only other point of significance that he shared with me was about the lack of passengers in our carriage. That situation had been engineered by the police to minimise the possibility of risk. Although I hadn't seen them since we left Istanbul, those two police officers also occupied cabins in this carriage. There was no one else in the carriage apart from them and us.

"I have to tell you, Marjorie, I struggle with this whole affair.

I have never been involved with something for so long and still not known who or what I was dealing with. Perhaps my superiors' opinion of me is correct. They had to send someone on this job in response to a spot of political pressure and to pacify the Turks. I got the job because I was the one person they had who wouldn't be missed if I was absent abroad."

His bitterness was obvious in his voice and on his face as Ralph spoke. My heart went out to him. Although I had no knowledge of his work, from what I had seen, he seemed quite astute and quietly confident as he went about his business. Perhaps his treatment by his superiors stemmed from something else. Ralph was no one's fool. That much I recognised in him early on. And he was not the sort that went around doffing his cap and trying to curry favour. "Do you like your job?" I asked. "Do you like being a detective?"

"It's what I know, and it's all I ever wanted to do. I like being a detective, investigating crime and obtaining justice for the victims. I don't like the politics and power mongering that goes on… the sucking-up-to-get-ahead stuff."

Any further discussion was curtailed by the rattle of the tea trolley advancing along the carriage. Ralph strode out into the corridor and gave some strange hand signal to Phillipe as he trundled the trolley loaded with our morning tea towards us. Then, a hand signal to me that was easier to understand. As I made to join Ralph in the corridor, he said, "We will have morning tea together in Sofia's compartment. We were still in Sofia's compartment when lunch was served in the dining car shortly after we left the station at Sofia for Crveni Krst.

The stops at Sofia and Crveni Krst were short, only 15 to 20 minutes, and we arrived at Belgrade at 6.45p.m. Dinner that night was delayed until we departed there at 7.30p.m. Although passengers were encouraged to leave the train and wander around the city during the long stop at Belgrade, traipsing around the city on a Saturday night held little appeal for us. Ever wary of what might still lurk out there, the three of us appeared content to remain on board as much as possible. However, as we discovered later that night, perhaps the train wasn't the safest haven.

After dinner, we congregated briefly in Sofia's compartment

before Ralph and I headed for our own cabins, perhaps to read for a while before settling down for the night. With our arrival at Zagreb scheduled for about an hour after midnight, it was likely my sleep would be disturbed again tonight. My poor sleep the previous night caught up with me and I read only a couple of pages before turning out the light. I think I found deep sleep in an instant. It wasn't our stop at Zagreb that dragged me from the depth of my slumbers.

A noise I couldn't identify woke me. As I struggled to persuade my eyes to open, I realised the noise was coming from somewhere on the train… was coming from within our carriage. I flew out of bed with the speed of a thousand gazelles and threw on my robe. I heard my mind screaming in my ear, "Now what…?" as I stood frozen to the spot in my cabin. My brain slowly shook off the sluggishness of sleep and kicked into gear.

There were so few people occupying this carriage that any strange noise would be immediate cause for alarm. My straining ears eventually identified the sounds as coming from a struggle taking place somewhere not too far from my cabin. Shrugging off indecision, I cracked open my cabin door. I couldn't see directly down the corridor unless I opened the door wider, and I wasn't about to do that until I knew what was going on out there. However, there were reflections on the glass in the windows close enough for me to see even with the door almost closed.

Although the images were blurry, the reflections were clear enough for me to make out a number of men engaged in a struggle somewhere along the corridor beyond Ralph's cabin. As I watched, shouting became mingled with the scuffle and thump of the fight. Then, a familiar voice rang out above the other sounds. "He is secured," Ralph yelled. Within a few seconds after that, the scuffle was over and men clambered to their feet, hauling up the spoils of their fight as they did so.

I counted a total of five men. At least, from this distance, I took them to be men. Two of their number appeared to be hand-cuffed and were being handled none too delicately. Whatever the situation was now appeared under control and I took a moment to weigh up the wisdom of going along the corridor to enquire about the incident. Having decided it seemed safe enough, I pulled the door wide open and then came to a standstill. I realised the train was slowing down. No. No. I thought. I don't want to spend hours stuck out in the middle of nowhere again as happened previously. I wanted to feel safe, whatever that meant and involved, that's what I wanted.

My watch was on the small table on the other side of my cabin. I ducked back and checked the time. Perhaps there was no cause for alarm. It was very nearly time for us to arrive at Zagreb. I went back to peer out the door again. The corridor was empty. There was no one in sight and nothing to indicate anything had happened out there. For an idle moment I wondered where they had taken the two men they had handcuffed, but it seemed logical they would be safely locked in one of the empty cabins.

Not sure what was happening, or what might happen any time soon, I remained standing in the doorway for about five minutes and almost begged for something or someone to enlighten me about the incident. The stars were not aligned in my favour. No one emerged from anywhere while I stood there in my doorway. Common sense took over. I closed my door and went back to bed although I knew sleep would not come again.

On the timetable, the stop at Zagreb was shown as about 15 minutes. As we were arriving at the station when I climbed back into bed, I would be starting to drift off by the time we pulled out from Zagreb. That was a comforting thought. I wouldn't have to endure being woken again by the train leaving the station. In spite of my best efforts, no amount of trying to relax and drift off to sleep produced the desired result. It is hard to tell how much time has elapsed when there is no reference point.

As I lay there in the dark waiting for my shoulders to relax and my eyelids to become heavy, it seemed we had been stopped for quite some time. Although I tried clearing my mind in my quest for sleep, something about our stop at Zagreb kept returning to bother me. I gave in to curiosity, got out of bed and checked my watch. The train had been stopped for a little over half an hour. That can't be right. Our timetable indicated no more than 15 minutes. So, why are we still parked at Zagreb? The first thing that came to mind was that something was amiss, and I had no doubt it had something to do with the scuffle that took place in our carriage earlier this evening.

I threw on my robe and went out into the corridor to see if anyone was around. The carriage was deserted and deathly quiet. In a display of bravado, I sauntered along the corridor towards the facilities at the far end. That exercise produced nothing to help explain our extended stay at Zagreb. As a last resort to put my mind at rest, I knocked on Ralph's door. There was no response. That only raised other questions. Was he so sound asleep he didn't hear, or was he not in his cabin at all? Whatever the situation was, I was none of the wiser about where Ralph was or why we were still at Zagreb.

That left me with only one option: go back to bed and try to get some sleep. I was still wide awake and tense as the train shuddered and creaked into life to begin the Ljubljana leg of the journey. Allowing for our delayed departure from Zagreb, we will have passed through Ljubljana and Jesenice, and be well on our way to Salzburg by the time breakfast arrives tomorrow morning. That was a lot of hours to be left wondering about what had happened. And that was the last thought I remember before my eyelids slid closed.

Although I expected a restless night, I slept soundly and until late. Breakfast found me not long out of bed and still in my robe. In record time, I dispatched breakfast, dressed and was on my way to Ralph's cabin. Philippe already was collecting the depleted breakfast trays when I reached the cabin. As I raised my arm to knock on Ralph's door, I noticed there was no tray outside his cabin. Perhaps he hadn't finished breakfast yet.

"I do not think you will get any response," Philippe said as I knocked on Ralph's door. "I could not wake him earlier when I came to deliver breakfast. He did not get much sleep last night so, perhaps he is still in bed." Okay, it sounded as though one of us knew something about the ruckus that went on last night. I decided to pursue the matter with Philippe.

"Wait up please, Philippe. Why did Mr Carter not get much sleep last night? I heard all the noise and saw something of the scuffle that went on in this carriage but, so far, nobody has said what it was all about. I very much need to know. So, if you know anything about what happened in this carriage last night, please tell me now."

Philippe looked uncomfortable and shuffled from foot to foot for a moment while he considered his answer. "I do not know what it was all about. I too heard the noise and came out to investigate. One of the other passengers instructed me to go back to my cabin and to stay there. It was not what I wanted to do. This carriage is my responsibility, but the man who told me to go back to my cabin had authority." Philippe shrugged and looked embarrassed as he added, "So, I did like I was told. However, I think whatever happened in this carriage is somehow connected with our delayed departure from Zagreb. That is all I know. This is all I can tell you." I followed a few paces behind as Philippe again trundled his trolley along the corridor.

As I walked past Sofia's door, I noticed her breakfast tray was not outside for collection. I knocked, and called to her through the door. There was no answer. Philippe stopped when he heard me at Sofia's door. He abandoned the trolley and started back towards me. There was still no response when I knocked again and called out a little louder. I held out my hands palms upwards towards Philippe in question. He nodded as he continued walking towards me. "Miss Elmas was there when I delivered breakfast." I gave him a withering look and he shrugged in return.

"Philippe, I get very nervous when my companions disappear while on this train. At the moment, both Mr Carter and Miss Elmas are missing. Did you deliver breakfast to the other two passengers in this carriage?"

"No, my supervisor brings their food. It is all part of this being so... so ... How do you English say it ... so secretive. I do not talk to them. I do not look after them, not even their food. Only my supervisor has anything to do with them – and Mr Carter of course."

"I see. I think the English word you're looking for is 'hush-hush' and that certainly is the word that seems to apply in this situation. And I find it a curious situation indeed." My stomach was a tight ball of nerves as I thought about the strange absence of my companions. This was not right. Something was wrong. I began to wonder if Ralph had been injured in the scuffle and maybe had been taken to hospital or for medical treatment while we were at Zagreb. What other explanation could there be for his absence? But that didn't explain the apparent disappearance of Sofia. This is no good. I need to be sure whether Ralph and Sofia are in their cabins or not.

"Do you have keys to every cabin in this carriage? Are you able to open every door there is?" Philippe gave a faint affirmative nod in response to each question, but a nervous confusion occupied his face. "That must be an enormous bunch of keys. It would be so heavy to carry them around all the time. How many keys do you have?"

He laughed, pulled out his keyring and spread the keys out across the palm of his hand. "Not too many keys and not too much weight to carry around; only three keys. This one is a master key that opens all the cabins and other doors passengers use. The middle one is the key to my cabin and the equipment room I use. This little one on the end opens the electrical and other services cabinets."

I leaned in as if to take a closer look at the keys, but instead snatched up the keyring by the key Philippe had indicated was the carriage's master key. Without wasting a moment, I turned on my heel and stepped up to Sofia's door. "No, Miss Leggett, I must not let anyone else have these keys. What are you doing? No, you cannot do that. You must not go into someone else's cabin. I cannot let you do this."

"Oh, but I must, Philippe. I must know if Miss Elmas is in her cabin or not. Now, look away if you want to be able to say you didn't see anything." I don't know whether he turned away or not. I already had the key in the lock, and turned it to unlock the door as I finished speaking. Sofia was not there. The breakfast tray Philippe delivered earlier remained untouched on the table where he had left it. So, whatever happened, it must have happened soon after Philippe did his breakfast run.

"Please, may I have the keys back now? This is most irregular. It will bring serious trouble for me."

"No it won't because nobody will know what's happened unless you tell them. I want to check on Mr Carter's cabin next to see if he is there." Like Sofia, Ralph was not in his cabin either.

In his case, Ralph's breakfast hadn't even made it into the cabin. "Neither Mr Carter nor Miss Elmas is in their cabin. We must look for them, Philippe. I fear something terrible has happened on board this train again. We need to check every cabin. Where do we start?"

"Perhaps they have gone to use the facilities. Maybe we should check their first."

"What, both of them gone to the facilities together? That's hardly likely is it? But you're right; perhaps we should start by checking that first." I strode down to the far end of the carriage where the facilities were located with Philippe following along at my heels. This is tricky, I thought. Which one of us should do the checking in there? Either way it could be embarrassing to whoever goes in to check. It can't be helped. Someone has to do it and it might as well be me. With my hand on the doorknob, I gave Philippe a nervous last look before I pushed the door open and marched in. There was no cause for alarm. The place was deserted.

"Okay, that eliminates two of the possibilities. My companions are not in their cabins and they are not in the facilities. I'm afraid it's time we checked all the other cabins." Philippe looked as concerned as I felt but he didn't argue. I walked across the corridor from the facilities to the first cabin on the other side of the carriage.

"No, not that one; we must not go into that one. It is for one of the 'hush hush' people." We will start with this one," Philippe said. He stood in front of the second cabin and pointed sternly at the door, indicating I should to unlock that door. Reluctant as I was to bypass the first cabin, it made sense not to upset Philippe too much this early in our search. But, if we didn't locate Ralph and Sofia in one of the other cabins, we would be coming back to this first cabin regardless of who supposedly occupied it.

Our trek through the carriage checking cabins took little time. With so few occupied, it required nothing more than a quick look inside to confirm there was no one there and that no one had been in there. We reached the cabin three from the steward's area and again Philippe insisted we could not look in that cabin. I was prepared to humour him until we had checked all the remaining cabins. As we confirmed that the last of them was empty, I turned to Philippe. "You haven't got anyone stashed in your cabin have you?"

"What… Me…? How could you ask if I had someone in my cabin? The disappearance of two of my passengers is a serious matter. My job could be on the line. Why would I hide them in my cabin?" The poor man was becoming increasingly upset with every word. It was time to put him out of his misery – or cause a heart attack.

"Right, well you haven't got them and they're not in my cabin, so where are they? We checked every other cabin – except two. It's time we checked those. No, don't argue with me. We must make a thorough job of it. Come on. Let's start with this one along here." I strode back along the corridor past the first three cabins to one of those occupied by one of our mysterious passengers. As I unlocked the door, I thought perhaps Philippe was going to have a heart attack.

"No, no. We must not do this. I have strict orders not to go into these cabins." His protest was a waste of time. I already had the door open. Surprise, surprise; there was no one inside. But, more than that, there were no belongings of any sort in the cabin either. I heard Philippe behind me gasp as he peered over my shoulder into the cabin. "What is this? It does not look like anyone has been in here, but I know there was somebody in this cabin. What has happened to them? Where have they gone, did they get off somewhere along the line?"

I did not like the way this was shaping up. "Well my friend, they either left the train somewhere along the way, or you have another missing passenger. Either way, this is not looking good. I am now concerned that something horrible happened on this train – in this carriage – somewhere between Belgrade and Zagreb. We have one more cabin to check before we know exactly how worried we should be about my missing companions."

Philippe pushed past me and rushed to the far end of the carriage to stand in front of the first cabin at that end immediately across from the facilities. I had to trot to keep up with his long strides, but we arrived at the cabin together. As I still had the keys, I did the honours and unlocked the door. There was no one in the cabin. However, this cabin was different. Someone's personal effects still cluttered the small space. While I poked around, being careful not to disturb things too much, Philippe stood just inside the doorway. I heard a soft keening sound. It was Philippe moaning in a low voice as he stood there wringing his hands.

"Stop it. For goodness sake man, pull yourself together. We need to think about this and try to work out what has happened." Philippe pulled back and blinked at me a few times as if he'd been slapped in the face, but he seemed to regain control.

"Yes, we need to think on this situation but, more than anything else, we need to find my missing passengers – or work out what happened to them." I think that sounds a bit like what I suggested but, not to worry, at least now I think we're both on the same page.

Out in the corridor again, I leaned up against the cabin and stared out the opposite window absentmindedly watching the scenery flashing by. It didn't take too much to work out that one of our 'special' passengers might not have been all he was supposed to be. It didn't take me long to add it all up. As I saw the situation, we had four passengers missing due to whatever circumstances have befallen them and one rotten egg who seemed to have decamped. Of course, I could be adding two and two together and coming up with five. But, somehow I don't think my calculations are wrong.

There was another place that we hadn't checked. The thought of it almost caused me to feel ill. I grabbed Philippe by the arm, dragged him back into my cabin and handed him my camera bag. Before he had time to question what it was all about, I was out in the corridor heading for Sofia's compartment.

Sofia's overcoat was hanging in the small closet in the compartment. I thrust my hand deep into the coat's right-hand pocket. My fingers touch cold steel and, in an involuntary movement, my hand flew out of the pocket again. "What is it ... What happened? What is in that pocket?" Philippe, who had observed my exploration of the coat pocket, had taken a couple of steps back as though we half expected a cobra or something similar to come writhing up out of the pocket.

"Philippe, do you know how to use a gun at all? Not a rifle, a handgun is what I mean."

"That is a strange question, and one that worries me. Why…" Philippe was now standing in the doorway eying off Sofia's coat in a way that indicated he still expected something unpleasant to materialise out of that pocket. I gave him a hard look and he went back to the question I'd asked.

"Yes, I do know how to use weapons, including handguns. I enlisted in the Army, but only managed to finish my basic training before my father became very ill. I had to resign to be with him and to run the business. It took about 12 months, but he surprised everyone by recovering. He wanted me to stay on in the business after he returned to work, but I did not really like that kind of work. Besides, now that he was back there was nothing for me to do, so I joined the police force. Three years later my father died. I resigned and went home to take care of things. I stayed there for another 10 years but then we had an offer to buy the business, a fantastic offer we couldn't refuse. So I was out of a job again and came to work on the train. But, to answer your question, yes I can use a handgun."

"Good, put your hand in that pocket and fish out the one that is in there."

"Eh…? What is in there?" Although he was still asking questions, Philippe slid his hand into the pocket and drew out the handgun. He let out some exclamation in French that I didn't understand and probably didn't want translated. "How did you know this was in here?"

"It's a long story and one I haven't got time to tell you right now. But, as we were boarding the train at Istanbul, Sofia's coat bumped against me and I knew something hard and heavy was in that pocket. Please check whether it's loaded."

As Philippe went through the motions of checking whatever it was he needed to check, I took a couple of steps back away from him. The sight of that handgun frightened me now was much as it did the first time I saw it. Philippe looked up startled as I moved away from him. "What is the matter? Yes, it is loaded, but the safety is engaged. It is perfectly safe."

"So you say, but those things terrify me. Please check the

other pockets to see if she brought extra bullets as well."

From the left-hand pocket of the coat, Philippe withdrew a small rectangular box which he scrutinised for a few moments. "Yes, this is the correct ammunition for this weapon and the box is nearly full." I think I heaved an audible sigh of relief, and then I realised Philippe was watching me intently. "What I think you have not told me, is why we need this handgun and why does it matter whether I know how to use it or not. What do you think is going to happen?"

"I honestly don't know the answers to any of that, Philippe. However, there is one place we still haven't searched but, before we go there, I need to go to Ralph's cabin again." Philippe stood in the doorway as I scrabbled around through Ralph's possessions. I started with his coat and other clothes in the closet and then moved on to his piece of hand luggage that looked like an oversized briefcase. Tucked in amongst the papers and other things in the case was the handgun Sofia had given me the night we were involved in rescuing Yasmin and her husband. I remember Ralph took it from me when he came to help us with the bloke who was trying to get away. It seems he had 'forgotten' to give it back to Sofia before we left Istanbul. Or, perhaps it was by design that the weapon accompanied him on this trip.

"Please check this weapon too, Philippe. Is it also loaded?" It was loaded, and I was tempted to flee the cabin as Philippe brandished it about, checking it out in a manner that seemed far too cavalier for my liking.

"There is nothing to fear. See here, the safety is engaged." With that, he flicked this little button thing and said, "See, the weapon will not fire unless you push the safety like that." He brandished the thing under my nose so I could see what he was talking about and, as enlightening as it was, I still didn't want to know about it.

"Thank you, Philippe. Please engage the safety again or whatever it is you need to do so it will not fire. I will carry it with me, but I need to know it's not going to go off at some stage and shoot someone, especially me – or you!" Philippe managed to re-engage the safety despite laughing so hard, and then handed the weapon to me. God, I hate this thing, but it might be handy to brandish about if we suddenly find ourselves in a threatening situation. Holding the weapon ever so gingerly, I slid it into my pocket and hoped that nothing went wrong and I suddenly ended up with a hole in my foot or something equally traumatic.

As I locked Ralph's door, Philippe queried me about that one last place where we hadn't looked. "I assume your master key will get us into the luggage carriage. Good, that is our next stop, and I think we might need to be careful. If my thinking is right, I am not sure what we might find in that carriage. You should keep your weapon ready. We might need to take photographs. That's why we are taking my camera bag with us."

When we were in the space between the sleeping and the luggage carriages, Philippe offered me the camera bag. I had expected to open the luggage carriage door as I had opened all the other doors in our search for Ralph and Sofia. Philippe had other ideas and would not be dissuaded. He took the keys from me, thrust the camera bag into my arms, and took a deep breath to steady himself before unlocking the door in front of us.

CHAPTER 18

Philippe presented a professional image as he eased open the door and, applying extreme caution, slipped into the luggage carriage. I couldn't help but think he was wasted as a train steward. A formidable image with his gun held at the ready, Philippe eased his way along the central aisle of the carriage. His performance helped me generate some courage. I tiptoed along behind Philippe. However, my weapon remained 'safe' in the depth of my pocket. My one concession towards being ready for anything that might come at us was to have my hand firmly in contact with the weapon.

Not too far into the carriage, we came to an abrupt halt. The hairs on the back of my neck stood up. I took a firm grip on the handgun in my pocket, all the while telling myself to be careful to avoid touching that safety thing that Philippe had educated me about. In a slow arc, Philippe swivelled his head from side to side. Like me, he was trying to pick up that sound again, that sound that now had us standing still half way along the central aisle. Breathe properly, I told myself as I realised I was taking short sharp breaths and was again in danger of fainting on the spot.

Then it came again, that sound we thought we had heard but couldn't be sure about. It was some sort of scraping sound, although 'scraping' might be an overstatement. It wasn't loud; just a soft rustle or rubbing sound. Philippe held up his hand, instructing me to stay where I was, then he began inching his way further along the aisle towards the other end of the carriage. A thump made me jump and brought Philippe to a halt again. It emanated from somewhere behind the rack of luggage to my right and sounded like something hitting the floor. Whatever created the noise, it wasn't hard. The sound seemed muffled somehow.

Close to the far end of the carriage, a gap existed between the wall and the end of the luggage rack. Philippe took one quick careful look around to the other side of the luggage rack and let out an exclamation. I couldn't see what was happening as

Philippe was hidden by the luggage rack. I wished I had devoted some time to learning French so I understood what he said. In hindsight, perhaps it's as well I didn't understand it. I don't think it was something I could use in polite company.

Unsure about what Philippe had found on the other side and equally unsure about what I should do, I tiptoed to the end of the luggage rack. After a few more moments of indecision, I risked a quick look at what lay on the other side of that rack. What I saw shocked me and I gasped in horror. Philippe looked up at me. "Miss Leggett, please to come and give me a hand here."

Ralph looked pale and helpless slumped down there on the floor. Both he and Sofia were bound hand and foot and gagged. A nasty gash at the hairline above the temple had bled down one side of Ralph's face. Sofia's eyes were as big as saucers. I rushed to her and removed the tape from across her mouth while Philippe dealt with freeing Ralph. At first, I thought Sofia had been rendered catatonic by her ordeal but, after a few seconds she managed to rasp out a thank you to me. A darkening bruise surrounded one eye and travelled down to cover most of her cheek.

I wasn't sure what the appropriate first-aid was but confined myself to rubbing Sofia's hands and ankles to encourage circulation again. A quick glance in Philippe's direction revealed him doing much the same for Ralph. Sofia drew my attention to an area a little further along the aisle from where they were. There, in a tangled heap on the floor lay another body. I caught my breath at the thought of a repeat of the scene I had witnessed behind the luggage rack on our previous trip on this train.

Not wanting to divert Philippe from ministering to Ralph's injuries, I got myself up on shaky legs and made my way along the aisle to investigate the body on the floor. The man lay face down with only one side of his face exposed to me. A large pool of blood was drying around him and its metallic smell rose up to meet me as I bent over him. I placed a hand on his uppermost shoulder and gently rolled him over a little way to expose the rest of his face. It only took me one quick glance to realise who the man was and I gently lowered him back to the way he was when I found him.

The bile rose and burned the back of my throat. After

swallowing hard a couple of times, I reached down to search for a carotid pulse. Perhaps it was because I was nervous, but my first attempt found no pulse. I tried again, and this time I found a pulse. It was weak, but it was there. The man was alive. When I returned to where Ralph and Sofia were, Ralph was trying to speak to Philippe but could utter nothing more than a raspy croak. I stated the obvious. "He needs water; they both need to drink some water."

Philippe looked up at me. "Perhaps you could... No. Please remain here to look after your companions while I go for some water and some first-aid material. I need to find my supervisor to ask him to have the police and an ambulance meet us at Salzburg.

"N-o-o-o," Ralph croaked. "No supervisor..." He made some strange gesture that swept across himself, Sofia and the man on the floor further along. Philippe looked confused. He lowered his head to position his mouth next to Ralph's ear and whispered something to Ralph that I could not hear. Then Philippe put his ear to Ralph's lips and, I assumed, whispered something to Philippe. Shock and anger registered on Philippe's face as he sprang to his feet. He quickly checked the other side of the luggage rack to confirm no one else was about to join us. Then he returned to where I remained with Ralph and the others, and I received my instructions.

"I am going to get water and first-aid supplies. You must guard these people while I am away. Be prepared to use your weapon. I have shown you how to do what's necessary. If anyone – anyone at all – other than me comes in here, you must shoot them. You MUST shoot them, or I fear none of you will survive." My mouth opened and closed a couple of times but no words came out.

My head was shaking in disbelief. What was Philippe trying to tell me? Then I felt a gentle tap on my arm. I looked down to see Ralph, still propped up against the end luggage rack, but with his hand extended towards me. "Yes, that is probably better. Marjorie, give Ralph your weapon. He will not hesitate to protect you all." With that, Philippe turned and walked away and out of our sight. I wrestled the handgun out of my pocket and gingerly handed it to Ralph who promptly set about checking it out. Satisfied it was loaded and ready to use, Ralph rested the weapon in his lap but maintained his grip on it.

It seemed like forever before Philippe returned. Long before his return I had begun to fear the worst. Perhaps he too had now met with foul play. If that were the case, what were we to do now? We couldn't expect to hide in here all the way to Paris or Calais, and whoever was responsible for the others being in here was likely to come back sometime between now and when the trip ended. Just when I felt I was nearing breaking point, I saw Ralph stiffen at the same time as I heard a faint noise in the carriage. With his left hand, Ralph waved me back towards the far end of the aisle, as he brought his right hand up and pointed his weapon at the end of the luggage rack where any intruder was likely to appear.

Then a soft whisper drifted through the luggage rack, and I felt as though a weight had suddenly slipped from my shoulders. "Do not panic. It is Philippe and I am alone." I noticed Ralph didn't relax, at least not so that I could see. He kept the gun trained on the gap at the end of the luggage rack. That weight that had slipped from my shoulders started to climb back on board. What did Ralph know that I didn't? If he wasn't relaxed, perhaps I had been a little premature in my belief that all was well.

A hand clutching a carafe of water came into view around the end of the luggage rack, and again Philippe announced himself as coming alone. Ralph lowered his weapon to his lap again, but didn't release his grip on it. And then it was all happening. Both Ralph and Sofia were given a few sips of water before Philippe poured some onto a cloth and began cleaning Ralph's wound.

More water to drink for Ralph and Sofia, and then Philippe and I were helping Ralph to his feet. He insisted on going to check out the man on the floor. I gave Ralph a report on the man. "Your police officer friend is alive – just – but he has been seriously injured and has lost a lot of blood." Ralph nodded his understanding of what I had told him but was not deterred from going to check for himself.

"The man is Captain Volkan. We met in the course of the incidents that happened on our way to Istanbul, and we worked together at the Istanbul end of things. In spite of his being so fit and well trained, the two of us were no match for what we encountered last night on this train. Is Sofia all right? I don't think I have heard her speak since she was untied. She is still in my custody and it remains my responsibility to deliver her safely to London." I said I thought she was in shock and that I would go back to talk to her. Before I could do that though, Philippe asked a question that made me stay where I was.

"Mr Carter, why did you not want me to talk to my supervisor about what was happening here, and why did you not want him to radio for the police to meet us at our next stop?"

"I'm sorry Philippe, but your supervisor is not all he appears to be. Just as the man who came on board with Captain Volkan is not a trustworthy policeman. That man, who was one of Volkan's fellow officers, and your supervisor are working for whoever is behind all of the murders that have occurred. I believe it was your supervisor who provided keys to the wrong people to allow them to commit the crimes that occurred on our trip to Istanbul. It was your supervisor who made it possible for what happened to us to occur last night. I do not want to alert him to the fact that our situation has changed, at least not until I have had time to think about what to do and to develop a strategy."

"Ralph, I saw a scuffle in the corridor of our carriage during the night. Is what happened to you an outcome of that incident? There seemed to be at least four men involved."

"Yes, and at one stage there was five of us. I don't want to spend time discussing it right now. I need time to think, and to work out how to get assistance for Captain Volkan. Philippe, it is important that you return to your post and appear to carry out your duties in the normal manner so as not to arouse the suspicions of your supervisor. I'm sorry, Marjorie, but you also must return to your cabin and carry on as if nothing has happened. I know that will worry you and you will be nervous the whole time, but that is the way it must be if all of us are to arrive safely at our destination."

Neither Philippe nor I was too keen on Ralph's requests. Our protests were to no avail, and he took the stern line with us, ordering us back to our cabins. I left my weapon with Ralph and Philippe kept the one we had taken from Sofia's compartment. Much as that handgun had terrified me, I found myself wishing

I still had it with me as I sat locked in my cabin. Every strange sound brought me out in a nervous sweat and I would rush to press myself against the wall near the door. The small bronze statue I bought to take home as a memento of my trip to Istanbul was the only suitable weapon I could find. Whenever a sound sent me scurrying to my post against the end wall near the door, that small statue was in my hand, although I doubted how effective it might be as a weapon.

The train was due at Salzburg at 11.30a.m. It would be a short stop, with the train to depart for Munich at midday. I made it back to my cabin and locked myself in when we were only a few minutes out from Salzburg. Ralph had insisted that we act as though everything was normal. For me, that meant I had to leave the safety of my cabin for lunch in the dining car shortly after we were underway from Salzburg. Although I knew my cabin provided only a false sense of security, it was all I had. Any-one wanting to come in undoubtedly would have a key, and my locked door would not be an obstacle for them.

At the appointed hour, I took myself off to the dining car for lunch. As I made my way through the train, I wondered how I was supposed to make having lunch look normal when my two companions and I always sit and eat together. The fact that I am alone and appearing to be unconcerned by the absence of my two friends should generate suspicions. The solution to my problem arrived in the last carriage before the dining car.

Three young English women travelling together scrambled out of their seats and collided with me. When we managed to untangle ourselves and had done the apologies and introduction stuff, they suggested we all lunch together. It was an offer I couldn't refuse. Besides, they seemed an interesting group and worth finding out more about. We still laughed about our undignified encounter as we entered the dining car.

Quite a few of the tables were occupied. I shepherded the women towards the table where I usually sat with my companions. It was unoccupied, so we claimed it and got on with the serious business of getting to know about each other while we waited for lunch to arrive. It was an enjoyable lunch made all the more so by lively and interesting conversation. The downside to the interlude was that I learned the three women were leaving the train at Munich. Damn! I was hoping to arrange to have dinner with them this evening.

As I made my way back to my cabin after saying goodbye to the women, I pondered how I might avoid being conspicuous when I arrived for dinner alone. So preoccupied with my thought was I that I blindly blundered into Philippe as he came out of his cabin. As we dusted ourselves off, Philippe commented, "You looked concerned about something. Has anything happened to worry you? I mean anything new, not what we already know about."

I gave him a brief explanation of my concern about going to the dining car alone. I thought it might attract the sort of attention we were trying to avoid. "You could request a tray in your cabin tonight instead of going to the dining car for dinner. I will bring the request form when I deliver afternoon tea." That might be an ideal solution, but the question is whether it might attract even more attention than my eating alone in the dining car. I need to give the matter more thought before afternoon teatime. As I turned to continue on my way to my cabin, I sensed the train was slowing down. Philippe acknowledged it as well and said he would go to find out what was happening.

We were due to arrive at Munich at about 4.15p.m., with only a short stop before heading off again for Paris. However, our Munich arrival time had increased a bit due to various delays along the way and now our forecast arrival time at that city was not until sometime after three o'clock. The train's slowing down out in the middle of nowhere, much as it did on our trip to Istanbul, suggested our arrival time would be even later. By the time I reached my cabin, the train had all but come to a complete stop.

About 15 minutes later, Philippe came to explain that the line was blocked by a land slip a short distance up ahead of us. It was not too serious. After the previous night's rain, just a few rocks and a tree had come down from the hillside and were blocking the line. Work was in progress on clearing the debris. Philippe was told the delay while they finished clearing the rocks from the track might be an hour to an hour and a half. I felt that now familiar reaction deep in the pit of my stomach as Philippe's news caused it to tighten and spasm.

"This is not good news, Philippe. A delay like this in the middle of nowhere is the idea opportunity for your supervisor and any of his colleagues in crime still on board to get rid of the problem they have in the luggage carriage. Do you remember a similar incident when my colleagues and I were on our way to Istanbul about a week ago?"

Philippe's eyes widened as recall kicked in. "We must hurry to do something, but what can we do? Apart from my supervisor, we do not know who else might be involved. We cannot watch everyone who is on the train."

My mind slipped into top gear as Philippe spoke. By the time he finished speaking, I had the makings of an idea, but it was only a sketchy outline and not yet a solid plan. There was no time to stand around discussing it. My rough plan would have to evolve and crystallise as we put it into operation. I took some comfort in something I read years ago. It suggested that plans often go awry when they are 'over-engineered' with every last detail worked out in advance. If that were true, my approach should work like a dream as there was not one concrete detail in my mind.

With Sofia's handgun tucked into the rear waistband of Philippe's trousers and hidden under his uniform jacket, we set off for the supervisor's cabin. "Why have you brought your handbag? Won't it get in the way?" Philippe asked as we neared the supervisor's office and I slung the handbag over my shoulder.

"A woman always has her handbag handy. She puts things she needs to keep safe in it, and she carries it with her because she never knows when she might need something that's in it." I received a strange look from Philippe, but we had reached the supervisor's cabin and, thankfully, there was no opportunity for him to pursue the matter further.

Philippe pressed himself hard against the wall adjacent to but out of sight from the supervisor's cabin door. I knocked and received something akin to an Arctic welcome. "As you can see, I am busy with another gentleman. What is it you wanted? Please make it quick, Miss… uhmm … Miss…."

"Leggett; the name is Leggett. I have a couple of things that I wish to speak to you about. Perhaps this gentleman could come back later, or wait outside for a few minutes until I leave. After that, he could come back in to complete his business with you." The 'gentleman' in question looked anything but that. A huge lump of a man, unshaven and roughly dressed, he had a livid red scar running from his cheekbone, across his cheek and under his chin to disappear beneath the crew neck of his jumper. Although I am no expert, it looked like a recent acquisition. This man looked more like a hardened criminal than a gentleman.

Neither the supervisor nor the man with him found my suggestion acceptable. I felt sure they weren't going to humour me when I was told in in something resembling gutter language that, if I knew what was good for me, I would leave the cabin now. Never much good at taking advice, I strode into the cabin, with the supervisor and his mate backing away as I advanced.

By the time I reached the middle of the cabin, the other pair was hard up against a bench built in to the rear wall. The bench served as a desk for the supervisor and was covered in pieces of paper. Scraps of paper also adorned the noticeboard mounted on the wall above the desk, next to what I assumed was a two-way radio. It was at that point that Philippe felt compelled to insert himself into proceedings.

Philippe rushed in with his weapon drawn and instructed both men to remain where they were and not to move. Of course they weren't about to comply, and the first one to make a move was the man with the scar. While I was still trying to recover from the shock of seeing Philippe behave in such an authoritative manner, I noticed a slight movement by the man with the scar. Not wanting to appear as though I was watching him, I tried to keep him within my peripheral vision.

Both of the men were telling Philippe he had made a mistake and urged him to put the weapon down and explain what the problem was. The supervisor and his mate had their hands in the air in response to the weapon Philip had aimed at them and, as they pleaded with him to put the weapon down, they emphasised their words by waving their hands around in the air. 'Scarface' seemed particularly agitated, but I noticed that, every time he moved his arms, he also managed to slide a centimetre or two further along the bench. By the time the exchange between Philippe and the two men was coming to an end, Scarface had moved some distance from the supervisor. He was in an ideal position to skirt around Philippe if he should decide to make a dash for it.

And that's exactly what he decided to do when Philippe's attention was focused on telling the supervisor what he thought of him. I was standing two or three paces behind Philippe and a little off to one side. When I realised it wouldn't take Scarface too much to get around Philippe on his way to the door, I moved over closer to Philippe but remained behind him. I had barely made the move when Scarface launched himself from the bench and barrelled straight towards me. I took a half step back and swung my handbag. Although he was a big man, Scarface was slightly bent over as he charged past Philippe. As a result of that, my handbag connected with the side of his head, although I wasn't aiming for there. I wasn't aiming for anywhere in particular. I just wanted to stop him.

Scarface hit the floor with a thump and lay still. I saw blood seeping from a wound on the side of his head. When I looked up, Philippe, mouth hanging open, was staring at me and my victim on the floor. Out of the corner of my eye, I saw the supervisor make the slightest move. I yelled Philippe, "Pay attention!" And I jerked my head in the direction of the supervisor. Philippe spun back to face the supervisor and again warned his boss about making any silly moves.

While Philippe brought his supervisor under control again I squatted down beside Scarface on the floor and began to check him out. I flicked back his jacket and revealed a handgun tucked in the waistband of his trousers. Using two fingers to grab it carefully I tried to remove it, but it was too heavy and I had to take a firmer grip. I waved the weapon at the supervisor. "Monsieur Supervisor, I am surprised this train allows passengers to carry such weapons." The supervisor blinked a few times but didn't respond.

The weapon was larger and heavier than any I have seen before, but then I am no expert. As I was examining it, I noticed the supervisor tense as if in readiness to bolt. Philippe was again watching what I was doing and not his supervisor. So, once more I reminded him to pay attention to the task in hand. At the same time, I thought it worthwhile to remind the supervisor that any attempt at escaping via the cabin door had the potential to prove fatal.

I babbled on as I continued to examine handgun. "I have not seen one such as this before. In some ways this weapon is different from the others I know, but at the same time, it is very similar. See, even this is similar. This safety mechanism is the same on many others … And when I push it like this, it is now ready to fire." I held the gun up so the supervisor could see as I went through the motion of taking the safety off.

"Monsieur Supervisor, I would not recommend you make any silly moves. Philippe will not hesitate to deal with you. And, should you manage to get around Philippe, I will shoot you. Let there be no mistake Monsieur, in the event of an attempt to escape, I … will … shoot you."

Was that really me threatened to shoot the supervisor? I couldn't believe I had uttered those words. I couldn't believe I was capable of uttering anything, so terrified was I by the whole situation. And yet, here I was handling this gun with nothing short of gay abandon, not to mention releasing the safety and threatening to shoot someone. Is this really me, Marjorie Leggett, and if it is, where has all this bravado come from?

The supervisor, accepting the reality of his situation, slumped against a bench. I watched as Philippe withdrew a length of thin rope from his pocket. Within moments, the supervisor's wrists were bound behind his back. "Do you know of someplace where we can lock them up safely?" I asked. Philippe nodded and said there was a small empty store room at the end of the carriage that would be ideal.

With one hand on the supervisor's shoulder and the other prodding him in the back with the gun, Philippe began shuffling the supervisor towards the door on his way to locking the supervisor in the storeroom. I was still going through Scarface's pockets when Philippe drew level with me. "What about this one?" Philippe asked, gesturing with his chin towards the man on the floor. I told him to take care of the supervisor and then come back to help me with Scarface. Philippe was only gone about a minute before he came bouncing back into the supervisor's office. "How could a woman's handbag inflict such a wound?" Philippe was crouched down examining Scarface's wound when he asked the question.

"Ah well, that depends on what the woman has in her handbag." With that, I opened my handbag and tipped it upside down. A one inch thick, eight inch square slab of marble dropped out and clattered on the floor. "The catering people probably wonder how one piece of the marble book ends that hold the menus has disappeared from the dining car. Unsure about my safety and feeling a bit vulnerable without a weapon of some sort, I followed my training from the London Underground and acquired a solid, heavy object to keep my handbag."

When his laughter subsided, Philippe became concerned. "He hasn't moved since you hit him. Is he still alive?" I checked the pulse and assured Philippe that Scarface was still alive and probably would regain consciousness at some point in time, but would have a terrible headache when he did. "Will he be all right if I put him in the storeroom with my supervisor?"

"I don't see why not… And I really don't care if he's not. However, we should search him first to make sure there are no keys, or weapons, or anything else that might be used to escape. And we should do the same to your supervisor." Philippe laughed and pulled number of objects from his pocket, including a keyring he was one step ahead of me and had already frisked the supervisor for any useful tools in might be carrying.

With the two men bound at wrists and ankles, we left them locked in the storeroom with a carafe of water for company and returned to the supervisor's office. "Do you know how to operate one of those?" I asked Philippe as I pointed to the radio mounted on the wall.

"I have used two way radios before. Their operation is all much the same, but it is call signs and who they connect to that is important and different for each situation. I can turn this machine on and use it, but I am not sure how to contact police, or whether the machine will only contact the company running this train. I suppose I will just have to try … Ah *bonne* … there are instructions pinned here on the board. Yes, I will be able to make a call to the police."

Perhaps you should do that now. The train sounds like it is getting ready to move off again. By the time you make the call, we should be underway again and I will be looking for my afternoon tea." Philippe murmured something about 'you English and your tea' as he got set to make the call. "By the way, I'm still of the opinion that dinner in my cabin might be a sound option." I left him to it and walked smartly back to my cabin. We might have taken two of the bad guys out of action, but we didn't know how many more of them might be on the train… and how safe or otherwise I might be now.

About 25 minutes later, I heard Philippe's trolley come rattling along the corridor. Afternoon tea in this carriage was quite a bit late this afternoon. As I got up to open the door for Philippe to bring in my tray, I saw the key lying on the table. I picked it up as I went past and still held it in my hand when Philippe brought in the tray.

Along with my afternoon tea tray, Philippe delivered the cabin meal request form. He indicated I needed to complete it now as the cut off time for such requests to be placed with the caterers was close. A vague idea drifted into focus as Philippe fussed about with placing my tray on the table and explaining the cabin meal request form to me. "Are those extra afternoon tea trays supposed to be for Miss Elmas and Mr Carter?"

"Yes. I think it best we continue to act as through we don't know anything has happened to them…" He gave me a knowing wink. "So, of course they must have afternoon tea." Good, I think my idea just became a plan.

Despite of all the thought I had expended on the matter, I remained in two minds as to how to deal with the matter of a solitary dinner appearance this evening. However, now under some pressure to make a decision, the way forward clarified. I grabbed a pen, filled in my details and ticked the appropriate boxes on the menu section of the form. Philippe took the form and said he would lodge it with the caterers and then return for my tray. When he came to collect my tray, Philippe confirmed I would be having dinner in my cabin tonight.

In his absence, I had collected the two trays meant for my companions and stacked them with my own tray ready for collection.

On Philippe's return to collect the trays, I carried the stack of trays out and slid them onto the trolley as soon as he arrived at my door. It was obvious he was a bit taken aback by my action. I explained it away by saying that I had taken up so much of his time this afternoon, I felt guilty and wanted to help in whatever way I could. Such a feeble explanation sounded hollow to me and I'm sure it didn't wash with Philippe either, but it was the best I could come up with at the time.

After telling me that dinner would be delivered around seven o'clock, Philippe and his trolley rattled off towards his end of the carriage. I called him back. "Is there any way we might be able to get Ralph to the supervisor's office so he can make a radio call? I think he might be keen to let Inspector Yazar know what has happened to Captain Volkan." We discussed the matter briefly but, in the end, decided against it as being too risky, and it would mean leaving Sofia and Captain Volkan alone and unprotected.

It was almost four o'clock when the train at last pulled into Munich. This was our last night on the train. After Munich there was about a seven-hour trip to Paris where we would spend the night at *Gare de Lyon* before being taken on to Calais in the morning. We were now running a good hour and a half late. However, according to my timetable, our stop at Munich was supposed to be for about two hours. They might be able to make up some time by shortening the length of that stop, but there was no indication so far that might occur. I hoped that, if Philippe managed to talk to the police on the radio, they and an ambulance might be waiting at the station. In which case, a two-hour stop might be a good thing.

I scanned the platform and watched the three young English women depart with their luggage to spend the next few days in Munich. Only a couple of other people left the train and no new passengers boarded. No police or ambulance type personnel were visible anywhere on the platform and there was no sound of extra people boarding the train from anywhere other than the platform.

As I stood with my nose pressed hard against the window to provide me with the maximum view of the platform, an uneasy feeling started to settle over me, and a whole flock of difficult questions flew in and settled in my mind. Had Philippe made the radio call, and had he spoken to the police? Why was there no police or ambulance waiting for us at the station? And what about Ralph and the others holed up in the luggage carriage, how do we get them off the train safely, where and when?

This feeling of helplessness was becoming more than I could bear. There had to be something we could do, but whatever that 'something' might be remained a mystery. But, it occurred to me that I could ask Philippe about that radio call he was supposed to make. That might answer some of the questions that were dogging me at the moment. I set off in search of Philippe but he appeared not to be in his cabin or anywhere in the steward's area at that end of the carriage.

About to give up and go back to my cabin, I was startled when Philippe came into the carriage through the adjoining door. He seemed a bit tense, maybe 'rattled' might be a better description, and I knew in an instant something was amiss. I didn't think it was that I had been looking for him and found him missing. It seemed as though whatever was bothering him had accompanied him from wherever he had been further along towards the front of the train.

He stopped when he saw me, but didn't say anything. After a moment, he wiped a hand across his now stubbly chin. "I have been looking for the police, but they have not come. There is no ambulance to take Captain Volkan for medical attention. I do not understand what has gone wrong." I felt sick as a possible explanation thundered into my mind. Philippe shook his head gently from side to side as he studied his boots. He too was searching for explanations. As the explanation that occurred to me grew and took on monumental proportions I stared at Philippe. He must have felt my eyes on him and gave up studying his boots to look at me and say, "I did call them. I did speak to the police and they were going to meet us here at Munich." His anguish was almost palpable, and my guilt at having doubted him even for that brief moment made me so ashamed.

CHAPTER 19

This was not a time for mental apologies or self-recrimination. It was a time for action. My pressing need was to check on the trio holed up in the luggage carriage. I needed to share with Philippe my concern for the welfare of those in the luggage carriage. A long stop in the middle of nowhere is an ideal opportunity for people to go missing off the train and, given we didn't know how many were involved in what was happening on board this train other than the two we had locked in the storeroom, we had no way of knowing how safe any of us was. I was about to explain all that to Philippe when he turned on his heel and made for the door. As he opened the door to exit the carriage, he said over his shoulder, "I will try calling the police again to find out why they weren't at the station."

I murmured, "Okay," as Philippe closed the door behind him. In response to some subconscious bidding, I thrust my hand into my pocket – my left pocket – and tightened my fingers around the key they found there. Philippe was right. It was worth trying to find out what happened at Munich, but I couldn't wait for him to come back. The weight in my right pocket was reassuring as I marched the length of the carriage.

A moment of truth confronted me at the far end of the carriage. The key I held in my hand I had taken from Scarface. Without any indication of what it might open, I had taken it in the hope it was a master key. My hand trembled as I lined up the key to insert it in the lock of the carriage's end door. Not known to resort to prayer in times of crisis, I considered giving it a try at that point. But there was no need. The key slid into the lock, and moments later I was standing in the inter-carriage space between the two carriages. As the key had unlocked the door at the end of the sleeping carriage, I assumed it was a master key and would get me into the luggage carriage.

The only sounds in the luggage carriage were the sounds of the train clattering along the rails and the beating of my heart which seemed to have stepped up a gear or two. I remembered Ralph was armed and I wanted to avoid getting myself shot. "Hello. Hello, it's me, Marjorie." No one responded; not a sound came from the other side of the luggage rack.

My instinct told me to get out of there as quickly as possible, but I couldn't leave until I knew what was on the other side of the luggage rack. As I wended my way towards the end of the rack, I softly kept announcing my presence. When I reached the end of the rack and still hadn't had any response, I tried calling individuals by name. "Ralph, Ralph Carter can you hear me?" No response. "Sofia, Miss Elmas, are you all right? Sofia, are you still there?"

There was only the width of the rack between me in the aisle on the other side, only a metre further to go before I could see into the aisle where I last saw my companions. I don't know which emotion was the strongest: terror at the thought of what might happen to me if I entered the other aisle or the fear of what I might find when I looked into that aisle. Why weren't they answering me or making some noise for me to hear? So close to finding out what the situation was in that next aisle, I willed myself on to the point where I could look around the corner.

No one was there, not Ralph or Sofia, nor the badly injured Captain Volkan. Although I had conjured up various worst-case scenarios in my mind, I had not anticipated this outcome. My mind refused to comprehend what I was seeing. Stupefied, I stood welded to where I stood, unable to go forward to inspect the aisle or to make a hasty exit from the carriage. For the best part of a minute, I just stood there stunned.

At last sensibility started to return. Perhaps they had moved into the aisle on the other side of the carriage. My mind refused to address the ongoing question of why they hadn't responded. I moved back to the centre aisle and, without any hesitation, crossed behind the other luggage rack to the aisle on the far side of the carriage. Somehow, I knew no one was there so didn't waste time on caution. I dragged myself back to the carriage door and let myself out into the inter-carriage space, locking the luggage carriage behind me.

What to do now kept running through my mind. What was there I could do? They were gone. I had let my friends down. I should have checked on them earlier when we stopped instead of locking myself safely in my cabin to avoid any unpleasant things happening to me. It was up to me to keep a lookout for them. But now they were gone. I would never see Ralph again, not that that mattered much in his world anyway. And I still did not know what any of this was about. I still did not know why my friends were taken from me.

The tears that had welled up in my eyes overflowed and came down my cheeks in torrents. Blinded by my tears, I fumbled with the lock but finally let myself back into the sleeping carriage and stumbled along the corridor towards my cabin. There was no one around. Well, who would there be? The only two people in this carriage now are Philippe and me. I felt light headed, my stomach churned and I didn't seem to be able to control my legs too well.

My reaction to the whole situation was to rush back to my cabin and lock myself in but, early into my staggered journey along the corridor, it occurred to me that this might not be the right thing to do. Philippe! Philippe, I need to tell Philippe about the luggage carriage… about the missing trio. A noise from one of the cabins startled me. I jumped and ended up pressed hard up against the window on the opposite side of the corridor from where I thought the noise had come.

There should be no noises coming from any of the cabins. Mine was the only one remaining that had an occupant, apart from Philippe's cabin at the far end of the carriage. I wanted to run, to gallop back to my cabin and lock myself in, but my feet wouldn't move. More noise, and then the carriage door yawned open. "Philippe…! What are you doing … Why are you in that cabin? I was coming to get you. Something terrible has happened." And then there was more noise.

"Marjorie… Are you all right? You look as white as a sheet. Come in, come in and sit down." There was Ralph standing in the doorway peering around Philippe to talk to me. There was no question. It was Ralph and that was Ralph's voice. For a brief moment, I thought I might faint. Then Philippe had me by the arm and supported me as he dragged me into the cabin. Sofia jumped up from the bunk where she had been sitting applying fresh dressings to Captain Volkan's wounds.

Sofia pushed Volkan's feet across to one side of the bunk and helped Philippe eased me down onto the space she had made. I sat there, unable to speak and not sure whether this was real or I was imagining things. Then Philippe crouched down in front of me and took both my hands in his. He looked up into my face and said, "Relax, Miss Leggett. Tell me please what is this terrible thing that has happened?"

"What … What terrible thing?" Not only was I incoherent I was inarticulate.

"Outside, you mentioned something terrible had happened. I think you are on your way to tell me about it when I met you in the corridor."

My mind swum back to that first moment when I encountered Philippe in the corridor, and every word I'd said came back to me. I gave something that sounded like a high-pitched cackle and slapped my hand to my mouth to prevent any more of that escaping. I swallowed hard a couple of times before I spoke. "I fear there was no terrible happening, just an old woman behaving irrationally. The three of you are here in this cabin, being looked after by Philippe, and all looking a lot better than when I last saw you – even the captain here."

"Marjorie, you are not irrational. Something upset you – frightened you. We need to know what it was, and whether we should be worried about it and prepare for something else unpleasant that might happen." Ralph had pushed Philippe to one side, and now stood looking down at me as he held my hands. His voice was soft and kind. I felt the tears welling up again.

"I was concerned that something might have happened to you while we were stopped along the track. I was about to ask Philippe to come with me to check on you when he went to try and make another radio call to find out why the police hadn't met us at Munich. So, I went to the luggage carriage alone and found no one there. You were all gone. There was no sign of you anywhere, and I feared the worst."

And then it all happened. How much shock can a person

stand in one day? Ralph threw his arms around me and hugged me to him. I buried my head in his chest and sobbed. "I thought I had lost you – and Sofia. I didn't know what to do." Sofia rushed over and perched on the edge of the bunk beside me. She threw her arms around me too and, for a few moments, the three of us remained locked in firm embrace. When we untangled ourselves, I rummaged in my pockets looking for a handkerchief. Ralph removed one from his pocket and handed it to me. He rubbed my shoulders as I mopped my tears and wiped my face.

"I am thinking we are all in need of coffee and something a little stronger," Philippe announced. "Do we all agree? Good, I will be back soon."

"That poor man, what must he think of me? I treated him as though he didn't care and wasn't interested in what might be happening to you down there in the luggage carriage, and all the time he had you safely installed in this empty cabin." Philippe was right, I did need something stronger than coffee. God, I have been such a silly old woman.

This evening, Philippe brought four meals to Sofia's compartment and Philippe joined Ralph, Sofia and me to dine in the rather cramped compartment. Volkan continued to drift in and out of consciousness and could not eat or drink. We wiped his mouth with ice cubes in a bid to get some fluid into him. The release of tension combined with the sadness of our last night on the train and last night with Philippe made for a strange evening. There were fits of laughter interspersed with periods of melancholia and nostalgia.

Nobody slept that evening. Our scheduled arrival around midnight at *Gare de Lyon* impacted by the delays encountered along the way saw us pull in to Paris around 2.00a.m. The police were waiting, as were two ambulances. Captain Volkan and Scarface were whisked away in the ambulances. Philippe's supervisor was manhandled into a police vehicle and also whisked away. A doctor came on board and checked out Ralph and Sofia. After attending to Ralph's wound and giving Sofia something to apply to her bruised face, he pronounced them both fit to be interviewed by police.

Philippe and I were surplus to requirements, although police said they would want to interview us later. I gained the impression they were interested in that slab of marble I had in my handbag and wanted to discuss it with me. We both returned to our cabins. There wasn't much of the night left, but I knew I would not be able to sleep. I think it was due to the shock I had earlier in the afternoon but there also was a degree of trepidation about how the rest of the night and our stay in Paris might pan out. A soft tap on the door startled me. I hesitated for a nervous moment before answering it.

Armed with a tray loaded with coffee and a bottle of 'something stronger', Philippe stood outside in the corridor. He gave me a sheepish smile and said, "I did not think you would be asleep either. May I come in?" Although not someone who indulges in alcohol on any regular basis, I decided that perhaps a small glass of brandy might prove beneficial. Philippe poured rather more than I expected into a glass and handed it to me. After inane salutations (led by Philippe), I lined up for my first sip.

The smell, or fumes, or whatever rising up out of the glass almost was enough to change my mind. But, Philippe had gone to the trouble and it would be rude not to accept his good intentions. I took my first tentative taste. The liquid burnt the back of my throat. There followed a few moments of coughing and spluttering until I got my breath back and I was sure I hadn't done myself any serious mischief. Philippe tried without too much success to stifle a smile.

"No. You must sip it, just a tiny sip. Then, hold it in your mouth and roll it around to enjoy its warmth before you swallow it." I felt embarrassed, not only because of the undignified performance my first taste produced, but because of my ignorance of how to drink brandy. My next tentative sip followed Philippe's instructions and I marvelled at the difference it made. Just as I was settling in to the sipping brandy and coffee routine, a knock on my door and someone calling my name interrupted the interlude.

"I wonder if I might have a word." It was the police officer I had assessed earlier as being the one in charge of the small squad that came aboard the train. Philippe rose and made to leave my cabin. "No, please Philippe, if you wouldn't mind staying... and if that is all right with you, Miss Leggett." All his officers were off interviewing other passengers on the train. He was reluctant to interview me alone – or to be alone in my cabin with me.

"Yes, please stay, Philippe. You know I have no French and I might need you to translate … to interpret for me." Philippe, as I spoke to him, stood with his back to the officer. He gave me a curt half bow sort of response – and an exaggerated wink – before turning to the officer to confirm he would stay. This lad was a bright one indeed. Philippe's abandoning the police force to work as a steward on this train was a loss for the police force.

There was no surprise when he opened the interview with questions about Scarface's injuries. I showed him the marble slab and explained that I had felt vulnerable and sought to protect myself with whatever weapon I could find. Then he moved onto the difficult stuff. He held up the plastic bag with a handgun in it and asked if I recognised the weapon.

"It looks much the same as the one I took from the man in the supervisor's cabin, but I don't know much about these guns and they might all look the same for all I know." The officer took the gun from the bag and held it out to me, telling me to take it and have a closer look at it. "No. No thank you, I can see it quite clearly from here." I leaned in and made a show of giving the weapon close scrutiny. "Yes, it is as I said before. It looks the same as the one I took from the man, but I couldn't say if it is the same gun."

"Do you not wish to take it and have a closer look at it? Maybe it would help you be certain about whether it is the same gun or not. Here, take it and examine it."

"No thank you. Just the sight of those things terrifies me." After I explained how I found the weapon, the officer questioned my familiarity with such weapons.

"Do know how to use a weapon such as this? Have you ever fired one?"

"Good Lord, no. I've never fired one. I'm not sure I would know how. However, from what I've seen in the movies, you pointed it at whatever you want to shoot and pull the trigger thing. Oh, yes, there is one other thing that I forgot about. See that thing there…" I pointed to the small button-like mechanism near the trigger. "I think that is some sort of safety device. As

Philippe explained it to me, it has to be in the right position for the weapon to fire."

"Why was it necessary to explain that to Miss Leggett?" The officer asked Philippe.

"When Miss Leggett removed the weapon from the man, I could see she was extremely nervous. She held the thing out in front of her like a bomb that might explode at any moment. I explained that it was safe and showed her that the safety was on. I don't think my explanation helped too much, so I took the weapon from her."

"And quite right you were to do that too. I know you said it was safe. But I couldn't help thinking it might go off at any moment and injure me or someone else, or blow a hole in the train or something. Anyway, Philippe needed something to help convince his supervisor to behave himself and not try doing anything too heroic." The officer seemed to consider my comments for a few moments before addressing one last question to Philippe.

"Did you need to fire the weapon or use it in any way?"

"I did not fire the weapon. I just waved it around prodded the supervisor in the back with it a couple of times to remind him I had the gun."

My interview ended shortly after, and the officer and Phillipe went to Philippe's cabin. I was pleased Philippe was there during my interview as he now knew what was said. It ensured he wouldn't say anything contradictory when they interviewed him. And why would he anyway? I hadn't told the officer anything that wasn't true... thanks to Philippe's quick thinking while we were having coffee and brandy.

We knew the police had Scarface's gun and would be keen to know all about it. During our raid on the supervisor's office, Philippe had the gun we took from Ralph's cabin. To be more precise, he had the gun Sofia had given me when we rescued her sister, and which Ralph later took from me. The weapon Philippe took to the supervisor's office was the gun I found in Sofia's cabin. In order to simplify life and avoid a whole lot of difficult question about where that gun came from, we hid it amongst my belongings.

That left none of us with the weapon in the event that anything else should go wrong. But it also opened the way for the telling of only the true part of the story of how a gun was involved in the incident that occurred in the supervisor's cabin. Well, it wasn't too much removed from the truth. No more than a forgetful old lady might wander from the correct facts.

Before too long, I heard voices coming along the corridor. I opened my door as they drew near. The two men paused in front of my cabin to say good night before the police officer continued on his way to the far end of the carriage. Philippe announced rather more loudly than necessary, "If it is okay, I will come in to collect the tray." My invitation to Philippe to come in for the tray was delivered at much the same volume as his request. I assumed our performance was all for the benefit of a police officer who must still be within earshot.

Philippe hesitated a few moments, and then seemed to relax before coming into my cabin. "The officer has left this carriage. I made sure he was gone before I came in. I think everything is good and they will not be back to ask us more questions. It is almost breakfast time, so I will go to see if the breakfast trays are ready. I shouldn't be gone long, and perhaps we could all breakfast in Miss Elmas' compartment when I return."

As soon as Philippe had departed for the dining car, I locked my cabin and took myself along the corridor to find my two companions. Ralph, continuing his custodial duties, was reading his book in Sofia's compartment while Sofia scribbled in her journal. "Philippe will return with breakfast soon. He suggests we all eat together in here."

"Will he continue with us all the way to Calais?" Ralph asked. I hadn't thought about it and had assumed that he would. However, now that Ralph had asked the question, I could see that there was a possibility Philippe would leave us before then. Therefore, one of the first questions we had for Philippe when he returned with breakfast was for how much longer he would remain our steward.

Breakfast was enjoyable despite a sombre undercurrent. Philippe explained that, shortly after breakfast, they would shunt us around to the *Gare du Nord* where we would be connected to another train. That train would take us through to Calais. Philippe would remain with us until we reached *Gare du Nord*. He would then have a couple of days off before the Direct Orient Express departed Paris on its next trip. We celebrated our last couple of hours with Philippe as best we could. His service was exemplary, and he had been so much more than a steward to us on this trip.

Sofia went to use the facilities at one point. I took the opportunity to thank Philippe for being so instrumental in keeping us all safe. Ralph said quietly, "Look, lad, it's none of my business but you are wasted as a steward on this train. You have a good head on your shoulders and would make an excellent police officer, or probably anything else you set your mind to."

It opened the way for a private conversation I had been hoping to have with Philippe. "Ralph is right. For what it's worth, in my opinion, you should give serious thought to returning to the police force. You have all of the qualities needed to succeed, and I too believe you are wasting your life on this train."

"There you go, Philippe. You can't get much better recommendation that that. You would make an excellent detective one day." Ralph tapped the side of his nose as he finished speaking.

Embarrassed by the conversation, Philippe fidgeted on his chair, before giving Ralph a solemn look. "Miss Leggett is the one who would make an excellent detective. She has the ability to pull all the clues together. Nobody could ask for a better friend. She would risk things – frightening things – to make sure her friends were safe."

Three embarrassed people sat around the table when Sofia returned. Her puzzled look made us all chuckle, but none of us was about to enlighten her. About ten minutes later, Philippe took his leave of us to take care of the last of his duties before leaving the train. Sofia and I hugged him. Ralph shook Philippe's hand and slapped him on the back, and then Philippe bolted from the compartment. But I had seen the moisture glistening in his eyes as he made his hasty departure. Philippe's departure also was our cue to pack and get ready to disembark the train for the last time.

We arrived at Calais just before midday and, with a minimum of fuss and bother, we were on our way to London. Our arrival at three o'clock provided the three of us with a little time alone to say goodbye. Although we all vowed to keep in touch, I suspect all travellers do that, but never do, or at least not beyond the first month or so afterwards. But, for us, our goodbyes were a little different. There was still the issue of the incident at the British Museum hanging about and perhaps a troubling time ahead for Sofia in its aftermath.

I knew we would keep in touch at least until that mess and all the other murders were resolved and Sofia was free to resume her normal life again. We had become a 'family' and, after what we had been through together, probably were a lot closer than some families. As the taxi ferried me back to my cottage, I nursed a heavy heart. It was sad to be parting with such special friends, but I was so looking forward to being home again.

CHAPTER 20

Over the subsequent three weeks, Ralph, Sofia and I met four times. Ralph was busy with the investigation of who was behind all the murders that occurred in that short preceding period. Sofia looked more haggard each time I saw her but, early in the third week after we returned to London, she was clear of any involvement in all of that had happened. I expected her to return to Istanbul immediately afterwards. However, she chose to stay and fulfil her original contract in relation to the exhibition of artefacts from the Ottoman Empire mounted in the British Museum. Connie and I booked in for a tour of the exhibition and an associated floor talk. I was ecstatic when it was Sofia who led the tour and delivered the talk.

While there was no question about my being happy to be home again and among my own things, I felt strangely unsettled. Connie and I continued to volunteer at the local library, but my life seemed lacking in some way. I kept busy tidying up the garden and spring cleaning the cottage, but it wasn't enough. That continued until Ralph and I lunched with Sofia and then took her to the station the day she left London to go home. Her departure left something of a hollow feeling in the pit of my stomach. I never imagined that standing on the platform waving her off as the train pulled out would be such an emotional thing.

Ralph must have experienced much the same feeling. We stopped waving and stood in silence for a moment watching the train disappear into the distance. Ralph took my arm and spun me away from the direction of the train. "I don't know about you, but I could do with a nice cup of tea about now. And I don't mean from somewhere here at the station. Come on, let's go and find somewhere to have a cuppa."

I allowed myself to be led away for a few paces before I stopped. "Are you sure it is appropriate for us to be doing this?"

"Doing what? We're only going for a cup of tea, nothing more. How can that be inappropriate?"

"I'm thinking of your wife and what she might make of something that, while quite innocent, might be interpreted otherwise." Ralph just about convulsed with laughter and tugged my arm to get me moving forward again.

"I assure you it will not bother my wife. We can discuss this over a cup of tea."

Not a word passed between us as we walked to a quiet little place that Ralph knew about not too far from the station. It was one of those lovely old fashioned places whose charm included wonderful service, good tea and delicious cakes. As soon as we ordered, Ralph adopted a stern demeanour. "Now what's all this about my wife's not approving of us taking tea together?" I was about to try brushing it aside but I could see he was serious and an honest answer was required.

A rambling honest answer is what he got about how I did not want to cause his wife any concern and did not want the possibility of a simple shared cup of tea to create tension in his marriage. Ralph broke into raucous laughter that caused the only other two customers to look up in alarm. He got himself under control that instant and apologised to the other patrons.

"My Dear Marjorie, us having a cup of tea together will not bother my wife in the least… because there isn't one to bother. I'm not married; never have been." I felt the heat climb up my cheeks and knew my face would be bright red with embarrassment. Ralph sought to easy my discomfort.

"Thank you for your consideration but, no, there is no Mrs Carter. At one time – a long time ago now – I thought there might be. However, if there is one thing I have learned in this life, it's that police officers and marriage don't get on together. Being a copper takes over your life. Well, it tends to if you are there for all the right reasons and hold strong to the ideals of what being a police officer means. From what I've seen, most women love the man but can't live with the man's job or, more to the point, what his life entails."

Somehow, his words did help. I relaxed and felt a little sad at the thought of what Ralph had hinted at: a love that had not matured into marriage maybe because of his chosen career. "I do not want to get involved in someone else's marriage ever again."

That was my thinking as I thought on Ralph's situation. But, it seems I was thinking aloud and I saw the quizzical look Ralph shot me.

"I sense a deep sadness there. Perhaps we are more alike than we know. Is your wound recent?" He voice was low, not much above a whisper, and I was taken aback by what he said. At first, I wondered whether detectives learn to read minds, but then I realised what had happened. My decision now was whether to share details of my 'wound' with Ralph or to keep them to myself. Whatever it was about Ralph, before I knew it, I was telling him my story.

"After spending more than 30 years working for the company, it was time to go. I worked myself up from being one of the girls in the office to the office manager and held that position for more than 20 years. My long-time affair – if that's the right word, or should it be 'relationship' – ended in disaster. He was the manager of one of the company's smaller branches, but had started his career in the same building as where I worked. The company frowned on 'romantic liaisons' – or any other closeness – between its employees. Our affair constituted grounds for dismissal in the company's eyes, so we took great care to conceal it. After some time, I hoped he might ask me to marry him, and again when he was made branch manager I hoped a proposal might follow. It never did. As years went by, and although our relationship continued, I began to accept that was all it would ever be. What I didn't know at the time was that he couldn't marry me regardless of whether any marriage proposal was forthcoming or not. He already had a wife for many years."

"Pretty shabby treatment I would say, but unfortunately not uncommon today. I hope the wounds have healed some since then and that you don't judge all men by the same yardstick." I tried to brush it aside as ancient history now but I don't think I convinced either of us of that.

It was a lengthy afternoon tea and, when it was time to leave, Ralph insisted on driving me home. No amount of protesting would persuade him otherwise. I have to admit to feeling pampered – special – as he drove me to my cottage and walked me to my door. As ever the perfect gentleman, he thanked me for a wonderful afternoon and turned to leave after I opened the door and stepped inside. As I watched, he reached the gate, stopped and then strode back. "Would you be interested in having dinner with me at some time?" he blurted out.

"I would enjoy that. Why don't we eat here? I could cook something. It wouldn't be up to restaurant standard but it would be quiet and we wouldn't have to worry about bookings." Ralph looked doubtful, so I hastened to reassure him. "I can cook, and I can manage a bit more than bangers and mash."

"It's not that. I don't doubt that you are a good cook. It's my job that's the concern. I wouldn't want you to go to all the trouble of preparing a meal for us only for me to have to cancel at the last minute because something had come up at work. If you don't mind short notice, it would be preferable for me, when I knew there was nothing work-wise happening to ring to say I'd pick you up in half an hour. We could pick a tentative evening in advance and see how it things go when the day arrives."

"I don't mind short notice and that sounds like a good approach. Let's choose an evening and see what happens." We settled on the following Friday night, or Saturday night if Ralph was late finishing off something on Friday. We said goodbye again, and I stood and watched him drive away. I floated through the cottage to the sitting room and collapsed into my favourite chair. I was so excited, I thought I might burst. Ralph wasn't married and he wanted to see me again – for dinner. I think that means we have a date.

After what seemed like extremely long days, the weekend finally arrived. My mounting excitement took a bit of a dive when Ralph called around lunchtime on Friday to say he would be delayed at work this evening and could we defer dinner until the following night. I knew this was a possibility, and I also knew this is what coppers' wives put up with all the time. Dinner on Saturday night would be fine with me I assured him, and I hoped I sounded relaxed about the change of plan.

Ralph picked me up on the dot of seven o'clock and took me to a little Italian restaurant in the next suburb that I'd never been to or even knew about. The food and service were outstanding.

And the cannelloni we had with coffee almost made me swoon. It was quite late when we arrived back at my cottage. I invited Ralph in for a coffee, more out of courtesy than the need for more coffee, but he refused, citing the late hour. On something akin to autopilot, I wafted through the cottage and my preparations for bed without any thought to what I was doing. It had been a wonderful night; good food, interesting conversation, and Ralph is such good company. We made tentative plans to do something together the next weekend. The plans would remain a bit loose ended until nearer the time, and when Ralph knew what he would be doing.

*****

Over the next few weeks, there were dinners and lunches, and we even took in a couple of shows together. It was all such a new experience for me to be out and about in public with a man. Then, one evening when we came out from a show, the weather that had threatened all day turned nasty. It was bucketing down and was quite a few degrees colder than when we went into the theatre. Ralph ran through the rain the couple of blocks to where his car was parked. He pulled up in front of the theatre, and I threw myself from under the relative shelter of the theatre's awning to land in the passenger's seat.

It still was raining heavily when we arrived back at my cottage. I insisted Ralph remain in the car while I made a dash for my front door. He brushed that aside. "I'm already soaked. A bit more rain won't make any difference. Hang on a minute, there's an umbrella in here somewhere." Always the gentleman, with his large black umbrella keeping at least some bits of me dry, he raced me to my front door and stood holding the umbrella over us as I fumbled with my keys.

By the time we were both inside, we were soaked through and freezing. The rain had become heavier. It was unthinkable to be out in such weather. After the central heating was going, I lit a fire. We removed what outer garments decency allowed and spread them out to dry. It was unthinkable that Ralph should drive home in such weather. Although he took some persuading, in the end he agreed. I took him through to the spare room, showed him the bathroom, and left him to make himself as comfortable as possible.

Next morning, the sky was black as midnight, but the rain had backed off to a miserable drizzle. The clothes we spread out the night before were almost dry. As soon as we finished breakfast, Ralph took his leave. Before dashing for his car with his umbrella held down low over his head he expressed his concern about what the neighbours might make of overnight stay. I didn't care. "Oh, I'm sure they noticed and there will be plenty of speculation, but it's of no concern to me. We are both adults and what we choose to do is nobody's business but ours… and it will stay that way as far as I am concerned."

Ralph chuckled. "I can imagine them tut-tutting over coffee about the scarlet woman in the neighbourhood and her goings on."

All the following week, I didn't see or hear from Ralph. The media was full of a major crime that occurred in the early hours of Monday morning. I noticed Ralph's name mentioned in the newspaper as being involved in the investigation of the crime and accepted that he was far too busy to think about me. Far from being disappointed by that, I felt some kind of thrill at seeing someone I thought so much of being involved in something being splashed all over the media.

The time that elapsed before I saw Ralph again allowed me some space to think about us, Ralph and I, and how that might work out if it were to come to something more. I explored it often during those ten days of absence. The conclusion I came to at the end of the period was exactly the same as the one I reached when I first thought about it: we would be perfect together!

At the end of the second week of no contact with Ralph, his investigation was finished and we went to dinner. As we lingered over our coffee, Ralph said he had the next few days off and suggested we go on a picnic the next day. I don't think I'd been on a picnic since I was a little girl but it sounded like a wonderful idea.

I was up early the next morning, prepared food, and put together a hamper including a thermos of tea, a couple of pieces of fruit and a couple of slices from a cake I'd made the day before.

We drove out into the country, through narrow leafy lanes and along back roads to an area in the foothills that overlooked rolling green fields running down the valley to a river below. Ralph set out a rug and a couple of fold up chairs in the shade of a patch of trees. We sipped tea and ate cake in comparative silence as we took in the vista before us and soaked up the peace and quiet around us.

While I packed up the mugs and thermos and put them back into the hamper, Ralph fetched from the car one of those folding card tables and set it up at our chairs. When we were settled again, it was time for conversation. We spoke very quietly, not much above whispers, for fear of damaging the tranquillity of the environment.

"That's a lovely little cottage you have. You showed good planning and foresight in getting yourself set up like that, and in such a nice neighbourhood," Ralph said.

"It was none of that. I inherited it." Ralph looked interested in my comment, so I explained how I came by the cottage. "I discovered an aunt I never knew I had. When my mother died, I thought I was the last one left of the family. A few days after Mum's funeral, I received a letter of condolence from a woman whom I didn't know. She must've suspected I wouldn't know anything about her so, at the end of the letter, she explained that she was my mother's sister. There had never been any mention of this woman. I didn't know she existed and was intrigued, so I went to meet her."

"Aunt Edith was a lovely old lady, not at all like my mother. Because of an indiscretion with a soldier around the start of World War I, she was thrown out of the family in disgrace and ostracised for life. We became close friends, maybe because we were much alike."

"Eh...? What was your indiscretion?"

"No, not alike in that way; just alike in that neither of us ever married. She was pregnant to a soldier who was killed early on in the War. After that and being thrown out by the family, she miscarried. That soldier was the love of her life. She never looked for anyone else. Anyway, we had some great times together until she became ill. The cancer was aggressive and didn't take long to complete its work. After she died, I discovered she had left the cottage and her car to me and provided me with a small annuity."

"Is that another common thing you had in common: losing the love of your life?"

"Good God, no, the one I lost wasn't fit to be that for anyone."

"How did you come to find out he was married? I assume that ended it all for you."

"It was a long time before I found out. We had been seeing one another for a long time with not a hint of anything more happening. Then, out of the blue, he proposed. I had gone off the idea by then and my life had become complicated. My seriously ill mother moved in with me. So, I couldn't accept the proposal at that time. He wasn't able to come to my apartment while my mother was there, but we still managed to see each other at work and share an occasional meal in some seedy back street eatery. After my mother passed away, I hoped the proposal might again be forthcoming. When it wasn't, I tried to encourage it. I wasn't successful. We carried on seeing each other but something had gone from the relationship. He had been transferred to another of the branch offices and we didn't see each other at work any-more."

"It would have been one morning about 12 months later. The office girls were talking amongst themselves before starting work for the day. I heard one of them mention that my lover's (why was it so hard to say that word?) wife had passed away after a long illness. Another girl asked when the funeral was and whether they should attend. The one who knew all about every-thing said there were no funeral arrangements yet as the family was waiting for an adult son currently studying at an overseas university to come home."

Ralph interrupted the story. "I think the problem at that time was that he knew he wanted you. Hence, the proposal that was made probably in the full knowledge of his wife's imminent demise. When you rejected his proposal, it gave him time to think about things. After that guilt got in the way of a further proposal until he was legally able to marry you."

"Yes, I tried to rationalise and justify things in just that way, but I don't think I ever convinced myself. Soon after that, a further promotion brought him back to where I worked and made him my boss. Going to work every day was difficult. I thought if I worked somewhere else – for a different employer – we wouldn't have to worry about people knowing about us. Applications for a few jobs were sent off. Most didn't do any good, but I had offers from two employers. Both of the positions sounded interesting and would suit my experience but, when the time came, I couldn't bring myself to accept either of them."

Ralph looked up at me from under his lashes. "Was it the job or the man that stopped you from leaving?"

"I still don't know, but I think it might have been fear of the unknown, particularly as I was getting on a bit in age. The relationship became a shadow of its former self, but it continued. It wasn't a satisfactory arrangement. I knew that, but I held onto it. There wasn't anything else to hold onto I suppose. If I'm honest, I suppose I hoped that when he came to terms with the loss of his wife, he might see fit to make an honest woman of me. So, we drifted along for another couple of years. Goodness knows how long it might have gone on if he hadn't come to see me that fateful night."

"If this is too uncomfortable to talk about, you don't have to go on. It doesn't make any difference. From my point of view, you are the woman I know, and whatever went before probably contributed in some way to making you what you are today."

"No, it's probably good that you do know how the story ended. It was a Wednesday night when he turned up unexpectedly at my unit. He seemed tense and ill at ease and remained distant. He didn't stay long, just long enough to share the good news. He was getting married on Saturday to the woman he'd been engaged to for the last five years, and he would be away from the office for the next three weeks while they were on their honeymoon. It's not surprising he didn't get round to proposing to me when, for some time before his wife died, he was already engaged to this other woman. It goes without saying that I threw him out that evening, and wondered how I was ever going to front up at work the next day. But I did and I survived the day after that as well. And then he was married and on his honeymoon for the next three weeks. All of this came in the week after I lost Aunt Edith.''

"You are a very strong woman to have survived that as well as you obviously did.''

"I'm not sure I did survive it, and certainly not well. I knew I couldn't go on working in that office once he returned after his honeymoon, but I didn't have another job to go to and financially I couldn't retire. That weekend, while he was busy getting himself married, I sent out applications for every possible job I found in the weekend papers. I knew that, even if I was successful with any of them, it would be weeks before I'd have something else to go to. However, my salvation arrived on the Monday after his wedding when the solicitor handling Aunt Edith' estate contacted me. That's when I learned of her bequest. I took time off work first thing on the Tuesday morning went to talk to the solicitors. By the time I'd returned to work, I'd made up my mind. About an hour later I handed in my resignation and terminated my employment with the company on the Friday before my former lover returned to work.''

"That took some guts. Did it all go well?''

"I moved into the cottage over that weekend and put my unit on the market. I just kept so busy the whole time, cleaning out my unit, organising what was left of Aunt Edith's possessions in the cottage, just doing everything and anything to keep busy so I didn't have time to think about the enormous step I'd taken. Although I'd been careful my whole working life, I couldn't have done it without the annuity. Did it go well…? All I can say is that settling into retirement was a slow and sometimes tedious process of transitioning to a whole new world. So ends the story of my disastrous love life.''

By the time the story of my unhappy relationship was told and discussed, it was time for lunch. Again we sat in silence, listening to the bird songs and the distant lowing of cattle. The air was heavy with the perfume of grasses and trees, and damp leaf litter.

Although I have no way of knowing where Ralph's thoughts took him, I suspect they wandered along much the same track as mine: reviewing what a fool I had been for so many years.

Ralph broke the silence causing me to jump. "You know, I reckon you and I have more in common than you had with your Aunt Edith." I raised my eyebrows at him in question and he continued. "We both had similar experiences in the past, and I suspect we both have been careful not to get burnt again." I encouraged him to explain and he did.

"A lass and I were part of a group of friends up Oxford way who used to knock about together. The lass and I were a bit sweet on each other when we were teenagers. Then I went away to join the police force and we lost touch. Several years later, we ran into each other again by accident, and almost straight away took up from where we left off. I was planning to ask her to marry me as soon as a promotion I was waiting on came through. Her birthday was coming up soon after I got the promotion. I planned to take her to dinner for her birthday and propose. However, in the week prior to that, we were called to a hold-up at a pub. The manager and a couple of the staff were knocked about in the incident, so we were interviewing all the patrons about what they saw. My girlfriend was one of the diners. She was there with another bloke and it was obvious they were more than friends. They coped well with the interview situation until she saw me."

"Oh dear, fate can be cruel as can coincidence. I take it things did not go well after that."

"No. We met up the next day for a 'please explain' session. It turned out she had been seeing that other bloke behind my back for months. I hadn't seen her for about three weeks before that night at the pub but there were phone calls. She seemed a bit distant during those calls. I put it down to the fact we hadn't seen much of each other for a while. I had been working every bit of overtime on offer so I could afford to buy a ring. She told me she and the other bloke were getting engaged as soon as she could get some time with me to tell me we were finished. They were married about three months later."

Silence descended on our picnic once more. After all, what is there to say in response to such a sad story? After a few minutes, it was my turn to break the silence. "You were right. We have much in common, not the least of which is the fact that neither of us has had much success in the 'romance stakes' of life.

Darkening skies and the distant rumble of thunder brought us back to reality. We loaded everything into the car in a flash and were on our way home when the first large drops of rain hit the windscreen.

CHAPTER 21

Life took on a new meaning. Connie noticed a new spring in my step and pestered me for information… particularly about that car that spends a lot of time outside my house. I'm sure everyone in the street had noticed it, and should not have been surprised when it started staying parked out front overnight… or when it progressed to parking in the driveway for the weekend.

As the months slipped by, Ralph seemed more settled in himself and I thought he was enjoying his job more than when I first met him. On a few occasions I asked about progress on the investigation into the murder at the British Museum that had Sofia under suspicion for some time. I knew he couldn't discuss it, but I couldn't help asking. All he would say was that it was progressing. The last time I asked, he was a little more expansive and added that Interpol were getting close to sorting it out. It was late in November when he made the simple announcement. The case had been solved and they were now wrapping up the last of the details.

With that out of the way, our attention turned to the coming Yuletide season. Neither of us had any family, so it was a foregone conclusion that we would spend Christmas together. In previous years, Ralph always made himself available to work over the Christmas break to allow other officers to spend time with their families without the unwanted intrusion of being called into work. I half expected Ralph to volunteer for 'Christmas duty' again this year, but that appears not to be the case.

On the weekend, as I dealt with the Christmas cards I wanted to send, Ralph sat buried in a lounge chair with the weekend papers. I don't have many cards to send, just a handful to former library volunteers now too old or too ill to continue volunteering. "I am going to send Christmas cards to Sofia and Philippe. I know Philippe was only a steward on the train, but he became more than that to us. Did you want those cards to be from the both of us?"

"Get them ready and I'll sign them before you seal the envelopes. By the way, I'd like us to go out to dinner tonight. There is something I want to talk to you about." My heart skipped a beat. What did he want to talk to me about that he couldn't do here? Ralph made a couple of phone calls before announcing we had a reservation at a rather more upmarket restaurant than we tended to patronise. I took great care choosing an outfit to wear that night as something in Ralph's behaviour suggested it was to be a special occasion.

Over a glass of wine while we waited for our entrées to arrive, Ralph eased my suffering by introducing the 'something' he wanted to talk to me about. "That murder at the museum and everything that followed from it made for something a bit different from the usual crime we deal with. It seems I handled the investigation with distinction. My promotion came through this week. I am now Detective Inspector Ralph Carter." He paused to allow the news to sink in.

I gasped and clapped my hands together. "That's wonderful news. I'm so happy for you; so proud of you. I had noticed you seemed happier in your career lately, and I was curious about it. So, tell me, what does this all mean for you now?"

"The main thing is that I command a bit more respect from some of the hierarchy and I have a couple of detectives under me when we are working a case. But, the big news is: I am being transferred."

"O-o-h…" That was all the response I could manage, and I couldn't hide the disappointment I felt. "Is the transfer a good career move, or are they just trying to sideline you?"

"God no, it's great. It means I will be in charge of a small team, but my own team. Of course, there is a downside to the transfer." Of course there is. There always is a 'but' involved, I thought, but I didn't interrupt and Ralph continued. "It means moving out of the city and finding somewhere new to live, and all that stuff that goes with relocating."

"Look on the bright side. It's a good opportunity to clear out all the unnecessary stuff you have accumulated since you have been in your current place. I couldn't believe the amount of stuff I threw out when I moved to the cottage." I tried to sound upbeat and positive about his relocation. "So, where will you be moving to?" His answer stunned me. Ralph's transfer was to the station in the suburb next to where I live.

The station there is still part of the Met, but it expanded over the last couple of years as what was once surrounding agricultural land was turned over to residential development. In recent times, they expanded the police precinct there with the addition of a new building. Ralph's transfer and his new team are part of that expansion, in a bid to curb the escalating crime rate in the now huge sprawling suburb.

"You will be working nice and close to me. When do you have to take up the position?"

"Well, I start there straight after New Years' Day. So, it appears I will be busy over Christmas packing up and looking for somewhere to live. I thought about staying in London until I found somewhere, but that wouldn't work. It's too far away from where I need to be when things happen."

"That's not a problem. You can stay with me until you work out what you want to do… or, alternatively, you could forget about looking for somewhere to live and move in with me on a permanent basis."

"That's a wonderful offer, but I don't think that would do your reputation much good. I couldn't do that to you." Further discussion was cut short by the arrival of food and waiters fussing about topping up glasses. I wanted them to finish and go away so we could return to our discussion. I revisited the question of Ralph's future accommodation as soon as everything around was quiet again.

"Ralph, I like your company. I love having you around. I'm not trying to own you or stake any claims on you. There is plenty of room in the cottage and you probably won't be there much anyway. Please give it some thought, at least as a short term solution to your accommodation problem."

The plate in front of Ralph held his undivided attention for a few moments before he responded. He sucked up a great slug of wine, cleared his throat and then looked directly at me. I didn't know how to react. It all looked like being so serious. "Your offer is most generous, Marjorie, but there is only one way I would consider taking you up on your offer of long-term accommodation in your cottage. Will you marry me?"

My fork clattered onto my plate. I blinked a few times as I replayed in my mind what Ralph had said. No words would come. I was stunned and I though my heart would burst.

"Please…," Ralph added when I hadn't uttered a word in response to his proposal.

Somehow I managed to croak, "Oh Ralph, yes. Yes please, of course I will marry you." Hot tears welled up and overflowed down my cheeks. I dabbed at them with my napkin, leaving a make-up smudge on the starched stark white napkin. Ralph wasn't watching my pathetic performance. How gallant of him, I thought, to look away while I sit here blubbering. That turned out not to be the case.

Ralph finished rummaging in his pocket. His hand covered whatever he wrestled from its depths. Then, he leaned across the table, opened his hand, and flipped open the tiny box cradled in his palm. I caught my breath… and more tears made their presence felt.

"I know it was presumptuous of me, but I had hoped… It was my mother's. If you prefer, we could look for something more to your liking."

"It is so beautiful… and so perfect." The delicate little ring sported a central deep, deep blue sapphire and a tiny diamond on each shoulder. Ralph slipped it on my finger. The diners at the neighbouring table, whose attention we had managed to grab, clapped wildly and raised their glasses to toast us. It was all so embarrassing… and so wonderful.

I don't remember much about the rest of the meal or the drive home. I can't remember ever being deliriously happy before. That night, as I lay in bed waiting for sleep to come, my mind conjured up a new issue for me to think about.

If Ralph were to be moving in, I would have to have a major clean-out and reorganise the cottage a bit to accommodate the man, my future husband, and his belongings. I look forward to that… And to breaking the news to Connie when she and her husband join us for a drink on Christmas morning.

A couple of days later, I retrieved my holiday journal for a few moments of reminiscing. There wasn't much to read. Abandoned early in the trip when other happenings took priority, the last sentence remained unfinished. It read: On the way to Istanbul… I snatched up a pen and completed it: *On the way to Istanbul…. I discovered love and happiness.*

The End

ABOUT THE AUTHOR

KAYLA DANOLI spent her early years traipsing around Australia and then Europe with her parents, and then completed her tertiary education in England before returning to Australia. There were a variety of jobs in various parts of Queensland before eventually making her way towards the coast. She now lives in a small coastal town on the Queensland coast where she works part-time on a charter vessel.

In the early days after settling in that small town, to fill in her spare time, both when at home and while on cruises, she started scribbling down her ideas for stories. These days, she writes whenever time permits. Her Harbour Plaza series, previously released in 2015 as monthly eBook episodes, was updated and extended and released in 2016 as the Harbour Plaza: built on dreams compilation. Revenge is not Enough, also released in 2016, was her first full-length novel.

Discover more about Kayla and her work by visiting

www.kayladanoli.com

or contact her at

contact@kayladanoli.com